M000304756

By Jen Silverman

The Island Dwellers

We Play Ourselves

Bath

There's Going to Be Trouble

THERE'S GOING

TO BE

TROUBLE

THERE'S GOING
TO BE
TROUBLE

A NOVEL

Jen Silverman

 Random House | New York

There's Going to Be Trouble is a work of fiction. Names, characters, places, and incidents are the products of the author's imagination or are used fictitiously. Any resemblance to actual events, locales, or persons, living or dead, is entirely coincidental.

Copyright © 2024 by Jen Silverman

All rights reserved.

Published in the United States by Random House, an imprint and division of Penguin Random House LLC, New York.

RANDOM HOUSE and the HOUSE colophon are registered trademarks of Penguin Random House LLC.

Grateful acknowledgment is made to poetryloverspage.com and Edward Bonver for permission to reprint "I Was Born in the Right Time" by Anna Akhmatova, originally published in Russian in 1913, translated to English by Yevgeny Bonver (2000), and edited by Dmitry Karshtedt (2001) and an excerpt from "You, Who Was Born" by Anna Akhmatova, originally published in Russian in 1956, translated to English by Yevgeny Bonver (2002), and edited by Tatiana Piotroff (2002). Used by permission.

LIBRARY OF CONGRESS CATALOGING-IN-PUBLICATION DATA
Names: Silverman, Jen, author.
Title: There's going to be trouble : a novel / Jen Silverman.
Other titles: There is going to be trouble
Description: First edition. | New York : Random House, [2024]
Identifiers: LCCN 2023014272 (print) | LCCN 2023014273 (ebook) |
ISBN 9780593448359 (hardback ; acid-free paper) |
ISBN 9780593448366 (ebook)
Subjects: LCSH: Fathers and daughters—Fiction. | Political activists—Fiction. | Social movements—Fiction. | LCGFT: Novels.
Classification: LCC PS3619.I55235 T47 2024 (print) |
LCC PS3619.I55235 (ebook) | DDC 812/.6—dc23/eng/20230327
LC record available at https://lccn.loc.gov/2023014272
LC ebook record available at https://lccn.loc.gov/2023014273

Printed in the United States of America on acid-free paper

randomhousebooks.com

1st Printing

First Edition

Book design by Betty Lew

For my parents, Mark and Sue:
scientists & humanists who have not
given up on the world

My mind is made up there's going to be trouble.

—ALLEN GINSBERG, "AMERICA"

Where do people go? Not after they die,
but when they are alive and well, where do they go?

—SALOME KOKOLADZE, "HOW WE ALL FALL"

THERE'S GOING
TO BE
TROUBLE

2018

1

MINERVA HUNTER STUMBLED INTO THE PROTEST BY ACCIDENT, A cacophony of voices swerving her off her path. All around her, bundled into jackets and scarves, other people hurried in ones and twos toward that sharp static swarming call. It was mid-November, a Saturday, and it sounded to Minnow's ears as if all of Paris had descended.

Curious, she followed the others down a narrow side street and then out onto a boulevard. It was densely packed, swollen with bodies. Children perched on their parents' shoulders, heads swiveling, faces bewildered and pleased. Minnow's eye picked out a bristling forest of placards hand-printed in French, long swooping banners, and far ahead, tall marionette puppets leaping and jerking above the crowd. The air was bright with excitement, as if everyone had shown up to the same surprise party.

Minnow knew that Paris was a city people mythologized, but she herself hadn't brought a lot of fantasy to it. She had taken a job here because the job had presented itself at the moment in which her American life dissolved. Had it been located on another planet, she would still have unhesitatingly agreed. But when she'd landed in Paris, in September, the city had been drenched in sunlight, and she had found herself sliding into it like a warm bath. Her first day, she'd walked through the sweeping corridor of trees that marched down the southern side of the Jardin des Plantes, and the beauty had shocked and soothed her. *Oh,* she'd thought then: *Paris.* Now, coming across this strange and brilliant crack in the city's nonchalant quiet, she thought again, *Oh,* and the surprise curled through her like pleasure.

Minnow pressed in closer and bodies shifted to permit her entrance. She brushed up against puffy down jackets, gleaming leather shoulders, bare arms and yellow construction vests. She recognized these from recent news broadcasts in which the French was spoken too quickly to catch but the day-glo yellow was unmistakable. The protestors were even calling themselves the *gilets jaunes,* or yellow vests—or maybe they were called that by others, she wasn't sure. She had seen them on TV more and more of late. The images slid past her, meant nearly nothing.

"Excusez-moi," Minnow said hesitantly to the nearest puffy jacket. It turned, and she found herself cheek to cheek with a woman in her sixties. "Qu'est-ce qui se passe ici?"

The woman was startled into a smile that grew broader as she took Minnow in. She answered Minnow's question with her own: "Vous êtes d'où?"

"America," Minnow said, a little apologetically, and the woman laughed.

"Ah, okay, America." The woman launched into a fast-paced explanation—something about a Facebook post, a video, a call to gather. Truckers, but also regular citizens, mothers and fathers, the workers. People who were hungry and angry, to whom nobody was listening. The woman made a sweeping gesture, triumphant. The gilets jaunes were gathered not only here but outside of Paris as well: partout, partout! "Vous voyez, Madame!" she cried.

She spoke even faster, and Minnow listened carefully but understood only the disdain, anger, sorrow. The woman interrupted herself when the man beside her started to shout a rhythmic phrase. She picked up the chant with swift efficiency and all at once everyone was shouting it, creating the effect that had drawn Minnow in in the first place, that of total concentrated synchronicity: "Macron démission! Macron démission!"

Glancing around, Minnow gave up estimating how many were present. Even as the crowd shuffled forward, it joined itself to yet another mass of bodies creeping along the avenue ahead, and the confluence forced all movement to a standstill.

Even ground to a halt, the crowd was like a great machine coordinating all its parts. People shouted and chanted and greeted each other. "La Marseillaise" started playing, coming from an unknown direction. After a few moments of bobbing on tiptoe, trying to see over the shoulders in front of her, Minnow grabbed the side of the nearest lamppost and pulled herself up onto the narrow metal lip where the lamp's wide base narrowed into its pole. Wedging her sneakers into the metal furrows, she clutched the pole tightly to keep from slipping and stared out over the crowd. She realized for the first time that she had emerged onto the Champs-Élysées, the long avenue leading up to the Arc de Triomphe. Turning to look in all directions, she made out the metal-and-glass bulge of the Grand Palais in the distance, and farther still, rising up on the opposite bank, the delicate lace of the Eiffel Tower.

The large marionettes were approaching down the aisle of the avenue, and people moved aside to make room. Lady Liberty beckoned with her long arms, torn bedsheet streamers floating from her wrists. The wind buffeted her, forcing the puppeteer to move side to side, laughing, as he tried to keep her upright. Minnow saw that he was a young man in a leather jacket with the collar turned up, dark hair falling into his eyes in messy tangles. He was almost directly beneath her now, his face upturned. She lowered her chin and as their eyes met unexpectedly, Minnow realized with a jolt that she recognized him. It was Charles Vernier.

Charles was a fellow teacher at the university where Minnow worked. He had only recently graduated from it himself. Minnow reassured herself that this was why the students all loved him; he had been one of them not so long before. It irked her how much they adored him, students who were impassive and unimpressed in her own classes, who intimidated her a little bit with their European sophistication. She imagined that they looked down on her as a boring, nearly middle-aged (no, say it! middle-aged!) American woman who had appeared after their semester had already begun, to cover literature classes they didn't particularly care for. Charles, on the other hand, exuded cool. He was in the Communication and Media Department, which sounded much more au courant than simple, stuffy English lit. When he taught, he rested one narrow blue-jeaned ass cheek on his desk, long legs sprawled out, and the students hung on his every word. Passing his classroom once, she had seen this—the girls who had packed the front row to bat their eyelashes at him, the boys as well. Her students sat in the back and couldn't be lured any closer.

The other teachers said Charles's family name, Vernier, as if Minnow might recognize it. This told her that he was not only wealthy, he was aristocratic. Even worse, Charles had the good fortune to be attractive, which irritated Minnow the most of all his sins. How devoted would his students be, she asked herself, if he were middle-aged, middle-class, and ferociously ugly?

Though she had met him briefly at a faculty welcome dinner and seen him from time to time in the halls, they had never spoken. She had felt as if she'd never registered for him, a state that she was sensitive to, as she was often overlooked: her quietness, her stillness, her way of folding herself into herself so that eyes would go right past her. These things were her fault, she knew, and it had only become worse since the incident at her previous job, after which she had been fired. This was how she thought of it: The Incident; though it was in truth not one event but a chain of them spilling outward into the public eye. Now she caught herself practicing a particular way of standing in which she sank her chin into her shoulders as if trying to disappear entirely. Charles, on the contrary, entered every room to the turning of heads. It surprised her to find him here, mixed in with a cheering crowd, content to be one of many.

His eyes firmly fixed on hers, she saw the exact moment in which he recognized her. His face went blank with surprise and he lost control of Lady Liberty, who soared high, seized by the wind. Minnow felt a rush of embarrassment, as if she had been caught somewhere she didn't belong. She jumped down from the lamppost into the crowd, her heart pounding. What did it matter, anyway? His opinion meant nothing to her; she didn't even know him. She turned her back on him and pushed off into the sea of bodies, seeking the safety of anonymity.

*

Later, when Minnow saw the images on television—armored squads of police as shiny as beetles, the Arc de Triomphe covered in the thick grayish haze of tear gas—she wouldn't recognize them. She had been insulated by the bodies around her and had seen none of what was occurring at the head of the crowd. And so the shift had come from seemingly nowhere.

One moment, she was standing with the sunlight beating down on the top of her hair. The next, the bodies gathered around her surged forward, wild and panicked. Minnow was briefly swept off her feet as a man's shoulder slammed into hers. She pushed at the man's back, but he was being shoved as well; there was no space for his body to fit into that wasn't Minnow's space. The thousand disparate bodies had become a single animal fighting itself. Thrown backward, Minnow slammed into someone's stomach, found her feet, and then was shunted to the side as the crowd shifted direction. People were trying to run, she realized, but there was nowhere to go, and whatever was happening at the front was translating backward in unforgiving electric pulses, bodies forced this way and that, colliding with each other, stepping on each other. Minnow pulled back as an elbow grazed her cheek—a woman losing her balance and falling but never hitting the ground because there was no space in which to do it. Suspended in a crush of strangers, the woman paddled, gasping.

Fear sparked in Minnow. She turned sideways and started squeezing her way through, but it was impossible; for every gap that opened up, a tidal change would press her in the opposite direction. She wished she had stayed near the lamppost, that she could climb back up it and out of the panicking mob. Someone was screaming, and now more people were screaming, and a strange smell caught the edge of Minnow's nostrils: an odd acrid warmth that made her cough.

Minnow began fighting in earnest, shoving against the wall of thrashing flesh. But she had gotten turned around, and she realized she wasn't sure in what direction she was trying to go. Someone nearby was shouting a warning that caused the bodies around her to crush against each other more tightly, but Minnow didn't understand the words, and her head had become wedged against the ribs of a towering man in a camo jacket. The man smelled pungently of cigarette smoke and onions, and then under that was an intensifying gunpowder smell that seemed to be drifting into the cracks between bodies, filling up the small pockets of oxygen with an itch that was beginning to burn. Tear gas, Minnow realized. She had never smelled it before, but it could be nothing else.

She started shouting and realized she couldn't hear herself above the chaos around her. The man against whom she was crushed was also bellowing, though she could only tell by the vibration of his ribs against the side of her face. Panic welled inside her. She began kicking out with her feet, making bruising contact with whatever was nearby; she could no longer think of the immutable wall as comprised of other humans. Her elbows were pinned to her sides, but she was kicking and kicking, and then suddenly, a sliver of space yawned open and someone grabbed her wrist and pulled her sideways through it. Gasping, Minnow followed the bruising grip, and with a lurch and a groan, she broke through into air. She tripped over the curb of the sidewalk and hit the ground on her knees, choking. Someone grabbed her shoulders and she looked up, eyes streaming, to see Charles.

"Come on," he said, already looking behind her. "We have to go."

He grabbed her arm and pulled her to her feet. Minnow didn't bother to look over her shoulder, she stumbled into a run after him as he tugged her. Bodies hurtled past, scattering in a variety of directions. Some people ran straight down the Champs-Élysées away from the Arc; others were sprinting down side streets, cutting into the park. She realized that another man was running next to Charles, keeping pace, and the three of them were now a unit.

"Use your sweater," Charles shouted. She turned toward him and saw through the haze of chemical tears that he had his scarf wrapped around the lower half of his face.

She pulled the neck of her sweater up over her nose and mouth, panting through the knit weave. As their feet slapped against the sidewalk and her lungs burned, the wail of sirens filtered into Minnow's

consciousness. She didn't know how long the sound had been puls-
ing, but now she was vividly aware of it. Charles grabbed her wrist
again, pulling her in a sharp left turn toward the looming mouth of a
side street. "Cops," he said breathlessly. The three of them peeled
down the alley. As they ran, Minnow found that her eyes were no
longer stinging, and the air tasted clearer through the neck of her
sweater.

Charles's friend was in the lead, and when he slowed to a walk,
Charles slowed as well. Minnow doubled over, hands on her knees,
gasping. She cleared her throat, spat onto the sidewalk, cleared her
throat again. Her heart was smashing into the walls of her chest and
she felt dizzy and elated. It was the elation she would never have
expected, but it rose up in her nonetheless.

"Are you all right?" Charles's chest heaved as he fought to steady
his own breathing, and his voice came out strangled.

"Yeah, I think so." Minnow reached for her breath. Then, remembering: "Thank you." And to his friend as well: "Both of you."

Up close, Charles's friend might have been in his mid-thirties,
closer to Minnow's age than to Charles's. He had a sharp face, eyes
like chips of blue paint. He nodded and Charles said, "It's nothing."

Charles *was* good-looking, even up close, hair blown wild, damp
and flushed. In the moment of having been saved by him, Minnow
felt less inclined to resent him; the body memory of being crushed
still lived in her ribs and lungs. She wondered if he would mention
knowing her from the university, and then she felt sudden doubt:
maybe he hadn't made that connection after all. Perhaps she had been
completely forgettable for him.

"You are all right?" Charles asked again, as if he wasn't sure.

"We know each other," Minnow said, before she could stop herself. "Don't we."

To her surprise, Charles flushed. "Yes," he said. "I did not know if
you remembered me."

"If *I* remembered *you*?" Right away, Minnow regretted showing
her surprise.

"We've never spoken," he said apologetically.

"*I* don't know her," his friend said, stepping in. He extended a hand and Minnow took it and found his grip dry and firm. "Luc," he said. "We have also never spoken."

"Minnow," Minnow said.

"Minnow like the fish?"

She wished she had begun with her full name, though she rarely used it. She sighed: "Minerva," she said. "Minerva Hunter. The nickname is a habit, and a bad one."

"Not so bad," Charles said with a glance at Luc. Luc was still holding Minnow's hand, and now he released it.

"It's cute," Luc said. *"Minou."* He laughed: "This is how we call a cat—minou, minou! Comme ça."

"Which way are you going?" Charles asked, breaking in. "We will walk you."

"Oh, that's not necessary . . ." But as Minnow glanced around, she realized she didn't know where she was.

Charles read her blank look correctly and smiled. "Which neighborhood do you live in?"

"The Cinquième—near the Jardin des Plantes."

"Charles lives in that direction as well," Luc said. "Saint-Germain."

"I'm still getting my bearings," Minnow admitted. Luc pivoted to another question: "How long have you been at the university?"

"A few months. I'm covering someone else's classes." And then, surprised: "How did you know I was at the university?"

She looked to Charles and, seeing him flush again, understood that he must have spoken to Luc of her. But what would he have said?

"You have the look of a professor," Luc said smoothly. "And you came from . . . let me guess. New York?"

"Luc thinks America is just two cities," Charles said. "New York and Los Angeles."

"I'm from neither." An image rose in front of her: the thick green of spring, cicadas screaming, the polished iron gates of Sewell School swung shut against her. Minnow had thought herself beyond that old pain, and it caught her by surprise this time, a tight band around her heart and throat.

"Neither New York nor L.A.?" Luc was making fun of himself. "But what else is there?"

Charles's eyes slid toward her, and the keenness of his gaze was unsettling. "It is the same in France," Charles said, and Minnow got the sense that he was covering for her somehow, covering over the lapse in her composure, as minuscule as it had been. "Except we have only one city, and that city is Paris. Everything else? Wasteland."

"According to our friend Macron," Luc added, pronouncing the French president's name with disdain, and they were safely steered into the territory of the political.

They reached a bridge leading back to the Left Bank. In the distance, the shriek of sirens rose and fell. The streets by the river here were oddly deserted, as if the teeming mass of life inside which they were only recently trapped had been raptured.

"Well," Minnow said, falling back on ceremony, "thank you for your help."

"Do you know how to get home from here?" Charles asked solicitously.

"Yes," she said, "of course." He quirked an eyebrow, and she smiled: "Maybe not *of course,* but: Yes, generally."

Luc extended his hand. They shook once again, his grip as tight and commanding as it had been earlier. After a hesitation, Charles extended his as well, a half-smile ghosting his face as if he were making fun of himself for the gesture.

"Now we have officially met," Charles said. His hand was surprisingly warm. Holding it, Minnow felt a giddy swell—what was this?—and, recognizing the sensation as desire, she dropped his hand in alarm.

Crossing the Pont de l'Archevêché, Minnow tried to walk as if she were unhurried but at the same time as if she had great purpose. When she reached the other side, she permitted herself to glance back. The street was empty. Charles and Luc had melted into the city as if they were never there.

*

Turning from the broad Boulevard Saint-Germain onto the narrower Rue Monge, Minnow found herself playing out the fantasy of calling her father. Though they were not currently speaking, the urge to call

him had not abated, and she often caught herself imagining how it
might go: Christopher Hunter, drawn in from the garden by the
sound of the ringing landline. He did not like or trust technology; he
owned an iPhone because she had made him buy it, but he was always
leaving it inside a thick padded pouch he had bought at the hardware
store. It would ring and ring from inside its pouch, and he would
never hear it, so she only ever called his landline. He would wipe his
hands on his patched jeans, contemplate the ringing. Perhaps enough
time would have passed that the harassment had stopped, the vul-
tures had dispersed, so Christopher could answer the call mid-ring
instead of making it go to the 1990s answering machine he had set up
in the wake of the Sewell incident. If he did pick up he would say,
"Hello?" with a tone of gruff suspicion that Minnow could replay
perfectly inside her head. "Who is this?"

"Minnow," Minnow would say, and then . . . what? What would
they say to each other? What was there to say? She sometimes uncon-
sciously jumped to the phrase *I'm sorry,* but it was always her next line
and never his, and the fact that this script was deeply embedded in
her made her furious.

Christopher was not an easy man. Minnow knew this about her
father. It was what other people had said of him throughout her
childhood—the neighbors, her teachers, even his colleagues at the
college where he taught chemistry, though she surmised their feelings
not by what they said but by the small furrow that appeared between
their eyebrows when they encountered him.

To Minnow, however, Christopher had been her whole world. It
wasn't just that he was her only parent. It was that he had turned the
full force of his attention on her—that keen, curious intelligence that
she had grown up admiring—and he had shaped the universe to her
understanding. His explanations were measured and thoughtful. He
gave her eyes to see and language with which to understand what she
saw. He gave her a pragmatic framework: logic, always logic. He often
deferred to her if she had constructed a pleasing argument for why,
for example, she should be allowed to buy a pet hamster, or why her
allowance should increase. (*Inflation,* Minnow had argued at seven,
having just learned the concept, and Christopher had laughed long

and hard before he agreed to the additional twenty-five cents.) He'd answered her questions honestly even when she was young enough that her friends' parents were still teaching them the shorthand lies that sufficed for information. And even *that* was a Christopher thought. He despised simple explanations to complicated things. He had taught Minnow that complicated things deserved complicated answers, and that hard things often had hard answers.

This was something he had said when, as a small child, she first asked about her mother: *Why do we not know where Mama is?* Her father had pulled her onto his lap, his arms circling her like balcony rails, and replied gravely, "That's a hard question, Minnow, and I don't have a good answer. But here are some of the things I know." It was only many years later that she appreciated how he began the list with: *She loves us very much, but she is not well.* Christopher was not sentimental, in fact he could be infuriatingly stoic, but he had always shown his daughter a great tenderness. In this case, his tenderness had been so great that he had betrayed his own first precept and erred on the side of deceit; as an adult, Minnow felt he could not have known whether or not her mother loved them still, nor was her mother exactly *unwell.*

Even now, when for the first time in her life she and her father were not in contact, Minnow still found herself talking to him in her head. She had spoken to him on the phone multiple times a week for her whole adult life. In her first months at Sewell, she had called him nearly every other night because she had been so lonely; even before the incident occurred, she had felt out of place there. When she landed in Paris, she had almost called him to tell him that she'd arrived safely, and then she had not. Every night after that, she made the decision not to, and it never came naturally. As she walked home from the protest, her body aching, her lungs raw, her thoughts slipped from what had just occurred to how she would have narrated it to her father, even though she knew he wouldn't have liked any of it: the uncontrolled nature of the crowds, the danger. The political aspect would have troubled him, too, though she herself did not understand the politics.

A memory came to mind: Minnow, in the sixth grade, preparing a presentation on the Vietnam War, and Christopher, incensed, beside himself with rage.

"What are they teaching you?" he kept demanding. "Why are they feeding you politics?"

Minnow was trying to explain that it was just history, it was just old things—but her father couldn't be reached. He had gone somewhere else in his eyes, a thing he did rarely. He called her teacher, and she remembered the timbre of his voice as he shouted at the man on the phone: "What are you teaching my daughter!"

A few minutes later, her father slammed down the phone. He paced the porch for a time, while Minnow sat in her room. She was not afraid of her father—she was certain of this, no matter how often the memory came to mind—but sometimes she was afraid of his sadness, how it could descend on him and operate him like a machine.

When Christopher reappeared at her bedroom door, he was regretful, exhausted. He sat on her bed and watched her at her little desk; she was drawing a timeline, using the edge of her ruler to keep her lines straight as she wrote in Major Events. She kept waiting for him to say something, but he was silent. Eventually, as if dredging the words up from a place deep inside him, he had said: "I'm sorry. I shouldn't have yelled."

"It's okay," she had said unhesitatingly. And then, wanting to comfort him: "It isn't politics, anyway, it's just history."

Christopher was quiet for so long that she thought he hadn't heard her, and then, as she was opening her mouth to repeat herself, he said: "It's history *now*. But back when it was happening, it was politics."

"But it isn't happening anymore," she assured him patiently.

Christopher studied her with eyes that were entirely different from hers: a lucid gray, in contrast to her deep brown. She had recently come to realize that she had her mother's eyes, though they rarely talked about her mother.

"No," he said at last. "No, it isn't happening anymore."

"So it's over," she said, wondering why he didn't seem comforted by this. She waited for him to agree with her that, yes, it was over, but his silence stretched out and out into the night around them. And it was this quality of silence that she remembered now, years afterward.

It was this moment, suspended in time, in which her child mind first skirted the edges of a new idea: that history, though no longer happening, might not be over.

*

In her Paris apartment that night, Minnow hunched on the floor, inches from the small corner television, staring in disbelief at the scenes playing on loop. A car, flipped and burning along the Champs-Élysées. Police charging a barricade. That looping wail of sirens, this time playing against a montage of smashed traffic lights swaying over streets in which park benches had been overturned or thrown through shop windows. A shot of someone on the ground—a woman, weeping, curled in a ball as panicked people ran past, sometimes stepping on her.

Minnow switched the channel but the same footage was everywhere. As she kept flipping, watching for a few seconds and then changing to the next, she realized that she was looking for Charles. On one of the channels the police were dragging a protestor away from the camera, masses of brown hair in his face as he kicked and struggled, and Minnow's heart leapt. But then, as the reporter gave chase, a thin, waifish face was revealed, eyeliner smudged by tears. Not Charles.

She cycled through the channels several more times before turning the television off. The night outside was eerily quiet, the stillness broken only by the sound of radiators clanking. Despite herself, her mind went back to the moment in which she had doubled over on the sidewalk, gasping for breath—how the pure blank of elation had seized her. When had she last felt that way? The night of the fire, had she felt that way? Had that been elation, or a rage so distilled, so refined, that it had coursed through her blood like jet fuel?

Minnow shook herself like a dog, walked to the wide French windows, undid the latch, pulled them open, and plunged her head into the cold night air. Far away a single siren lifted and fell, a bright thread. Her heart rose to meet it, and for a moment she tasted it again: the burn of tear gas and the buzz of exultation.

1968

2

THE PROTESTORS WERE STILL THERE WHEN KEEN PASSED BY, driving slowly so that he could see. Their mouths were elongated, their faces pulled into ovals, and for a moment, with his car windows rolled up and Bob Dylan playing at top volume, he couldn't tell if they were shouting or singing. Then he slowed as the stoplight changed and he could hear their chanting.

Keen turned down Dylan for a moment, although he already knew what they were saying. Though it was possible that their concerns might involve Vietnam, nuclear testing, or civil rights, Keen had seen this group before and he knew whose name they would be shouting. And indeed, when he switched Dylan off midchord, there it was: *Down with Cavener!*—the name of his advisor.

The light changed and Keen hit the gas again, rounding the corner. The protestors fell into his rearview, and he glanced once to see them: the bearish guy with the red beard was there, as he was most days, and so was the skinny girl with the long yellow coat and flyaway brown hair. She always seemed to be thrusting her sign above the others, propelled by the force of her outrage. Keen looked for her every time.

Keen had never asked Cavener what he thought of all this. None of the grad students or postdocs dared to bring it up, and there were only two undergrads permitted in Cavener's lab, particularly clever specimens who rarely spoke. Cavener had won a Nobel Prize, and Keen often thought that if he himself ever won a Nobel Prize, he wouldn't care what other people thought of him either. Keen was thin-skinned, and he cared a great deal; even that morning, hearing two girls laughing behind him in line at the coffee shop, he had become flustered and left before he'd ordered his coffee. But Keen was thrilled by the idea of being so important that, even in this sea of things to protest, you would be singled out for special attention. Maybe Cavener didn't mind it either: a constant reminder of how important he and his discoveries were.

It made Keen secretly even prouder of working for Cavener, although their work involved none of the things that made Cavener protestable: weapons of war, for example, or compounds found in napalm. No, Keen had spent the last year trying to synthesize tetro-dotoxin, a compound that appeared organically in the venom of puffer fish but was particularly hard to manufacture because of its sulfur bridge. He didn't know why Cavener wanted it synthesized, and he wasn't sure there was even a use awaiting it; sometimes Cavener just had them do these things because it was good for them. An older graduate student, Priya, had explained this to him, a little conde-scendingly, when he had asked her if synthesized puffer fish venom would find its way into chemical weaponry. Priya's projects were more complex and important, and Keen nourished the envy that they might bear real-world results.

The protestors didn't know the details of Cavener's lab, but they knew what the school newspaper had reported: that Cavener was consulting for the federal government and that, twenty-five years ear-lier, as a young prodigy, he had been involved in research that may have resulted in the nuclear bombs used in Hiroshima and Nagasaki. He would have been nineteen then, painfully young and overedu-cated; he had gone to college at twelve, said the newspaper, although this was the one rumor that Cavener had rolled his eyes at and dis-proven aloud: "It was fourteen," he had said grumpily, "and don't read that trash in my lab."

Keen was the only one who thought that being the object of pro-test was exciting. Arjun and Masaki, whose benches shared the corner space in which Keen worked, made no mystery of the fact that the protests upset them. Masaki was irritated by the emotionalism of it, he said. The protestors didn't know what they were protesting; their information was thin and their response melodramatic. He had also become a target for a few of them. Apparently, a white girl had come up to him the week before as he entered the lab, asking if he felt that he was betraying his country by working for someone who had bombed it. "She meant Japan," Masaki told them drily, "and even when I *said* I was from Oakland, she gave me this whole *But your ancestors*. Which—I mean, let's talk about *your* ancestors, ya dig?" He had drawled out the *ya dig* in a mockery of her speech patterns, but to Keen, who often whispered these same speech patterns to himself alone in the bathroom, it made Masaki sound particularly cool.

Arjun's complaint was that two times now, working in Cavener's lab had gotten him unlaid. "What's unlaid?" Keen had asked, and Arjun had said sardonically: "The opposite of *laid*."

Arjun had gone on to explain that he had been on a promising date with an English grad student only to have it end when he mentioned he was a graduate student in organic chemistry—"Wait, isn't there a war criminal working there?" she had asked. When he had tried to explain that Cavener wasn't a war criminal in any conventional understanding of the term, she had ended the date. The second girl had been an undergrad theatre major—"I thought I'd try prettier and dumber"—and she had been impressed when he said he was in chem, only to ask tentatively, minutes later, "You don't work for that guy they're all talking about, do you?" Arjun had lost his temper at that point, he admitted, which Keen thought might have been why he got himself unlaid.

The truth was, Keen wished he had a sex life to have gotten disrupted. He appreciated the excuse the protests offered him. When his friends asked about women, he got to repeat what he had heard Arjun say: "It's like *Lysistrata,* my man, they're all on a sex strike against science." Only Keen knew that even if their lab had not had its own small cabal of picketers, he probably still would not be having sex.

He hadn't had sex since his junior year of undergrad, when he'd had a serious girlfriend for three semesters. It had seemed like a miracle to him, this project of dating someone—you got to have sex regularly; it was a hobby you could do together like bicycling or jogging, except it was *sex!* When the relationship ended, he had thought he was devastated in the specific, only to realize later that he was just lonely in general. He had loved being a person who got to do the things that girlfriend-havers got to do—which wasn't *just* the carnal; he had also liked regularly telling someone how his day was—but the sex had been mind-blowing. Or: sex as a concept had blown his mind. Having only had it with one person, he wasn't sure how their particular endeavors had ranked in terms of all that could be accomplished.

Keen wasn't shy, but he was timid. He thought of the difference in this way: he could talk to anyone, given the chance, and he could make people laugh. He was quick, he enjoyed doing favors without asking for any in return, and so he was also used to being liked. Hence: not shy. But when it came to women who he found attractive, words stuck in his throat. And as he hesitated and worried and tried to gather the courage to thrust himself onto their radar, they would invariably start dating someone far bolder.

Keen's roommate Sheila—a philosophy grad student—had told Keen on numerous occasions that he was hopeless. "You just have to let them know you think they're *foxy*," Sheila had said. Sheila had no problem getting dates. "All anybody wants to be is *foxy*, especially at a school where all they hear is that they're *smart*."

Keen had taken this advice to heart but still had not managed to put it into action. And so the ire of the protestors made him feel safe. If nobody at his lab was getting laid, then he wasn't particularly defective for his celibacy. It had been three weeks now that they had stood in the rain and the wind with their placards. Every time he drove past them, he felt their presence as encouragement. As a cog in the machine of Cavener's lab, he was facilitating what they felt the need to protest against and so, in a way, they were a sign that he mattered.

*

When Keen left lab ten hours later, night was falling and the protestors were getting routed by the police. Normally there were six of them, but now Keen could only see four protestors squared off against four policemen, though they didn't seem equally matched. Two were women—one couldn't have been more than five feet tall, the other was the thin brunette with the yellow coat, who, though tall, looked wispy. Keen was driving so slowly that the light changed to red before he had reached it, giving him an excuse to stop and watch.

Two policemen had their hands on the red-bearded man and they were dragging him down the sidewalk, presumably toward their car. He was cursing and flailing, and even as Keen watched, a third police-man brought his baton down hard on the back of red-beard's neck. Red-beard's legs gave out and he pitched forward, and Keen made a pained noise out loud, flinching back into the firm warmth of the driver's seat. The girl in the yellow coat screamed, a feral banshee shriek of rage, and launched herself at the cop with the baton. Sur-prised and equally enraged, he grabbed her by the hair, pulling her away from him to hit her, but she was too close for him to get enough elbow room to swing. She clung to his blue-uniformed body—was she *biting* him? Keen leaned forward, trying to see, and a symphony of horns rose up behind him. The light had changed and three or four cars were waiting impatiently for him to move.

The blare of the horns startled both police and protestors. At the sound, the girl in the yellow coat let go of the cop with the baton and leapt backward; as he grabbed for her, she ran directly toward Keen. Keen had started to press the gas but now hit the brakes, afraid that he would run her over. As she came soaring past him, the side of her thigh connected with the front of his car. She skidded over the top of the hood, landed on the other side, and without missing a beat started tugging savagely at the door to the passenger seat. Shocked into immediate response, Keen unlocked the side door and she flung her-self inside.

"Drive, drive, drive!" she shouted, and indeed now all four of the police were turning toward Keen's car. Two were still holding red-beard, who was slumped between them, and one had seized the smaller woman under the arms and was simply holding her off the ground as if she were a child. The cop with the baton started running toward them, waving his arms, and that was when Keen floored it and they sailed through the intersection.

He went several blocks before they spoke. Once they had crossed the river and he was driving without any direction, the girl turned and gave him such a conspiratorial smile that Keen had the feeling she was going to say they had met before. Instead, she just said: "Right on."

"Are you okay?"

"Me?"

"Well . . . I mean, yeah, it looked like maybe that cop was hitting you? Uh, and then I guess I hit you with my car?"

"Oh, that." She smiled, waved a hand. "No, I'm fine. He didn't get any good ones in."

"I'm glad. I'm Keen, by the way."

"Keen," she said. "It's a pleasure. More than usual, given the circumstances. I'm Olya."

"Olya," Keen repeated. "Is that a Russian name?"

"My mom is—was—Russian." She narrowed her gaze at him. "Have a problem with that?"

"No," Keen said.

"The way you said it . . ."

"I like Chekhov," Keen said lamely, and she burst out laughing.

"Of course you do. What are you, an actor?"

"I don't like the plays. Nothing happens in the plays. I like the stories." And then, flattered to have been taken for an actor: "I'm a grad student, actually."

"Nothing happens in the stories either," Olya said.

"I guess not. But I like that Chekhov was a doctor," Keen said. "He was a scientist but also a humanist. He looked at people really closely in a bunch of ways—their bodies, their maladies, but then also their . . . you know, souls, I guess." He was embarrassed to have used the word *soul* in a casual conversation, but Olya leaned back in the seat, arms folded and her eyebrow lifted.

"All right," she said, "I'll bite. Are you a doctor?"

"Oh, no," Keen demurred, feeling like he was making a hash of the conversation. "No, no."

"Well, what are you? Other than a car owner?"

Keen half winced and half smiled. "Well . . . I think I'm one of the people you're protesting, actually."

Olya's other eyebrow went up, and now she turned in the passenger seat, giving him her full attention. "*You're* with the ROTC?"

"What? No! I'm a scientist—I'm one of Cavener's grad students."

"Ohhh," Olya said. And then: "I coordinate a few different protests, you know."

"Oh," Keen said weakly. "I didn't know."

"Yeah, it's not just Cavener. He's not the only bad guy." Olya studied Keen and he resisted the urge to look back at her, keeping his eyes on the road. He didn't know where they were going; he was just driving aimlessly now, around the outer rim of Brookline. "So, you're . . . chem?"

"That's right."

"How delicious," Olya said. He snuck a glance at her and saw she was smiling. "What're you doing, making napalm?"

"No, none of the stuff we do is . . . uh, useful, actually."

Olya laughed out loud, her head tilting back. He saw the pink flash of her tongue, and a dizzying abyss briefly opened in his abdomen like a trapdoor. He blinked hard at the road.

"You know why we're protesting him though, right?" Olya said, suddenly fierce. "I mean I hope you know what he's done, your teacher."

"I've read your signs," Keen said, "and one of you threw a pamphlet at me a while ago? But I think your facts are kinda precarious, to be honest."

He waited for Olya to get upset, but instead she looked pleased. "You read it?"

"Sorry?"

"You got a pamphlet thrown at you and you read it?"

"Yeah," Keen said. "I like to read. I'll read anything."

Olya faced forward again, gazing out the windshield, but the half-smile had returned. "Groovy," she said. Keen waited for her to return to the subject of Cavener, but she was quiet. He felt the first creeping dread of awkwardness enter the air between them. There hadn't been time before this, he had just been reacting to the immediacy of her presence, but now a silence extended and Keen began to curse himself for not knowing what to say next.

"Where are we going?" he asked at last.

"I was about to ask you that," Olya said. "Are you taking me to some parking lot to shoot me and chop up my body?"

"No!" Keen said, dismayed, and then realized he had taken her deadpan joke seriously and felt stupid. He made his tone brisk and businesslike: "Where should I drop you?"

"So the taxi service is door-to-door," Olya said. "How impressive. Unless you're a cop, trying to figure out where I live."

"Look, you're the one who got in *my* car. So if I'm a cop, you made my job phenomenally easy."

Olya grinned. "You're not a cop."

"How do you know?"

"You haven't asked me anything," Olya said. "You haven't tried to pump me for a single detail. Which means you're a bad conversationalist, but also not a cop."

"I asked your name!" Keen protested, feeling both pleased and embarrassed, and Olya shook her finger at him.

"Ah-ah—you volunteered *your* name, and then I gave you mine."

"Well, maybe that's a technique I learned in cop school!"

"Maybe," Olya said. "I'll give you that, *maybe*." She leaned into the window as Keen turned from Commonwealth onto Winchester. "Oh, I know where we are. You can drop me in Coolidge Corner. It's two minutes away, do you know where it is?"

"Sure. What're your streets?"

"And *that*," Olya said, "is a cop question." But before Keen could defend himself, she was telling him: "Wellman—it's actually just off Winchester."

Olya had him circle the block a few times while she checked in the rearview and side mirrors. She said she was seeing if they were being followed, and Keen felt a thrill of alarm, but the road was empty behind them, and when Olya pronounced all clear, they shared a smile of relief.

Keen was prepared to drop her on the corner but she took him down Wellman to a big olive-green Victorian with a dilapidated gate standing half-open. Paint peeled off it in strips.

"This is me." Olya undid her seatbelt. "Gonna remember the address?"

"No," Keen said, defensive, preparing for another cop joke, but this time Olya said: "Well, you should, because I'm inviting you to dinner."

"Oh." Keen was taken aback. "You are?"

"As a thank-you," Olya said. "And to lecture you about the evils of the academic-corporate hierarchies in which you're clearly embedded. But mostly to say thank you. Will you come?"

"Yes," Keen said. "When?"

Olya shrugged. "Tomorrow, the next night, it doesn't matter." And then: "Come tomorrow, actually, since that's my night to cook. I'm not sure I'd trust a dinner guest to some of the others."

"Tomorrow," Keen said, and wasn't able to prevent the sincerity in his tone, as if he were making a more meaningful promise. She gave him a thoughtful look. She seemed to be receiving and retaining a great deal of information at high speed. Then she smiled and opened the car door.

"Tomorrow," she repeated, and slammed the door shut behind her. Keen watched her walk up the sidewalk to the gate. It was broken, he realized; that was why it was standing open. She slipped past, trying not to dislodge it, and he waited until she had gained the front steps and was fumbling with her key before he pulled away. All the way home he said the address to himself—5 Wellman Street—until it had taken on the shape and weight of an incantation.

2018

3

THE NIGHT AFTER THE PROTEST, MINNOW HAD A NIGHTMARE about Katie Curtis. She had had this nightmare again and again during the last weeks at Sewell, but not since she had landed in Paris. In the dream, she had just dropped Katie Curtis off outside the Sewell gates. Katie was in her fleece and leggings, still a little dazed from the morning's activities but clear-headed enough to not want Minnow to come as far as the dorms. Minnow could smell the faintest whiff of gasoline and then, stronger by the second, the full stink of burning. Minnow looked at her former student, wondering if she could smell the burning, too, but Katie had already turned toward the open gates and was gazing through them with her wide anxious eyes, ready to return to her life as she knew it. She didn't seem to know that there was danger. "Wait," Minnow said to her, but even as smoke thickened the air, Katie was already walking through the gates. She walked into the smoke, unseeing. *"Wait!"* Minnow called, but Katie did not hear her and did not turn, and that was when Minnow awoke, sweat washing down her body, and found that it was dawn.

The apartment was quiet, and she lay still, letting her nerves settle, reminding herself where she was, object by object. The exposed beams running the length of the ceiling. The white plaster walls, cracked. In a few hours, sunlight would spread itself like oil across the rough old floorboards, the woodstove, the battered red couch. In several more hours, Minnow would be at the university, ensconced in the hard, granular details of her life here, what had become her real life. For now, the apartment cradled a soothing dark. *All right,* Minnow thought. *All right.*

She tried to go back to sleep, but the dream of Katie stayed with her. And even after she got up and dressed, even as she made her Nespresso and stood on the balcony to drink it, the dream hung over her shoulder like a shadow. Below her, a girl in a trench coat and Doc Martens passed, a large sketchbook self-consciously tucked under her arm. An early-morning Beaux-Arts student, Minnow surmised, watching her duck into the just-opened gates of the Jardin.

Katie had liked to draw. It was an unrelated detail; there were so many of them that came to Minnow from time to time, when she allowed it. Unrelated because they had nothing to do with what had happened, and so when Minnow had been made to "run through the details, one more time," they were things she never mentioned. How Katie had doodled in class; how she had been good enough that Minnow had asked her if she had ever considered art school; how she had replied shyly that her parents would never consider it. How Katie had looked and acted so much younger than she was, although she was in fact quite young already. How Minnow had watched her sometimes, walking on campus with a backpack that was ugly and unfashionably large, and had wondered how she ended up here.

Katie was not wealthy, though most of the students at Sewell were. There were other scholarship kids, but they didn't come from families like Katie's: strict in their religion, wary of education, wary of the world outside the family. Minnow had gathered this from what Katie didn't say as much as from what she did. Another unrelated detail: that Katie had been named for her grandmother, a woman who had had six children by age twenty, and who had died before she was twenty-three. "And now there's me," Katie had said, the second week of class, in Minnow's office. She had come to ask about a different assignment than the one given; for religious reasons, she explained, she did not feel comfortable reading or writing about Faust. "Mephistopheles is *literally* Satan," she had explained, arms folded. But when the conversation turned to her background and she understood Minnow's curiosity to be without judgment, she had relaxed into self-disclosure and had mentioned her grandmother: "I have her whole name, first *and* middle, but my life is totally different. Isn't that weird? Like, she wouldn't even have recognized it."

Minnow had felt what Katie was trying to say. Minnow often thought about all that she had received from her father, though in her own case, she was still making her life resemble his: the small town, the teaching appointment. Sometimes it felt uneasy to her how much she had received from him and kept. She had not said any of this though. Instead, she had tried to guide Katie past her prejudices, turning the conversation back to the assignment and reframing Satan as metaphor. But Katie had held firm.

"Evil is *evil*," she'd said. "There's nothing metaphorical about evil. People do bad things—"

"Yes," Minnow had said, "*people* do—"

"—because Satan acts on them," Katie had finished triumphantly.

Minnow had been struck by Katie's certainty. Minnow could not remember being so confident on any subject at Katie's age. Her friends had been ready to rebel, thrilled at the prospect of throwing themselves in the face of the adult world. But Minnow couldn't help looking at them through Christopher's eyes and seeing them as silly and performative with their piercings, their politics, their promiscuity. In return, they had called her square, boring, a daddy's girl. They had salacious nights filled with drugs and boys, but those stories made their way to Minnow only months later, painfully out-of-date. When she asked why nobody had told her, they'd demur and pretend to have forgotten. But once, in college, her roommate had said, blunt enough to bruise: "I mean, you tell your dad *everything*."

Torn between the clarity of her father's opinions and the realization that her friends expected her to embrace murkier, less defensible positions, Minnow had been consumed by anxiety. And so, when Katie explained calmly that she could not read Faust (or, later, that she could not write a paper on *Orlando,* as that would be condoning homosexuality), even as Minnow tried to explain to Katie why she was wrong, she was mesmerized by Katie's confidence that she was right. Each time, she caved to that confidence, giving her different assignments but warning her that she would eventually be required to read things that made her uncomfortable, and that part of courting an education was courting discomfort. Katie had accepted this with a nod, although Minnow hadn't known if the girl was agreeing or not. But when she had left Minnow's office, there had been a warmth between them, and the warmth grew.

Later these were the details that mattered to Minnow, though they mattered to nobody else.

Later, after everything that was going to happen had happened, Minnow wondered if Katie still felt so sure of her rightness, or if she, too, had had her certainty stripped away.

*

Minnow's sensation of having escaped to Paris made it hard to tell that she was lonely, at first. Everything was something to be figured out, from the frequently out-of-order hot water in her apartment to the question of groceries. In Paris, it turned out, everything you wanted was sold at a shop different from the shop you were in. After a few days, Minnow began to understand the art of specialization: the cheese shop sold only cheese, the bread shop sold only bread, the vegetable stands sold only vegetables. A few more days and she stumbled across the ubiquitous French grocery stores—Carrefour and Monoprix—that mimicked American grocery stores with their jumbled abundance and walls of refrigerators. But by then, Minnow had begun to form habits, going to the same four stalls on the Rue Mouffetard for her bread, cheese, vegetables, and wine—and since the habits felt like they were keeping her tethered to the beginnings of a life, she clung to them.

Minnow's errands were not without anxieties, and that also helped distract from the loneliness. The man who sold roast chickens on the Rue Mouffetard spoke carefully and clearly, and though her heart sped up every time she opened her mouth, she was usually able to conduct the transaction in French. At the boulangerie, on the other hand, the woman behind the counter would mumble or ask unexpected questions rapidly. "Le ticket?" she demanded once, sternly, and Minnow fell into an abyss of confusion, learning only a week later that she had been asked if she wanted her receipt.

She had adjusted to the university rapidly, perhaps because her fellow teachers were incurious about her, and their lack of curiosity created a space inside which she felt safe. They knew she was only a stopgap measure, not staying beyond the spring if Felice's mother did well with her surgeries. Minnow knew Felice from graduate school, though they hadn't spoken much in recent years. Felice had called Minnow out of the blue, two weeks into the semester, and asked if she would take the classes—"I wouldn't ask," she had said delicately, "except I rather imagined you might want . . . a change." Minnow had expected her to say "an escape" or even "asylum," and the delicacy of the word *change* nearly brought Minnow to tears.

"Yes," she said, choosing not to ask Felice how much she had followed of the last few months' proceedings, which had become national news. Some, clearly. Maybe all. "I'll take your classes, thank you, yes."

The university sat on the border of the Sixth and Seventh Arrondissements; or rather, its buildings were scattered throughout the city, but the one in which Minnow taught sat on top of a Carrefour and across the street from a mattress store. "This isn't the Sorbonne," Felice had warned. "I wouldn't call it glamorous. And the money's not great, to be frank. But . . ." And again she spoke with delicacy, not following the *but* with anything, and Minnow had repeated, "Yes, that sounds fine."

Felice had not lied. The first time Minnow saw the location of the building, she had blinked with dismay, and the dismay had only intensified upon swiping her key card and letting herself in through two sets of prisonlike double doors to a series of damp, scuffed hallways. A fluorescent flicker added a pale lemon wash to everything, and as Minnow peered into classrooms, sniffed air that had a subterranean aroma, and at last made her way to Felice's office, she thought: *All right, it's bleak.* The office door had a small Xerox-paper sign with her name on it—MINERVA HUNTER—but the ink from the printer was uneven and striated; the cartridge clearly needed replacing. Sitting in the office with the door shut, each opposing wall an arm's length away, Minnow couldn't help but summon an image of where she had been a few short months ago: Sewell School. Elaborate stone buildings writhing with ivy, classrooms with high, lofted ceilings and sun spilling in. Then she opened her eyes, and relief swamped her instead of dismay. She was so far away from that now. None of them would know where to find her, even if anyone was looking. And with that thought, the bad fluorescents and dirty tile and heavy air began to feel not suffocating, but liberating.

Minnow's apartment was in the Fifth, located where the Rue Lacépède intersected the Rue Geoffroy-Saint-Hilaire. Rushing to the outdoor market on the Rue Mouffetard, she had passed Hemingway's first apartment many times before she noticed the small plaque on the door. Yes, a plaque, but such a small one. The neighborhood was rich with history, it did not need to make overmuch of what it had. Minnow's own apartment building came with a plaque on the outer wall, though the building was so old that the plaque was tarnished past the point of legibility. Minnow did not know what had happened here that required declaration, but the fact that it could have been anything lent the space a certain grandeur.

Felice had provided a list of various sublets and had been surprised when Minnow chose this one. "There's not even a *dishwasher*," Felice had written in an email whose subject line was BAD IDEA? "And it's kind of far from the university, if you plan to walk."

It must have been a former chambre de bonne, a maid's room tucked under the mansard roof. Minnow had gazed at the pixelated images of a minuscule sleeping loft atop a rickety spiral of stairs, a nook so concealed it resembled a child's hiding place. All the other apartments had felt open and exposed, with their wide walls and tall windows. Minnow had not examined her wounded-animal impulse too closely; she had only replied to Felice without hesitation: "I'll take it."

A small balcony faced onto the great iron gates of the Rue Cuvier entrance to the Jardin des Plantes. Minnow sat on the postage-stamp-sized balcony for hours, watching hungrily as people jogged and walked and yanked their dogs into and out of the Jardin. She did her best not to think at all, and it helped to have other people to project her attention onto. But sometimes the streets were empty, and there was no distraction, and it was always then that she considered calling her father.

Christopher had spent time in Paris once, as a young man. This was in the seventies, Minnow knew, though she wasn't sure where her mother fell on the timeline. She guessed that this was during the period of their first long separation, before they came back together to create Minnow. This time was painful for Christopher; he had mentioned it only once. When he spoke of Paris, he was careful not to mention her mother at all. Instead, he told her of the blissful seven days he had spent as the invited speaker for an international chemistry conference. He had been an associate professor at the time, not yet tenured. "I was so broke," he said, laughing. "I had no business being there!" But he had been given a daily stipend for the conference, and had unexpectedly found himself flush with money—more of it every morning!—creating the brief illusion of wealth.

"What did you do with it?" Minnow had asked, and Christopher told her that he had walked up and down a row of fancy storefronts, working up the courage to go in, after which he had bought three leather jackets. Three in a row—"Nobody needs *three* leather jackets!" he'd said, as if still horrified by his own profligacy. But each one had been a slightly different shade of brown—tawny, mahogany, and deep chestnut—each one tailored differently, ridiculously chic. Christopher had worn the chestnut one on his walk back to the hotel, staring at himself in window after window, amazed by his reflection.

For the next several days, he had eaten only bread and cheese, buying the ubiquitous daily baguette for under a dollar, and a round of cheese for a little more. He told her that he had skipped any meals the conference did not provide for free, and while others lingered over restaurant lunches, he walked the aisles of the Jardin des Plantes, wrapped in his leather armor. Sometimes he sat on a bench and tore off hunks of baguette, scattering crumbs for the pigeons. The image stayed with her, resurfacing as soon as she was here: her father, younger even than she was now, scattering crumbs across the Jardin because he had wanted beauty more than the frugal pragmatism by which he normally lived. This was so unlike him that she had never forgotten it. Minnow had wanted to separate herself from him by coming here—wasn't that at least some of what she had wanted?—and yet this was the neighborhood she had chosen, with its proximity to the one landmark he had staked out as his own before she was even born.

*

It was midweek before Minnow saw Charles again. She looked for him in the hallways of the university, listened for the sound of his voice when she passed classrooms with their doors ajar. She wasn't sure what she would say if she did see him, but anticipation hummed under her skin anyway. Their schedules must have been in opposition though, because she saw no trace of him until that Wednesday afternoon, when he sought her out.

She was sitting at a café across the square from the university, and she didn't see him until he was standing over her small table. "Do you mind if I join you?"

Minnow took in the lift of his cheekbones and the thin, mobile shape of his mouth.

"Charles," she said, startled.

"Are you waiting for someone?"

"No, not at all." Minnow measured the tone of her voice—did she sound too encouraging? Too enthusiastic? "No," she said again, drier, making up for it. Charles sat across from her. It was a very small table, and his knees jostled hers as he shifted in his equally small plastic seat. He gestured to the server, and when she came over, he asked for an espresso and then courteously inquired if he could get Minnow another one.

"Oh, I'm fine," she said.

When the server left, Charles leaned back in his tiny chair and looked her straight in the eye. "I have wanted to ask you," he said, with a half-smile, "what you thought."

"What I thought?"

"Of la manifestation." He corrected himself: "The protest."

Minnow considered the question. Though his tone was light, it was not casual.

"It intrigued me," she said.

"It *intrigued* you." Charles's mouth widened into a pleased smile.

"I don't understand all the issues, but I—I guess I was moved by the idea that all of those people want change so much that they showed up." Minnow hesitated, and then: "Or . . . not even that they *want* change but that they must believe it's *possible*. Otherwise they would have stayed home."

Minnow glanced away, self-conscious, but Charles was nodding. "Yes," he said. And then: "When I saw you fall—in the crowd— I thought you would be scared. But when I reached you, you weren't at all."

"Of course I was," Minnow said, but he shook his head.

"No, you looked—*illuminée*. What is the word?"

Minnow smiled. "Illuminated? It's the same in English."

"Illuminated, then," Charles said, and laughed at himself, a huff of breath. "For us, this word also means *mystique, un peu fou*." He lifted an eyebrow at Minnow: "Or *folle*."

Minnow knew the French word for *crazy* and she smiled back at him. "Only a little?"

Warmth deepened between them.

"You didn't say what *you* were doing there," she said. "With a puppet, no less."

Charles grinned. "Luc used to be an actor. Some of his old friends are with a theatre, a political collective. At the first protest—the Saturday before last—I did not know how many people there would be. And to see how many . . . filling the streets, filling the avenues—were you there?" Minnow shook her head. "Luc said to me, 'This is the most important thing that is happening. It will change the country.' He had a sense. But I did not believe him, until I saw with my own eyes. And then last Saturday—to see even more. No wonder the police came back with violence. We frightened them with our numbers, and all they can do with fear is become violent."

"What is the end goal?" Minnow asked.

Charles tilted his head. "The end goal?"

Minnow felt foolish, as if she'd asked the wrong question and revealed herself to be the tourist she was. "I just mean . . . Macron levied a fuel tax, right? And the protests are—people are angry about the taxes?"

Charles considered. "A fuel tax," he said. "Maybe. That was a spark to the tinder. But more than that—Luc says Macron thinks that the people are so stupid, he can talk circles around them. But people aren't stupid when it comes to their own suffering. They know when the money for groceries goes to gas, when hospitals are closing in their towns because the government has cut off the funding. They know when they're being dismissed or condescended to by men who don't care if they live or die. They know because the answer to 'We are starving' is 'Be quiet.' The answer to 'We have no jobs' is 'Drive slower.'" Charles saw the confusion on her face and said: "The speed limit—Macron changed the speed limit in the countryside. Luc says it's all games of control, and people know when they're being played with."

Minnow opened her mouth to ask Charles why Luc had so much to say on this topic but closed it again. She saw Luc in her mind as he had been that Saturday: lean, wolfish, his sharp blue gaze raking over her when he asked—with studied innocence—about her time at the university. Luc had been letting her know that Charles spoke about her; he had enjoyed her brief confusion and Charles's embarrassment. She did not read him as a man who spoke without knowing exactly what he meant to provoke.

"How do you know Luc?" Minnow asked.

"We met years ago. I was in lycée—high school—I went to some stupid meeting—you know, full of students who think politics is what you put on your social media. Luc was there—he was not a student—and I listened to him and I thought: *This man is real.* And I was right."

"Real," Minnow mused. "What makes him real?"

"He comes from factory workers, outside of Paris. For us at the meeting, we were debating ideas. We were passionate about our ideas, yes, but they cost us nothing. But Luc understands cost, and the question of what kind of country France wants to be—this is a question that has been built on the backs of his father, his grandfather. After the meeting he was smoking outside, and I asked if he would get a drink." He made a gesture: *And there you have it.* "From there, we were friends."

Minnow became aware that she felt a distrust of Luc that she couldn't justify. She had met him only briefly—in a moment when he had helped her, even. Looking at Charles, guileless in his admiration, Minnow chose to smile.

"I was lucky for you both on Saturday," she said, diplomatically.

"He asked me about you." Charles was deliberately looking away as he said this, moving his small espresso cup with one finger, then the other.

"I hope you said you didn't know much to tell."

Charles smiled and his eyes lifted to hers. "I said I would like to know more."

Minnow felt the current shifting between them. "What would you like to know?"

"Are you married?"

"No." Minnow waited, but he was quiet. "You aren't going to ask about a boyfriend next?" she teased.

"I care less about a boyfriend," Charles said. "Husbands are more complicated."

Minnow burst out laughing, surprising herself and then Charles. She couldn't remember the last time she had laughed in public. She was certain now that Charles was flirting with her. Though the possibility still existed to interpret this as a joke, it was not one. She would of course shut it down—it was not to be taken seriously, Charles was so young, and then they worked together, too—but a pleasant warmth traveled through her nonetheless. She heard herself ask, in a tone that was so light and blasé she did not sound like herself: "Are you in the habit of dating married women?"

"Habit, no," Charles said. "But these things happen."

Minnow felt her eyebrow climb. But then of course it was different here, wasn't it? And Minnow herself had been a late bloomer.

"I've never dated a married woman," she said, intending to joke, but Charles took her statement at face value. His gaze flickered back to her as he asked, "Is that the direction in which your interests lie?"

"That is not the direction in which my interests lie," Minnow replied, and then had to ask: "How old are you?"

Charles blinked. "Twenty-three."

"You're almost the age of my students. *Our* students."

"But I am not a student," Charles returned.

"No," Minnow agreed slowly. "Evidently not."

A silence extended between them, and then Charles broke it cautiously: "Forgive me if I've offended you."

"Offended, no. I'm not used to how—direct—people can be here. And also . . . it's been some time since . . ." She stopped herself. There were many ways that sentence could have finished itself, and all of them were too revealing. She changed the subject, aware of her clumsiness as she did so: "So Luc was the one who told you about the protests?"

Charles's eyes rested briefly on her face, as if he saw exactly what she was doing, but he responded easily. "We knew something was coming. For many weeks now, there was talk. On Facebook, yes—all the videos, Jacline Mouraud, Ghislain Coutard—and you would click and see: 'A hundred thousand people have watched this video.' And then one day later: 'Six million people have watched this video.'" Charles laughed. "When you have the undivided attention of so many, something will happen, and the only question is when."

"And what," Minnow suggested, but Charles shook his head.

"The what still remains to be seen. This is a beginning, and beginnings can go anywhere." After a moment, in what was almost a confession: "My father does not believe in the protests. He thinks if you are in the streets, you're up to no good."

Minnow smiled. "That sounds like my father," she said ruefully.

"What does your father do?"

"He's a chemistry professor—or he was. He's retired now."

"Mine is a lawyer," Charles said. "A well-positioned one, a public figure—you may know this already." He paused, studying her, as if the thought of what she might have heard about his father troubled him. She shook her head, implying she had heard nothing. Though the other teachers gossiped about Charles from time to time, it was never with her, and she had retained almost nothing.

"He and Macron went to school together—did you know this?"

"No," Minnow said. "I don't know anything about your family. We just met."

Charles laughed, but there was a bitter edge to it. "How refreshing," he said. "There are many people I haven't even met, but they know many details about my father—perhaps even more than I do."

"Are they friends, then? Your father and the president?"

Charles hesitated. "Yes," he said, "and then, no, who knows? Do powerful men have friends? Or do they have allies and advisors?"

"I don't know the answer to that," Minnow said, "I'm not a powerful man." She was trying to make a joke out of it to counteract the bitterness in his voice, but he didn't smile. Instead he leaned across the table toward her, his voice lower but intense.

"When I was in high school, I asked my father for advice. I was in a stupid situation, a popular classmate asking to cheat off me. My father, this man whom I love very much, whose opinion helps shape the country in small ways every day—he said to me: 'Well, what do you have to gain, what do you have to lose?' He laid it out for me like that: 'Who is your classmate? Ah, okay, his father works at the Ministry of Culture. Is he kind to you? No? Okay, but if he owes you a debt, he must then be kind to you.' And so on. Everything in my father's world is a strategy, a transaction, the world has no wider scope beyond that. If these are the only men speaking, then no wonder we are stuck in time, hundreds of years standing in the same place."

Minnow was quiet, and when she did not speak, Charles's voice softened. The anger was gone now, though the intensity remained.

"I am beginning to ask myself: What world do you want to live in? How must the people in that world be treated? What must you do to ensure that this is the version that comes to pass? We keep doing the same things again and again—and *your* country, too, what I see in the news, it's the same thing again and again. We go in circles, a hundred years pass and the same people are starving, the same people die. What if it could change?"

Minnow could feel the dazzling force of Charles's attention. She thought of her previous life at Sewell, where men had clustered along the road to her apartment with their chants and signs. She thought of Katie Curtis, looking up at her with brown eyes so wide they appeared stunned. She thought of what it had felt like to understand for the first time how much of her life would no longer be in her control. She made herself focus on Charles and realized that he was waiting for an answer. She had assumed that he was employing rhetorical flourishes. Were they actually questions?

"Wouldn't that require something of us?" Charles asked. He *was* asking.

"Yes," she heard herself say.

"Yes?"

"Yes, it would require something. Of us."

In the silence their eyes met, and electricity leapt like a circuit snapping shut. Minnow saw all his potential laid bare for her like fresh wood or new sheets, a thing that is clean deciding how it would like to be used. She envied him that. Then they forced their gaze apart—down at the café table, at the street, in any direction but at each other.

1968

4

THE BIG VICTORIAN SMELLED LIKE LENTILS, CUMIN, INCENSE, AND age—the comforting, stifling mustiness of an old house. Standing awkwardly in the doorway, a bottle of wine in hand, Keen inhaled the mingling odors as the stocky red-bearded man in front of him blinked suspiciously. "I don't know you," the man said.

"Olya invited me," Keen explained, apologetically. Then, unable to stop himself: "Are you all right?"

"What do you mean am *I* all right?"

"I saw you . . . when the cops . . . I was passing, but . . ." Keen's voice trailed away, since a scowl was deepening on the other man's face. He opened his mouth to try and extricate himself but Olya appeared in the hallway, wrapped in a faded blue apron.

"Keen!" she said, with what seemed to be real delight. "Look at you, right on time."

It was the first time Keen had seen her without her bulky yellow coat, and he took in her details with a quick and hungry eye. She was all angles: her button-down man's shirt, sleeves rolled to mid-bicep, the thin planes of her bare wrists, the line of her neck, the definition of her jaw.

"Hi," he said, and held out the bottle of wine.

"For us?" she asked, pleased. "How polite. Ethan, isn't that nice?"

The red-bearded man, Ethan, grunted. "You know this guy?"

"No," Olya said, "I just like it when strangers pop up with booze. Keen, come in. Ethan, don't be a cock-hole."

Ethan stepped aside, barely, and Keen followed Olya into the house, taking in its many badly lit rooms leading off from the hallway, mismatched chairs, and handmade rag rugs. The smell of incense intensified, and under it he caught the humid whiff of feet. Books piled everywhere: on top of chairs, beneath them, riding the edges of a staircase that led up into a vast gloom. Olya took him into a large kitchen with uneven yellow linoleum flooring and a gas range crouching in the corner. Somewhere along the way Ethan had peeled off into a shadowy side room, and when Keen realized he was no longer with them, he felt a profound relief.

"So he's all right?" he asked Olya.

"Ethan? Yeah, he's always like that."

"No, I mean—it looked like the cops hit him pretty hard."

"Oh! That!" Olya was stirring a large pot of something on the burner, but she looked up at Keen with interest. "Yeah, they did actually. He's got some crazy bruises. So you're pro-Cavener but you're not pro-cop."

"I don't really think of it in terms of *pro* and *anti*," Keen objected, as Olya gestured him over to a tall stool in the corner. He perched, feeling pleased at being directed by her but a little silly to have his legs dangling. He arranged himself so that he could rest his legs on the ground, in what he hoped was a casual but commanding posture.

"I mean, those are the most fundamental terms." Olya pried the cork out of the bottle Keen had brought and poured a liberal amount into two jam jars. She handed him one. "Right? Either you're for or you're against, it's basically the root of all human nature, to choose a side."

"I don't think that's true," Keen said. "I think it's our animal nature to reduce everything to this tribal thing—for or against—and it's the root of our *human* nature to entertain nuance and context."

Olya laughed, delighted. "You're wrong, of course, but you're *very* educated," she teased. "It's actually a marvel to watch their education at work in you. You wield it like the weapon it was designed to be."

"I like to think of it as *my* education," Keen said mildly, trying not to show the irritation that rose up in him.

"Of course you do," Olya agreed, "because that's how they've trained you."

"Okay." Keen rocked forward. "And what about you? How's their education treating *you?*"

Olya smiled. "Badly. It fucked with my head and it took a long time to unlearn."

"This is a funny place to unlearn it, here in their midst."

"On the contrary, it's the only place. You've got to go into the heart of the cave to look the monster in the face."

Keen snorted. "So what's your major? Philosophy?"

"I dropped out," Olya said, defiantly. "But before I dropped out, it was Russian literature, because I thought: *Well that's one field in which they can't implant their thoughts in me, since I already have my own.* But they tried anyway, of course."

"I don't know about the humanities," Keen said, "but science isn't about implanting thoughts, it's about getting at the truth. A truth that is so concrete, so tangible, that you don't need to spend your time convincing people of things because if they just looked they could see it for themselves."

"That's pretty," Olya said, stirring. "That's a very pretty way to think of it."

"It's not *pretty.*" Keen was nettled enough that, this time, he showed it. "It's *accurate.*"

"Something I'm learning about accuracy is that it's not about the stone you're throwing or the mark you hit." The teasing note was gone from Olya's voice, and she sounded very serious. "It depends on where you're standing when you throw the stone."

"I don't know what that means."

"It means that things can look very convincing from where you stand," Olya said. "But if you shift even one step to the left or the right, they begin to look very different. And you have to start asking a lot of questions about what you assumed and what you intended."

"But that's the point of science," Keen protested. "It doesn't matter where you're standing, once a thing has been tested and proved, the truth is the truth whether or not you're even there to see it." He heard a pleading note enter his voice and shut his mouth abruptly, sitting back on the stool.

He expected Olya to make fun of him, but she didn't. She remained silent, chopping a fat yellow root that was dyeing her fingertips, the knife, and the cutting board a rich gold. Keen couldn't stop himself. "Do you not believe in scientific proof?" he asked. "Do you just think everything is relative no matter what the data shows?"

Olya glanced at him. "No," she said. "I believe it's not possible to separate a thing out from how it's used. What you're talking about is pure science, a world of numbers that add up and physical laws that order the cosmos. In that world, the one you're describing, humans don't even exist—or they aren't necessary. What I'm talking about is the world we're actually in, where a scientific discovery is immediately absorbed and deployed by humans and corporations and armies, and you end up with napalm and nuclear bombs and bioweapons."

"So you don't think people should make discoveries because other people might misuse them?"

"No," Olya said. "I think people who misuse discoveries should be punished."

"Oh." Keen felt as if he should have been able to follow the argument she was making; it was simple logic, after all. But at the same time he felt the presence of some other meaning running alongside it, just under the surface, and the sensation unsettled him. In the end he was unsure whether they had agreed or disagreed, or on what terms.

*

Dinner was held at a long wooden table full of the clamor of voices, the clatter of silverware and plates, spoons scraping against bowls of stew. Two cast-iron pans full of turmeric rice and beans rested on folded towels, one at each end of the table. Olya placed Keen at an end as well, between her and a girl named Daisy who was from California and had come to study geology. "That's rocks," Daisy said, and Keen, stunned at the idea that she believed herself to be conversing with someone who didn't know what geology was, automatically replied, "Oh wow," and then searingly wished that he had said something else.

He had expected Olya to announce him (or denounce him) as a chemistry student, and for the whole table to turn on him like a pack of ravening wolves, but she didn't and nobody asked what he was doing there. It seemed to be a common thing for someone new to show up at dinner. Eventually Daisy asked what he did, and Keen evaded the question by asking Daisy how long she had been living in Boston. As she replied, he saw Olya's flickering smile come and go, but she only reached over to serve him more salad.

Ethan was sitting at the far end and Keen watched him from time to time, intimidated and curious. Though he didn't seem in a much better humor, he was seated next to a tall, striking boy with a hard jaw and large glasses who was delivering a low stream of commentary. From time to time something the boy said would make Ethan smile despite himself.

Olya saw him looking. "That's Peter," she said, keeping her own voice beneath the orchestral crash of table-wide conversation. "He's the other original."

"Original?"

"It was me and him and Ethan that got the house. It was going to be torn down and we went to the landlord and asked if he'd rent to us for cheap if we fixed it up. Ethan's dad owns a construction company so Ethan can do drywall, even some roofing, that kind of thing. And we lied and said that Peter's dad is an electrician, so we could fix the wiring without the landlord needing to pay anyone."

"Did you actually fix it up?"

Olya laughed. "I'm insulted," she said. "Can't you tell?"

"No, no, I mean . . . it looks great," Keen fumbled.

"I'm kidding," Olya said, "it's a shithole, I know. But it's *our* shithole—and yeah, we did fix it up. I mean, we didn't do anything to code, but Peter rewired a whole floor, and it hasn't blown out yet."

"So his dad *is* an electrician?"

Olya grinned. "No, his dad is in jail. He built some bombs and put them in the wrong places. But he *did* concern himself with wiring, and so does Peter."

"Wait, really?" Keen stopped eating, scanning Olya to see if she was joking.

"Which part?" And then: "Oh, you mean the bombs? Yeah, really."

"Who did he want to bomb?"

Olya sighed. "Well, that's the problematic part," she said. "He wanted to bomb Jews, but he didn't know any—they're from Oklahoma—so he made a few bombs and thought he'd start out just seeing how it went. He put one in a bank—which was owned by a Christian guy, by the way, but, you know, he made that age-old facile connection, money and Jews—and he put another one in an auto-body shop."

"An autobody shop?"

"Yeah, he owed them money and ultimately it was easier to blow them up than pay them." Olya shrugged. "So says Peter, who should know—he was there for it. When Peter tells this story, he always says: 'The reasoning was faulty, but the wiring was impeccable.'" She laughed: "He's a craftsman, our Peter. More wine?"

As she poured for Keen, he studied Peter with renewed interest. Peter was gesturing with one long and capable hand as he said something to Ethan, and Ethan's face had softened into a smile before he realized Keen was looking at them. The smile slid off his face and he directed a hard look straight down the table. Keen glanced away, embarrassed, afraid that he had looked like he was trying to eavesdrop.

Keen remembered Olya in the kitchen saying, "I think people who misuse discoveries should be punished," and he turned back to her, a newly unsettled feeling under his ribs.

"You aren't . . . ?"

"What?"

"I mean . . . you guys aren't . . . *bombing* anybody, are you?"

He expected Olya to either laugh or get angry, but she did neither. Instead she just looked at him coolly. "Now that, Keen, *is* a cop question."

"Only if the answer is yes."

"Is that something you were gonna ask me anyway, or are you asking because of what I said about Peter?"

"Peter," Keen admitted, "but also . . . I don't know, you seem to have a lot of convictions."

"Convictions and bombs aren't the same thing."

"No, not always."

"In fact, it's the people *without* convictions who most often resort to the bombs," Olya informed him severely—and then, as if she felt that she had made her point sufficiently, she answered his question. "No, we aren't bombing anybody. Are you disappointed?"

"I don't know," Keen said. "It depends what dessert is."

Olya laughed out loud and Keen felt the immediacy of eyes on him. When he glanced up, both Ethan and Peter were watching him, their heads close together, blond hair against copper. Peter looked curious, Ethan hostile. Olya didn't seem to notice.

"Noted," she said. "The man is a gourmand."

Daisy returned her attention to them just then, and the man next to Olya—an excitable actor named Lawrence who said he specialized in "performance as absurdist disruption"—joined them as well. Keen found himself folded into a series of conversations that never really ended, just opened themselves to include more people saying other things, turning and flowing and changing direction midsentence, so that the things you thought were being discussed were not what was being discussed anymore. At one point, Daisy turned to him, having been holding forth for some time: "Sorry, what's your name?" "Keen," he replied, and she continued from there: "As Keen was saying, there's been a real influx of Eastern philosophy, which America has immediately moved to corporatize—" as if it was every day that she ate dinner beside someone for sixty minutes without knowing their name. As if his name and occupation were the least important things about him.

*

In the kitchen afterward, Keen insisted on helping wash dishes and was rewarded with another of Olya's surprised, pleased smiles. These weren't the teasing ones, or even the ones that acknowledged that Keen had scored a point with a well-turned argument. They seemed to come from a different place entirely, and they blossomed over Olya's face, unfolding into deeper sweetness the longer they lasted, making her look younger and more vulnerable. When she smiled at him like that, Keen felt that he was getting a glimpse of whoever Olya had been as a child, and something in the center of his chest expanded in a quick painful pulse.

"Normally the cook does the dishes," Olya said, perched on the stool observing him.

"Doesn't it go the other way? I thought cooks never clean."

"Ah, not in this house. We believe in just getting the suffering out of the way. One day a week, you will cook, you will clean. Your life will be rendered a misery of obligation. The other six days, you bask in your freedom like a little lizard."

"So there are seven of you who live here?"

"I should have remembered," Olya said drily. "I'm talking to a numbers guy. We are indeed seven. Me, Peter, Ethan, Daisy, her boyfriend Jonno, who you didn't properly meet—he was the one yelling about the Rolling Stones—Lawrence, who you met, and Molly, who was sitting on the other side of Peter. They're not usually all home at once, so you lucked out. But for a few years, there were only five— Daisy and Jonno are relatively new."

"So what was your philosophy of suffering when there were more days than humans?"

"Ah," Olya said, "then we would draw straws weekly, and two people would suffer twice as much as everybody else."

"Did people who had to do it twice get taken out of the drawing for the next week?"

Olya gave him a raised eyebrow. "I see you're still married to the concept of fairness, in direct contravention to everything happening in the world around you."

"Oh come on," Keen said. "Not wanting to cook and clean twice a week for two weeks in a row isn't exactly a big moral statement, it's just common sense."

Olya grinned. "*Two?* I once got my straw pulled every week for six weeks straight."

"You're kidding."

"Nope. Just me. Everybody else was rotating on and off, and I was the fucking hunchback of Notre Dame, running up and down the stairs with my mop and bucket."

"Why didn't you just take your name out of the hat?"

"Because part of communal living is agreeing to a set of rules that hold society together," Olya said, serious. "If you've agreed to the rules when they're working for you, you can't suddenly withdraw your participation when they aren't."

"But I thought that was your whole thing," Keen said, "changing the world because the systems are broken."

Olya cocked her head to one side. "Yes, but you see, the house-keeping system wasn't broken, it was working very well. For six weeks, my suffering was doubled and the suffering of those around me was reduced. They had no incentive to abandon the intentional commu-nity we were creating, and when the time came for their straws to be pulled several weeks in a row, they continued to cook and clean despite being frustrated. The house remained clean, food was on the table every night, the community stayed together. What part of that looks broken?"

"The part where your suffering was doubled," Keen said, "for six weeks in a row." He had initially felt silly using the word *suffering* to describe housework, but now he felt righteous in his argument.

"Ah, a rugged individualist." Olya bowed her head toward Keen, and now the mocking tone was back. "I should have guessed. Men of science, you know, advancing society one carefully honed career at a time."

Keen wanted to say something brilliant and cutting but he couldn't find it, and he was so flustered and irritated that in the end he just said, "Ah, fuck off." This was not a way he had been raised to speak to women, but it was perhaps the best thing he could have said, because Olya burst out laughing.

"Keen," she said. "Look at you. You are full of surprises." And under her maddening, mocking, tender gaze, Keen believed her, for the first time felt that he was, and that it was marvelous.

*

She walked him to his car at the end of the night. He was halfway through thanking her for the meal when she interrupted him.

"You'll have to come back," she said.

"Really?"

"Yes, really. Unless this was all too much for you."

"No!" Keen protested, flushing. "It was . . ." He wanted to say *perfect* but stopped himself just in time.

"Good," Olya said, as if she had heard him anyway. And she leaned in—everything in him constricted itself to a dizzying point of exalted anticipation—and her lips brushed the side of his cheek. "Good night," she said, turning back toward the broken gate and the broad flagstones.

In the car, disappointment swamped him. If only he had turned his face. If only *he* had been the one to lean in for a kiss and therefore could have chosen where to place it. But with the disappointment came exhilaration, and he replayed the kiss he had gotten again and again the whole drive home. Later, lying in bed, he replayed it still: the way her face had come so close to his that he couldn't even take her in with his eyes, but only with the entirety of his senses; her chapped lips and her citrusy smell, the nutty scent of turmeric and cooking oil caught in her hair; that same hair falling into his face as she kissed his cheek. For those three seconds, she had filled his whole world.

2018

5

SOMEBODY WAS RINGING MINNOW'S BUZZER INSISTENTLY, AND the sound brought her up out of a deep sleep. For a moment she had no idea where she was. The buzzer was an urgent summoning, and the urgency made her frantic. She knocked over the bedside lamp, and as it hit the floor, she realized she was in Paris, in the Cinquième, in bed. Saturday night. And the buzzer was ringing, still.

She got out of bed, careful not to step on the fallen lamp, and fumbled for the wall switch. Dull light flooded the little sleeping loft, penetrating only partway down the tightly corkscrewed stairs. Clinging to the railing, Minnow made her way down and into the kitchen, turning on lights as she went, and hit the speaker button.

"Oui?" she asked, warily. Outside the French windows, the darkness was broken only by streetlights. It might be the middle of the night or early morning.

The tinny voice that came back to her was that of Charles. "Minnow, j'suis désolé."

"Charles?" Minnow blinked at the speaker. "What are you—*why* are you downstairs?"

"I need help." Charles sounded out of breath. "Please, can you—"

"I'm coming," she said.

She saw Luc first, leaning against the entryway to her building. His head was bowed and he had one hand clamped over his face. Blood seeped from between his fingers, inky and thick.

"Jesus," Minnow said, and Charles's face separated out from the darkness. Minnow realized that Luc's other arm was slung around Charles's neck, that Charles was holding him upright.

"I'm sorry," Charles said again. "We were close by and we—can we—"

"Yes," Minnow said, "Jesus, okay, yes." Cold air whipped them as she held the door and Charles and Luc staggered past her. "There's no elevator, I'm on the top floor."

Charles spoke to Luc in French, low and patient, easing him up one stair, then the next. Now the landing, turning him, talking him up the next flight. Minnow followed behind, feeling as though she were sleepwalking. Up ahead, Luc faltered and Charles staggered under him, and Minnow bounded up, steadying them. A moment, in which Charles breathed and Luc moaned.

"Can you put your arm around me?" she asked Luc, and he mumbled something indistinct.

"He won't take his hand off his face," Charles said.

Minnow opened her mouth to ask what had happened and then set it aside. She slid an arm around Luc's waist and he sagged against her. Even with Charles supporting him from the right he was heavier than she had imagined; he had seemed so lanky and thin when she met him the Saturday before. Between the two of them they half carried him up the stairs, and with each step he inhaled sharply, his body tight with pain.

When they reached the warmth of her apartment, she moved around the space hastily, turning on other lights as Charles navigated Luc to the couch. Luc sank down, head in both hands, and Charles turned to Minnow.

"Bandages," he said, "and hot water. Do you have . . ."

"Yeah, yes. In the kitchen."

Charles followed Minnow into the narrow kitchen as she rifled the cabinets for Band-Aids and antiseptic ointment, anything that could be used.

"Charles, what the fuck happened?"

"He got hit in the face with a flashball."

"A what?"

"An LBD40—they're like these . . . j'sais pas how to . . . lanceur de

balle de défense, like a rubber bullet mais c'est bien pire que ça."
Charles caught himself, found English again. "They aim for the faces,
I saw cops doing it all night on purpose, aiming for the faces."

"You were—there was another protest?"

"Yes, near here. They came at us, and Luc . . ." Charles shook his
head. "He wouldn't back down, he caught it in the face."

"I'm not a doctor," Minnow said helplessly. "If it's serious, you
need to take him to a doctor."

"He won't go, I tried—but we heard they're standing outside the
hospitals, like a dragnet, making arrests, I don't know if that's true
but . . ." His voice subsided and he took a deep breath, then another.
Minnow realized that he was panicking. "I didn't know where to go."

"All right," Minnow said, calming him. "It's all right."

They were both quiet, staring at each other across the unforgiving
fluorescent glare of the overhead light. Charles was beautiful. Minnow tried not to put words to this thought, tried not even to let it
enter the room, but it existed in a series of fragments: the high slant
of his cheekbones, the sharpness of his chin, the slight frown line
between his large eyes, the way his hair, matted by sweat and blood,
framed his face. Blood?

"You're bleeding," Minnow said.

"Am I?" He reached up and touched the side of his head. "I think
that's from Luc?"

"Were you hit?"

"I'm not sure. It was chaos, chaos. Luc got a text, they needed bodies. I said we shouldn't go, things were getting—people were throwing whatever they could—I saw a park bench go through a store
window—but Luc said—Luc always needs to *push,* he thinks . . . And
then when we got there . . ." Charles's voice soared and he made an
effort to calm himself.

"Let me see." Minnow moved closer to him, lifted her fingertips to
his hair. He permitted it. Gently, she combed her fingers through the
tangles, feeling dried blood. She prodded gently at the side of his
head, but the skin was firm and whole under her fingers.

"Does this hurt?"

"No."

"But you feel this? It isn't numb?"

"Yes," Charles said tightly, his eyes landing on hers for a briefest moment. "I feel it." He dropped his gaze to the floor, and Minnow dropped her hand as well.

"I think it's Luc's blood," she said.

"Luc," Charles said abruptly, as if remembering something long forgotten, although only a minute had passed. He took the bandages Minnow had found and left the kitchen, and she soaked a washcloth and filled a small cereal bowl with warm water. Back in the living room, Charles was kneeling in front of Luc, talking softly. When Minnow entered, he moved back, ceding the floor to her as if she knew what she was doing. She knelt where Charles had been, facing Luc, though she did not know what came next.

As if obeying a command, Luc lowered his hand from his eye. Behind her she heard Charles's stifled intake of breath, but at first she didn't know what she was looking at. Then she began to piece it together. Luc's face, the right side of his face. When she had met him a week ago, there had been a whole forehead, a bright blue eye, a smooth expanse of skin. Now the flesh was distorted and swollen, puffed strangely and mottled with bruises, everything slicked over in dry blood layered with wet blood. Where was all that blood coming from? And her eye followed it to his forehead, below the hairline, where she found a gaping absence. Luc's head had produced a hole the size of a golf ball, from which oozed blood so dark it was black.

"Is it bad?" Luc slurred.

"No," Charles said from just behind Minnow, but she could hear the fear in his voice. "Pas si grave."

"Minou?" Luc asked. He sounded scared now, too, as if the fear was catching up with the pain. "Minou, is it bad?"

"It can be fixed," Minnow said, without any knowledge of whether this was true, "but you have to go to a doctor, Luc, I'm not a doctor."

"Je ne vois rien," Luc said, "from my right eye, nothing."

"Hold still." Minnow took Luc's chin in her fingers and tilted his face toward the lamp. The hole was terrible, it was like a devouring mouth in a place no mouth should be. She tore her eyes away and studied his right eye socket instead. His eyebrow was so swollen that it produced a Cro-Magnon ridge, and below it, his eyelid was glued shut with blood. As gently as she could, Minnow brushed the wet washcloth over his eyelid, taking care not to go above it. Luc whimpered. She dipped the washcloth into the cereal bowl and this time she squeezed water over his eyelid instead of touching it with the cloth. Water mixed with blood and flowed down his cheek, but he was quiet. She dipped the washcloth and squeezed it, dipped and squeezed, and gradually Luc's eyelid became visible, the layers of blood removed like varnish.

"Try to open it now," she said.

She could feel Charles at her back, tense. Luc's eyelashes fluttered, and his eyelid lifted. The electric blue of his eye was caught in a red net of burst veins, but it seemed whole. He blinked, blinked again, and his voice was shaky with relief when he said, "I can see."

"Thank God," Charles said behind her, fervent.

"I can see!" Luc grabbed Minnow's forearm, exhilarated. "Oh my god, you saved my eye!"

"No, no," Minnow said, "it was just the blood"—but he wasn't listening, he was full of a celebratory high.

"Ils ont cru qu'ils allaient me rendre borgne but fuck them, man, fuck them!" He wanted to get up, but Minnow grabbed his arms: "Luc, please sit down! You're still hurt"—and with that, the elation ebbed and he felt the pain descend again.

"Oh god," he said, sitting heavily. "It's my head. Is it my head?"

"Yes," Minnow said firmly, "you have a big fucking hole in your head so you need to take it easy."

She had Luc's attention again, and with it came a new docility. He put himself into her hands wholeheartedly. The bleeding seemed to have stopped, but she worried that if she removed too much of the crust of dirt and dried blood, it would start again. She cleaned blood off his eyelids and cheeks as best she could, avoiding the wound itself. She didn't know how deep it was or what to do with it, she had never seen anything like it. Charles said nothing, occasionally handing her things she asked for: a fresh washcloth, a new bowl of water, the ointment. After what felt like a long time, Minnow sat back on her heels, the blood-soaked washcloth in her hand. She studied Luc's face; already, new bruises were coming up in mottled reds and indigos and deep purples. Luc's blood was tacky on her fingers and on her jeans, though she wasn't sure how it had gotten there.

"Well?" Luc asked.

"I've done what I can," she said. "You should go to an emergency room." And, as he opened his mouth to protest: "The night is over, they must be done making arrests. And if anyone asks questions, just say you got hit by accident—what can they prove?"

It was dawn now. The light outside the windows was a gray haze, and though the streets remained mostly empty, there was a wakefulness in the air—the sound of a dog barking, someone running by, their footsteps clattering. Luc and Charles shared a glance and then, slowly, Luc nodded. "Give me a minute."

Charles withdrew into the kitchen, gesturing Minnow after him. She followed, turning off the overhead lights so that the room was filled with the dim underwater blue of dawn. The kitchen window pointed out into a cluster of red-tiled roofs, stubbled with short pipe-mouths and little chimneys on which pigeons were huddled against the cold. From here Minnow could see stones crumbling, shattered tiles, broken concrete sidings, as if all that held these old buildings together was a sense of duty in the face of such endless history.

"He's lucky," Charles said. "When people get hit there"—he tapped his temple—"or here"—his cheek—"usually they lose the eye."

"Usually? This is a usual thing?"

"Last time and this time," Charles said, "we are seeing it. Our friend Martin, his hand blew off."

"His *hand*?"

"The grenade, it landed right beside him. He thought, *Oh no, I will lose a leg!* He picked it up to throw it away and *boom!*" Charles shrugged. "If he did nothing, he would have lost the leg, so . . . an arm or a leg, I guess, is your choice."

"But," Minnow began, and then subsided, unsure what her objection would have been. After a moment, she asked, gently, "You *will* take Luc to a hospital?" Charles nodded. "He's concussed, with an injury like that. Do you know what that means, a concussion? I don't know the French word, but if he were to go home and go to sleep right now, he could die."

"I understand," Charles said.

"He doesn't seem to."

"He understands as well, but he has charges. Is that the word?"

"Charges?" Minnow asked. "Like . . . criminal charges?"

"Yes—a situation from before. That's why he's so worried about the police."

Minnow sighed. "Great. Well, if he dies of a concussion, the charges won't matter, will they?"

Charles tilted his head to one side, taking her in. "You are very . . . certain," he said, with wonder.

Minnow was surprised into laughing. "*Certain?* I thought I was— what did you say? *Mystique* and a little crazy."

Charles smiled. "When I first saw you at l'université . . . you were walking down a hallway and I started to say hello, but you just kept walking. Right away, I was curious about you. The way you looked—so strong, and kind of pissed off."

"I don't remember that," Minnow said, flushing. "Did you really try to say hello?"

Charles waved it away. "No matter. I wanted to know: *Who is that woman?* And then I saw you last weekend, climbing the lamppost, your whole spirit was present. And now—we come to your apartment in the middle of the night, like this, and you are . . . unflapped? How do you say. As if you do this all the time, sew people up in the night, no problem. You say: *Do this, do that*— You have no *Why the fuck did you come here?* Just what to do next. Very certain. You are full of mystery, Minou."

Minnow opened her mouth to say that the word was *unflappable,* then hesitated, feeling she should point out that she had only washed Luc's face, nothing had been sewn. But the details were beside the point, she should just tell him he was wrong. She was neither mysterious nor particularly certain about anything. She had relied on her father for certainty and Christopher had always been willing to provide it; his opinions were bedrock, and in general she had done what he suggested. She had even taken the job at Sewell because he thought it was a good idea. Somehow, Charles had misunderstood her completely.

And then she thought of Katie Curtis. What the girl had asked of her, and how she had complied. Had she not been certain then? Though later everyone had questioned her motives, though later she had come to question her own, in that moment she had felt that what she was doing was right. For that whole strange day, she had been the image of whoever Charles thought she was now. And the thought filled her with a strange joy, like drawing a line between two distant points and then finding that those points were actually much closer than she'd believed.

Charles was waiting for a reply, Minnow could see that. He had given her a gift with this admission—not only in how he had seen her, but that he had been trying to understand her. And then a new thought occurred to her. It had been living at the back of her mind this whole time as a general confusion, but she hadn't had time to recognize it.

"How did you know where I live?"

"I looked it up."

"You—how did you look it up? Tonight, you looked it up?"

"I looked it up," he said, meeting her gaze directly, "in the database. There is an admin directory. If you check the box, they don't put your address. But sometimes people forget to check the box, so . . ."

"I don't remember a box."

He allowed the corner of his mouth to swerve into a smile, despite himself. "You are very good with head wounds and very bad with paperwork."

"I'm bad with both," Minnow said. "So . . . you looked up my address while Luc was bleeding out? Just in case I lived nearby?"

"No," Charles admitted, still meeting her eyes steadily, "I looked it up last week. After we had coffee. Just in case I might accidentally run into you, on purpose."

They stared at each other in the dim kitchen. Minnow felt the leap and crackle between them. She wanted him to look away first, and then she wondered if she did want that. Charles opened his mouth, but before he could say anything, Luc limped into the kitchen, bracing himself heavily against the wall.

"Okay," he said. "Let's go."

Charles spoke to him rapidly in French and Luc replied. This time Minnow listened closely but caught only a few words—something about a telephone call, *I told him,* something about *les flics,* which she had learned from her students was a word for cops. Charles nodded, turned back to Minnow. "Thank you," he said, and Luc echoed it: "Thank you," as if they were both leaving after a successful dinner party.

"Be careful," Minnow said, and though she addressed them both, it was Charles who replied with a small private smile.

"And you," he said.

Minnow stood in the doorway as they descended the stairs. Charles glanced up once, when they reached the bottom, and then the two of them turned the corner and were gone.

*

Christopher had not liked Minnow's first boyfriend, and he had not liked her last one. The ones in between he had not met, though Minnow thought it was fair to assume he would not have liked them either. She felt that he saw them all as interlopers, though he had never said this directly.

The first one was named Victor, and he had been Minnow's best friend in her junior year of high school. Although it was not yet clear to Minnow that Victor was gay, it was clear to them both that they had joined forces to protect each other from ridicule. Minnow was the kind of shy that meant she was mostly ignored, only pushed into the lockers every so often, but Victor was fat and witty and unable to sink into himself and vanish the way Minnow did, so he bore the brunt of the bullying. They sat together on the bus, since neither of them belonged to the subset of wealthy children whose parents bought them cars, and they sat together during lunch. When they shared classes, which was not often—Victor was in AP math classes but remedial English, and Minnow was the opposite—they sat at the back of the classroom and passed each other notes. Somehow the concentrated high beam of Victor's attention counteracted the sneers of everyone around them. When Minnow was with Victor, she felt that she existed. It was a fraction of the feeling she got around her father—as if with Victor she existed as an outline, and with her father she came into full being. But Minnow knew what it was like to create a world with a single other person and escape into it, and so her friendship with Victor felt safe and familiar.

Christopher never said he disliked Victor, but something shifted in his face when Minnow talked about him. He never remembered details she shared from the funny stories Victor had told her or the ideas Victor had had. Occasionally, when she was trying to tell Christopher about one of Victor's opinions, Christopher would interrupt her: "What do *you* think? Not what *he* thinks, what *you* think." Minnow learned that the in-jokes she shared with Victor could not be shared with her father; and likewise, if she told Victor things her father said that seemed particularly clever or intriguing to her, he wrinkled his nose and looked confused. It baffled her that her experiences of her father and of Victor did not translate from one to the other. She couldn't understand how they had no interest in each other despite the fact that they made up the entirety of her social world.

On the eve of the junior prom, Christopher had sat Minnow down, nominally to talk to her about sex. "You're too young," Christopher said, addressing the rubber tree in its large terra-cotta pot, his eyes never meeting Minnow's. "So don't do it. But if and when you do, especially if that's soon, make sure you use condoms. And you can say stop at any time—it doesn't matter how far it goes, you have the right to say stop. If anybody ever doesn't listen to you, that's a crime and you should tell me, or someone you trust."

Minnow had been so horrified and embarrassed that she didn't retain much that Christopher said on the topic, but eventually, Christopher had taken a left turn and landed in much stranger territory. He had tried to talk to Minnow about love, and this she remembered vividly. He explained that it is possible to feel very sure that you are in love and that you will be in love forever, but that all feelings are changeable and these ones most of all, so no future plans should ever be built upon them. Love didn't exist as often as you thought it did, he said, and even when it did, it rarely existed for two people in the same way.

Minnow had not understood what it was that Christopher was trying to do with this conversation. Even now, she wasn't sure. It was an odd thing to tell a high school junior, especially if Victor actually *had* been her first love. But at the time she nodded and nodded, waited until he was finished, and then she asked him: "Was that how it was with you and Mom?" She remembered this clearly, because they spoke so rarely about her mother.

Christopher had stared at her for a long moment in silence, stricken. And then he gathered himself and said no, they had been very much in love. One had to be in love in order to produce a child.

"That has nothing to do with love," Minnow protested. "That has to do with biology."

Christopher had been thrown off by this. Minnow watched him stumble over his words as he explained that what he meant was that he and her mother had a lot of history between them and a deep understanding of each other. That when they realized she was pregnant, their desire to have and raise the child had been a response to that history and that understanding, even if ultimately Minnow's mother had not been able to stay and see it through. This was how Minnow had first learned that she was a mistake.

Minnow had not asked what specifically prevented her mother from "seeing it through." Later, when she was in college and even after, she would find herself asking Christopher sneak-attack questions about her mother: What was her major? What kind of music did she listen to? But as a junior in high school, Minnow was still too angry to ask questions. She had learned her anger over time, starting in elementary school when she was asked repeatedly where her mother was, and why it was always her father who showed up to drop-off and pickup and parent-teacher meetings. She had nursed this anger into a hard shape as she chose crueler and crueler answers to the questions, more and more often wielded by girls who sought to shame her. "My mom is dead," she told them, deadpan. "She's in prison. She's in a mental asylum. She's dangerous, we're hiding from her." She tried to refuse their attempts at humiliating her by pushing the boundaries of humiliating herself. By high school, her anger manifested in silence, a refusal to ask the questions to which she most wanted answers. And so: "She couldn't see it through," Christopher said, and Minnow said nothing.

Though Christopher had made himself address the topics of love and sex that once, he did not do it again. Not as it concerned Minnow, and certainly not as it concerned his own life. Throughout her childhood and adolescence, Minnow saw that he was friendly with women—lately, one of their neighbors, an avid gardener in her seventies, and when he still taught, there were one or two female colleagues whom he particularly respected. But he did not invite people over to the house; it was too private a sanctum for outsiders. Minnow had never seen him date.

She had discussed this with Jack, once, one of the boyfriends that Christopher did not meet. Then again, Jack was not a boyfriend exactly. Minnow was thirty-six, living in New York after grad school and before Sewell. Jack was the roommate she had found through a friend of a friend. Unlike in her relationship with Victor, she had assumed Jack would be gay. She discovered he was not when, one night, watching a movie on the couch, he leaned over and kissed her. After that, they'd fallen into a pattern of having sex whenever one or both of them was lonely, sad, or drunk.

They were lying in Jack's bed together as Minnow talked about how sad it made her that Christopher would never find love. She was thinking of herself more than her father as she said this, however. Jack had told her earlier that evening that he was starting to sort of get serious with a hot IT tech from Queens, and that sooner or later they would need to stop sleeping together, though it could technically be on the later side as long as Minnow was cool—and this had filled her with the malaise of abandonment. And so she said, of her father: "I just think it's sad that things went so badly with my mom that he decided he was . . . you know, done."

"What do you mean *done*?"

"Like, she left him, and the possibility for love left him. He doesn't date—"

"You don't know that," Jack objected.

"Of course I do. He's never once said—"

"But he might not tell you, right? I mean, you're his kid. Like, maybe that's just not something he discusses with you."

Minnow blinked up at Jack, dismayed. The idea that Christopher had a whole part of his life that she wouldn't know about struck her as nauseating and impossible.

"No," she said, "we don't really have secrets from each other."

Jack made a noise in the dark, like a snort that got swallowed. "*If* that's true," he said, "then maybe that's part of the problem. Yours and his." And then he had refused to talk about this more—"You're just going to get upset"—until Minnow, insisting that he continue the conversation, or at the very least that he tell her more about the IT tech from Queens, had become as upset as Jack predicted.

Minnow's last boyfriend had been very much like Christopher, though she told herself she didn't see the similarities until after they'd broken up. If she had subconsciously believed this would make Christopher like him, it had not. His name was Kenneth, and he was ten years older than she was, a mathematician at Columbia. Kenneth was the consummate authority on all things in their life together—politics, books, whether a movie was bad or good, the exact amount of time to roast a duck. He understood leases and mortgages and Roth IRAs and taxes. He had introduced her to his accountant, and they spent three afternoons sitting at the large round table in his Ninety-sixth Street apartment while his accountant sorted through the scraps of paper Minnow had remembered to save and made lists of the papers she would need from previous employers. All of this had been in the first few months of dating, and Minnow had been amazed by how Kenneth lived: solidly, deliberately, well.

In the second year of their relationship, Minnow had taken him home to Christopher. She always spent the holidays with her father and this had been a source of tension the previous year, as Kenneth had imagined all kinds of Christmas activities for them to do together, only to discover that Minnow was already spoken for. When she extended the invitation this second time, Kenneth understood that it was not a casual one, and he accepted with a mixture of grace and resentment.

Within an hour of Kenneth's installment in her father's house, Christopher met Minnow in the kitchen with a sour look on his face.

"What's wrong?" Minnow asked.

"Wrong? Nothing's wrong." And then, after a moment in which she knew to wait for more: "He tried to talk to me about *baseball*."

"Is that so bad? He likes baseball."

"Mathematicians have so little imagination," Christopher muttered, and ducked back out. Things had not improved from there. At dinner, sitting around the small kitchen table with both men, Minnow found herself thinking back to her junior year of high school, in which she had sat at this same table trying to tell Christopher about what she and Victor talked about at school while her father refused to find Victor interesting.

The visit had lasted for three arduous days, and on the morning of the fourth, Kenneth told Minnow that he couldn't take it anymore. They were scheduled to stay at Christopher's through the New Year.

"He *hates* me," Kenneth said. He was not prone to overstatements, and Minnow had been caught off guard by the frustration in his voice.

"Ken, he doesn't hate you, I promise. He's just—he can be tricky with strangers."

"I'm not a stranger! I'm your partner!"

"I know, I know that. But you have to understand—he doesn't really see a lot of people." As Kenneth turned an unconvinced face toward her, Minnow tried harder. "I just mean, he doesn't really let people in; *everybody* is sort of a stranger to him. Except me."

"Can you hear yourself?" Kenneth demanded. "That's not normal!"

"Careful how you talk about my father," Minnow shot back. Kenneth had been visibly surprised. They never fought, they weren't even a couple who raised their voices to each other.

"I'm sorry," he said. "This whole thing is just really stressing me out." They had ended up inventing a burst pipe in his apartment that he needed to rush back to New York and handle. Christopher was so visibly relieved by Kenneth's departure that it was clear he wouldn't question the story.

The rest of the holiday had been peaceful, and Minnow had found herself enjoying it in a way that was not possible as a trio. She and Christopher cooked together, played their favorite big band records on Christopher's ancient record player, rewatched the movies they watched every year, and went to bed early. When Kenneth and Minnow texted, she said that she missed him, and was aware of lying.

Kenneth was the one to end the relationship, several weeks after the failed Christmas visit. The conversation began calmly and amicably over a breakfast that Kenneth had made. He offered that they'd grown apart, that they didn't share many interests, and that Minnow had just opened her job search to include positions out of state, which would inevitably force their relationship to a reckoning anyway if she landed one. "We'd either break up or get married, right?" Kenneth said, reasonably. "And I don't think we're getting married. Do you?"

"I guess not," Minnow said, and then she saw the look of hurt on Kenneth's face and was swamped in confusion. Was she supposed to be fighting for this?

"I mean, when exactly did you check out?" he demanded. "Because you could have saved us all some time and just told me."

"Ken," Minnow said, striving for the reasonable tone with which they'd started. "*You're* the one breaking up with *me*."

"I'm breaking up with you because you won't break up with me!" Kenneth's voice soared, for the second time in their relationship.

"Do you not want to break up?"

"What do *you* want?"

Minnow stared down at her cold eggs and damp toast, bewildered into silence. Underneath the bewilderment was a discomfiting edge of truth that she had managed to ignore: she wanted to break up.

"I don't know," she said instead. She was not in the habit of telling Kenneth things he didn't want to hear.

"But that's bullshit!" And now he was yelling, and she stared at him in open astonishment. Her eyes kept going to the shock of brown hair sticking straight up from the center of his head—how it bobbed agreeably as anger gripped and shook him. "That's such bullshit, Minnow! You never actually say the things you're thinking, but I can *see* that you're thinking them! You just—sort of *swallow* yourself, you just say the things you think I want you to say, or you say things you've heard your dad say—"

"That's not true!" Minnow cried out, knowing it was true and feeling like it was unfair of him to say it out loud, regardless. But he kept going, implacable.

"You hated *The Martian,* I could tell you hated it, but after you talked to him on the phone, you started saying you liked it! And I *know* you don't garden, you don't even water our plants! But that time we were having dinner with the Vickys you were saying all these things about how we should be growing our own *food,* all this shit that your dad said at Christmas, as if—"

"Oh my god!" Minnow was matching Kenneth in volume now. "This is absurd! You're leaving because sometimes I agree with my father?"

"No," Kenneth shouted, "I'm leaving because there isn't any *space,* there's none for me and there's not even any space for *you,* your dad takes up all the fucking space!"

In the silence that followed, Kenneth looked surprised and ill. He tried to walk that one back almost immediately. He'd apologized, he'd said that he hadn't meant to bring her father into it. That this wasn't her fault, obviously, or anybody's fault, they just weren't working out. But Minnow found herself thinking about his words again and again in the weeks after the breakup. She knew what he meant. It wasn't like she didn't know what he meant. Other boyfriends, though less serious, had said similar things. Fucking *Jack* had implied it. And boyfriends who had not said anything had still been the ones to leave. But she hadn't thought it was a bad thing for Christopher to loom so large in her life. It was a normal thing; it was the way her life looked.

Right after the relationship ended, Minnow had been called to interview at Sewell. When they offered her the job several weeks later, she called her father. "Go," he said, and she went.

But Paris—that had been her own decision. And Charles—young and bright, reckless and unpredictable—no, he was nothing like Christopher. Christopher would not approve of him at all. And so finally, Minnow's world was one of her own making.

1968

6

KEEN SAW OLYA AGAIN AFTER THAT NIGHT, AND AGAIN. SHE INVITED him back to the house for a subsequent dinner, and when he'd asked daringly if she would meet him for a coffee in Cambridge, she had agreed without hesitation. They began to meet up for lunches or occasional film screenings in Harvard Square. Olya invited Keen to come with her and Daisy to a teach-in about Vietnam in which the audience was alternately harangued and cajoled by an economics professor, a philosophy professor, and a feral-looking individual who Olya whispered was a former student turned activist. Keen was fascinated by both the people speaking and the people who had come to listen, and the words themselves fueled his own conviction that the war was a waste.

Keen would not have called himself political. He had gotten a grudging educational deferment from the Wisconsin draft board that would last only for the next two years, after which they'd said he could consider himself educated enough to go to war. Although he knew he would apply for a second deferment and likely get it—Harvard, after all—he remained outraged by the idea that all of one's years of painstakingly accumulated knowledge could add up to no more than landmine fodder. But it wasn't only that. When he thought about any of the boys he'd gone to high school with, most of whom didn't have college degrees and therefore had been shipped off back at the beginning, the waste made him sick.

When he said this to Olya, however, thinking she might approve, she came back with: "Yes, and when I think about what we've done to *that* country, and *those* boys, *those* women and *those* kids, that makes me sick, too." Keen protested that he hadn't meant the Vietnamese were expendable, he just hadn't been talking about them at that moment, to which Olya had returned, acidly: "Yes, and that's my point." Often their political exchanges ended this way, but sometimes he recovered with a retort that surprised and therefore delighted her. It was those second kinds of exchanges that he lived for but rarely achieved.

For all of Olya's willingness to spend time together, Keen wasn't sure what he meant to her. He had no doubts on the subject of what she meant to him. She had come to occupy the largest portion of his waking mind. He stored her facts the way he had stored small treasures as a kid: coins and shells so precious they could only be accumulated and placed under his bed to be looked at when he was alone. Olya rarely talked about herself in terms of her details—she preferred to talk about her opinions, her convictions. But every once in a while she would mention something: an older brother ("In Vietnam?" Keen had asked, daring, and Olya had been silent for a moment and then grimaced and nodded); her mother (a theatre director who had fled from Russia before Olya was born); an older ex-boyfriend who owned his own dry-goods store. Keen would store each new kernel of information to chew on later.

So: he knew how he felt, but there was no way to tell if it was reciprocated. They didn't flirt, insofar as he could tell. Mostly they argued. When he told his roommate Sheila this, she said, "Arguing can be a kind of flirting," but Keen wasn't sure. Olya argued with everyone. He had seen her arguing with Jonno over the medicinal use of psychedelics, with Daisy over whether the British Museum was a site of stored knowledge or a treasure-house of pillaged goods, and even with red-bearded Ethan over whose turn it was to clean the toilets ("It's called a schedule, Ethan! Read it!"). And so when Olya challenged Keen, he had no way of knowing whether Olya thought they were doing anything other than arguing.

At the lab, Keen brought Olya up to Masaki and Arjun, although he didn't mention that she was an activist. He said she was a graduate student in Russian literature, and they made appreciative noises and asked whether she was a full-throated communist or just "vaguely pink" and how far the two of them had gone. Keen refused to answer either question, but in such a way that implied the answers were titillating, and Arjun and Masaki were pleased on his behalf.

Late fall became early winter, and Keen realized that Olya was exerting an influence on him. Normally he would have been so buried in lab work that he would have ignored what was happening on campus. Now he was paying more attention, and what he saw he found himself noticing with her eyes.

Student protestors and faculty had been clashing over the presence of ROTC on campus all fall. The students demanded to know why they should tolerate an overexpanded military machine on their campus; the faculty protested that routing ROTC was excessive. Harvard had also started offering its first Black history class—Soc. Sci. 5, or The Afro-American Experience—but to the derision of much of the Black student body, it was being taught by a white man. "You might as well call it Black People I Have Heard About," Olya jeered at the dinner table, having gotten ahold of the syllabus. "And to make it even better, half the books are written by white guys!" Keen had to agree that a class titled The Afro-American Experience taught by a man who did not have one bordered on the ridiculous, although previously it would never have occurred to him to have an opinion on something happening in the Sociology Department.

Keen was also introduced to the *Old Mole,* an underground newspaper whose inaugural issue came out that September. Olya enjoyed bringing him copies and he read them eagerly at his lab bench during the tedious parts of his experiments. He thrilled to its anarchic rhythms, and felt his heartbeat quicken when, in the masthead of each issue, he saw the Marx quote from which its name had come: "We recognize our old friend, our old mole, who knows so well how to work underground, suddenly to appear: THE REVOLUTION." In its pages Keen enjoyed reviews of recent films, articles with titles like "The Hip Radical" or "Lyrics of Stones & Beatles and Various Notes from the Underground," and a variety of exposés on the much-hated college president, Nathan Pusey. To Keen's disappointment, the exposés never seemed to expose much, other than various sneering things he had said about student activists. The most thrilling reveal so far had been a quote from Pusey's report to the board of overseers, in which he wrote of the students: "Safe within the sanctuary of an ordered society, dreaming of glory, they play at being revolutionaries and fancy themselves rising to positions of command to stop the debris as the structures of society come crashing down."

President Pusey wasn't entirely wrong, Keen thought, though he had perhaps missed a few key points—that society had stopped being ordered some time ago and that nobody seemed to be playing. And this thought, Keen realized, bore Olya's influence most of all—an influence he made no attempt to resist.

*

Keen heard of what Olya termed "the Dow action" only a few days before it happened. Olya had been taking him to readings and teach-ins, but she hadn't spoken about the protests in which she was involved, and he mostly didn't ask. The few times he had, it had felt as if she was suspicious of his intentions, and so he had let it alone. He had not seen either her or Ethan again among the Cavener protestors—who had lasted only another ten days before being per-manently evicted by the police—but he knew Olya would not have stopped protesting his lab just because they were friends now. He assumed instead that she had found somewhere more pressing to be, and when she brought up the Dow action, he realized he had been right.

Olya brought it up the way she brought up most things: bluntly, leaning forward with her chin jutted, challenging him to a scrap. A job recruiter from Dow Chemical was coming to campus, she informed him, despite his colleague having been chased away the October before. Keen didn't know about this and Olya described it for him: three hundred Harvard and Radcliffe demonstrators gather-ing in Mallinckrodt Hall, taking it as their own, imprisoning the Dow representative in a conference room for seven hours.

"In Mallinckrodt?" Keen demanded, amazed and laughing. "Where was I for this?"

"I don't know," Olya said, not laughing. "Where were you?"

"Probably in the lab. We're in the basement, I must've missed the whole thing."

Olya went on to explain that, as the manufacturers of napalm, Dow and their representatives couldn't be permitted to set foot back on campus. She and one of the leaders of the local Students for a Democratic Society chapter, a junior named Dwight Beachum, had been organizing an action wherein the job recruiter would be stopped in the parking lot and prevented from getting out of his car.

"How are you going to do that?" Keen asked, expecting a metaphor, but Olya only looked at him coolly and replied: "How does anyone prevent anyone from getting out of a car?"

"Wait," Keen said, "you mean literally?" and Olya replied, as if he were disappointing her: "Yes, Keen, literally."

They were at 5 Wellman, what Keen had begun calling *the Commune,* although Olya rolled her eyes whenever he said it. The heat had stopped working a few days before, leaving the house bitterly cold, and they were sitting in the kitchen with the oven turned on and the door open. "This is how Sylvia Plath died," Olya had said gravely as they'd settled themselves around the grime-encrusted oven mouth, and Daisy, passing through, had offered: "I think she was properly *inside* though, Ol."

Now, hands wrapped around a chipped mug of tea, pinioned under her gaze, Keen asked, "So what happened to the students who imprisoned the last guy in Mallinckrodt? Did they get suspended?"

It was not the right question. Olya sighed. "What's your point?"

"No," Keen said, "I didn't have a point! I was just asking."

The afternoon had started so well between them. He had had a few hours to kill before he needed to return to his experiment, and so Olya had met him in Harvard Square and they'd gotten lunch, then wandered the aisles of Olya's favorite used bookstore. Things had been easy and gentle, and Olya had been in a good mood. And now suddenly he was putting his foot in his mouth with every turn.

"I mean, you can't *defend* Dow," Olya challenged him. "I know you're all about *chemistry* but they're a bunch of criminals. What they're doing is . . . I mean, it's antiscience. It's *beneath* science."

"I know," Keen said.

Olya was quiet for a moment, and then she asked, "Did you just agree with me?"

"We don't disagree about that."

"You're not going to defend their right to . . . I don't know, make use of existing synthetic chemicals or something?"

"No," Keen said. "I don't think that's what science should be used for either."

"Oh." Olya seemed so disarmed that Keen wondered what she had taken him for, if she had constructed a Keen in her head that didn't match his actual details. Sometimes he worried that all of his bare facts arranged in her hands added up to a person who he wasn't. After a moment, she said: "You should come with us."

"Tell me when and I'll come."

"Will you really?" Olya looked amazed, and Keen felt both pleased and foolish.

"Olya, do you still think I'm a secret cop or some kind of square?"

"You *are* square," she said, then hastened to add: "Not in a bad way. And not a cop, obviously. You didn't even know I was organizing anything until I told you."

"Maybe I knew but I was playing it cool," Keen suggested, and as he had intended, Olya laughed. She was still laughing when Ethan came in, slamming the side door and shaking rain off his jacket.

"Ethan!" she said cheerfully, and he nodded at her, then took in Keen and grunted. Keen had run into Ethan many times now, and Ethan never seemed any more pleased to see him. He always seemed pleased to see Olya though, and when Keen mentioned this to Sheila, she had delivered a knowing "Ohhh" that made Keen uneasy for days.

Olya gestured to the kettle, still steaming, and the canisters of loose-leaf tea scattered across the dirty countertop. "You want tea?"

"I'm good," Ethan said.

"I'm telling Keen about the Dow action."

Ethan peered at Keen, then back to Olya. "Okayyy," he said, in a voice that was so clearly dubious that Keen wondered if he should remind Ethan that he could hear him.

"He's going to come with us," Olya said.

"Okayyy," Ethan said again.

"Don't get too excited," Keen said in the unimpressed-but-in-command voice that he had begun cultivating around Olya when he felt particularly exposed.

Ethan blinked at him, raindrops still beaded on his pale eyelashes. "Okay," he said, "I won't." Then, turning back to Olya as if Keen weren't there: "Hey, Dwight wants to talk to you."

"What about?"

Ethan flickered his eyes at Keen: *Not in front of him.* Keen felt a flush stain his cheeks.

"Well, he knows where to find me," Olya said. "Is he coming for dinner?"

"It's not like that," Ethan said. "He wants to *talk* with you."

"Dwight just likes the feeling of being official," Olya said, unimpressed. She caught the twitch of Ethan's gaze toward Keen again. "Oh, I'll say it in front of him, I'll say it in front of anyone! I'll say it to Dwight! Dwight wants people to come to the *Mole* office and sit around with the blinds drawn and smoke, so he can feel like Truman fucking Capote meets Mata Hari, and he doesn't give a shit if anything actually gets done. I'm busy getting things *done,* he can come to me! And you can tell him that."

Ethan blinked again, and despite the expressionlessness of his face, Keen couldn't help but pick up a quiet tenderness when he said, "Well, all right then."

"All right then!" Olya said and laughed. Watching Ethan smiling back at her with just his eyes, Keen remembered Sheila's knowing "Ohhh" and felt heat sweep through his body. Alarmed, Keen tracked the slight nausea that accompanied it, the prickle in his throat. Was he ill? And then: *Oh,* he thought, *this is jealousy.* He had never had occasion to feel it before. He had not known it could be so visceral.

"You never told me when the action was," he said a little too loudly. Olya's attention swung back toward him like a warm headlight.

"Thursday. Dow reserved space upstairs at Mallinckrodt starting at noon, so we'll be in the lot by eleven." And then, with a smile: "You'll probably already be there, huh. Down in the basement, toiling away for the advancement of science."

"I probably will be," Keen admitted, "but this time I'll come upstairs."

"See that you do," Olya ordered mock-severely, but her eyes stayed on him even though Ethan was there too, and Keen found himself counting the seconds that her attention remained with him instead of drifting back to Ethan—counting the seconds and finding each one a victory.

*

On Thursday morning, when Keen said he was going upstairs for the Dow action, Arjun and Masaki looked at him like he was crazy.

"A Dow *action*," Arjun repeated. "What's the action?"

"Keeping the Dow guy from recruiting here," Keen said.

"What the fuck do you care if he recruits here?" Arjun demanded.

"It's not right," Keen said, a bit lamely. He wished he had access to more stirring language, but faced with a challenge by two other scientists, his rhetoric deserted him.

" 'It's not right,' " Arjun repeated. "What, are you gonna go protest ROTC, too?"

"I don't have time," Keen said, "but if I *did* have time, I would, because I don't think ROTC is right either. Military pipelines don't belong on civilian campuses."

"Okay, *well*." Arjun turned away, but Masaki surprised Keen.

"I mean, sure," he said from his bench. He had been using a gas chromatographer, and he kept his eyes fastened on his work but turned the side of his face partially toward Keen. "Fuck those guys, for real."

"Oh, I didn't realize there was an SDS down here," Arjun said sardonically.

"You're just mad about those dirty hippies screaming at us," Masaki said, without heat. "Which was annoying, granted. But you know what else is annoying? My number came up again, and now I gotta go talk to the draft board. And they're gonna be all suspicious, like, *Well what are you, a Viet Cong sympathizer?* because they're a bunch of white cats, so to them, I might as well be Vietnamese. And I'm gonna have a motherfuck of a time explaining that I don't want to go shoot other guys in a jungle *not only* because I don't wanna shoot Asian guys in a jungle, or *any* guys in a jungle, but *also* because I am contributing to advanced human understanding over here. So honestly fuck all of them, and fuck the ROTC, and fuck Dow."

Arjun and Keen were both quiet, impressed by Masaki's biting yet laconic delivery. After a moment, Keen said: "I'm sorry, man."

"Don't be," Masaki said. "It won't help. And probably you're up next." And then: "So what's the action?"

"They're keeping him from getting out of his car," Keen said, feeling a little silly as he said it out loud, but to his surprise, Masaki set his beaker down hard on the wooden tabletop and said: "Good. Keep him in his goddamn car and send him home."

*

The parking lot was crowded when Keen arrived, maybe two hundred people gathered around its edges. Many of them were carrying signs: DOW GO HOME, and: DIVEST FROM DOW, and: SCIENCE NOT VIO-LENCE, and, most tellingly, a sign that had no words at all but was just a large printed image of a man who had been badly burned, presumably by napalm. In the middle, on a makeshift platform, Keen made out Olya, Peter, and a short round man who did indeed resemble Truman Capote and could only have been Dwight Beachum.

Standing in the boisterous crowd, the air electric and carnival, Keen realized it had been a long time since he had been so surrounded by others. Partially by necessity and partially by design, his schedules and rhythms had managed to winnow the reality of crowds out of his life. He was only ever in rooms with scattered handfuls of people, except for large lecture courses, and even then he was usually running late from the lab. When he slipped in, he'd sit by himself in a back corner, with empty rows of chairs around him. His life was normally small enough that the people around him were always distinct in all their individual details. In this crowd, there was no detail, just a mass of data: numbers of arms and legs and faces, so many pairs of eyes, so

many signs, so many bullhorns. It struck Keen as unexpectedly exhilarating, as if he, too, had been untethered from his individual details
and remade in multiplicity.

Dwight was shouting into a bullhorn about the perils and travails
of revolution, and as Keen returned his attention to the stage, Peter
took the bullhorn and spoke into it tersely and laconically. "We've got
to trap that bastard in his car," Peter said. "Don't get crazy, no breaking his windows, none of that kinda thing. We need order and control to make our point, and if that's not the gig you're here for, clear
out."

He tried to hand the bullhorn to Olya, but she waved it away. She
was kneeling on the edge of the platform speaking to a man on the
ground, his face tilted to bring his ear close to her mouth. That was
more her speed, Keen thought with admiration—Olya let other people make the speeches, because she was giving orders. Then he realized that the man listening to her so avidly was Ethan, and a tight
explosive feeling swept through him, as if all of his organs were two
sizes too big and squeezing up against the walls of his chest.

"Pretty great, isn't it?"

Keen jumped and realized that Daisy was standing next to him.

"What is?"

Daisy gestured to the press of humanity. "This is work, right here.
What you're seeing. This is trust made tangible. People who picked
up the phone and said, *Since you're the one calling, I* will *be there.*
Olya's good at what she does."

"Is this all Olya?" Keen felt a flush of desire to talk about her, to
say her name casually out loud.

"Well, it sure as hell wasn't Dwight." And then she reconsidered.
"No, it was probably Dwight to a degree. He has his whole crowd. It
isn't my scene, but they're good to show up and yell when you tell
them to."

"What *is* your whole scene?" Keen asked. "Other than geology?"

Daisy smiled. "We recognize our old friend, who knows so well
how to work underground," she said languidly.

"*You're* in the *Old Mole*?"

Daisy gave him a conspiratorial wink, and even though it wasn't actually a secret—it was just something Keen hadn't realized—he felt the warm pleasure of being in the know. When he looked back at the platform, Olya had vanished, as had Ethan. Dwight remained and was leading a series of chants. Keen scanned the bodies to the right and left, trying to locate Olya and Ethan. He imagined the two of them, arms linked to prevent being pulled apart by the shifts of the crowd. He wished wholeheartedly that Olya was beside him. Maybe there could be a kind of stampede, and then he would have to link his arm through hers to keep her from being knocked over, and they would stay that way, even after the danger had passed.

"Oh shit!" The excitement in Daisy's voice cut through his thoughts. "Here he is!" Even as she spoke, Keen felt anticipation moving through the crowd, building like static between bodies. A tan Oldsmobile pulled up and, confronted with the unanticipated presence of so many people, hesitated at the mouth of the parking lot. Twenty or thirty students massed behind the car, preventing it from backing out. Keen and Daisy pushed closer, everyone wanting to see the face of the driver when he realized he could neither go forward nor back.

Dwight launched the crowd into a new chant—"No napalm in Vietnam!"—and Keen found himself shouting it as well, resting against its comforting slant rhyme. Next to him, Daisy bounced on the toes of her sneakers, keeping time. The chant died down and Dwight said into the bullhorn: "The atrocities you peddle are not welcome on this campus!" and as everyone around him cheered, Keen felt sound travel through him, from the earth up his spine. He had not planned to make a single sound—and yet he yelped, and then, unable to hear his own voice in the amalgamation of voices, he roared. He couldn't remember the last time he had raised his voice above a conversational tone. He shot a bashful look at Daisy but her head was tilted back, her hair swinging and her little earlobes showing. She was screaming at the top of her lungs like they were at a Beatles concert.

The Dow man started honking his horn, frustrated, really leaning on it. He inched the car forward and the crowd packed around his fenders and wheels, trapping him like a fly in amber. Keen caught a glimpse of a few boys laughing as they pounded on the car windows with their fists. Another pulse, flesh against flesh, and Keen found himself next to Peter. Peter was carrying a bullhorn in one hand, in the other a camera. Keen expected to be ignored in the way that Ethan would have ignored him, but instead Peter thrust the bullhorn at Keen—"Hold this a sec." Startled, Keen accepted it, and Peter lifted the camera to his eye, aiming at the Dow man. "Gotta get closer," he yelled and began pushing through the bodies buffering him from the car. Keen and Daisy followed in his wake.

Near the car, Keen had to tuck the bullhorn into the crook of his arm in order to plug his ears against the maddening honking. Then the honking stopped abruptly and the Dow recruiter began trying to open the door on the driver's side. With a gleeful roar, the protestors nearest to him slammed their bodies against his car in response, accidentally rocking it. The rocking of the car set off something feral and playful, as if the idea hadn't occurred to them before. They started rocking the Oldsmobile back and forth between them, not enough to flip it, but enough that Keen could see the recruiter's anger turning into pure alarm. He was still trying to get his door open, but it was pinioned in place. Swearing, he cranked his window down and stuck his head out, and the nearest protestors permitted this, mostly because they were curious to hear what he had to say and eager for the chance to clash with him more directly.

Peter was thrilled by this turn of events. Even before the Dow recruiter started shouting—and he was, for the sake of entertainment, allowed to shout without interruption for nearly sixty seconds—Peter crouched beside the car, shooting steadily through a roll of film. The recruiter started by calling them hooligans and thugs, no-goodniks (this got some laughter, which infuriated him more) and draft dodgers. Then, when his car started rocking again, he called them bastards and sons of bitches. This got ironic cheers and more laughter. Dwight wanted to make a speech, and he kept beginning to—"Sir, if you are wondering why you have been detained in this manner"—but the energy of the crowd was up, the rocking of the car had excited them, and nobody had patience for Dwight's sermonizing. People started shouting over him, telling the recruiter to pack it in, go home, fuck off, and Dwight gave up on making himself heard.

The recruiter was now kneeling in the driver's seat, the majority of his body thrust out of the open window as far as he could get it, his face brick red and his moustache trembling as he shouted. The sight of him half in, half out of the car whipped Peter into an artistic frenzy. He elbowed people aside, bodychecked them, removed them physically from his shot, and Keen followed him, bullhorn under his arm, otherwise unsure what to do. Daisy was gone by now, lost in the tides, but maybe Peter would lead him to Olya. Olya must be close by; Keen didn't think she would miss being right at the front, if only to see this man's face as he understood how powerless he was against what she had unleashed upon him.

The Dow man didn't know who to look at as he railed against them, and so he kept swiveling his head from side to side, trying to address them all. It was by sheer coincidence that eventually his gaze met Keen's, and he addressed his furious harangue directly at Keen: "Antisocial elements with no appreciation for, for, for advances, for technological, scientific advancement—"

Something snapped in Keen. He didn't even think. The hand with the bullhorn rose to his mouth and he said into it, forcefully: "Don't talk to me about science!"

It was such an odd thing to say, and it came out so loudly, that the people around him went quiet. Peter, kneeling by the car tire and shooting upward into the recruiter's face, turned and looked at Keen with interest.

The recruiter heard Keen and stared at him in surprise and then, relieved at having only one person to address in this many-headed hydra, said: "Now, look here, son—" but Keen cut him off again. A dull anger was throbbing through him, although he couldn't have said where it had come from; it felt in a way as if it had always been there.

"I'm not your son," he said into the bullhorn. He wasn't shouting, he was talking slowly and clearly, and all other sound seemed to die away around him, a rippling outward of stillness. People were shushing each other, leaning in. "You work in science? You don't understand a goddamn thing about it. You want to talk about *advancement*? We've got bodies burned beyond recognition, what's advancing other than your career?"

"Who the hell are you?" The recruiter spluttered, taken aback by Keen's cold, steady voice. The shouting was something that he could understand—it was part of the dance between protestor and pro-testee, to be shouted at and to shout back—but Keen was talking through the bullhorn as if they were having a private conversation, and the listening hush of the crowd was unsettling.

"I'm a scientist," Keen said. "I'm an organic chemist." These were bold claims to make for someone who had not yet obtained his grad-uate degree, but he had no sense of exaggerating. He was defending tenets that he held firmly, that he had dedicated his life to upholding. "You're here to talk about scientific advancement," Keen said, "but I bet you can't tell me what's in napalm. Go on, what's its chemical composition?"

The recruiter tried to respond in kind. "If you want to hear what I have to say," he shouted, "why don't you tell your little friends to get away from my car?"

"I want to hear you answer that one question," Keen said, "and then I'll know if I want to hear what you have to say. So, go on. What is it?"

The crowd murmured behind him, a ripple of delight. Keen real-ized that he had forgotten about them completely. The recruiter was furious now. Keen had backed him into a corner with a question he couldn't answer. There was no place to hide, so he tried to bluff his way through.

"It's a fluid," he said impatiently, "an incendiary fluid. Now, you want our boys on the ground being shot at, or you want a fluid that can fall from the air, clear the way for your friends?"

Keen ignored this rhetorical flourish. He spoke through the bull-horn with the same steely calm that he used when, from time to time, an undergraduate assistant ruined an experiment they had been run-ning for days.

"Napalm is composed of gasoline—C_8H_{18}—used for its low flash point and ease of access; benzene—C_6H_6; and polystyrene—

C8H8—a thickening agent you get by processing petroleum." Power gathered in his voice, he felt as if he were delivering a sermon from on high, and still the crowd stayed with him, rapt. "Inside napalm you have two combustion reactions happening simultaneously: octane is being burned at a fast rate and benzene is burning at a slower rate. And the styrene acts as an inhibitor on each, creating a slow, hot burn, and it acts as a sticking agent—it makes the napalm adhere to clothing and skin, you can't get it off you, it creates fourth- or fifth-degree burns, and then you die. Horribly. Agonizingly and inhumanly. *That's* the answer to the question I asked you."

Keen swung toward the crowd now, his back to the recruiter even though he kept addressing him, and as he did so he felt a wild thrill rising through him. "You come to this campus trying to recruit us to work for a company that pumps out toxins and hires people who don't understand anything other than money," he said. "You're a used car salesman for deadly weapons. You don't know how the car works, but you want to sell it to us so we can drive it off the cliff. We don't want it. We don't need it. We don't need to hear a word you have to say because you know nothing of value. Get the hell back in your car and get out of here!"

And then the crowd roared. It was the sound of an army coalescing before a general. It was a sound that Keen had only heard in the movies, and one that he would replay for himself again and again in the days—and even months—to follow. It was a single full-throated howl of allegiance, and when Keen heard it, he lifted one fist in the air—a gesture he had never before performed, had only witnessed. The crowd rocketed its fists in the air in answer; it stomped; it screamed; it loved him right then, how it loved him.

The recruiter pulled himself back through the window into his car. There was no further argument to be had, and he was ready to leave. Keen, mouth wet with victory, lifted the bullhorn again and shouted: "Let him go!"

The students who had been plastered to the back and sides of the Oldsmobile stepped aside, their bodies channeling the purity of Keen's command. The Dow man slammed into reverse and shot backward, the nearest protestors pulling their feet out of the way. His tires screeched in the road; he spun the steering wheel; he shot away. The parking lot spilled over with exultation. Strangers turned toward Keen, grabbing his shoulders, his arms, his hair, touching him the way you touch a religious ikon, rubbing him for luck. And all of that, which seemed to Keen the astonishing pinnacle of a joy he never thought he'd reach in his lifetime, was eclipsed by the sight of Olya running across the parking lot, her face bright with delight, her smile wider than the day, her hands outstretched toward him.

2018

7

IT WAS AFTER THE NIGHT THAT CHARLES AND LUC CAME TO HER door that Minnow began to think of Charles at times she shouldn't, in ways she shouldn't.

The curve of his shoulder. The jut of his jaw. The delicate hand-span of skin revealed between jeans and shirt when his jacket hiked up. She imagined him naked. She banished the image immediately, then brought it back. Twenty-three, he would be lean and taut in all the places that Kenneth had not been. That Minnow, at thirty-eight, no longer was. She imagined him standing under the sloped ceiling of her sleeping loft, turning toward her, that V of muscle that cuts down into the pelvis, the long planes of his body. In the shower, she turned the water up hotter and hotter, it left angry red streaks on her skin but she barely felt it.

That long Sunday expanse after Charles and Luc left her apartment at dawn, Minnow lost swaths of time: standing in the shower; sitting on the edge of her bed in the little sleeping loft, underwear in hand, having been distracted in the act of putting it on; standing in the kitchen holding the milk bottle in her hand until she realized the outside of the glass was beaded with condensation. Desire had flooded in: wild, inescapable. It had not lived in her like this before, never like this, in the form of a prolonged swoop, like flying.

What was it about Charles? It was maddening. She was reminded of when a limb has fallen asleep, unbeknownst to you, and for the short period in which the blood rushes back in, your attention can go nowhere else. What was it she wanted from him, she wondered. A relationship? Impossible. He was too young; he was a stranger; what did she know about him, anyway? This wasn't real life, this was a stopover between what had ended and whatever was coming next. And though she wasn't permanent faculty, she would be there at least through the spring. If things went badly between them it would make work harder and more stressful. After Sewell, the idea of being whispered about made nausea lift in her stomach.

So, what, then? Sex? Impossible. How embarrassing. And yet . . . Her mind wandered. In her sleeping loft, the image of Charles turned toward her again and again, presenting himself to her eyes. She tried not to take the fantasy further. It felt like a violation, to direct his imagined body through paces he knew nothing about. Instead, she began to imagine herself through his eyes, and that gave her as much of a thrill, perhaps even more. As she put on her clothes, she imagined him gazing at her. As she walked to the markets on the Rue Mouffetard, she imagined him across the street, watching her walk. What had he said about seeing her walking down the hallway that first time? That she had looked certain? And when he'd seen her perched on the lamppost: *Your whole spirit was present.* And she had felt that way, too, hadn't she? She had felt her whole spirit.

Delicately, Minnow circled the picture he'd given her of herself: a mysterious older woman, intimidating, maybe even glamorous in how unflappable she was. And that was another Charles word, though he had said *unflapped.* Replaying the moment, Minnow smiled every time.

Before this, when she had thought of herself at all, she had seen herself as she was by the end of Sewell: disgraced, alone. But picturing Charles's gaze, she felt herself become someone else entirely. That night in bed, running the pads of her fingertips over her ribs, her sternum, her breasts, she began by imagining that her hands were his. But after some time, she realized she was no longer thinking of the touch at all. Instead she was imagining the body being touched: a new idea, a possibility, a reckless and daring stranger to whom she was becoming reintroduced.

*

When classes started again on Monday, she worked to avoid him. This wasn't hard, as their schedules had never aligned, and yet now she found herself flinching as she rounded corners, glancing down the hallway before she stepped out from the safety of her little office. On Tuesday, she wondered if it might not be better, after all, to run into him. She was building an entire fantasy in her head, and it needed to be punctured, after which she could move on. They could be friendly colleagues. And besides, she should ask about Luc. That was the responsible thing to do. If she saw Charles, she would call out to him, she decided. She would act perfectly normal, and just inquire after Luc's health.

On Wednesday morning, she went looking for him.

The English Department, where Minnow was, shared a rabbit warren of small offices and bespectacled older faculty members with Comparative Literature. By contrast, Communication and Media—though technically also under their departmental umbrella—was young and hip. As she wandered the wider better-lit halls, she passed a series of open-doored offices occupied by professors in their late twenties who wore cool sneakers and had cool hair. Even when Minnow had been in her late twenties, she had not felt young or hip. Now, passing a woman who held a phone to her half-shaven head and spoke Italian into it, Minnow wondered if she herself should get a haircut. Her hair was the same indeterminate length it always was—above the shoulders, below the ears. What if she shaved the sides? Or at the very least a pixie cut, one of those expensive ultra-French ones that look as if you took your kitchen scissors and did it yourself.

"Je peux vous aider?"

Startled, Minnow turned. A young man in torn jeans—why were the jeans always torn?—looked up at her amiably from his laptop.

"I'm looking for Charles Vernier's office," Minnow said, feeling like she was incriminating herself. But the man just gestured farther down the hall: "At the end," he said, turning back to his laptop.

The door was closed when Minnow approached, and she heard

voices behind it. He was talking to someone in French, probably one of his students. She imagined him across the desk from a girl who was nearly his own age, who would of course find him very attractive. Would they understand each other better than Minnow did her students, given their shared generational touchstones? Was this a girl who came to his office hours regularly, in the hopes of spending time alone with him? Or was it a student who had done something wrong? How would Charles handle a situation like that—cheating, for example? Would he think of the story he had told her, his father's response to his own childhood temptation? Would this make him harsher, or more lenient?

Walking back to her floor, Minnow wondered if Charles and his student were actually talking about the protests. Her own students had been watching on the news, or they had gone, or they had friends and siblings who had gone. In this morning's class, they hadn't wanted to talk about *The Awakening,* they'd wanted to shout at each other on the subject of whether or not the university should shut down in solidarity with *les manifs*. A vocal handful had been in favor, while an equally vocal handful wanted to know why their exams should be interrupted by French rednecks. When the first handful shouted that this rampant classism was part of the problem, the second handful had volleyed back that if you wanted to talk about problematic *isms,* the gilets jaunes were racist, sexist, *and* anti-Semitic, or at least factions of their mysterious membership were. After this, class had devolved into a pandemonium that Minnow could not corral.

Alone in her office, at her desk, Minnow brought up a search engine. On impulse, she typed "gilet jaune" and "head injury." An endless scroll of websites appeared, above which an image bar displayed thumbnails of people's faces wrapped in bandages. Minnow hesitated and then clicked on one and it enlarged: a woman whose purple eye was swollen shut, her nose shattered. She clicked on the next: a man who had lost all of his bottom teeth. His jaw was bent sideways, his bloody mouth gaped at the camera.

Just then, Charles's voice startled her from the doorway. "Hi."

Minnow jumped and shut her laptop in the same instinctual moment. Immediately, she wished she had done neither.

"Charles," she said.

"Aidan told me someone was looking for me," he said. "I hoped it was you."

And there it was—the vivid spark of whatever was between them. Minnow had spent the past two days simultaneously fanning the flames and telling herself it was her own invention.

"What if it wasn't?" she asked.

"Not to worry," Charles said, "as *I* am looking for *you*."

"And why is that?"

"Janet sent me. She's throwing a dinner for the faculty this Friday— she's having me deliver her invitations so that nobody will say no to her face."

Janet was the department head; fast-moving and brittle, always on the way to somewhere else. It was clear to all that Charles was her favorite.

"A dinner," Minnow repeated thoughtfully. She hated dinners. Then she questioned herself: Did she really? Or was this, too, the aftermath of Sewell? She felt like she didn't know how to talk to people now—either the people she knew or the ones she didn't. With the people she knew, there was so much that wasn't being said. With strangers, there was so much she wasn't saying.

"Please come," Charles said, into her hesitation. And then he smiled at her: "I'm speaking for Janet, of course."

"And Janet is saying 'Please come'?"

"Janet is saying 'Please come.' "

In the silence between them, Minnow tried not to think of all the fantasies of Charles that she had entertained. She felt her cheeks getting hot. "How is Luc?"

"He had a surgery—he wanted me to say thank you."

"A surgery! Will he be okay?"

"Yeah—his eye socket cracked but his eye is okay. They had to put a plate in his face, like a titanium thing. He's the bionic man now."

"And he didn't have any, uh . . . issues?" She meant with the police, and Charles understood.

"No," Charles said. "No issues."

"Well . . . that's good."

Charles shifted in the doorway. "I want to apologize," he said.

"For what?"

"I should not have looked up your address. Nor, most likely, come to your house."

"'Most likely'?" Minnow asked, letting the words remain Charles's, and the corners of his mouth twitched upward. He fought the smile.

"It is very likely," he agreed, "that I was—how would you say? Impulsive."

Though his tone was playful, Minnow felt a plunge of disappointment. Had he imagined her, as well, but in the context of an apology that would need to be delivered?

"Well," she said, "please thank Janet for the invitation."

Charles studied her for a moment, and then nodded. "I will tell her you're coming," he said.

*

Janet's apartment was in the Sixième, on a block that looked expensive. Her building was beside a tiny natural-wine store and across from a pair of jewelry boutiques. Janet greeted Minnow at the door, taking her coat with one hand and the bottle of wine she offered up with the other—"How lovely," she said, leaning in to kiss Minnow's cheeks, choosing the Parisian style of greeting over the English. Janet's accent was hard to place; it wasn't American and it wasn't quite British. Wherever she had come from, she had managed to set herself up nicely here—the Sixième *and* a French wife. Minnow had imagined Janet might marry someone similarly crisp and aloof, but then she had met Janet's wife, Samira, at a faculty lunch and found her to be the opposite: easy, languid, mischievous. Down the long entryway, the muffle of voices drifted toward them. Minnow found herself instinctively listening for Charles and felt a wash of irritation at herself.

"All is well?" Janet asked, leading her down the hall toward the living room. "You've settled in?"

"Yes," Minnow said, "thank you."

"Minnow!" Samira exclaimed. "Welcome! Here, join us on the couch."

"I'll get you a glass." Janet whisked herself away to the kitchen and Minnow sat awkwardly on the couch, joining a small gathering of faculty members whose exact occupations escaped her: Asako, Franz, Olivier. Charles had not yet arrived.

"How are you?" Asako asked Minnow politely, and when Minnow said she was fine, thank you, the conversation returned to what it had been right before her arrival—namely, complaints about students in general and in the particular. Janet returned to hand Minnow a glass of red wine, and Minnow sat nodding and sipping, furrowing her brow at the right intervals, wondering why she had come. No, the most annoying part was that she knew exactly why she had come, and it was stupid—beyond stupid.

The arrival of newcomers created chaos again—fragmentary greetings, people sitting and standing, wineglasses fetched, coats taken, new configurations around the living room. Franz's boyfriend, Nicolas, was a young dancer in a thick cable-knit sweater that nearly swallowed him. When Nicolas gracefully lowered himself beside Franz on the divan, Olivier busied himself in his phone and then—in a slightly elevated voice—told Minnow that he was receiving texts from an old flame who was in town. He didn't lift his eyes from his phone as he said this, so that the comment could have been directed anywhere. Proximity made Minnow feel the pressure of responding; unsure what to say, she mustered a polite "Ah," as she remembered that Felice had once mentioned Franz and Olivier in the context of coupledom. The other two arrivals were an American couple, Pooya and Jacob, who began most of their sentences with *we* and handed phrases back and forth like polyphonic table tennis. Charles arrived last, windblown and breathless, and Minnow felt a shameful relief when he leaned in to kiss Janet on both cheeks.

Janet directed them all to the long dining room table and seated them—Samira at one end, Minnow to her left, Olivier and Franz as far apart as possible. She placed Charles beside her at the other end, where Charles spoke to Janet swiftly in French, with the cheeky confidence of a favored son, and Janet smiled back at him. Minnow had never seen her so effusive. She raised her glass in a toast to them all and to the end of the semester and to Minnow, who had been so kind as to join them, and as everyone clinked glasses, Charles's eyes found Minnow's across the length of the table as if he were lifting his solely to her.

Samira passed platters around the table, and Pooya and Jacob began apologizing for their delay. The subway line nearest to them had been shut down, they said, in advance of the coming Saturday protest.

"This is how the normal people get punished," Jacob added, accepting a platter of couscous and beginning to serve himself from it. "Every Saturday some people get to smash up the city and then *other* people—"

"Can't get to their dinner parties?" Charles asked, drily.

"When you put it like that," Jacob protested, "it sounds silly. But—"

"We just wonder if it's all going a bit far," Pooya said, "which we both—I mean, obviously we're in favor of—but *every* Saturday?"

Franz leaned forward, grinning. "I heard a woman on the subway platform the other day, she said she was outraged about what is happening to this city. Outraged! Her companion asks her, 'Do you mean *les manifestations*?' She replies, 'What manifs? I mean that my favorite wine store has been closed the last three weekends.'" He turned to Pooya and Jacob: "And *this*," he said, theatrically, "is why it must be *every* Saturday."

"I don't get it," Jacob said.

"Pour que les bourgeois comprennent," Franz said to Nicolas, who nodded somberly at him.

"You aren't exactly one to pass judgment on the bourgeois," Olivier said acerbically, his eyes darting between Nicolas and Franz.

"Oh," Franz said, rising to the challenge, "let me guess, Olivier. You think the manifs are bad manners and everybody should just stay home."

"Don't be reductive," Olivier said. "And don't try to paint me as some kind of conservative for saying that smashing windows and setting cars on fire isn't exactly furthering the dialogue."

"That's what we feel!" Pooya cried, relieved. "We're not *anti*protest, obviously, but—"

"But just anti-inconvenience?" Franz asked, faux-helpfully.

"Oh my god," Olivier began, irritated, but Janet intervened gracefully: "Did anybody listen to Macron's speech on Monday?"

"Oh yes," Charles said. "His concessions package."

"You say it as if it's nothing," Olivier objected, "but that's a fifteen-billion-euro package. It has a rise in the minimum wage, it has—"

"Not everyone is eligible," Charles said, cutting him off. "It's pure theatre—big gesture, no substance."

"So, what do you want?" Jacob demanded. "You want them to burn the whole city down? Like Pooya says, we're all about peaceful protest, but—"

"It can't stay peaceful when the police have weapons of war," Minnow said, and then everyone was looking at her. Most of them were surprised—they had not expected her to join the conversation, and neither had she—but Charles was looking straight down the table at her, with the same look on his face as when he had toasted her.

"What weapons of war?" Olivier demanded.

"They've got fist-sized rubber bullets and they're aiming for the eyes, people are getting their faces smashed in." Minnow took a breath but found she couldn't stop: "They've got grenades, they're throwing them into the crowds and people are losing hands and legs. How is it supposed to stay peaceful when the police are creating a war zone?"

"Is that true?" Jacob asked doubtfully.

"Of course it's true," Charles said, exhilaration in his voice.

And Pooya: "Where are you reading that? I'm not reading that."

"Even if it is true, what do you want them to do," Olivier asked, "just wave the gilets jaunes over to the Sixième, smash the windows, grab what you like, have a good time?"

Minnow knew this wasn't her argument, and yet she couldn't stop herself. "I'm just saying that there seem to be a large number of people in this country who believe that the government doesn't care if they live or die, and every time some college kid gets shot in the face, it proves that they're right."

"If you would like to talk about children getting shot," Olivier snapped, "why don't we talk about *your* country?" And then Janet had her hands up.

"My friends!" she said. "We're here to celebrate. And of course this is Paris, so no celebration is complete without an argument, but even so . . ."

Pooya pushed through. "All this talk about weapons and police—but who are the gilets jaunes? What do we know about them? I look at them, I'll tell you what I see. A mob of angry white men. And for my money, that doesn't usually end well." Jacob was staring uncomfortably at his plate and Pooya caught his discomfort. "Sorry, but you know what I mean," she said to him.

"No, no," Jacob said, too heartily. "You're absolutely right—I mean, I'm a white man and *I* don't even like mobs of white men!"

"They're not all white," Charles objected.

"Not *all*," Pooya conceded, "but you can't deny that it's most."

"But that is so American," Olivier said impatiently, "how everything so neatly returns to a question of race. Your original sin is not ours. In this country we also contend with *other* realities—"

"That's interesting," Samira cut in sweetly, "because, as the only Algerian of origin at the table, I would certainly call France's history in North Africa one in which race plays a large part."

"I thought you didn't believe in the gilets jaunes," Franz said to Olivier, who looked briefly confused, as if he had forgotten on which side of the argument he fell.

"I'm not saying that I do," Olivier said. "I'm not saying that at all."

"But look." Charles pressed on, eyes on Pooya: "The march on the twenty-fourth that set out from l'Opéra, its focus was feminism. Was that not also a gilet jaune action? And this Saturday, CLAQ and Comité Adama are marching—" He turned to Minnow, explaining: "CLAQ is the Queer Liberation, and Comité Adama formed after the police killed Adama Traoré. They're working-class, mostly Black and Arab." Then back to Pooya: "Is this not a gilet jaune march if both of them are marching with the gilets jaunes? Are they not *also* gilets jaunes?"

Pooya was unimpressed. "Are you trying to tell me that just because you have CLAQ and Comité Adama marching next to rednecks and racists, that this somehow is not a movement whose majority is still rednecks and racists?"

Charles opened his mouth, his eyes flashing, but Franz cut in neatly: "Janet, you must have an opinion on this." Franz was searching for a place to put down a large earthenware tagine and Nicolas leaned over to make room, jostling the table. Everyone snatched for their glasses, and as Olivier's wine leapt over the edge of his, he snapped, "Careful." Minnow could feel the tension in the air, but when she looked at Janet, she seemed as calm and composed as if she were at the front of a classroom.

"Well," Janet said thoughtfully, "on the one hand, there is a poujadiste quality that concerns me—rural, conservative, antitax. And when Le Pen tries to claim it, that also gives me pause."

"Exactly," Pooya said. "I mean, to hear Marine Le Pen tell it, they're her right-wing special forces."

"That said, *they* don't necessarily seem to think they are." Janet frowned at her plate. "Pooya, your question is the right one: What do we know about them? And the answer is, very little, to be sure. Which invites us to read in comparisons that scare us as well as ones that flatter us, depending on who we are. You might say it's somewhat slippery of them to permit this, but perhaps they just don't give a fuck what we think, and that's the point. They're past debates and conversations, they're done with talking. They're in the streets, let that speak for itself."

"They released talking points," Charles objected. "Last week."

"There are forty-two directives," Olivier said, with some glee. "And nobody's reading them. Like it or not, what happens in the street says it all."

"Well, it says different things depending on who's listening," Samira said, "which is the point, and the problem."

"Or maybe it's the invitation," Minnow said, quietly.

They all turned toward her again, as if they'd forgotten she was present. Samira gave her a delicately arched eyebrow.

"I just mean . . . if you don't have to be a card-carrying anything to participate—I mean, it's for anybody, then. Right? It's for everybody. All you have to do is show up. Any time you get more specific, someone like me goes, Oh, well, I'm not this, I'm not that, this doesn't apply to me." Minnow shrugged. "With this . . . all you have to do is arrive, and you're in the right place. It's kind of brilliant."

She realized, as her eyes skated over their faces, that Charles was listening to her the way she had seen his students listen to him: rapt, captured. The realization sent adrenaline rushing through Minnow. But Pooya narrowed her eyes at Minnow across the table.

"'Brilliant,'" she repeated. "But what would you say, Minnow, about *who* is arriving?"

"What is the question," Olivier broke in, "whether this is a right-wing riot or a left-wing riot?" He made a gesture at all of them: "Would you like it better if it was a cadre of librarians smashing all the windows?" And then, to Franz: "I bet you would."

"What would *you* like?" Franz asked, cuttingly. "If the whole city burned to the ground and you got to crow about the dangers of populism from the safety of a dinner party?"

"No," Olivier said tightly, "I'd like it if you had the courtesy to tell me what the fuck you want, *ever,* at *any* point, before all of a sudden you have a boyfriend and we're all supposed to sit around the dinner table together."

"All right," Janet said, at the same time as Samira said, "Olivier," and Asako began, "Okay, well, let's just—" but Olivier cut through them all: "Because seven days ago you were sucking me off in the back of a Monoprix, Franz, so I'm just a little *confused* about your *boyfriend.*"

"A *Monoprix?*" Samira demanded, laughing despite herself. "*Really?*"—even as Franz's voice rushed to fill the silence. He and Olivier started shouting at each other in French and German, and Nicolas stared fixedly at the tablecloth, as if this were a summer storm and he was waiting for it to pass.

Minnow and Charles caught eyes, and Charles's mouth twitched. "Cigarette?" he asked, low.

Without waiting for a reply, Charles slid his chair back. Minnow followed suit, feeling self-conscious as Janet's eyes tracked them to the balcony. Out in the fresh air, Charles closed the double doors gently and the cacophony of voices dulled.

"My mother has a theory," he said, "that in any relationship there is the fire and the rain. The fire flares up, the rain damps it down. In relationships that are fire-fire, it all burns out fast. In rain-rain, you drown. But fire and rain . . ." Charles smiled. "Franz and Olivier, they are fire-fire. I remember, even when I was a student, you could hear them shouting at each other from their offices."

"Is it strange to be their colleague now?" Minnow asked. "After having been their student?"

"I was never their student. I was Janet's." He offered her a cigarette and she shook her head. "Janet is fire, of course. Samira is rain."

"And what are you?" Minnow asked, and then wondered if she should have.

But Charles considered the question seriously. "I was raised to be rain," he said. "We all were, so that my father could be fire. But it remains to be seen, doesn't it? And you?"

Minnow hesitated, and then: "I think for most of my life I would have said rain, but . . . It's starting to occur to me that the answer might be fire."

Minnow could feel the tightly reined electricity of his body beside her. He was closer than she had realized. *In one more minute,* Minnow thought, *I will step away. In one more minute, we'll go back to the others.* They stood. She listened to the sound of his breathing. A car horn below, two plaintive bursts. And then his hand was on her face. Gentle. His fingertips against the side of her cheek, locating the line of her jaw.

"Charles," she said. She thought her voice would be firm, but it was not.

"Oui," he said, and then he kissed her.

She had expected it, but still she was shocked by the softness of his mouth, bitter with tobacco and sweet with wine, and she thought, as she had before: *Any second now I will end this. Any second now, I'll tell him to stop.* But that second passed, and then the next one. Both of his hands were cupping her face and she felt the length of his fingers, the metal of the balcony railing digging into her back, his heart slamming against the thinness of his shirt—or maybe it was hers, she wasn't sure. And then, only then, did she put her hands on his arms. And slowly, taking the gesture for what it was, he took a step back.

"We can't do this," Minnow said, at the same time as Charles said, "I can't stop thinking about you." Hearing what she had said even as he spoke, he demanded, "Why not?"

"Charles, we work together—we—"

"We do *not* work together, we work in the same building."

"Well—yes, and—"

"And what? On s'en fout! That has not stopped Franz and Olivier."

"And I'm older than you are. Much."

"Look," Charles said, "Macron and his wife have twenty-four years between them. You do not have twenty-four years on me."

"I thought you hated him," Minnow said, amused. "And *he's* your defense?"

"His wife was his high school teacher," Charles said. "She broke up her marriage for him when he was her student, still! Age means nothing when there is deep feeling."

Off-balanced by the phrase, Minnow wanted to ask Charles if he was implying that what he had for her was deep feeling. A crush, she had assumed. A flirtation, even. But the implication of more left her uncertain how to respond, and so she defaulted to the simple question of age. "I'm thirty-eight. I'm almost twice your age."

"That is some *very* loose math," Charles scolded her. "Fifteen years is not so bad."

"Isn't it?" Minnow shook her head. "It's quite a chasm, even when there's . . . interest."

"I did not say *interest*," Charles corrected her. They stared at each other in the dim light, both of them solemn. Below, a group of rowdy teens passed in the street, shoulder to shoulder. An older woman, pushing a trolley. A man on his phone, walking his dog. Nobody looked up.

"Charles," Minnow said, thrilled and exasperated at the same time. "You don't know me. How can you know that you have feelings, let alone deep ones?"

Charles smiled at her. It was the sudden shift that she had seen before, a smile of such guileless charm that of course you would want to turn toward it. He opened his mouth to speak, but—

"There you two are!" Janet stood in the double doors. Over her shoulder, Minnow could see that the dinner party had recovered. Franz and Nicolas were talking to each other gently on the couch, and Pooya was looking at something on Olivier's phone.

"Here we are," Charles said, turning the smile onto Janet instead. He moved toward the doors and Minnow moved with him, as if nothing had happened out on the balcony, as if they'd just been biding their time until they might be summoned.

1968

8

THAT NIGHT, MORE PEOPLE FIT INTO 5 WELLMAN THAN KEEN HAD
imagined possible. By the time he arrived, revelers were spilling out of
the front door, packing the torn scrap of discolored grass that mas-
queraded as a lawn, holding cans of beer and shouting at each other
over the music. Someone had carried a battery-powered radio outside
and set the volume as high as it would go. Someone else had put Janis
Joplin on the record player inside, in the living room. From certain
places in the house, you could hear the two soundtracks grinding
against each other.

Keen didn't like parties, or noise, and as soon as he made his way
through the press of bodies and into the front hall, he wished he
hadn't. The clear whiff of whiskey let him know that liquor had
already been spilled, and Janis up against the Rolling Stones was
threatening to give him a headache. He stood on the third stair gazing
around the sea of clamoring bodies and saw no one he recognized,
certainly not Olya. Maybe he should go home, he thought. He could
always tell her that he'd come and hadn't managed to find her. Or
maybe, even better, she might call asking where *he* was.

"Keen! There you are!"

He spun around to look up the stairs and saw Olya laughing at the
top of the second-floor landing.

"What are you doing up there?" Keen asked stupidly, as if she
didn't live here.

"I got a drink spilled down my shirt," Olya said. She descended toward him and, when she was close enough, surprised him by giving him a hug. It was a little awkward since she was standing two steps above him, but also somehow sweet. His head rested briefly against her collarbone.

"I'm glad you came," she said, releasing him. "You want a drink?"

"Sure." Keen did not want a drink. He did not want either of them to plunge into the noisy fray. Keen wanted to escape back up the stairs with Olya, into the welcoming darkness of wherever she had changed her shirt.

But Olya grabbed his hand and pulled him with her. "Kitchen," she said. "Let's get aggressive." And she propelled them forward, throwing elbows, shoving her way through the crowd. Keen was forced to let go of her hand to block the flailing arm of someone deep in conversation, but he stayed as close to her as he could.

When he entered the kitchen, it erupted in a cheer. He assumed the cheer was for Olya, but then he saw all the faces turned toward him, beaming, and he blushed to the roots of his hair. Someone said *Awww*, and then people were laughing, thumping him on the back and shoulders as if this were a reprise of the parking lot, except half of these people hadn't been there, it turned out; they had heard of him through other people. Keen was being talked about, he realized, and he wasn't sure what to do with the information. He had never in his life, to his knowledge, been the subject of other people's conversations.

"Good work," someone said, and someone else: "I heard you were amazing," and a third person, patting Keen's arm as if they were friends: "Peter got some great pictures of you."

"Of *me*?" Keen asked, genuinely shocked, and this occasioned another laugh, as if he were performing a required modesty.

"They *are* good pictures," Olya said at his elbow, handing him a can of room-temperature beer. "You'll probably be on the cover of the *Old Mole* by Monday."

"I'd rather not," Keen stammered, thinking of Cavener (did Cavener read the *Old Mole*?), or Arjun, or Masaki, or really anyone else. "Can we not?"

The people around him were no longer listening, but Olya looked into his face quizzically, realizing that he was sincere. "But they're such good pictures, Keen."

Keen was prevented from responding by Ethan, who had swum through the crowd to the drinks counter: "I didn't know you were a chemist, Keen."

It was the first time Ethan had ever addressed him by name; Keen hadn't been certain that Ethan knew what his name was.

"I am," Keen said, uncertainly. "A grad student, anyway." He glanced at Olya. He had assumed that she would have mentioned this by now. If she had not, did that mean she had been ashamed of him?

"So you're okay with chemical weaponry, just not in the hands of Dow?" Ethan folded his arms across his broad chest.

"Ethan, come on," Olya said impatiently.

"Like, Cavener for instance," Ethan said, and Keen thought, *Oh, you bastard.* "You're okay with him?"

"I don't think science should be used to manufacture weapons," Keen replied coolly.

"Right," Ethan said, "but in the world we *actually* live in, it is. And in that actual world, Harvard isn't an 'institute of higher learning,' it's a corporation, selling its students and knowledge and *products,* its scientific *products,* to the military machine. So. How do you feel about that?"

The kitchen was sinking into quiet. Ethan's voice wasn't lifted theatrically high, but it was gruff and strong and it carried, the aggressive tone perhaps more than the words, and people broke off their own conversations to listen.

"Ethan," Olya said again, but he shook his head at her.

"I know you like the guy," he said. "That's fine. And everybody's so crazy about what he said today, and that's also fine. But I wanna hear what he has to say about every day other than today when he's in that lab, churning out weapons for Uncle Sam."

Keen was taken by two conflicting sensations: a soaring glee that Ethan had admitted that Olya liked Keen, and then a raw irritation.

"So what do you think should happen?" he shot back. "We should all stop learning, stop contributing to a body of knowledge because it might get misused? Everybody should go back to the Dark Ages?

They still had weapons in the Dark Ages, you know, they had clubs—should we disallow trees because you can make a club from them?"

He had given Olya a version of this argument and she hadn't liked it, but Ethan's lips pressed together in genuine anger. "What weak rhetorical bullshit," he said.

He would have said more, but Peter stepped in. Keen hadn't realized Peter was there; for such a tall man, he seemed to have an uncanny ability to become invisible within a crowd. He put a hand on Ethan's shoulder and said something so quietly that Keen, only a few feet away, couldn't hear it. A moment suspended itself in which Ethan refused to look at Peter, keeping his jaw tight and his eyes trained on Keen. And then he swung away, brushing Peter's hand off and shouldering his way through the packed kitchen. The silence fragmented into a chatter of voices, people asking each other what had just happened—"Wait, *what* did he say?" "The guy Keen is a chemist." "Well yeah, he said that this afternoon."—and soon they would be talking about other things entirely.

Olya touched the back of Keen's hand with the back of her own. Though it was subtle, he felt a shiver travel the length of his body. "Let's get out of here," she said.

*

When she took him up the darkened stairwell, the luck of it filled his throat with sweetness. It was all that he had wanted. No matter what was or wasn't waiting at the top, he felt that a dream was coming true.

They climbed endlessly, reaching the unlit top floor where Olya navigated by touch, her fingers whispering against wallpaper so old that it was peeling off in sheets. When a fringe of disintegrating wallpaper grazed Keen's hand, he yelped and she laughed.

"Everything up here is falling apart," she said. "That's why I don't dare turn on a light: I might burn the house down."

"I thought Peter was good at wiring," Keen joked, keeping his hands away from the walls.

"Peter didn't do the top-floor wiring." Olya smiled. "Ethan and I did. We wanted to be of use. Clearly the goal was not accomplished."

Keen wondered at the casual grouping, that Ethan and she had been a duo with a shared goal. Did it mean nothing, or everything? He searched for a casual way to ask without seeming like he was asking and couldn't find it. Ahead of him, Olya pushed a door open. "Wait a minute, there's shit all over, you'll break your neck. Just stay where you are."

Keen stood obediently still and listened to Olya stepping on or around things, colliding with what sounded like a metal wastebasket, cursing. The room flooded in soft blue light, and Olya looked up at him from where she was kneeling, having plugged in a long string of Christmas lights. The lights wound around the walls of the room, over the windows and bed, dyeing everything a pale indigo: Olya's skin, a clutter of books and unstrung guitars, a broken drum kit. With a harsher light the bedroom might have seemed like an abandoned storeroom, but in the tender blue glow, it seemed like a magical and unlikely place.

"Voilà." Olya stood. "My bedroom."

"Very nice," Keen said.

" 'Very nice,' " Olya teased. "What do you like best, the furniture or the décor?"

At a different moment, Keen would have been embarrassed, wondering what you were supposed to say when a girl took you to her bedroom. But in this moment, Keen felt buoyed by the events of the afternoon and by the fact that he was the one with whom Olya had chosen to sneak away from the party. So instead of overthinking, he smiled and said, "Mostly the inhabitant," and to his surprise, she seemed to flush and look away.

"There's nowhere to sit," she said. "The floor, I guess. Or the bed." She got off the floor and sat on the edge of the twin bed, as if testing it. "The bed is fine," she said, "if you're fine."

"I'm fine," Keen assured her. He crossed to her and sat on the edge of the mattress, a few inches away. Together they stared at the far wall, the windows with the lights hanging over them. Outside, night had fallen completely, and the voices out on the lawn carried cleanly upward.

"Sorry about Ethan," Olya said.

"It's okay." Keen waited, but when Olya offered no more explanation he pressed: "Did I do something to offend him?"

"No, not really. He's tricky." Olya hesitated and then: "And things between us are . . . at the moment also tricky."

"Did you date?"

Olya snorted. "How traditional of you." But then the humor drained away and she said, "We were . . . together, I guess, for a while. And then we stopped being together, and we're trying to be friends. Which is easier some days than others."

"Why did you stop?"

"It's complicated," Olya replied automatically, and then: "Actually no, it isn't. His anger—the amount of it, the way it takes over—I couldn't handle that. I can handle it as a friend, but not . . ." Her voice trailed away. Then: "I understand anger, I think it's useful. I'm angry a lot of the time and it keeps me from despair, actually—the worst thing is despair, because you just fold in on yourself. My mother went from anger to despair and in the end, it killed her. But I think . . . to be too angry—to *become* your anger instead of using it . . . that's also a death of a sort. Does this make sense? Ethan is not who he was when we met. Ethan *is* his anger now."

"Why is he so angry?" Keen asked. When she looked at him, he made a gesture: "I know, the war, the planet, injustice—but actually, why?"

Olya smiled, just the tiniest twitch of her mouth. "And there's the biggest difference between you. To you, all of those things are extrinsic—they're topics. To Ethan, they're personal, intimate betrayals."

"Okay," Keen said slowly. "But that can't be the whole story."

Olya considered and then moved her shoulders in a thin shrug. "You want childhood trauma? That's Peter—it didn't make him particularly angry though. Ethan believes in justice, and the lack of it makes him crazy." She laughed then, without much humor. "Peter doesn't believe in justice because he's never seen it in practice, so he's doing great."

Keen opened his mouth and then closed it again. After a moment,

Olya said: "But if what you're really asking about is the moment in which he changed . . . That was after the tent city, this past April."

Keen frowned. He hadn't read the news back then, but he had seen the papers spread out in the dining hall. He could summon an uncertain image of a front-page photograph, a grouping of tents in a parking lot.

"They leveled a bunch of houses in the South End," Olya explained. "Evicted people, smashed it all down, made a parking lot. And Mel— Mel King, you haven't met him, he's a community activist—he got a protest together, hundreds of people. Put up tents, shanties, made signs calling the place Tent City."

Olya smiled, remembering. "I mean, it was cool. There was always music playing, we got some lights up, grilled some burgers. Ethan was living there—only the guys could stay overnight, so we didn't get charged with impropriety—and he got to know everybody. The cops came a few times to try and evict us, but it didn't seem to stick— the guys who got arrested would just come back, and the tent city stayed.

"It was only a few days in total, but I think Ethan—he started to see what things could really be. Like, if you were hungry, there was food. If you were lonely, there was company. Some guys got a bit drunk and out of hand and then other guys sat them down—you know, they weren't *criminalized*, it was just *You can't behave like that, you're hurting people.* You know? *This is a community, we're here for you but you have to be here for us.* And then they'd . . . shape up, basically." Olya grinned suddenly. "This one guy grabbed my ass as I walked past—like, a real handful—and some guys sat him down, talked to him about what if I was his sister, you know, would he feel like I'd been treated respectfully. And he apologized. Full on: 'That wasn't respectful and I'm sorry.' Talk about a brave new world.

"Anyway, so that went on for a bit. And Ethan was—he's never been what I'd call *optimistic*, but for the first time, I'd show up in the morning and he'd have this big smile on his face. He'd be running around making sure folks had water, supplies, checking in with people who were detoxing—if somebody's tent fell down, he'd be there to put it back up. It was like he had found a world he could *want* to be in, and he was giving it everything he had. And then on the last day of April, the cops came back and cleared it all out."

Keen remembered the protest he'd first seen—Ethan getting a club to the back of the head—and he winced. "Did he get hurt?"

Olya shook her head. "No, it was peaceable. The cops said 'You have to go' and everybody just packed up and left, like, *Okay we made our point, we're out*. And I think *that's* what broke his heart. He had been thinking of this as a world, a universe, a new way to live. And he was the only one."

"But he must've known it couldn't last forever."

Olya tilted her head to one side. "Why?" she asked. "Why couldn't it have lasted forever?"

Keen opened his mouth to say *Well, you were occupying a parking lot?* and closed it again. He knew her well enough by then to know that she hadn't been talking about the tent city anymore, exactly; she'd been talking about a way of living and thinking. "What if he bought a tract of land? I mean, so many people are doing that, I hear. Making these little communities on tracts of land?"

"We were trying with this," Olya said, gesturing to the house around them. "This was our tract of land."

"And it seems to be working," Keen said. When silence followed this statement, he asked, "Isn't it?"

Olya considered his question carefully. He watched her do it. And then she decided not to answer, and he saw that as well. Instead, she leaned down to fish under her bed and retrieved a book. Keen blinked at it, surprised, as Olya thumbed through, opening to a dog-eared page. She cleared her throat, self-consciously but with humor, and read:

"'I was born in the right time, in whole. / Only this time is one that is blessed. / But great God did not let my poor soul / live without deceit on this earth. / And therefore it's dark in my house. / And therefore, all of my friends / like sad birds, in the evening aroused / sing of love, that was never on land.'"

She closed the book again and crooked a wicked eyebrow at Keen. "Aroused in the evening," she said, "but loveless revolutionaries by morning. Ethan should have read more poetry."

Keen couldn't help himself from laughing. "That was poetry?"

"Yes," Olya said. "Oh yes, my friend. *That* was poetry." She placed the book back under her bed and lay down, her head on the pillow, her body arranged in a long straight line with her hands clasped on her stomach.

"Make yourself at home," she offered, with a quirk to her lips, and Keen understood this for the challenge it was. After only a second of hesitation, he stretched out beside her. He clasped his hands as well and stared down the bed at the wall facing them.

"So," Olya said to his right. "What's *your* deal?"

"My deal?" Keen shook his head. "What you see is what you get, I'm boring."

"See, but I don't think that's true," Olya said. "That keeps proving itself not to be true."

"Well, I'm glad you think so, but you're in the minority."

"No," Olya said, "especially not after today. You enjoyed that, by the way, didn't you."

Keen smiled. "Yeah," he admitted. "At the time I was just so . . . mad. But afterwards, I enjoyed it."

"I saw that," Olya said, but she wasn't teasing him. "It wasn't actually about the scene for you—the crowd, the bullhorn, all of that. You can tell when people are all about the scene. And you were just—something about the way you were talking to him, I could tell how angry you were. How much it mattered to you."

"It's hard to explain," Keen said slowly. "I mean—you and I have argued about science, how it gets used or misused—and what Ethan was saying downstairs, I get that. But what I don't know how to explain is . . . this wonderful thing of the universe, how it orders itself, how it finds balance. How intricate its parts are, the ways in which it's talking to itself—the chemistry of cells, amoebas, rocks, and trees—it's all just a sustained conversation the universe is having with itself. Or that's how it feels to me. My dad . . ." Keen hesitated, not sure if he wanted to open this can of worms, and then plunged ahead. It was easier lying beside Olya, not looking at her but feeling her listen.

"My dad is a preacher—like an old-school holy spirit kinda guy. I grew up in Wisconsin but he's from Kentucky, and for him the church has always been everything. I mean, literally everything, because he grew up dirt-poor, so sometimes the only place they were getting food, clothing, heat—that was the church. But also, it ordered his way of understanding the world. God created a masterpiece, you know? And when you receive the world as a masterpiece, you see what's beautiful first, and what's horrifying afterwards, and everything that's horrifying can feel like an aberration—the Devil at work disrupting God's plan.

"You might think my dad and I wouldn't understand each other—and we don't, in a lot of ways—but we both find a great beauty in order. The difference is he thinks the order is God's, and I don't believe in God. I believe there are provable answers to the questions of why and how things work. I believe that when you uncover answers with impeccable methods, those answers can become bedrock. And when you make decisions based on that bedrock—instead of ego or hope or fear—you make the right decisions. I think correct data is the best thing you can give someone else, because it isn't polluted by . . ." Keen searched for the words. "Whatever is bad in you, I guess. Science doesn't care who you are or what you want. There are just answers. But you have to always put the truth ahead of yourself—always. So when people fundamentally misunderstand it—when people want to twist its uses—that offends me. That's the only way I can put it. I find it obscene. What that recruiter was here for, what he was offering—that is obscene."

Keen fell silent. Beside him, he heard Olya's steady breathing. He felt, to his surprise, like crying. He had never said any of these things out loud before. He had never had anyone to say them to. After what felt like a long time, he felt the backs of Olya's fingers against his again, a caress so light that you could almost miss it. Keen lay, nearly holding his breath, and then Olya's hand slipped into his own, her fingers slotting through his. They lay motionless, holding hands.

"I wish my mother had had God or science," Olya said. "Anything, really. We all need something larger than ourselves or else we fall into our smallness and we drown."

"Did she pass?" Keen's voice was almost a whisper in the room.

"She killed herself." Olya's voice was just as hushed. "Don't say you're sorry, please. I sort of can't take that response anymore."

Keen nodded. Finding no other words available, he held her hand more tightly. He wondered if she would reject that as well, but she tightened her grip on him.

"How long ago?"

"I was in high school. I was the one who found her, actually. Which I think was not her plan. I was supposed to go to a friend's house after school, and my mom called her sister and asked her to come by around five. But I realized I'd forgotten something—I can't even remember what now—and I stopped home on the way to my friend's. And there she was." Keen darted a glance at her face and saw that her eyes were large and her gaze was directed at the doorway, as if she were seeing her mother there. "In the kitchen. That was her favorite room in the house because it was always warm—she would read at the kitchen table—and that's where I found her."

Later, Keen didn't know whether it was the right thing to do or not. But he rolled over onto his side, and as she turned toward him, troubled and questioning, he took her face in his hands and kissed her. For a long moment he felt her beneath him, neither pulling away nor participating, and he felt that he must have miscalculated. He knew he should release her, possibly apologize. But instead he kept kissing her, as if he were trying to convince her, pouring the whole of his focused desire, his admiration, his awe of her into the kiss—as if this was the language in which he would make his argument. After a moment she reached up and hooked her hand around the back of his head, and pulled him closer in.

It went quickly after that. She undid the buttons of his shirt with hard, fast fingers, yanked at it so he had to sit up and disengage his arms from the sleeves. She pulled her own shirt over her head with the same impatience; having made up her mind, she was leaving no time to unmake it. He was distracted by the reckless beauty of her, all that skin supple and outrageously cyan in those stupid, lovely lights, the shadows dyed ultramarine under her breasts and in the cups of her collarbone. She reached for his jeans, and he undid the snap and zipper, pulled them off and kicked them onto the floor. It was only when he was in his boxers and she was naked—a kind of nakedness that felt new to Keen, a nakedness more daringly exposed than other humans could achieve—that he slowed them down.

"Are you sure?" he asked her.

She looked at him, wry. "Are you scared of taking my virginity?"

"Are you a virgin?" Keen asked, alarmed, and she burst out laughing.

"No," she said, "I'm not a virgin. Are you?"

"No." Keen bit back the desire to confess that he had only had sex with one other person. He was ashamed of this most of the time, and here with her, someone who was on the cutting edge of the era, it felt like a nearly pathological condition.

"Well, good," Olya said sweetly, "we can be unvirginal together."

Keen took his boxers off; he fumbled with them; he fumbled; she took his hips in her hands and swung him back toward her; she did not fumble; her fingertips were light and certain as they found his skin and traced its lines: shoulder to chest, sternum to stomach; thigh to the back of the knee; knee back up to thigh. She drew him, and he became real. She drew him in, and he gave himself to her utterly, yieldingly, whatever she wanted he would do, and he did.

2018

9

MINNOW ARRIVED AT SEWELL SCHOOL IN THE FALL, AND IT WAS the following spring when Katie Curtis slipped into her classroom at the end of the day, after all the other students had filed out, and asked for Minnow's help.

Minnow was packing up her bag and simultaneously texting her landlord about the leaky faucet. Her first week in the apartment, she had asked him about the squeaky door hinges and he had said, heartily, "That's easy, honey, just get your husband to put some grease on it." She had replied, "I don't have a husband," and had been faced with his embarrassment, which seemed to be less for himself and more for her, that she could be her age and a spinster. She encountered the expectation often, here in the South, that she would be a wife, a mother, something other than what she was.

Her first few months, she had called Christopher most nights to complain about some new way in which she was made to feel out of place and wrong. Christopher was patient, pointing out gently that one could feel out of place anywhere, that it was only by finding and focusing on what you love that you start to feel *in* a place. "You like your students," he'd remind her night after night, as if he wasn't repeating himself. "Don't you like them?" "Yes," she'd admit, and then he'd ask her to tell him the things she had done that day that had given her some sense of belonging. Now, texting her landlord about the eternally dripping sink, Minnow was already rehearsing what she would say to Christopher that night on the phone—*It's like he doesn't want to fix anything in the apartment until I'm married!* And then, standing before her, there was Katie.

She had come to a stop in front of Minnow's desk with her small face very pale in the late afternoon shadow. Around three or four, the sun switched sides and then the lecture hall swam in darkness. Minnow tried not to turn on the overhead fluorescents until the gloom was absolutely unbearable, and so, appearing out of that underwater murk, Katie seemed particularly bloodless, almost spectral.

"Katie!" Minnow put her phone down, startled. "What can I do for you?"

"I need to talk to you," Katie said.

"All right." Minnow arranged her face into an encouraging shape. "What's up?"

Katie shifted a little, looking over her shoulder. Minnow realized that she was uneasy—no, more than uneasy, she looked sick.

"Sweetheart," Minnow said, surprising them both with the endearment. "What's wrong?"

She thought that Katie might burst into tears, but Katie took a gulp of air like a diver before a dive and spoke all at once: "I need your help and I need you to promise you won't tell anyone."

Minnow blinked. "I mean, before I promise, I'd need to know that—"

"No," Katie said, "I need you to promise."

"But if someone is hurting you, or—"

"No one is hurting me. If you don't promise, I'm leaving."

"If you leave, I won't be able to help you," Minnow pointed out, but instead of loosening Katie's resolve, it seemed to make her harder.

"No," Katie said, "I guess you won't."

Minnow studied the girl. How bad could it be? Drugs? Hard to imagine. There was the whole God thing. But regardless, Katie's desire for privacy didn't outweigh her need for help.

"Okay," Minnow said slowly. "I promise."

Katie looked as if she hadn't expected Minnow to agree, and her small face folded again, tears threatening. But when she spoke, she was steady and succinct. "I need you to drive me somewhere. Next week, Tuesday, eight A.M. Are you free then?"

"Uh . . . Yes, I guess I—Katie, where am I taking you?"

And that was when Katie said it, although she called it a "procedure" at first—"I need to get a procedure"—and it took Minnow another minute to understand that Katie was pregnant; that for months she had vacillated between denial and panic, not knowing what to do or who to tell; that finally she had made an appointment for an abortion at a clinic just across state lines, though it was against everything she had been raised to believe and did in fact believe; and that she needed Minnow to take her there and back, and never say a word.

*

Later, the story became that Minnow had said yes immediately, but this was not the case. That day in the classroom, Minnow had told Katie that she needed to think about it. Katie had nodded, accepting this, and then Minnow had asked her the question that was pressing on her: "Why did you come to me?" When Katie hesitated, Minnow had wondered if she shouldn't have asked, but then Katie replied, her voice firm though small.

"You aren't from here," she said. "And you—even when I say things that I know you don't agree with—you still listen." She darted a glance at Minnow. "I guess I thought—even if you thought I was bad—you'd listen."

"Katie," Minnow protested. "I don't think you're bad. It's just . . . given your age, and . . . It's complicated."

"That's what I mean," Katie said simply. "For you it's complicated. For everyone else, it's bad." She had been staring down at her sneakers, but now she met Minnow's eyes. "I guess—even if you don't help me—I needed to tell someone who wouldn't think I was bad."

That night, alone in her apartment, Minnow paced the cramped stretch of worn carpet.

Katie was clear on what she needed. Should Minnow not take her at face value? True, she wasn't an adult. But adulthood wasn't a guarantor of clarity; Minnow knew that firsthand. Minnow would have felt better if Katie's mother knew, or perhaps if Katie had explained to her the context in which the pregnancy had happened. But it was just that: *Minnow* would have felt better. Did Minnow need to feel comfortable in order to help Katie do something that the girl had already determined was necessary?

For a moment, Minnow wished she could call her mother, and the sensation surprised her greatly because she couldn't remember the last time she had felt it. Decades ago, maybe. She remembered the last time that Christopher had asked her if she wanted to be in contact with her mother. She had just moved to New York; she had not yet met Jack. The question had been hypothetical because the latest address they had was on a postcard that dated back to when Minnow was still in college. Minnow had not read it then—she was too angry—but Christopher had saved it, as he read and saved each of her mother's communiqués that occasionally arrived in their mailbox, always from a different address. Even so: "We could find her," Christopher had said, soberly. "If that's something you want."

"*She* doesn't want it," Minnow had said bitterly. "Clearly."

But Christopher had shaken his head. He was not someone who lied to spare Minnow's feelings, so she had listened reluctantly when he said that he disagreed. "Your mother likes to punish herself," he had said. "Or she—she chooses certain ways to punish herself, and she calls them values. Or that's how she used to be, I don't know how she is now. But I think if you reached out to her, if it was something you wanted, she would want to hear from you."

"Is that something *you* want?" Minnow asked, wondering if she was being given a directive in the form of a suggestion, but Christopher shook his head.

"No," he said, "that's entirely your choice, my love."

Minnow had not taken Christopher up on the offer. But now she imagined briefly what it might be like if she had tracked her mother down back then. She might pick up the phone, dial a number, and her mother would pick up at the other end and tell her what to do. But would she trust the advice? Advice only mattered as much as the person giving it; her mother had found herself pregnant, delivered Minnow, and vanished back into the ether.

Christopher was the one Minnow always called, but now she felt herself hesitating. Christopher would want to know the details and particulars—who was at fault and who should be notified and what courses of action were available to be considered—and these were not the questions that Katie had brought to her. Simply just the one: *Will you help?*

Minnow closed her eyes, cleared her mind. She thought about how Katie had stood patiently, waiting for Minnow to look up from her phone. How she must have been filled with the unbearable weight of her secret, a secret that she had kept for many weeks, even as she slowly came to understand what was happening. How the desire to tell must have moved in her—a seismic shift, an instinct toward breaking open. And she had chosen Minnow. She had looked at Minnow and seen someone who was trustworthy. Someone whose inability to belong here was an opportunity and not a failure. Seeing this, Katie had placed herself in Minnow's hands.

And this, in the end, was the answer.

In the morning, she called Katie on her cellphone, and as soon as Katie picked up, Minnow said: "I'll take you."

A silence, then Katie's shaky voice said, "Thank you." And that was the only time that Minnow heard her cry. She may have cried later, when it all blew up, but Minnow didn't know, because by then they were forbidden from being in contact.

*

Afterward, Minnow would remember the day in broad strokes, as something of a fever dream. But at the time it was filled with hard, granular details: the navy leggings and oversized pink fleece that Katie was wearing when Minnow picked her up down the road from the school; how the fleece was both too warm for the season and so large that it made Katie disappear inside it. The three traffic lights that they hit, one after the other, on their way out of town, and how on the third light Katie glanced sideways at Minnow, her small face pulled tight with worry, and asked: "Do you think this is a sign?" And Minnow, who had been about to make a joke, had realized in time that Katie meant a sign from God and that she was, in fact, dead serious. "No," Minnow had said gently, "I think it's just the way the lights are programmed." The length of the drive to the clinic, during which

sprawling green fields were replaced by towns were replaced by sub-
urbs were replaced by fields again.

The clinic wasn't hard to find, although Minnow had been prepared for it to be hidden. Instead, it sat openly in a complex of nail
salons and sandwich shops. She pulled into the parking lot, which
held only a few other cars, and the engine ticked and clicked when
she turned it off. Katie sat, enveloped in her pink cloud, staring
straight ahead at the windshield. Minnow wondered if Katie had
changed her mind. But then Katie pushed the car door open and
stepped out, still silent, and Minnow saw that she was shaking.

A straggling line of protestors stood along the road running past
the clinic. At a glance, Minnow caught their signs and placards, pictures of mangled fetuses and the ubiquity of the word *God.* Minnow
wanted to protect Katie from seeing all of this, but it was too late.
Katie's eyes fastened on the signs, and she stood motionless. Only the
twitching of her too-long sleeves communicated that her fists were
clenching and unclenching within.

A young woman walked over to them and Minnow tensed immediately, but she greeted them with easy warmth: "Hi, I'm with the
clinic, and I'd love to walk you in, if that's okay with you?" She looked
trustworthy in a button-down flannel and blue jeans, small earrings
shaped like honeybees in her earlobes. Katie looked at her and then
her gaze flickered back to the line of protestors.

"Are they here for me?"

The woman's face filled with weary tenderness. "No, honey," she
said briskly, "they're always here. We just don't pay them any mind
when we walk in, okay?"

Minnow and the escort stood on either side of Katie like body-
guards as they approached the clinic. She could feel Katie's body
vibrating like a reed as they got within earshot of the protestors. It
was not that the shouting began then, as it had been a background
wash of noise this whole time, but rather that it found its target. It
directed itself, it sharpened itself against the three of them. The escort
kept Katie engaged in a low easy conversation as they walked her past
a security guard and into the clinic. Minnow caught only fragments—
it seemed that the two of them were talking about leggings, a brand

that the escort preferred, and Katie was taking the conversation seriously, her little face focused into a frown as she explained why she liked the ones she was wearing.

Inside the waiting room, a handful of women sat scattered across the chairs. Most of them were looking at their phones, a few at magazines. Some sat with other women; a couple had men with them, who looked determined but uneasy. Minnow tried not to stare but she couldn't help taking in the range of their ages—girls who looked as if they were Katie's age and women who might have been Minnow's. It was hard to know at a glance who was there for herself and who was there for someone else.

The escort led them to the check-in desk where Katie was given a sheaf of forms to sign. The escort referred to Minnow once, casually, as "Mom," and both Katie and Minnow looked at her in a kind of shock, both of them hesitating until it was too late to correct her and the interaction had moved on and they were being ushered to a bank of maroon vinyl chairs. The padded seats were torn, stuffing escaping. Sometimes a nurse appeared in the doorway with a clipboard and called out names, and then women stood up and followed her. Once, the nurse called a man's name, and one of the men whom Minnow had taken for a guilty boyfriend stood up alone and followed the nurse down the hallway. Minnow realized that he must be trans, and that he must have been there not as someone's companion but for himself.

Minnow took in the torn seats and the scuffed floors and the word *underfunded* came to mind. She wondered briefly if this was a good idea. Katie had chosen the clinic for its location, presumably—but were there even reviews for clinics? *Five stars, took a baby right out of me.* Minnow felt her own palms starting to sweat. Katie glanced at her, and Minnow knew she wanted comfort, but all Katie said was "You don't have to stay."

"I don't mind," Minnow said. "Do you want me to go?"

Katie shook her head, staring back down at the floor. They didn't speak further until the nurse reappeared in the doorway and called Katie's name. Then she looked at Minnow once more. In that moment, her eyes were wide and her face was as open as water.

"I don't wanna die," she said. Her voice was so hushed that Minnow didn't understand her at first, and then she did, and she felt her heart turn over.

"You're going to be fine," Minnow said firmly. "I promise you, you're not gonna die." And then, not even knowing if this was allowed: "Do you want me to come in?" But Katie shook her head. "I'll be right here when you get out," Minnow said. She wasn't sure if Katie heard her, because the girl was already following the nurse out of the waiting room and down a hall, and then she was gone.

Minnow waited alone. Time passed. She looked at her phone. She stared at the wall-mounted TV as it flickered its array of images: E. coli in romaine lettuce, an Ebola outbreak in the Congo, a mass shooting in Western Australia. She checked her email on her phone; a student wanted to know if she was in her office and if he might stop by to hand in a late paper. She glanced around the clinic waiting room, trying not to make eye contact with any of the others, before emailing back that he could leave his paper in her mailbox. She stepped outside the clinic to get a granola bar from her car and then, seeing that the crowd of protestors had grown, she regretted it. She went to her car anyway and sat in the back, doors locked and windows rolled up, and watched the ebb and flow of people walking by.

A lull settled, in which no women arrived to be ferried from car to door. The protestors seemed content to take a break, and Minnow was surprised to see them leaning on their signs, chatting easily with each other as if they were at a mixer. A heavyset woman with a perm told a joke, and the men around her laughed. As Minnow chewed her granola bar, a skinny teenage girl with a LIFE IS A GIFT T-shirt bummed a cigarette from the clinic escort who had walked them in. Minnow remembered how they had shouted at Katie, how Katie— sandwiched between Minnow and the escort—had shivered. It was hard to put those images side by side: screaming at Katie, then telling jokes on the sidewalk. Protecting Katie, then giving a protestor a cigarette. It seemed to Minnow that she had wandered into an ecosystem she didn't understand and had, in her misinterpretation, over-simplified.

Minnow returned to the waiting room after a time. As she crossed the lot, she felt her presence clocked by the protestors, some of whom started chanting half-heartedly again. She wondered if they recognized her and felt that it was unfair to have to put in all that work twice for the same person. Back in the waiting room, the TV was moving rapidly through a series of commercials: for Burger King, for Range Rover, and (to Minnow's horror and amusement) for a birth control pill that encouraged a trio of teenage girls to twirl happily on a beach.

After what felt like a lifetime, Katie emerged from the hallway in her leggings and giant fleece, clutching a packet of papers. Minnow went to her immediately as a brisk but friendly nurse was explaining that Katie should call the number in the packet if she had any questions. The nurse turned Katie over to Minnow with a nod and returned to the hallway. Katie appeared a little groggy, but fundamentally herself.

"Hi," Minnow said.

"Hi."

"Do you need anything before we go?"

Katie shook her head. "They gave me antibiotics," she said. "I think we can just leave."

Out into the parking lot again. The protestors picked up the volume when they saw Katie coming. A different escort met them at the doors and walked them to the car; Minnow didn't recognize her. She seemed harder-edged than the first one, and when a guy in a camo-patterned windbreaker tried calling out to Katie—"Hey, little girl!"— the escort shouted over her shoulder, "Deuteronomy 23:1!"

"What's that?" Katie asked, startled into curiosity, and the escort recited, with some pleasure: "No one whose testicles are crushed shall enter the assembly of the Lord." She grinned wolfishly: "Camo Guy is super Jesus-y, so I like to keep him on his toes—I used to be super Jesus-y, too."

They settled in Minnow's car. Katie sat very still, her hands folded in her lap, until Minnow reminded her gently, "Seatbelt," and then she pulled it around her.

"Are you in pain?"

"They gave me painkillers."

"Am I taking you to the dorm?"

Katie nodded. "But down the road," she said softly. "Where you picked me up."

"Right," Minnow said.

They drove for a time with the radio turned low. Minnow thought that Katie had fallen asleep, but she spoke suddenly, her voice not much louder than the radio. "Do you think I'm going to hell?"

"No," Minnow said gently. "I don't think that."

"Because you don't believe in hell?"

Minnow nodded, keeping her eyes fixed on the road. They were passing through one of the long stretches of green fields dotted with billboards.

"Then it doesn't help," Katie said sadly. "Because I do."

"You think you're going to hell?" Minnow asked, not sure she wanted to hear the answer, and not surprised when Katie bobbed her head yes. "Why?"

"Because," Katie said. "This is a sin. Obviously. Like, the worst."

"But don't you think it's possible that God is on your side?"

Katie frowned. "It doesn't work like that."

"Why not?"

When Katie didn't reply, Minnow shrugged. "I don't know how it works," she said. "You know more than I do, I guess. But I just feel like . . . if God made you, He also made doctors, and He made the clinic, and He made me, and He made my car, and He made road-ways, and He put us all together in the same place at the same time. You know?"

Katie didn't say anything more after that. Minnow wondered if she had made a misstep, but when she snuck a glance at Katie's face, the girl looked pensive. Later she was asleep, her head lolling against the back of the seat. She slept the rest of the way, waking up only when Minnow shook her shoulder gently: "We're here." And for a moment, hazy from sleep, Katie began to smile at her—a shockingly sweet smile—before she woke up completely and her face froze in a surprised, troubled mask.

Minnow thought later that if she had known that this was the last time she would see Katie Curtis, she might have said more. She might have said that you have to be on your own side, whether or not God is. She might have said that you don't have to believe in hell to believe in the ways in which people tell stories to exert control over one another, and the ways in which those stories become codified into systems. Or perhaps there would have been no point to any of that. Maybe all she should have said was *Call me. If anything happens that makes you scared, call me.* But she didn't, and so when Katie was at her most frightened, she went elsewhere—and so this was the last time they spoke.

*

The first time Minnow saw Jim, he was standing in front of her car window, shouting. He was staring straight at her, the veins in his forehead distended. This was the day that the protests started, and so they were still local and small in number—the out-of-towners had not yet been bused in. It was four days after Katie had gone to Health Services with cramps and bleeding, where, terrified and guilt-stricken, she had blurted out the whole story: the abortion, the clinic, who had taken her there. That morning, Minnow had seen the first of the handouts going around, stuck under windshield wipers and doors, thumbtacked to the bulletin boards just inside the school buildings— a grainy, badly xeroxed photograph of Minnow taken from the faculty home page, and then the headline: DO YOU WANT HER NEAR YOUR CHILDREN? She had not read past the headline.

Jim was leading a small cluster of protestors in a chant on the island of grass between the Dean's office and the faculty parking lot. Minnow drove past them, sliding farther and farther down in her seat as she was required to slow, to turn. But nobody pointed to her—they were all focused on Jim, who had a bullhorn and was giving a speech. "My niece never asked for this," he was saying. "My niece has always been guided by God." After she parked her car, Minnow put her headphones on and walked quickly toward the university, hair in front of her eyes, head down. She caught a few more of Jim's words— *criminal* and *murderous*—but she managed to hear as little as possible.

Three more days passed before Minnow saw Jim again. By then, the world had turned upside down in a way that felt so far outside the scope of her imagination that each day brought constant bewilderment. She had heard her name on the radio; she had changed the channel and heard it again, as a group of cheerful strangers debated what she had done and why she had done it. Emails had started pouring in—a heady mixture of requests from liberal media outlets for interviews and quotations and death threats from people who seemed under the impression that Minnow had held Katie down and performed the abortion herself. With the emails came the texts and calls from friends, former classmates, some former teachers even—most of whom seemed impressed and worried about her. Kenneth had called, wanting to know if she was safe and asking if she should leave town. Jack had texted: *Baller move, dude.* Her small group of college friends, who had never before found much to admire in her, revived a group thread to which they sent missives: *You're a goddamn hero* and: *Ruth Bader Mins-burg?!*

Minnow was pleased and confused by this show of support, but unsure how to respond. It always felt nice to be told that she was impressive by people who, though they loved her, had most often thought of her as unremarkable and self-effacing. At the same time, Minnow knew she hadn't done anything. Or rather, she had done exactly what Katie had asked, no more and no less, and she had done it because Katie had asked her, not because she was defending a set of principles in the face of another set of principles. Oddly, perhaps unbelievably, the idea of driving Katie as a political act hadn't even occurred to her. So how to respond?

I'm all right, she said. And: *Thank you.* And: *How did you even hear about this?* But she quickly stopped asking the last question, because she realized the story had been picked up and was being told and retold, in a variety of mirror-image narrative variations, across America's media networks.

She was a saint, upholding women's rights in a backward conservative town. She was a whore, teaching her students to go whoring. She was a leader and a steadfast rebel. She was a murderer and probably a lesbian. She saw her name as *Minna, Minnie,* and occasionally her actual full name—*Minerva.* A lady on the radio said, "And get this, people call her *Minnow*—seems like a little fish to make such a big wave," and her cohost laughed heartily. It was like middle school all over again, except scarier.

She kept wanting to call her father and then hesitating. Christopher didn't watch television and he didn't read the newspapers. He listened to NPR, and NPR had contacted Minnow for an interview, but she hadn't written back—maybe they hadn't run the segment? Maybe, Minnow told herself, everything would stop, like an out-of-control car careening to a halt, and then she would never need to have told Christopher. But at the same time, as she ricocheted between excitement and alarm, she wished for comfort, and Christopher was where comfort had always come from.

The morning after a segment on CNN, in which an unflattering recent picture of Minnow was displayed—sallow and shifty, eyes blurred in a badly timed blink—a college friend texted Minnow in alarm. *Um, your home address is all over Twitter. You might wanna close down your accounts and scrub the net—get IT to help you out.* Leaving her apartment to find the Sewell IT office, Minnow saw Jim again. He was standing on the small square of lawn in front of her building, an old brick structure on the southern edge of campus. He was alone, and he was neither shouting nor brandishing a placard. He was just standing there, arms crossed, staring up at Minnow's apartment. For the first time, fear lanced through her—real fear, walking-alone-at-night-and-hearing-footsteps-behind-you fear, not the baffled anxiety she had felt hearing her name on the radio.

She saw Jim again that evening, coming back from the IT office, where a seemingly awed twentysomething had helped Minnow shut down all her social media accounts, change her passwords, shore up her email, and sign up for an expensive service that existed to scrub personal information from the global bulletin board of the internet. Minnow was nearing the safe haven of her apartment building when she saw Jim leaning against a low brick wall, looking down at his phone. He conspicuously didn't look at her, nor did he turn his head as she walked past. She understood that he was displaying himself to her—*I can be anywhere I want to be, I can be wherever you are*—but that he was doing nothing that could warrant a complaint. She walked past him, her body rigid, her hands folded into fists. Every hair on her arms stood up and adrenaline pumped through her veins. As she got to the end of the small walkway that widened into a larger path, she looked back over her shoulder, and he was staring right at her. His face was utterly blank and his eyes were narrow and bright. For a moment they exchanged stares, giving each other nothing, and then she turned her head and kept walking.

*

The first time the dean called her in, he seemed completely at a loss, though not unsympathetic. Dean Kaye was a man in his late forties who prided himself on being reasonable; he had stylish wire-rimmed spectacles and sandy hair that was getting long enough to be feathery. Minnow knew that he was originally from California, and though it was San Diego and not San Francisco, she imagined that they might still be on the same side of this matter.

Dean Kaye had Minnow sit in the leather armchair across from his desk, and then he stood, and then he sat, and then he cleared his throat, and Minnow realized that he was crawling out of his skin with discomfort. He asked Minnow if she knew why he had wanted to speak to her, and she said that she thought so, and that seemed to fill him with relief. Without ever using the word *abortion*, he told Minnow very sternly that she should never take the place of a parent where students were concerned; that these sorts of things opened them up to legal action—although, he hastened to add, nobody had mentioned that as of yet. He was speaking with the Curtis family later that day and he hoped to be able to clear up any misunderstandings around Minnow's intentions.

"My intentions?" Minnow asked.

"Exactly," the dean said. "Maybe you didn't even know where you were taking her. Maybe she wasn't clear with you. You know?"

"She was pretty clear," Minnow began, but the dean kept talking.

"Maybe it was framed as a doctor's appointment, you know what I mean? She had an appointment, it could have been a dentist, you drove her to—"

"An abortion clinic," Minnow said drily.

"Right, well—you know, maybe you thought it was a place like Planned Parenthood, where they treat a lot of different things, medically speaking." The dean ran his hand through his hair, but this time his eyes were fastened on Minnow. "I just think it's important to be clear about the . . . the ways in which there was a lack of clarity. You didn't have all the information, you know what I mean?"

Minnow blinked at the dean and he blinked back. There were dark circles under his eyes.

"Is Katie okay?" she asked. "I heard she had some bleeding."

The dean flinched a little at *bleeding*, but he said: "Yes, she's fine. She went home, she's with her mother."

"She went home?"

"It sounds as if she may be taking a leave of absence this semester."

"So they *pulled* her home." Minnow sat up straighter in the slippery leather chair. "Are they going to let her come back?"

"Miss Hunter." The dean sighed, but his face was not unsympathetic. "Katie's family . . . They have a very strict faith. And that faith is something that is incompatible with much of the behavior that other students Katie's age find acceptable. And I don't even mean . . ." Once again he didn't say the word *abortion*, but finding himself in the space where it existed, he selected a different path. "I don't know that they will find Katie's continued placement here compatible with their values, and that pains me, frankly. Situations like this—incompatibilities between the values of the family and the desires of the student—those happen from time to time, and they pain me. But the scope of my powers is . . . limited." For a moment he looked genuinely pained, staring down at his desktop, and then he looked back up at Minnow and his face was stern again.

"And the scope of yours," he said, "is *very* limited. Do you understand that?"

"Yes," Minnow said. "I understand that."

"All right," Dean Kaye said, and he let her go.

The second time she was summoned to his office was two weeks later. This was after all the media coverage was well underway; after pro-life organizations from out of town had come in and started organizing. This was after Jim had started to be everywhere; after he had appeared in the local newspaper, calling for Minnow's arrest, and Minnow had learned his name—Jim Curtis—and exactly who he was. This was before Christopher had called her, and later Minnow would be grateful for that at least; if she had gone into that second meeting knowing how her father felt, she would have crumbled.

This time, the circles under Dean Kaye's eyes were a deep purple, and he looked defeated. Minnow knew that she must look the same. She had been sleeping badly, and sometimes not at all. He had her sit, and he offered her tea or coffee, which was how she knew that this conversation would be a much harder one. She accepted the offer of a glass of water, and he left the office briefly to fetch one for each of them. He had never brought her water before.

When he was sitting across from her, he cleared his throat a few times, rubbed his palm over his face, and then started talking. His voice was low and measured, and he spoke as if he had spent time deciding what he wanted to say, and as if his purpose were to download that statement to Minnow as quickly as possible. He said that the situation had escalated and was clearly untenable; that Minnow must be aware of the community unrest and the national interest that was serving to fuel that situation; that classes were being disrupted—not just Minnow's but the classes of other teachers as well; that the life of the campus was being disrupted; that the question of legal action was unfortunately very much on the table, as concerned both Sewell School and Minnow herself; that he and the leadership and board of Sewell School had found themselves in a situation that nobody wanted to be in, wherein certain concessions would be required from them. He took a breath here, and Minnow noted that he had used the word *situation* three times, and the word *abortion* not at all.

"Legal action?" Minnow asked. "Do I need a lawyer?"

Dean Kaye sighed, a sigh that seemed to come from the depths of his soul. He said that he would be remiss in his duties to her if he told her *not* to get a lawyer. But that so far it seemed as if Katie's parents had not been convinced to press legal charges, although he knew that other members of her family were advocating in that direction. *Jim*, Minnow thought. *That son of a bitch*. However, this was contingent on the school taking certain actions, and on Minnow taking certain actions.

"What actions?" Minnow asked warily.

The dean looked her in the eyes then. His were a very light green, and with his glasses askew and his hair falling into his forehead, he reminded her of Christopher. "We think it would be best for us to part ways," he said. "Of course you would be choosing to move on— this would not be a termination that was on your record. And we would be able to put our energies toward promoting healing within our community."

Minnow was quiet, turning the words over in her head. Was she surprised? She felt that she was, and yet she knew she shouldn't have been. "Let me understand this," Minnow said, and her voice was unexpectedly cool. "You're firing me."

"We are *not* firing you," the dean said rapidly.

"You are requiring me to leave, or *else* you'll fire me."

Dean Kaye blinked several times in succession. He had short, bristling eyelashes. "We are attempting to protect you, and the institution, and the other students here. And we don't see a way to do that by moving forward together."

"Because if you don't fire me, you'll get sued. Maybe."

"Because," the dean said, not unkindly, "a lot of parents have expressed their deep concerns about your—role in Katie's choices."

"My *role*?" Minnow heard her voice lift and worked to bring it back under her control. "My *role* was that we got in my car and I drove it."

"I understand that this is your position, but there's concern that you suggested an abortion as an option, or that you found the place and made the appointment—you took her across state lines, Miss Hunter!—or even that she was on the fence and you convinced her to do it. That you had a particular political agenda, a particular axe to grind, and Katie was a victim of that agenda."

"But that's not true," Minnow said. "None of that is true. When she came to me, she had already—"

"I believe you," the dean cut her off. "I do believe you. And yet that doesn't change the conversations that are happening. With the board. With other faculty. And of course with the media. As you must be aware."

"So you just need this to go away," Minnow said slowly. "And it goes away if I go away. Did I get that right?"

She thought that Dean Kaye wouldn't answer her, or that he would insist on using words and phrases that slipped around the edges of what was happening. But when he looked at her, she understood that he had come to the end of his ability to navigate the situation, and that he was now willing to do many things, the least of which was answer her question candidly.

"Yes, Minnow," he said. "I think unfortunately that's where we are."

"What if I fight this?" she asked. "Concretely speaking, I'm not certain you have legal grounds to fire me."

"A lapse of judgment as concerns a minor that resulted in a breach of the school's expected standards for its teachers," the dean said, without hesitation. "Those would be the grounds. And is that enough? I'm not a lawyer. But you should know that those conversations are being had. Making this bigger and uglier doesn't benefit you, Minnow. It doesn't benefit us, of course, but it certainly doesn't benefit you."

Minnow opened her mouth but the dean kept speaking:

"This kind of visibility and pressure on Katie and her family isn't the best thing for them either. And putting us onto litigious footing with each other—Minnow, nobody would call that a victory, not for any of the parties involved. So I asked the board not to be hasty in their actions. To give you a chance to do—for yourself as much as us—the right thing."

In the silence, Minnow heard voices lifted on the main green, shouting, cheering. Students playing, she thought, a frisbee game. And then she caught the rhythm of chanting and realized with a sinking heart that it must be protestors again, more protestors standing by the main gate. The school had recently forbade them from entering the campus itself, so now they stood on the main drive that led up to the school gates. Their numbers had swelled over the past few days alone—a West Virginia church was busing its congregants in.

"Minnow?" Dean Kaye's voice was gentle. He had made his point, and so he could afford to be gentle.

"If you'll excuse me," Minnow said, standing. The dean didn't press her. He stood as well, and remained standing as she walked out.

*

Christopher called her that night, before she could call him. When she picked up, he launched in, and at first she almost did not recognize his voice, it was so unsteady with rage.

"What have you done? Minnow, what did you do?"

"I can explain," Minnow began, but Christopher was shouting. Her father, who almost never raised his voice to her, seemed to have lost control.

"Why are these men on my lawn, Minnow? Why are they banging on the door and asking to talk to me! They're going through my *mail*—one of them was in my *garden*—"

"Dad, I'm sorry," Minnow said. "I never imagined—"

"They're saying you took some little girl to get an *abortion*?"

"She's sixteen," Minnow said, lifting her own voice to be heard. But surprisingly, this silenced Christopher, and then:

"So it's true."

"I don't know all of what was said to you." Minnow's legs were shaking and she had to sit down. "But a student of mine came to me and *asked*—"

"Oh god," Christopher groaned.

"Dad, listen to me, she asked for help—"

"Help? You call that help? You had no business taking her!" Christopher tried to bring his voice down; she could hear the effort. "Minnow, that is *insane,* it is *insane* that you thought you should drive a *teenager* to an *abortion* clinic in *another state*—"

"Katie was asking the one adult she could trust! What was I supposed to do?" Minnow was on her feet again, pacing the apartment, swinging from wall to wall with the phone clutched in her bloodless, sweating hand. "Listen to me, I'm sorry—I'm truly sorry and I know that things are—blown way out of proportion right now, and people are really—I didn't expect, obviously, that this would get so—"

Christopher was shouting again: "What *did* you expect?"

Minnow felt her eyes fill with tears. "What should I have done?" she demanded.

"Stay out of it," Christopher said without hesitating.

"She was my student!"

"All the more reason to stay out of it."

"Dad—"

"Minnow, there are people who want to hurt you. Do you hear me? You have made yourself the face of some whole—some whole political *thing*—you have handed everybody a story that they can use however they want. And they will! Do you understand what you've done? People aren't thinking of you as a person anymore! You've thrown away your security and safety and—*my* safety, *my* security—"

Minnow fought to keep her voice level. "Are *you* unsafe? Are people threatening *you*?"

"There are men climbing my fucking fence!" Christopher yelled, and Minnow was speechless. She had never heard him swear. "They're trying to ask me fucking questions about who I raised and how I raised you! You didn't have *any* thought about what this would do to you or to me. You created a mob and put us both in front of it."

Something in Minnow snapped. "I can't believe you!" she shrieked. "I'm sorry reporters are in your *garden*, Dad, I'm sorry they're asking you questions, because I know privacy is your whole *religion*, like, heaven forbid anybody ask you a fucking *question*—but men are sending me death threats! Okay? So don't—don't talk to me like you're the only one facing down a mob."

Christopher's voice dropped and cooled, pure ice, but all he said was: "You need to leave that place."

"I'm not going anywhere. They can't drive me out."

"They *are* driving you out," Christopher said. "How do you not understand this? They'll do it with violence if they can't do it otherwise. You don't know how these people work!"

Minnow had had the same fear, and unable to answer this, she pivoted back to what hurt her the most. "I thought you of all people would understand."

"Understand?" Christopher almost spat the word. "What am I meant to understand?"

"That they're crucifying me for showing this girl some compassion, and the least you can do is agree that they're wrong! Even if there are men in your garden, even if they drive me out of here—even if they win, it matters that they're *wrong*."

Christopher's voice was quiet when he said, "I *know* you aren't stupid, Minnow, but what's worse than stupidity is naïveté, and currently you're trading in both."

Minnow hung up the phone, although later it would feel to her that her father was the one who had ended the conversation. The walls of the apartment were closing in on her; she felt the tightness in the room, the lack of air. She dropped her phone on the table, wanting to throw it, and stormed toward the door. At the foot of the apartment building stairs, sunk into the sticky June night, she stopped. She had nowhere to go, nothing to do there. She leaned back against the side of the building and inhaled deeply: grass, earth, the smell of bricks yielding the last of their sun-heat from a day of being baked.

Minnow closed her eyes, exhaled, opened them again. *How did I get here?* she asked herself. She sank down into a crouch. The back of the building pointed out at the small residents-only parking lot in which, two days ago, her windshield had been smashed. The single streetlight that looked over the lot had been out for the entirety of the time Minnow lived here, but it had never occurred to her to be nervous as she walked to and from her car. Now the idea of navigating the unlit parking lot at night made her stomach seize. When her car came back from the shop, she'd have to figure out where else to park it—a garage, some covered shelter. When the car came back, how much longer would she be living here? Even if she could fight to stay, did she want to? Minnow imagined this night spooling out into a series of other nights: months and years of nights in which she was isolated from everyone around her. The thought made her body feel like it was filling with cement.

Out in the parking lot, Minnow's eye caught a tiny flicker, like a red firefly. She squinted at it, at first idly, and then a jolt of recognition slammed the pit of her stomach. She caught the dark shape of a car, parked in the back corner of the lot, nearly sunk in shadow. Inside it, the glowing tip of a cigarette, brightening and then fading as its owner inhaled and exhaled. Someone was sitting out there in the driver's seat, smoking. Someone was watching her from the safe cover of the dark.

Minnow's heart was racing and she put a hand over her chest to calm it. If she got up and walked over to the lot, would he drive away? If she bent down to the driver's side window, what would he do, Minnow wondered—her mind already conjuring Jim's square jaw, strong nose, that throbbing vein, his straw-colored hair—what would he do if she put her face to the glass and met him head-on?

1968

10

AFTER THEIR NIGHT TOGETHER, KEEN WAS WITH OLYA AS MUCH AS she would allow him to be. She never made him feel unwelcome, though there were days when she wouldn't pick up the phone, she wouldn't be summoned. He respected those disappearances, although he missed her badly during them. But he learned to wait for her to emerge on her own, and by doing so, he felt himself winning her trust.

It became mid-October, and then Halloween. Keen missed the party at 5 Wellman because he was stuck in lab, redoing an experiment that had gone badly. It became November, and then Thanksgiving. Sheila left for home, and Keen did not, as he usually did not, but this time Olya and Peter invited him over. He spent the whole day in the kitchen, pressed into service as a sous-chef. Later, sitting at the long wooden table, studying the dishes of turkey, sweet potatoes, a chunky tofu curry, Keen felt pleasure seize him: he belonged here. Ethan was away, which was a relief. The house was full of people he liked, and they were lulled into a good-humored lassitude by food and warmth.

Early December brought a renewed sense of fervor. SDS circulated a petition demanding that the university deny ROTC the use of its facilities and that it replace ROTC scholarships with university ones. This was a subject of much discussion around the table at 5 Wellman. As demands were made and rebuffed in a choreography of negotiation, Peter reported that a professor of philosophy had agreed to present SDS demands at a faculty meeting after the SDS members themselves were denied access. At another dinner, Daisy read aloud a letter to the dean that the SDS Anti-War Committee had drafted, her voice ringing out as she declaimed: "It is an absurdity that the question of ROTC's retention may be considered at a meeting from which virtually all those who have voiced opposition to ROTC are excluded."

"We've got to rally," Peter said, and Olya replied grimly: "Oh, we're going to." Not for Olya were the lyrical and slightly hysterical dinner-table conversations about how they were living in the end-times. This was the domain of Daisy and Jonno and certainly Dwight Beachum, who Keen had now met (Dwight had shaken his hand firmly, pumping it like a crank, and said, "Good show with that Dow man" several times in a row).

Though Olya would tolerate theatrics, at a certain point she would break in with hard disdain in her voice. When she did this, everyone would fall deferentially silent, and then she would lay out a series of pragmatic actions: a rally that would exert pressure on a particularly sensitive bureaucrat, another activist group that was already organizing and needed their support. Olya sometimes drew flowcharts on large sheets of butcher paper, illustrating what they might do given a set of circumstances in which a public action met a variety of responses. And Keen, as someone who had always appreciated the cleanness of data, who had drawn many of his own flowcharts and diagrams, loved her most in these moments, when he could appreciate the diamond-hard, multifaceted clarity of her mind.

Early in the first of week of December, the SDS held a rally on the steps of University Hall during the faculty meeting from which they'd been excluded. Keen stopped by between experiments, bringing Olya a sandwich and coffee, and they huddled shivering in their coats while a series of somber-faced young men made speeches that they had clearly spent a great deal of time preparing. Olya groaned, balling up the wax sandwich paper in her hand. "The cause is righteous," she said drily, "but the men are *self*-righteous."

Later in the month, frustrated by being repeatedly refused entrance at the faculty meetings, a group of students took over Paine Hall and held a sit-in. This was one of the few large-scale actions that Olya didn't participate in. Instead, she stopped by Keen's lab. He remembered it clearly because it was the first time she had ever come to him instead of letting him go to her.

Arjun was gone for the day, but Masaki was there finishing up some work. When she stuck her head tentatively around the doorway, it was Masaki who saw her first, and Keen heard the open curiosity in his voice when he asked, "Can I help you?"

"I'm looking for Keen." Olya sounded oddly uncertain. Joy surged through Keen and he stood so quickly he nearly knocked over the test tube into which he was pipetting.

"Back here," he said, ablaze with eagerness.

Olya entered the lab gingerly, glancing around at the subterranean, windowless walls, the wooden benches, the high, scuffed tabletops with their precision instruments, their fragile glassware. "Hi," she said.

"Hi," Keen said, and then they were quiet, self-conscious.

"Hi," Masaki said behind them, and this broke the tension. They all laughed and Keen introduced Olya and Masaki to each other.

"So this is where you spend your time," Olya said. "Synthesizing nuclear weaponry and eternal youth."

"Nuclear weaponry is next door," Masaki said. "Eternal youth, we'll take it."

Olya drifted back toward Masaki's bench, and Keen felt irrational jealousy. Masaki was good-looking, Masaki was funny. But she had come here for Keen, he reminded himself.

"What're *you* working on?"

"Absolutely nothing of interest," Masaki said promptly. "But I speak three languages and I can juggle, so I promise you that I, myself, am fascinating."

Olya laughed, swinging back toward Keen. "And you're doing . . . puffer fish toxins."

"Puffer fish toxins," Masaki said, "but he has no hobbies and he's not very exciting."

Keen smiled. "Good memory," he said to Olya. And to Masaki, a little smugly: "I told her I was working on tetrodotoxin months ago."

Olya tapped her temple. "I'm a steel trap." She came to stand over

Keen's shoulder again, regarding his setup with interest. "So, what is all of this?"

"Well," Keen said, "I'm looking at sulfur bonds—or, more accurately, trying to make them exist so I can see them."

"What department are you?" Masaki vied for her attention once again.

Olya turned back to him with a cocky smile. "None whatsoever. But I was protesting you guys in September, I'm not sure if you remember."

Masaki's eyebrows lifted. "Oh yeah, I remember."

"And now here I am in enemy territory."

"Your friends were real assholes," Masaki said, matter-of-factly. "I don't remember you, though."

Olya shrugged. "They weren't all my friends," she said, "but we had similar goals at the time. Your advisor is a real asshole, but I imagine you might say the same thing—that you share similar goals at the moment?"

There was a breathless beat in which Keen wondered if a fight was going to break out, and then Masaki laughed, shaking his head.

"What're you doing with this one?" he asked her, gesturing toward Keen. "He's too nice for you." But he said it like a compliment to Olya and not to Keen, and she smiled back at him.

"That's what *you* think," she said. "I've seen a different side." And Keen filled with mute pleasure.

It was only later when they were walking toward their favorite diner, shivering in the cold, that he thought to ask her what she was doing at the lab, and why she hadn't been at the sit-in. She took her time in answering, but when she did, she didn't equivocate.

"It's just for show," she said. "It's starting to be just for show, all that ROTC-SDS stuff."

"I thought you were all about it?"

"They're sitting in because they aren't permitted at a faculty meeting?" Olya made a grunt of disgust. "Who the fuck cares? Why are we even going to faculty meetings? To make our case to people who already despise us, so we can be ignored? And Dwight—I mean, he loves a sit-in, and God bless, I guess, but . . ." Her voice trailed off and she glared at the sidewalk. When she raised her gaze back to Keen, it was cautious. He remembered that later, the caution in her eyes, like she was trying to decide whether or not to say what she wanted to say.

"I just think," she said, slowly, "that there's more we could do."

"More like what?"

Again, the hesitation. And then she must have decided against saying whatever it was, because her tone grew cooler and breezier, and she said, "I guess that's the question," and changed the topic.

*

On the matter of sex: they were having it.

Not in the way Keen had had it with his undergraduate girlfriend, where it was understood that it was a regular activity they could enjoy together. But sometimes, if they were alone in Olya's room, she would turn to him with that slow, teasing smile and ask if he wanted to, mostly to see him blush. Keen was never as comfortable talking about sex as Olya was. Conversations about what they enjoyed or might want to do made him stammer with discomfort. He preferred when she would just kiss him and he could fall into her like a small planet around its sun, and no language was needed at all.

Other times they listened to music and talked. Then, even if Keen advertised his interest with light moments of physical contact, Olya did not seem to notice what he was doing. He took the lack of noticing for what it was—not a lapse in perceptiveness but a communication in and of itself—and after one or two tentative forays, he would stop. Something about Olya felt tenuous to him, as if he might lose everything by pushing his luck too far.

Keen didn't know where he and Olya stood, because they never talked about it. Although this bothered him more and more, he tried to follow her lead here as in other matters. When she introduced him to people he didn't know at the long wooden table, she always said: "This is our friend Keen"—claiming him for the whole house. Sometimes she would say, "Keen, who ran off the Dow guy, you might've heard." He listened to the words she used and didn't use, to what her tone did and didn't do, and although he fluctuated between elation and despair on a regular basis, he felt no clearer about which was warranted.

But then there were days and evenings in which everything between them was bright and electric and effortless. When everything Keen said or did made Olya respond with pleasure; when Keen lay with his head against Olya's shoulder, her hair tickling his eyes and nose, inhaling the clean, soapy, orange-y scent of her, and during these days and evenings he became certain that Olya felt for him what he felt for her, and that they would end up together.

Keen didn't entertain the words *marriage* or *wife* when he thought these things, although it was what he meant by *together*. In lieu of thinking the words themselves, he let himself fantasize outrageously traditional things: going down on one knee in the lentil-and-feet-smelling kitchen of 5 Wellman; Olya wearing his thin gold band on her finger, and Keen catching a glimpse of it at a protest, knowing she was his regardless of who else had her attention and efforts. The fantasies embarrassed him at the same time as they thrilled him.

Once, when they were lying in bed together, he described to Olya how they might someday drive cross-country in his old VW bug. He told her how they would camp in Yosemite, how they'd stand on the rim of the Grand Canyon, how each night they would stare up at the stars as the campfire burned out. Olya laughed and asked, "Will we be needing to read Jack Kerouac as well?" and Keen realized, with a start, that in his mind they had been on their honeymoon. He had described the honeymoon to Olya in all its details without letting her in on the most important part of it.

But: "That's not a no," he replied hopefully, speaking to her tone and not her question. She laughed and shoved his bare shoulder, as if they were both in on the same joke, but Keen knew right then that they weren't, and he did his best to bury this knowledge before the sun came up.

Ethan was around like a sore thumb or a lingering cough, always on the outskirts of Keen's awareness. Ethan didn't confront him again in the way that he had during the post-Dow party, but at dinner he always seemed to be digging up facts that contradicted whatever Keen said, laying groundwork that went in the opposite direction from wherever Keen was going. Olya rarely spoke of him to Keen, but Peter did once, to Keen's surprise.

The two of them were sitting on the small lip of roof that jutted out over the back porch. They had been assigned the task of reapplying the roofing tar to combat a persistent leak that appeared whenever it rained—or rather, Peter had been assigned the task and Keen, who still felt the need to be useful, had volunteered to help him. For the first five minutes they were quiet, focused on their work. Peter pointed out to Keen where the rain would run off the leaf-choked gutter, cascading down the side of the house, and Keen suggested they tackle the gutters next. Peter gave him an amused glance and then, imitating a conversation between neighbors: " 'Who fixed your roof?' 'A PhD in chemistry.' "

" 'Who wired your house?' " Keen returned, extending the joke, and Peter grinned.

"We're less proud of that," Peter said. "Above the second floor, anyway." But that seemed to have put him in mind of Ethan, whose work the top-floor wiring was, because eventually he said, with a casualness that belied itself: "It probably doesn't seem like it, but Ethan's doing his best—about you and Olya."

Keen focused on dipping his brush in the tar and letting the excess gather at the end of the brush. "Has he said anything?"

"No," Peter said, "but I know him. And look, I'm not—you know, I have eyes, I can see that he's being a dick. But I can also see that he's trying." He sighed. "I don't know why I'm saying this, it's not like you'll ever be friends."

"But things are over with him and Olya," Keen said, without meaning to. "Right?"

He had expected Peter would say, "Yes, of course," but instead Peter shot him a glance. "That's more of a question for Olya, no?"

For a moment, Keen felt light-headed. Then he rallied. "Is that a question I *should* be asking Olya?"

"I dunno, man," Peter said, "is monogamy your fetish?"

"*Fetish*, I don't know." Keen clung to his tar brush as if it would steady him. "But it's something I think can be good. Maybe it's not in vogue, but . . . Two people who have an understanding, who aren't— who are only . . ." His voice trailed off. He thought Peter might challenge him on an ideological basis, but Peter was quiet, painting. "I mean, wouldn't *you* want to know?" he asked. "If you were—if you were seeing a girl and you . . . it felt real to you . . . Wouldn't you want her to be seeing only you?"

Peter considered this, and then, with just a ghost of a smile around his lips, he said: "Well, it wouldn't be girls for me, so."

Keen blinked at the siding, and blinked again, as Peter's meaning came to him. "Oh," he said, wonderingly. Keen had never met a homosexual before, at least not to his knowledge. He knew they existed, but it had never occurred to him that one might self-identify so casually. Keen darted a sideways glance at Peter, to see what he looked like—had the confession changed him in some way?

Peter was looking directly at him, and, catching Keen's darting glance, he laughed out loud. "You should know," he said, "you're not my type. Before you panic."

"I'm not panicking," Keen said immediately.

"You are a little bit?"

Called out so openly, Keen had no choice but to be honest. "I've never met one before," he said. And then, hearing his own rudeness: "That wasn't . . . I didn't mean . . ."

"You definitely have," Peter said, smiling. "Met one, I mean. Possibly many. Though I believe you that *you* wouldn't have known it."

"Wow," Keen said and felt immediately stupid. But when Peter laughed at him, the warmth remained. "Does Olya know?"

"Of course."

"Ethan knows?"

"Everybody here knows. It isn't a thing that I'm particularly trying to hide."

"Are people . . . Aren't you worried that people will . . ."

"Outside of here," Peter said patiently, "I'm cautious. Where I come from, you have to be *really* cautious. But I lived in San Francisco for a few years before this, and that was great."

"San Francisco," Keen echoed, impressed. He had never been, but it was a city that loomed large in his imagination as a stronghold of both adventure and vice.

"You're learning all kinds of things about me today," Peter teased. "Good thing you signed up for roof duty."

"It *is* a good thing," Keen said, and they smiled at each other. And then his mind went back to the question from which he had been wholly distracted: "So . . . *are* they—Olya and Ethan—still . . ."

He thought Peter would answer him this time. But after a pause: "Just talk to her," Peter said. And that directive unsettled Keen entirely, because it felt like an answer.

*

Keen meant to talk to her, he was waiting for the right moment, but Christmas came and, to his shock, Olya went away. It had not occurred to him that she had anywhere to go; he'd never imagined her having a real life outside of 5 Wellman. When Keen showed up to find her gone, Daisy informed him that Olya had left to spend a week with her father in Baltimore. Keen had also never imagined that Olya might have a father; she seemed sui generis. He learned that her father was a contractor, that he had remarried after her mother's death, and that Olya had a half brother, before Daisy ran out of information, and Keen went home bereft.

The week before the New Year stretched out in a bleak limbo of filthy snow, freezing rain, and a piercing loneliness that Keen hadn't felt since before he'd met Olya. He spent New Year's Eve in the lab. Arjun was there as well, and when the clock turned to midnight, they toasted each other with warm champagne that they'd been storing on Masaki's bench while he was away.

Olya came back on the second day of January. Keen had been worried he wouldn't hear from her right away, but she called and invited him to dinner that night. Even then he didn't have a chance to bring up the topic of Ethan because the house was full of inhabitants and their guests, everyone exuberantly relieved to have returned from wherever they had been. Keen stayed until nearly two in the morning but had no opportunity to be alone with Olya. The same was true of

January third, a Friday, and then the weekend was a wash because there was a protest. Olya was galvanized by excitement, and when Keen suggested they slip away for dinner she said she didn't have time.

And then on Monday the sixth, a letter arrived like a bomb falling out of the white winter sky. It was addressed to Christopher Hunter, and he knew what it was from the envelope alone. But still, upon opening it, he held it in his hands and studied it as if it were an alien object.

The first typewritten line read: *GREETING: You are hereby ordered to report for induction into the Armed Forces of the United States, and to report to the home office of Green Bend, Wisconsin, on* **May 15** *at* **12:30** P.M. *for forwarding to an Armed Forces Induction Station.* Scanning the page with increasing panic, Keen saw that the letter was purportedly from the president of the United States, and this made him laugh out loud, a little crazily.

"This is insane," Keen said, and then again, "This is crazy," as if he were arguing with the draft board already. "I haven't finished my degree, you said I had two more years to finish my degree."

When Sheila got home from class, Keen accosted her in the hallway, letter in hand. He had been waiting desperately to talk to someone about it; when he had called 5 Wellman, the phone had rung and rung until he hung up.

"Tell me this is crazy," Keen said as Sheila read the letter. "They can't do this, right?"

"I'm not sure," Sheila said, frowning. "You'll have to write to them."

"I'll write to them, I'm writing to them, my god will I write to them." Keen paced the apartment, filled with manic energy. "They have to listen to me, they'll listen to me, right? Do you think they'll listen? They said—they already *said*—that I could finish, that if my grades—if it's physics or chem or engineering, they let you finish!"

Sheila's face was folded into small lines of concern and sympathy, but she was not the kind of person who told gentle lies. "They called up my friend Will in the fall, and he was in engineering. And a few days ago they called this guy Nathan—also engineering."

"Called them *up?*" Keen heard the note of hysteria in his voice and fought to tamp it down. "I mean, do they have to *go?*"

"Will definitely did," Sheila said. "He applied for a deferment and he got denied."

"Oh fuck." Keen sank into the battered secondhand armchair in their little living room.

"With Nathan, I don't know yet," Sheila offered. "Maybe they'll give him the deferment. I don't know Will's specific circumstances"— but Keen heard no comfort there.

"I can't go," he said. "I can't go to some war I don't even—I can't *shoot* people, Sheila." But what he was imagining, even as he said that, was the reverse: bullets speeding at him, the thickness of jungle, disease, landmines, death. All of it directed against him, Keen, who didn't even like hiking in the woods, who didn't like group activities, who had always had difficulty making friends with other men, especially those who were not scientists.

"Maybe you won't have to," Sheila said hopefully. "I mean, they gave you a deferment once before."

"I can't go," Keen repeated quietly, the hysterical energy draining out of him. Dread settled in his chest like a weight. He put his head in his hands, and after a moment, Sheila crossed to him and rested her hand gently in his hair. "It'll be all right," she said, which was the closest Sheila ever got to a lie, and in that moment Keen was so desperate for comfort that he pretended the hand in his hair was Olya's.

*

He went to 5 Wellman early the next morning, skipping a nine A.M. seminar that he had never before skipped. Olya, Peter, Ethan, and Daisy were sitting around one end of the long table drinking milky coffee, the remains of breakfast spread out in front of them. He might have guessed that this meant something was afoot—normally they didn't eat breakfast together, or even at all—but he was so consumed by misery that it barely registered.

Daisy was the one who answered the door, and when she saw him, she exclaimed, "What's wrong?" Olya said this as well as soon as Keen entered the dining room: "Keen, you look terrible, what's wrong?" At the far back of his mind, he felt a vague satisfaction: that she could see his suffering written across his face, that she felt concern.

"I got called up," Keen said.

"Oh no." Olya's response was so heartfelt that the satisfaction drained away and something in Keen sank. She had just made it real for him.

"Burn it," Peter said. "Fuck them."

"I can't do that," Keen replied automatically.

"Why not?" This was Ethan, and though the words were challenging, his tone held an odd sympathy. "A bunch of us burned our draft cards in front of ROTC in September."

"Sit down," Daisy offered gently, saving Keen from the embarrassingly square explanation that he didn't want to go to prison, that he didn't know what good burning paper did when he was already in a registry, that there were a hundred ways in which this country made you do what it wanted in the end. These were his father's opinions, he was aware—for a man of God, Roger Hunter was both a pessimist and a realist—but Keen held them as well.

Keen sank into an empty wooden chair and Peter poured a mug of coffee for him. "It's still hot," Peter said, and the kindness in his voice made Keen's eyes sting. Keen blinked hard and took a sip of coffee.

"Fuck them," Olya said. "Fuck them all." Her dismay had been swiftly chased by anger, and Keen tried to find this comforting but could not. "And they have the nerve to keep sending their propagandists here."

"Who's coming now?" Keen asked listlessly, and then caught the touch of eyes above his head—Olya, Ethan, Peter, Daisy: all interconnected in a network of glances. When he asked again, he was genuinely curious: "Wait, who's coming?"

"Andrew Hungerford," Peter said.

"I don't—do I know who that is?"

Another network of glances, but briefer. "He's a historian," Peter began, before Olya said ferociously: "If you can call him that."

"*He* calls himself that," Peter said patiently but Olya cut in again: "He's a mouthpiece for their fascist military talking points."

"He's giving a lecture," Daisy said, "in March."

"Okay . . ."

Olya picked the explanation up with disdain. "The topic of his lecture is 'The Ethical Obligations of Super-Power Countries: How Manifest Resources Oblige Global Intervention.' He's basically coming to make the argument that we couldn't ethically be doing anything other than sending American boys to kill Vietnamese ones."

"And you're protesting?" Keen asked, a little wearily. He didn't care about Andrew Hungerford in the face of the threat that had been leveled against him—against the normal rhythms of his life, against his *work*. Who would finish his *work*? And then he thought piercingly of Olya. If he was sent to the army, how would he see Olya?

"We're disrupting," Olya said, and now the thing that was in her glance was in her voice. Keen looked from her to Peter, then to Ethan, and to Daisy.

"We're discussing a disruption," Daisy said.

"So, a protest," Keen clarified.

"A manner of a protest," Daisy evaded.

Ethan broke in. "Look," he said firmly, meeting Keen's eyes across the table. "You might not wanna know the answers to the questions you're asking. Or, if you keep asking, you might get answers you don't want to have gotten."

Ethan wasn't being hostile for once, but his authoritative tone was like sandpaper over Keen's nerves. "What's that supposed to mean?" Keen snapped.

"It means," Peter said gently from his end of the table, "that in the event of . . . legal difficulty, you would be liable."

"Legal . . . like getting arrested?" Keen turned from one face to the next, wild with the abandonment of being outside the tight circle of their knowing. "Are you trying to get arrested?"

"Well," Daisy began, but Peter interrupted smoothly.

"In the event that there were arrests, it would be likely—given what we're discussing—that it would lead to prosecution. Which is different from catch and release."

"I want to know." Keen heard the hurt clearly in his own voice, how much he sounded like a child whose friends were all going off without him.

"Just tell him." Ethan was bored and surly, as if he'd done his duty toward Keen and Keen had failed to appreciate it. "If he wants to know so badly, just tell him."

They all looked to Olya, understanding that Keen was her responsibility. She was leaning forward with her elbows on the table, looking at Keen as directly as she ever had, as if she was trying to X-ray layers of muscle and tissue and bone, stare through him to some small sliver of core that would tell her what she needed to know. Keen met her gaze, trying not to waver under its force. *Don't leave me alone,* he said with his eyes. *Don't let me be sent away from you, don't go anywhere I can't go.*

"All right," Olya said out loud. "All right. Let's tell him."

And—as morning unfolded into early afternoon and Keen's coffee cooled in his hands, and Olya spread drawings and diagrams across the tabletop, and their voices rose and fell in argument and excitement, finding and losing harmony and then finding it again—they told him what they planned to do.

2018

11

LUC AND FOUR OTHERS WERE STANDING BY THE FOUNTAIN AS MIN-
now and Charles approached, bathed in the clear morning light. "It
is the hero of the hour," Luc cried out, seeing Minnow approach.
"Viens, Minou, je te fais la bise."

Half of Luc's head was swathed in bandages; on his unbandaged
left side, deep purple bruising created islands and valleys. She leaned
toward him and they kissed on each cheek. His lips were very dry, and
the bandages brushed her skin. She caught a medical smell, the clean
pungency of antiseptic and iron.

"Should you be here?" Minnow asked, worried, but Luc was
already laughing.

"It takes more than a bullet in the face to keep me off the streets,"
he said. "I'm a cockroach."

"Minnow," Charles said, taking over again, "may I introduce you
to Rémy, Sophie, Flora, Julie." He gestured from face to face and they
smiled and nodded back at her. Flora looked to be about Charles's
age. She was wearing multiple gold stud earrings that traveled up the
curve of her ear. It was hard to place Sophie's age; she was wrapped in
a voluminous sweater, and she leaned in to kiss Minnow's cheeks with
brief efficiency. Julie, in her thirties, was put together in a way that
surprised Minnow: more real estate agent than protestor. Rémy was a
stocky man in his forties, prematurely balding, and he shook Minnow's hand heartily with both of his.

"This is Minnow," Charles said. He might have said more, but Luc cut in with flair: "She saved my life."

"I really did not," Minnow objected, but Flora was already smiling, shaking her head at Minnow.

"We heard all about it. You are too modest."

"No, Charles was the one who saved your life," Minnow told Luc. "He got you out of there."

"Charles," Luc said. There was teasing in his voice, an older brother speaking to a younger one. "Didn't I say to you, 'Tu m'as sauvé la vie'? Or have I been ungrateful?"

"Ce n'était rien," Charles said roughly, dismissing it.

Flora and Rémy laughed, but Luc took up the challenge: "That's what my mother also says when the subject of my life comes up."

Charles rolled his eyes, but he was grinning. To Minnow he said: "Luc has a number of routines—if you stay for under an hour, you'll see him run through them all. There is the Bad Luck routine, there is the Good Luck routine, there is the My Mother Hates Me routine—"

"Ah, but what are we doing talking?" Luc cut Charles off deliberately. "Allons-y! Is anyone else coming?"

"Alain said he'd join us," Charles said, "but the Métro is closed, so he might not make it." To Minnow: "He lives in the Seventeenth." Minnow nodded sagely, as if she knew where the areas of the city lay in relation to each other.

"They're trying to keep us from gathering," Flora said in disgust. "I've heard they've already made a bunch of arrests."

"Arrests?" Julie's voice soared in indignation. "For what?"

Luc had been staring at his phone, but he lifted his face at this. "That's what I'm getting, too—they're grabbing people coming into the city. The word is ten thousand cops got sent in for the weekend, but my guy thinks it's fewer—seven thousand, maybe."

"Seven thousand cops?" Minnow asked, amazed. "For the weekend?"

"Did you see they removed the benches?" This was Julie. "I noticed when I was walking over here—all the public benches are gone."

"God knows you can't have a revolution without a bench," Luc said, and then they were off, Luc leading the way. Minnow was happy to take up the rear, and Charles fell back to walk beside her.

"I'm glad you came," Charles said.

He had asked her the night before, as they left Janet's dinner party. They had left at the same time, Minnow gathering her coat and then realizing that Charles was gathering his. She had wondered if he would mention the kiss, even if he would try it again. Instead, he had walked her to the corner before asking her, with sober formality, if she would come to the protest the next day. Luc was gathering some friends, he'd told her—Luc was the informal organizer of a small band of agitators. Charles had used this word with a smile, so Minnow hadn't been sure if he was joking, or what exactly Luc was in charge of. She had hesitated, but the heat of the dinner party was still with her, the argument around the table and the side of it she had found herself on. How it had felt good to be on that side, in a way she hadn't expected. And the kiss, like a reward. And so here she was, though a low unease roiled in her stomach.

"Do you think it's going to end up like last week?"

"You mean the violence?" Charles lifted a shoulder. "The problem now is the media is saying everyone in the street is a casseur—that we are all here to tear down the city." He shrugged. "So if you are police, you behave differently when you see the people standing across from you as criminals, not citizens."

"And do you think there will be violence from us?"

Charles considered. "I hope not," he said. "We are stronger when we don't help them to discredit us."

"This is where Charles and I disagree," Luc said. He had dropped back to walk with them. "I think, the more they fear us, the more seriously they take us."

"This from the man who needed head surgery," Charles said wearily.

"But that is what I mean," Luc argued. "That first time, we were— what is the English? *sitting ducks*. We thought, *If we're doing nothing wrong, we can't be harmed.* Now I know better, so now I say"—he turned toward Charles—"strike first and strike hard."

Charles opened his mouth, but whatever he might have said was interrupted by Luc's phone ringing. Luc picked up and spoke rapidly, listened, and then gestured to their small group, steering them down a side street. Overhead, a helicopter wheeled and turned, and Minnow tracked it with her eyes.

"Change of plans," Luc said without breaking stride, also glancing upward at the helicopter. "We go to Bastille."

As they walked, Minnow became aware of a deep and permeating hush. Gone was the normal busyness of a Saturday in the weeks before Christmas, gone was the rattle of the Métro under their feet and the congestion of traffic aboveground. Shops were closed—many had boards over the glass, but a few had yellow construction vests arranged in the front windows, presumably a plea of solidarity to keep from being broken. They walked past the Banque de France, each of its large windows entirely covered in sheets of gray metal. They passed other congregations of pedestrians, all walking in the same direction, but there was an air of caution—people glanced at each other, nodded, but that was all. A dark-blue armored vehicle rumbled past. Its tires were large and deeply grooved and its snub muzzle jutted pugilistically.

"What was that?" Minnow asked, turning uneasily between Charles and Luc.

"VBRG," Charles answered.

And Luc: "We used that shit in Kosovo. And now here it is, on the streets of Paris."

They arrived at one end of the Boulevard Beaumarchais, where a crowd was milling. A man wearing a yellow construction vest over a gray hoodie stood on top of a metal garbage bin, steadied by his friends, shouting in French. When he finished, people near him hooted and whistled and applauded, and a short chant broke out: *Macron démission!* Another man shouted out, "Foutons le bordel!" and the crowd around him cheered that as well. Luc led them along the packed boulevard toward the Place de la Bastille, where Minnow saw more of the VBRGs parked diagonally, surrounded by men wearing black metal riot gear and helmets equipped with face shields. The men in armor were watchful; they walked from one truck to the next, busy and idle at the same time.

Charles followed her gaze. "CRS," he said. "Well, a mix. Those are the CRS over there, the Star Wars–looking guys, and those ones are gendarmes mobiles."

"What are CRS?" Minnow asked.

"Riot cops," Luc said, "but worse than that. Compagnies Républicaines de Sécurité—you know what they say: CRS, SS."

"It's from the protests of '68," Charles explained. "That they're just like the SS, the Nazis."

Luc turned his head, like a dog feeling the wind change. "Tiens," he said, "they're on the move."

Even as he spoke, one of the cobalt tanks detached from the others and rumbled off down a side street, though the group of armed men remained. Luc's phone rang again and he picked up: "Ouais?" He listened, his forehead furrowing. "Ouais, j'arrive." When he hung up, he turned back to them: "They're calling for reinforcements on the Champs-Élysées."

They walked all over the city that day. Minnow quickly lost track of where she was. None of what she saw seemed part of a whole picture; it existed in fragments and juxtapositions, windows into a hundred different worlds. On one boulevard, a group of men carrying a banner that read POUVOIR D'ACHAT = POUVOIR VIVRE were singing with boisterous enthusiasm. Another group of men carried a large placard that read ILS ESSAIENT DE NOUS ENTERRER, ILS NE SAVENT PAS QUE NOUS SOMMES DES GRAINES. Around the corner, a group of college-aged girls were pulling yellow vests over their hoodies and jackets. Around another corner, a joyful knot of teens were pulling on balaclavas. A news anchor stood in the middle of the street talking into her microphone as people poured past her, and the balaclava-clad boys, spotting her, took turns darting into the background over her shoulder and waving at the camera.

They passed a fruit stall that had been demolished; clementines had rolled into the street to be trampled into bright splashes of orange against the gray asphalt. She tilted her head back and saw the faces of people standing at their balconies looking down into the street. Some were laughing and some looked grave. A group of men marched by wearing Guy Fawkes masks, some turned around on the backs of their heads so that Minnow could watch their manic plastic smiles receding into the distance. Sirens wailed, sometimes close by, sometimes farther off. Trap music blasted from a speaker tucked inside a man's backpack. A young woman in a yellow vest held the elbow of an older woman who was sobbing. A plainclothes policeman, recognizable only by the red band around his arm, was holding her other elbow. Oddly, both of them seemed to be trying to console her. Minnow saw people wearing dust masks, people wearing gas masks, people with wet T-shirts wrapped around the lower half of their faces. As they walked, she began to recognize the chemical sweetness in the air, the lingering tang of tear gas clinging to people's clothes. She saw men wearing Winnie the Pooh heads, and one woman wearing the head of a giant plush squid. Messages were written on the backs of yellow vests and she found herself reading them: names of fallen comrades, dates of the previous protests that the wearer had attended, ACTE 2, ACTE 3. Sometimes Minnow just saw the phrase MACRON DÉMISSION. On the back of one vest was scrawled, in cheeky English: HERE COMES THE SUN.

Luc was often texting, and then he would relay the contents to Charles and the others in quick low French. Minnow wondered who he was talking to, though she didn't feel that she could ask. She had imagined Luc as the ringleader of a small group of friends, but it was quickly becoming apparent that he had embedded himself in something larger. He was a hub of information, receiving it only to redirect it this way and that. He didn't translate for Minnow, and she didn't ask him to; she felt the bodies around her communicating what she needed to know. When danger was close, fear would travel like a current through flesh; it was always in those moments that she knew something was coming, and then a crowd would sweep down a side street toward them, fleeing, and they would be borne along in its current, clinging to each other's hands to keep from being pulled apart.

As the day progressed, signs of destruction became more and more evident, although their band seemed to be slipping between skirmishes, arriving after one had ended or before another had begun. They arrived at one intersection to find it strewn with capsized metal barricades; at another, a traffic light was broken and swinging and the air was acrid with tear gas. A rack of city bikes had been looted, the bicycles with their kelly-green fenders kicked here and there until the street corner looked like the bedroom floor of a giant child who had had a tantrum. As they passed, Minnow saw a handful of tourists scurrying into the open doorway of a charcuterie bar that closed and locked behind them. On the Avenue de Friedland, people were dancing in front of a wall of flame, their forms blurred and unwieldy. It took Minnow a moment to realize that they had created a burning barricade from trees in planters, stolen from a boarded-up nearby restaurant. A group of gilets jaunes were prizing panels off the Tunisair storefront; another group had taken a hammer to the plywood covering a bank window. Minnow could feel Charles's disapproval and Luc's elation without either having said a word. The distinct sound of breaking glass punctuated their silence, and everyone stood back to watch the large windows avalanche downward in a spray of fragments.

A man slid past them in a Freddy Krueger mask, and Minnow caught the warning glint of metal; he was carrying a hunting knife in his hand, and then the crowd swallowed him. Shouting startled her, and she spun to see two contingents facing off. One seemed to be young men, white, stocky, clad in leather. A pirate flag flew over them, and Minnow would have laughed if their faces didn't immediately make her think of Sewell, the protestors standing outside the school, the look on Jim's face as he watched her walk past. The other contingent was also mostly men, though less unified, and they began to shove forward, attempting to push back the pirates. The crowd roared, and on sheer impulse, Minnow threw her head back and roared with them. Her voice rose up through her legs, through the base of her spine, through her stomach, into her lungs; her body vibrated with the force of it, her mouth was whole with sound. When she stopped to draw breath she saw Luc was looking straight at her, laughing in delight. But Charles was already steering her past them.

"Fachos and antifas," he said in her ear. "Worthy fight, but not our own."

"Fachos?"

"Fascists." This was Luc, on Minnow's other side. "Here, this way."

The crowd surged, sirens wailing, and within seconds, Minnow realized that she knew no one around her. It had happened as swiftly as a slippage: Charles and the others vanishing like mist.

"Charles?" Minnow shouted his name and felt the lining of her throat burn. The smell of tear gas had become stronger. She tried to see over the heads of the bodies around her—by now she knew that the clouds of tear gas came with police. All day long, they had created kettles along barricaded avenues and dead-end streets, circling crowds neatly like fish in a net. "Charles!"

A hand on her arm tugged her and she wheeled toward it to see Luc.

"Thought we lost you," he said.

"Where's Charles?"

"Over there," Luc said, and then his brow furrowed. "Or he was. Putain." He held his phone to his ear, keeping his grip on Minnow's arm. "He's not picking up. Let me try Rémy."

Rémy didn't pick up either. Luc steered them down a warren of side streets. The tear gas smell was thinner here, replaced by a new stink, one that it took Minnow time to place: the stench of burning rubber. As they came out into a plaza, she saw a burning car on its side, flames leaping into the darkening sky, smoke belching upward. She had to cover her nose and mouth with the neck of her shirt.

"Fuck," Luc said, pulling her around the edge of the plaza. "That's gonna blow." They ran up a new side street, their sneakers drumming on the pavement. Outside a Carrefour, a small crowd was gathered, ferrying alcohol out of the smashed glass doors and distributing it on the street. A man handed Minnow an unopened bottle of wine and she was so startled that she took it and then was unsure what to do with it. Luc glanced over, laughing.

"Drinks for the road?"

"He just . . . gave it to me."

Luc smiled. "That's the part Charles hates," he said. "The smashing and grabbing."

"But you don't?"

"Charles and I grew up very differently." Luc shrugged. "I understand the instinct, to smash and grab. And who cares, businesses have insurance, stores have insurance, anything that is not an actual human, there is a safety net." Luc took the bottle from Minnow and twisted off the cap. "This is going to be terrible wine," he told her. "It won't even deserve the name." He tipped the bottle to his mouth and took a grimacing swallow.

"Bad?"

"I would use this to strip paint." Luc took another pull and handed the bottle to Minnow. She accepted it and drank as well. The taste was acidic, thin and sour, but it didn't taste much worse than the cheap wine she used to buy at Trader Joe's.

"Here you are, in the heart of the resistance." Luc flashed her a winning smile. "What are your thoughts on the day's events?"

"I don't understand what's happening," Minnow admitted. "Nothing seems . . . planned, by us or by them, it's all just happening, and then other things happen."

"Chaos is happening," Luc instructed her. "Chaos is a good tool because it can't be derailed. We don't control it, they don't control it." And then, with some amusement, he added: "I heard your *us*, mon professeur."

Minnow extended the bottle to him, and he took it without hesitation and drank. They were passing another burning car now, this one an SUV seemingly full of firewood. Luc covered his face with his arm and Minnow followed suit, holding her breath until they were on the other side, the wind blowing away from them. He nodded his head toward a side street and Minnow turned with him. She thought the conversation had ended, but he surprised her by continuing, his tone as casual as if he were discussing the weather.

"Where Charles and I disagree is that he believes that we can be reasonable, we can have reasonable conversations and the country will change. And I know that reasonable conversations do nothing but generate more reasonable conversations. There is a time to be unreasonable if we want more than conversation. I come from men who all lived the same life over and over again until it wore them out. Men talking in Paris did not change what their lives looked like, or what mine would have been if I'd stayed. But action—violence, even—*that* creates change, because if it goes far enough, reasonable men will do anything to make it stop." Luc eyed Minnow. "No?"

"Yes," Minnow said. The drift of burning rubber seared her in-breath, and she coughed.

"Yes?" Luc sounded surprised and pleased.

"I burned someone's house down once," Minnow said matter-of-factly.

Luc burst out laughing, until it turned to coughing as well. "Was he in it?"

"It was his garage," Minnow amended. "He was home, but I didn't kill him, I wasn't trying to kill him."

"Does Charles know this?"

"No," Minnow said, "in fact, nobody knows. Except now you, I guess." Sewell flashed before her eyes, the thickness of trees, crickets screaming; she blinked and the pavement reasserted itself.

Luc rinsed his mouth with wine and spat onto the sidewalk. He handed it to her and, a little appalled and thrilled, she did the same, getting the burned-rubber taste out of her mouth.

"My father worked at a factory," Luc began. They were walking uphill now, through a winding alley. "Forty years—he started when he was thirteen alongside his father. I started when I was seventeen—I finished high school, you see, and neither of them did."

"You worked in a factory?"

"You seem surprised, but I'm good with my hands."

"I don't know you well, but I can't imagine you taking orders."

Luc grinned. "Well, I couldn't imagine it either, as it turns out. But that's not the story I am telling you. So, my father. He has worked his way up, he goes from being on the line to handling specialty machines. And then one day—I am eighteen—he gets injured. A heavy container falls, my father is standing too near . . ." Luc winced. "The spine breaks, they say he might not walk again. This is how the pain pills start, but—that is also another story. His boss says, 'Well, we hired a man who can stand and walk, we need a man who can stand and walk.' He lets my father go. Just like that: forty years, and—nothing."

"Can he do that?"

"Whether or not he *can,* he *does.* And so—I am eighteen, remember, I am going to this factory every day, working with my hands, my sweat, and I come home at night and see what lies ahead for me: my father, dazed with drugs and pain, lying in bed. And this eats at me, it eats at me, I see his boss on the floor sometimes walking through, my father cannot walk but this man is strolling past. I see him in his office, sitting at his desk, my father cannot sit but this man is sitting. And I decide to kill him."

Minnow darted a look at Luc. She realized it had become dusk now, and it was hard to make out the expression on his face. The side street deposited them on a wider sidewalk, where a group of men were building a barricade out of a set of expensive-looking dining room chairs. Luc's voice was easy and untroubled, but as they passed under a set of traffic lights that hadn't been smashed, she could make out a muscle leaping in his jaw.

"I have never killed a man before, so I don't have much to go on. Movies, that's all. I take my father's hunting rifle, I wait until evening, I leave the house. I bike to the house of my father's boss. I leave the bike in a ditch, I walk with my gun to a stand of trees near his door. It is growing dark, he will come home for dinner, I will step out and shoot him. This is my plan. I don't know what happens after I shoot him, what to do with the body, or with his wife and kids hearing the gunshot—all of this, I don't plan that far. But the moment of the bullet hitting his head—that part I rehearse, I play it in my mind again and again, rewind and play like a tape, you remember cassette tapes?"

Minnow nodded, unsure what to say.

Luc nodded. "So . . . I sit by his door, I imagine his death, I am ready to pull the trigger. But as I wait . . . it occurs to me: If I kill him, so what? They will put another man in his position. A new man, an interchangeable man. These men, you swap them out one for another, you tell them what to say and the same voice comes out of their throats. Do you know what I mean?" Luc shook his head. "You kill this man a hundred times, and a hundred times a new man takes his place. And this is how it works, this system. And then it occurs to me, eighteen years old with my hunting rifle by his door . . . you must change what is above the man. The individual means nothing. The forces above him—*they* are what must be killed."

Luc shoved his hands in his pockets and turned toward Minnow. "And I quit the factory and I quit my family and I came to Paris," he said, singsong, as if he were telling a fairy tale.

They had come to a broad avenue that was oddly empty. Trash cans had been kicked over and trash blew freely in the street. A nearby travel agency had managed to get by unscathed, its great sheets of plywood still successfully guarding the window glass behind them, though the wood itself was tagged with paint: MACRON T'ES FOUTU, LES GUEUX SONT DANS LA RUE. Luc followed her eyes to the tag and smiled.

"Nice."

"What does it mean?"

"It means: *Macron you're fucked, the peasants are in the streets.* Very theatrical—but hey, it's all about the symbols." Luc laughed suddenly: "As you know very well, having burned down a garage."

Minnow shifted the bottle of wine from hand to hand. It was still heavy, although she and Luc had been passing it back and forth.

"And you didn't kill him? Your boss?"

"It would have meant so little."

Minnow hesitated. Something in Luc's eyes made her feel as if she had glimpsed him clearly, but now he was hiding again. "You just left?"

Luc nodded.

The wind had come up cold, and Minnow pulled her jacket tighter. They had been walking for so long, she had not noticed until now that her feet hurt or that her body was aching. She was not hungry, though she hadn't eaten since that morning. It was as if she had stepped through a door and everything on the other side was luminous and strange. The city had been rendered unfamiliar, punctuated by fires leaping and crackling.

Minnow hefted the bottle in her hand for one more moment, and then threw it, cleanly. It smashed against the plywood, splattering dark wine like blood across the face of the wood. It had hit near DANS and erased the last three words, so that the sign now read, MACRON T'ES FOUTU, LES GUEUX SONT.

Minnow turned toward Luc and saw that both his eyebrows were raised. "Somebody is going to stand in front of this sign for hours, now," he said. " 'Les gueux sont quoi? Mais quoi encore?' " Luc shoved his hands in his pockets and found a pack of cigarettes. He took one, offered the pack to her. Minnow took one as well.

"Charles thinks things can stay separate—your family in one box, your principles in one box, your government in one box. A revolution of little boxes, and you can move between them." He lit her cigarette for her. "Have you met his family?"

"We just work together," Minnow said guiltily.

Luc laughed out loud. "Oh," he said, "all right. You just work together."

"We do!"

"The thing about Charles," Luc began, and then a shape swam at them out of the darkness, bewildering and close, and Minnow yelped in alarm as its hands fastened around Luc's shoulders. Luc spun, fists rising, and then saw who it was.

"Putain," Luc said, and Charles shook him gently, laughing, then leaned over to give Minnow a rough kiss on the cheek. Charles was luminous with exhilaration; he smelled like sweat and gasoline.

"Je vous ai trouvés!" he crowed.

"What happened?" Minnow asked. "Are you okay?"

"Yes, yes—my phone got lost. I was with Rémy, he tried to call Luc, but we got separated—I don't know where the girls are. Minou, ça va?"

"Yes," Minnow said. Her head spun with wine and the sweet searing smoke that seemed to follow them everywhere. Whatever Luc had been going to say was lost; he tucked it away as easily as he did everything. He and Charles spoke quickly in French—Minnow made out some names and locations: Rue de l'Arcade, République, le Sacré-Cœur—and then the piercing blast of a police whistle interrupted them. All three of them turned as one, alarmed, to see a line of policemen running down the avenue in their direction. When Minnow swung to look over her shoulder, she saw a new grouping of gilets jaunes had formed on the other side of them, tearing at the plywood covering a bank of store windows.

"Let's go!"

Charles seized Minnow's hand. Minnow ran with him; the wind blew her hair around her face, whipping into her eyes. It was hard to know if they were running away from the police or toward something else, and perhaps Luc and Charles were not in agreement about either the away or the toward. But Minnow felt the running sweep her up again, the rhythm of her feet striking the pavement, Charles's fingers holding hers so tightly that, even when she skidded on the rain-wet pavement, he didn't let go.

*

It was deep in the airless space between night and late night when Charles walked Minnow home. The streets were cold and empty and the city hung loose around her. She had realized a few times throughout the long day and night that she was happy, although it wasn't a thought she was used to having, and every time she had it, she was unsure what to do with it. They walked side by side, Charles's shoulder occasionally brushing against hers. Desire moved in her, tidal. She had to break the silence, it was becoming dangerous, a space inside which the possibility of touch increased itself.

"Are you an only child?"

"No, two brothers." Charles smiled. "Both lawyers, like my father."

"Very impressive."

"Oh, completely. I am, of course, the disappointment. Perhaps you guessed."

Minnow shook her head, surprised. "No," she said. Nothing about Charles—the way he moved through the university, the way he was adored—smelled of disappointment.

"And you," Charles asked. "Brothers, sisters?"

"It was always just me and my dad."

"Did your mother pass away?"

The narrow street widened into a small plaza. A church with heavy columns sat back in an apron of shadow; Minnow caught the shapes of men sleeping on the steps.

"She left my father right after I was born. I mean, she wrote to us sometimes, but . . . that kind of petered out."

"And your father, did he stay in touch with her?"

"I don't think so, no. She was always on the move. I'm not sure he would've known how to reach her, even if we'd really needed to." Minnow remembered finding a thin stack of postcards rubber-banded together, one of the summers that she was back from college. What had struck her most was how unremarkable the messages were. "Best wishes from Alaska," her mother had written on one, and no more. On another she'd written a sentence about lying in the back of a VW bug and seeing the stars at night; the postmark on this was Montana. In the third she'd written, "Happy birthday to my big girl," post-marked Oklahoma. In the fourth was a message to Christopher: "Keen," she had written, "melancholy tonight. Give our girl a kiss." The last postcard had shown a stream with salmon leaping, grizzly bears standing haunch-deep in the water, *Yosemite* emblazoned across the pastoral scene. On the back, she had simply signed her name.

"It's sad," Charles said softly. She hadn't realized how close to her he was, but the backs of his fingers slid against hers. She didn't pull away.

"Is it?"

"Of course it is. No?" His eyes searched her face.

"I guess it is," Minnow said, "but *I'm* not sad. I mean, I didn't know her."

"She's your mother," Charles suggested delicately, not as if he were correcting her—which she would have bristled at—but as if he were offering her a claim that she wasn't taking for herself.

"My dad—he was always . . . enough. He was all the parent I could want."

"You're very close?"

"Yes." And then Minnow amended: "We were." Regret rose in her as soon as she said the words, and she corrected herself, defensively, deceitfully: "We *are*."

"I envy that," Charles said. "My father and I . . . We do not understand each other."

"It sounded from Luc like you were close with your family?" Minnow hadn't meant to mention that she and Luc had spoken of Charles,
but Charles didn't seem perturbed.

"Luc has renounced his family," he said slowly. "I don't blame him
for this—he suffered very much, as a child. But for me . . ." He made
a gesture: *What can you do.* "I look at my hands, I see my mother's
hands. I look in the mirror, I see my father's chin. My handwriting, it
is my mother's. The books I love, I was given them by my father. For
me there is no separation—who I am, who they are, what they made.
So . . . when Luc asks me to put my family on one side and me on the
other, how do I do that?"

"Is he asking you to do that?" Minnow tilted her head.

Charles sighed, shoving his hands into his pockets. They were
both moving slowly now, achy and stiff. A pounding exhaustion
worked its way up Minnow's feet, through her calves and thighs and
into her lower back. She felt like an unstrung marionette.

"It is complicated," he said. "Who my father is in all of this. I told
you—sometimes Macron calls him?"

Minnow nodded her head.

"And so my father gives him advice. Just sometimes. Off the
record, you know, nothing official. Just a friend to a friend, that sort
of thing. But what is wrong with this country—he is up to his elbows
in it, my father. Macron is a clever banker, he tells the people they are
rolling in abundance when they are starving; he says that he has heard
the voice of the people and he stops taking money from one pot, but
all the while he steals it from another. And my father is a clever lawyer. Sometimes he laughs to us, me and my brothers, at how simple
people are, how easily led—how if Macron tells the country that the
sun is shining on a rainy day, half of them will put away their umbrel-
las. My father is not a bad man, but he is in part responsible for what
is bad."

Sympathy moved in her. "For what it's worth," Minnow said, "my
father and I don't understand each other either. Not at the moment,
possibly not for a while. Though I didn't realize it for years, I guess."

She wished they hadn't begun the conversation about their families. It had been easier when they were flirting. This was honest in a way that could only draw them close.

"Well," Charles said, lightening his tone as if he knew what she was thinking. "As they say: La seule chose plus tragique que la guerre, c'est la famille." He spoke slowly so that Minnow could follow, and when she did, she laughed out loud.

" 'The only thing more tragic than war is family'? Who says that, Balzac?"

"Luc," Charles admitted. "Luc said that." And they both burst out laughing, their voices echoing in the empty streets.

As they reached the Fifth, holiday lights appeared, strung like canopies over the streets, single white tiara-like stars studding the centers. Minnow watched Charles walking with his hands in his pockets, laughter lingering in the lines around his eyes and his mouth. His arm brushed hers as they rounded a corner, then brushed hers again, but she didn't step back. The day was still in her, in the smells that clung to her clothes and skin, but also in the recklessness throbbing through her. When she took Charles's hand, she took it firmly, as if she knew what she was doing.

*

This is how it happened, when it happened.

They entered her apartment; she knelt to take her shoes off. When she rose again, Charles caught her face in his hands and kissed her. It was not a surprise, but it was a shock. She returned the kiss and felt relief pour through them both like adrenaline.

Charles was not what she expected, although she hadn't known what to expect. He was eager and confident, playful in ways that disarmed her. In the quiet dark of the sleeping loft, he pulled his shirt over his head with one hand, undid his jeans and dispensed with them easily. He stepped forward naked, despite the fact that she had removed only her shoes, and he kissed her again—first her mouth, and then his lips found the unguarded hollow where jaw became throat. She stood still in the spinning darkness and let him. She could smell the cigarettes on his fingers as they slipped over her lips, across the edge of her jaw, down her throat, dipping into the neck of her T-shirt and then up again, holding her face firmly as they kissed. And yet he was willing to be led; he made no attempt to undress her, and when she began to undress herself, he fell back, sitting on the bed—watching her intently, even seriously. She removed her shirt, her jeans, unfastened her bra, stepped out of her underwear. She thought she would feel self-conscious under the steadiness of his gaze, but instead she felt exhilarated.

Charles rose up from the bed and stepped into her, his bare chest and shoulder and thigh pressed up against hers. The skin between them lifted and fell, hammered by breath. After a moment, she raised the flat of her cheek to the flat of his. She could feel him smile. "Hello," he said, and his arms lifted around her, and he swung her toward the bed. The backs of her knees hit the edge of the bed, and when she went down, he fell with her, his arms on either side of her, suspended just above her, pinning her to the mattress with his tight, coiled weight and lowering his mouth to hers.

He was a good listener. He yielded easily when she rolled on top of him, laying himself open beneath her. She sank onto him, and he tilted his head back, eyes closed, the fine long line of his throat exposed, fully at her disposal. He was so willingly vulnerable that she found herself watching him, even as pleasure mounted in her stomach, made it hard to focus—she scoured his face and found that it was entirely open, nothing obscured, no secrets. Was it because he was so young? And he was young, she reminded herself punishingly. *Say the word: he is young, Minnow. When he is your age he'll have all the secrets in the world, his face will be guarded, his armor will be—*

He opened his eyes and looked at her, languid and dazed, pupils blown wide. Pleasure spiraled up through her, using her as its conduit, and flung her throat open; she cried out and every thought fled.

When she opened her eyes, she was under him again; he was lying between her legs, half-raised onto his arms, looking down at her. He smiled, sweet. Muscles rippled in his arms as he shifted, his damp hair falling into his eyes.

"Je veux te lécher," he said, casually. A moment, while she put the words together and he watched her face for a yes or a no. She nodded, and without further hesitation he slid down her, his long hands coming to rest on her hips, holding them in place, his face disappearing between her legs. At the first touch of his tongue, she bucked up into his mouth, oversensitized.

"Wait," she said, and he stilled. "I don't think . . . It's too soon."

She heard the smile in his voice. "On peut essayer autre chose?"

Time was devouring itself, time was on fast-forward. It felt like only minutes later that she became a raw channel for pleasure once again. Charles rested briefly, his head pillowed against her inner thigh, his breath gentle on her skin.

She had not expected that he would be so experienced, but then, *Why not*, she thought, he was a beautiful boy in a permissive city. She had been raised very differently, it had taken her a long time to think of sex as something that required skill and technique, active participation. So much of the sex she had had at Charles's age had been akin to sitting in the passenger seat while somebody else drove, feeling content to be in the car but wondering how long the trip would take. What Charles wanted, she understood, was to give himself to her like a gift, again and again, barely waiting for her to feel a lack before he was there, ready to spread himself out like a feast. What kind of a man would he be, she wondered, her fingers carding through his hair as they breathed. Or was he already who he was?

Charles's tongue carving up the curve of her inner thigh, bringing her back to the moment. "On remet le couvert?" he suggested.

"I don't know what that means," Minnow admitted.

"Let me give you," Charles said slyly, "some context clues."

1969

12

IN THE WEEKS THAT FOLLOWED, KEEN EXPERIENCED A BLANKETING depression unlike anything he had ever felt before. The feeling was akin to being in a car driving backward down a long road, everything in the windshield growing smaller and smaller. At first he went to class and to the lab, but then he found himself so exhausted that he would just come back to his apartment and sleep for long unbroken swathes of time. Eventually he stopped going to class at all and went only to the lab, where he set experiments in motion and then returned to bed. He felt far away from his work, incurious about what it would yield, and that was new for him.

He had written and mailed a letter to the Wisconsin draft board the day after receiving their summons, and then, panicking, looked up the number for the home office in Green Bend, Wisconsin, and called that as well. He spoke to a middle-aged woman, who was not unkind but who confirmed multiple times that he had received a valid summons before saying, as if he were a particularly slow child: "I don't know what to tell you, hon, it sounds like you've been called up."

"But I'm in graduate school," he said, simultaneously pleading and trying to impress her. "I'm at Harvard, I was told I'd receive a deferment until graduation."

She let him finish but then circled back to the beginning of the conversation: "But you received a summons. It sounds like you've been called."

"But it was a mistake!"

"It doesn't sound like a mistake to me. You say you got a summons?"

As the days passed without a response to his letter, he stopped being able to sleep. Instead, he lay in bed staring up at the ceiling and imagining himself at war. He was ashamed of many things about himself, but his fear of fighting wasn't one of them. He thought it would be unnatural if he felt any other way about the prospect of being killed or being required to kill someone else. He imagined burning his draft card, as Ethan had suggested. But then what? He imagined going to Canada. But then what? His lab wasn't in Canada, and neither was Olya. And what would his father say? Roger Hunter wasn't a hawk, but he had served in the Korean War. And his father, Keen's grandfather, had served in World War I. How could Keen refuse the call to duty? How could he answer it?

Somewhere in the morass of his exhaustion and anguish, Keen felt his senses begin to sharpen, although he had expected the opposite. He began to notice what he couldn't help but see, though he had never seen it before: that ignorance, delusion, and corruption underlay everything around him, from the lab to the university to the city of Cambridge to the greater Boston area to the country to the world.

Walking home from the lab one afternoon, he passed a cluster of middle-aged women at the bus shelter, making small talk as they waited, and he stared at them in hatred, thinking: *How can you stand around gossiping when my life is on the line?* Around him, people went to movies and went to dinner and laughed at their friends' jokes, and the juxtaposition of that normalcy with his terror was mystifying. Did people not *know*? he wondered. How had he not spent every waking second thinking about this before now?

He could no longer listen to the radio, because everything the disc jockeys said between the songs made him nauseous and enraged. If they talked about the war, then he was nauseous; if they did not, he was enraged. When he stood in line at the coffee shop and listened to students posturing with their political opinions, he wanted to scream in their faces: *You don't know anything!*—as if he had already been to the war and come back, as if he had already seen the things they were debating.

But it got worse than that, his unforgiving clarity. He began to see how tenuous it was, this thing of participating in society: how all of it hinged on a series of unspoken pressures that came to bear on individuals, so that they would not make choices that benefited themselves but instead would make choices that benefited those who had more power. Sitting in the cafeteria one day, he watched student workers ferry dirty dishes that hadn't been properly bused by other students. The more he watched, the more it seemed ridiculous to him that their occupation should be to move the half-eaten sandwiches and picked-over pasta crusting the dishes of wealthier peers. How had this come to be?

Differently ridiculous, but equally so, was the mailman, whose job was to drive pieces of paper all over town and drop them into boxes. Most ridiculous of all were the pieces of paper, which had commands written on them: pay me, pay her, buy this, sell that. How was it that a piece of paper, scrawled on by someone in an office far away, could affect the life of whoever had received it? Why did the whims of distant bureaucrats have the power to reroute the intimate workings of a daily life? Because of fear, Keen thought—fear and self-interest and greed. People didn't want to be the ones ferrying dishes and receiving slips of paper, they wanted to be the ones abandoning their half-eaten meals and writing summonses. And so, in order to someday reach the top of a ladder to which they incorrectly imagined they might have access, they were willing to tolerate any amount of injustice, absurdity, and abuse. No, Keen corrected himself, they were willing to tolerate any amount of injustice, absurdity, and abuse in order that they might someday inflict injustice, absurdity, and abuse on those beneath them.

He felt himself get further and further from the world. He thought about Olya constantly, but days passed in which they didn't speak, and without warning it had been a week. Because he wasn't sleeping, he had stopped being certain of where days began and ended; they all seemed to spill into one another, becoming long ellipses of sun and dark and sun. He had the desire to go to 5 Wellman, but exhaustion swamped him before he could leave the apartment. He knew that Olya called and left messages for him because when Sheila was home, she wrote them down and left them on the fridge:

Olya called, looking for you, 5 pm.
Olya called, says plz call her back, 8 pm.
Olya called, asked if you're alive? 10 am.

Keen found his mind going back to the last conversation he had had with Olya—or, to be more precise, the last conversation she and Ethan and Peter and Daisy had had with him. "There's no way the university will listen," they had said, "to yet another protest, yet another petition. They don't even read those things anymore," they had said. Someone had said—had it been Olya?—"A petition is a waste of paper." They had used phrases like *increasingly radical tactics* and *a necessary militancy* and *use the tactics of the state against the state.* They had sketched for him a possible and then a probable progression of events: Andrew Hungerford's arrival at the lecture hall, the planting of student operatives ahead of time, the uprising and takeover of the building with Andrew Hungerford inside it.

"We held that first Dow guy for seven hours," Peter had said. "Let's hold Andrew for seventeen. Or twenty-seven."

"And then what?" Keen had asked.

"And then we let him go," Peter had said with a shrug. "And make a statement. Why he wasn't permitted to lecture, why his ideas are toxic and injurious to decency."

"No," Ethan had said, "fuck that, we get him on camera. We interrogate him, on camera. Who's paying him? Who's subsidizing these little speeches? Who's bankrolling what he's trotting out as a philosophy? He's not a thinker, he's a drone in the pocket of the military corporation—let's get him to admit *that,* and then we let him go."

This had occasioned fierce debate around the breakfast table, and Keen had lapsed back into his own thoughts. What did occupying a building matter, he had thought, when he was in danger of forfeiting his entire life?

But now, as the days passed and Keen was left with nothing but time, he turned over the name Andrew Hungerford in his mind. He tried to match it with a face. What might be the face of a man arguing that the unimaginable waste of human lives was a moral necessity? Keen gave him jowls one day, gaunt cheeks and hollow eye sockets the next. As his fixation with the unknown Andrew Hungerford grew, he stopped trying to imagine his visual attributes and instead began having long conversations with the man in his head.

"You think the United States has a moral obligation to disrupt my life?" he would say, glaring at the sloped ceiling above his bed, with its old yellow water stain. "You think we have a moral obligation to disrupt the lives of others?"

"We didn't choose the war," Andrew Hungerford would reply, "but how can we refuse to answer the call of duty when it comes?"

"Simple," Keen would shoot back, "it isn't our duty."

"But you don't believe in the primacy of the individual over the common good," Andrew would chide, "I know you don't. You went into science not for the satisfaction of your own tiny, selfish mind but so that you could work to advance general knowledge, the conditions of the community in which you live."

"Don't talk to me about science when you're the one suggesting it's our duty to nuke some poor farmers into the ground!"

"It's our duty to prevent the spread of communism from Asia to the West. Communism is a philosophy of attrition. It pretends to consider the collective, but in reality, it serves to erase the individual."

"But you want me to die!" Keen would wail; sooner or later he would always wail that line. "You want me to be erased!"

"But what makes you so special?" Andrew Hungerford would ask him, and sometimes there would be pity in his voice. "What makes you so special, that everyone else should be sacrificed to the great god of carnage, but not you?"

"Because I'm smart, I'm fucking smart, there are so many virtues I don't have, but I am smarter than most of the people I've ever met in my life, and I don't want that to be wasted."

And then Andrew Hungerford would smirk a little, and his tone would be heavy with condescension when he said: "There are many kinds of intelligence, Christopher; the kind you have, while admirable, is not necessarily preferable when considered in the vast scheme of what serves the collective good."

In truth, he knew nothing about Andrew Hungerford's philosophy beyond the title of his lecture as Olya had remembered it, and so the more he argued with Andrew Hungerford, the more the other man's arguments resembled what Keen imagined his father might say. And the more like his father Andrew Hungerford sounded, the more Keen found himself unable to back down from these arguments, even though they were self-generated. Sometimes he would pace the floor of his bedroom, he would twist his lips and snarl and mutter half sentences while all the time, in his mind, he was facing off against the shadow of a man whose face kept changing and who had, clutched in his meaty fist, a copy of the summons Keen had received.

*

It was during this stretch of days that he had his first and only fight with Sheila. It escalated in leaps and bounds, until he and Sheila were screaming at each other across the tight enclosure of their living room. It was nighttime; she had returned from a study session and found the trash overflowing, the dishes unwashed. Keen was normally tidy to the point of meticulousness, and when Sheila brought the fetid catastrophe of their apartment to his attention, it frightened him that he hadn't even noticed.

"You have to live your *life*," Sheila was shouting at him. "You can't just decide to stop participating because you're scared of something that might happen four months from now!"

"No," Keen shouted back at her, "that's where you're wrong! We have to shut down all the things that seem normal—classes and jobs and work and—otherwise things just keep on churning. People going about their lives isn't normal, it's obscene." He had been saying versions of this in his head to Andrew Hungerford for a week or so now, and so he delivered all of this to Sheila in a tone of which Dwight Beachum himself would have been proud.

Sheila was less impressed. "This is ridiculous!" she groaned. "Keen, you're not showering, you're not going to class—this isn't philosophy, it's depression!"

"What are *you* doing?" Keen hissed at her. "Reading Chaucer and going on dates? It's all burning down, Sheila. What are you *doing*?"

"What the fuck are *you* doing?" Sheila bellowed at him, goaded to anger. "Wake the fuck up, Christopher, men have been getting drafted for three years, you just haven't had to properly pay attention because you got a pass! And you know *why* you got a pass? Because you have a taste for school and your parents had enough money to make sure that got put to good use. You think you're having revelations? You're just waking up to the reality everybody *else* has been in."

"Maybe," Keen said, so angry that he had become strangely calm. "Maybe that's true. But now I'm awake, and I can't just go back to sleep."

"All you do is sleep!" Sheila yelled at him. In the end Sheila stormed out, slamming the door, and went to stay with her new boyfriend.

Alone in the apartment, Keen sat on the couch with both hands over his racing heart and wondered if he was having a heart attack. He felt faint, hot and cold, his palms tingled, and when he brought them to his face they were damp. Eventually he curled on his side on the thin dirty rug, his hands still cupping his chest, and like that, improbably, he drifted off. When he woke up, it was still night and Sheila was still gone, but he didn't feel like he was going to die anymore. He felt numb and empty.

He got up and went to the refrigerator, but there was nothing in it. He located a box of shredded wheat in the cupboard, returned to the patch of rug where he'd slept, and ate the shredded wheat squares dry out of the box with his fingers.

"Something has to change," he said to the heavy air in the apartment. He wasn't talking to Andrew Hungerford anymore, although he felt the shadow of him nearby; he was talking to himself, with all the kindness he could muster. "I can't live like this." He thought of Olya then, how she had looked in the dark of her bedroom when she said: "We all need something larger than ourselves, or else we fall into our smallness and we drown."

"How do you do it?" he asked. "How do you find what's large enough?" And this time he was talking to Olya, although of course she did not reply.

*

He had planned to return to 5 Wellman, but the morning after the fight with Sheila, Olya showed up at his door.

The knocking woke him up. It was late morning and he was asleep on the rug, his head throbbing, sunlight pouring unforgivingly across his face. He thought that Sheila must have forgotten her key, having left in such a hurry, and he hurried to his feet, then stood swaying, dizzy. The knocking had stopped, but it started again, slow and steady. He made his way across the room, steadying himself on walls and furniture, and opened the door to see Olya standing there, cheeks bright with cold, wrapped in her too-thin but achingly familiar yellow coat.

He stared at her, and for a long moment, she stared at him.

"Olya," he croaked.

"Keen," she said, and her voice was gentler than it had ever been. "I'm going to come in."

"Okay," he said automatically, and then: "Please, please come in."

He stepped back and she entered. She hesitated, glancing around his apartment, taking it in. He could see it through her eyes and the mess was appalling. It wasn't even mess but dirt—no wonder Sheila had reached the end of her patience.

"So this is where you live," Olya said, neutrally.

"I didn't know you were coming."

"Well, I called you thirty times and left an entire life's worth of messages with your increasingly grumpy . . . girlfriend?—but I didn't hear from you, so . . ."

"Roommate," Keen said immediately, alarmed and addressing the thing that mattered most. "Sheila is my roommate."

"Okay," Olya said, as if she didn't care either way. "I mean, I'm just glad you aren't dead."

She waited, implacable, and Keen realized what she was waiting for. "I'm sorry," he said. "I wasn't . . . It wasn't . . . I sort of . . ." His voice trailed away hopelessly. He didn't have the words for the thing that had been happening to him. But whatever Olya saw in him softened her. She turned away, peeling her coat off and draping it over the back of the armchair.

"I'll make some coffee," she said. "Do you have coffee here?"

"I think so," Keen said. "Usually we do."

"I'll make it," Olya said. "Go sit down."

He took the opportunity to splash water on his face, brush his teeth, change his shirt. When he returned to the living room, Olya was sitting in the armchair with a mug in her hands, and a second mug was waiting on the wooden arm of the lumpy couch.

"You had instant," she informed him.

"Thank you for making it." They sat across from each other. Keen focused on sipping coffee so that he wouldn't have to look at her. "I don't want you to misunderstand about Sheila," Keen said, surprising himself by starting there. "She's not my girlfriend."

Something shifted in Olya's face. She looked both tender and wary when she said, choosing her words, "I believe you, obviously. But for the record, *if* she were, whatever she was would be fine to me."

"Okay," Keen said, realizing they were about to have the conversation he had been trying to have for six weeks now. "But I don't think it would be fine to *me*, because you're the one who . . . You're the one. For me."

He jolted to a halt and stared at his mug again, his face burning.

"Keen," Olya said quietly, and he heard the affection in her voice and maybe the apology.

He had to ask: "Is it not like that for you?"

"I really like you."

"But?"

"But nothing."

"But Ethan?"

Olya sipped her coffee, and then, slowly: "Ethan has nothing to do with you. And you have nothing to do with Ethan."

"But you and Ethan are . . . ? You have been . . . ?"

Olya sighed. "Ethan and I are entwined in each other's lives," she said. "I think sex is a pretty simple way to talk about the intricacy of human connections. And I think this societal regulation of when women get to have sex and with whom and how much—I don't think that has anything to do with human connection. That has to do with control. Bodies as chattel."

Keen was sure she was right, and also, he didn't give a fuck. "So you *are* sleeping with Ethan," he said, as if he had somehow not managed to grasp that basic fact until now.

"Sometimes Ethan and I share that," she said. "And sometimes we share other things. And sometimes you and I share that. And sometimes we share other things. The more people who love us and who we love, the richer our lives are. Don't you understand that?"

Keen was distracted by the one word: *love.* And instead of pressing further into the dark, he let himself swerve, he let himself be carried by it, and he heard himself sound moth-wing fragile and wholly pathetic as he asked, "Do you love me, then?"

After a moment, Olya smiled. "Yes," she said. "Don't you love me?" And:

"Yes," Keen said, fervent, a promise that Olya wasn't asking for: "Yes, I do, I love you."

He could have stayed there, in that moment, forever. He wanted to tell her about the days that had passed, the conversations he had had with the man he had invented. He wanted to tell her how he had started to see the world anew, and how, in its unforgiving light, he did not understand how any of us keep looking, how we don't all just close our eyes in despair. He wanted to tell her what Sheila had said and how she was right: he *was* late to a disaster that had been unfolding for centuries—not just this particular war, or the long line of wars that had preceded it, but the disaster of human society, the lies we tell each other about what is required of all of us in order to participate, about the normalcy of things that should never be normal. He wanted to ask her to give him guidance for whatever came next, whatever was required to understand the world he lived in—and to change it, or change himself if he could not change the world, or change them both. But:

"I want to go with you," Keen said. "When you stage your disruption, I want to come too."

2018

13

THE TRUE STORY OF THE FIRE WAS, IN CERTAIN WAYS, A TRUE STORY about Minnow—but it was one that she did not understand at first. It was a window that opened up, showed her to herself completely, and then closed again. Minnow had thought about it obsessively in the weeks and months that followed, because she didn't know if she liked or disliked what she had seen. It was not that she had never before felt such rage, but rather that it had never before occurred to her to act on it. Late at night in bed, she summoned the memory again and again, holding it in her mind like a talisman. That had been a Minnow who existed. That Minnow had been real, even if nobody else knew what she had done.

It happened in part because the world moved on, but the town did not. This was the reality that Minnow had not known to expect when her life at Sewell first turned upside down. One day, nearly two weeks into the chaos, she woke up to a world of quiet. There were fourteen emails in her inbox, eight of which were advertisements and six of which were from people she knew. There were no requests for comment, no requests to be interviewed, no death threats. Nobody was asking her to do anything. She turned on the radio and did not hear her name. She turned on the television and discovered that a minor celebrity had drunkenly driven his car off the side of the highway in the romantic company of a major celebrity to whom he wasn't married, and every head in the country had turned with a whip-sharp synchronicity. Minnow was no longer news. Minnow had been forgotten.

What she hadn't expected was how forsaken she would feel after the outside letters of support stopped and the wordless disapproval of the town settled in. Walking through the grocery store, she felt the weight of eyes on her. When she wished the cashier a good day, the woman cast her gaze elsewhere and didn't respond. Loading bags into the back of her car, she glanced up to see a middle-aged man frowning at her as he worked his car into the adjacent parking space. He got out of the car, facing her directly, and she felt a jolt of adrenaline in her chest—was he going to approach?—but he just walked away shaking his head.

Minnow wondered, after the fact, if her fixation on Jim would have been different if she had not felt abandoned. Jim was so visible. Jim had not forgotten her. Jim was not hating her quietly, he was standing where she would see him, shouting into bullhorns and waving placards—by her apartment building, by her car, by the campus gates. He was the one person in the town who would speak to her, of her, against her. By doing so, he admitted that she existed. The force and focus of his loathing did for her what she was not able to do for herself. It grounded her completely.

The first time she went to Jim's home was after her second conversation with Dean Kaye, after the fight with Christopher, and after she was suspended from her classes—"In order to limit disruptions while we wait for your decision," said the dean in an email. And it was after Minnow had seen Jim sitting in his car in the little parking lot, the cherry of his cigarette glowing in the dark. All this had happened, one thing after another, and at the end of it, Minnow had used up her anxious, cautious pragmatism and landed in a new world of rage and instinct.

It wasn't hard to find where Jim lived. She simply looked it up. It was midafternoon, her car freshly out of the shop, its windshield repaired from the brick that had gone through it. She was walking to where she had parked and glancing around every corner for Jim, and when she did not see him, she looked up where to find him.

His house, from the outside, looked like any of the houses around it. The siding was a weathered green that, under the sun, had lightened to a shade of pea soup. The stretch of lawn in front was tawny and dry. A picket fence stood along one side of it and then abruptly gave up, as if exhausted. A car sat in the driveway, and Minnow blinked at it. How harmless it looked, a medium-sized Ford. She had reconstructed Jim's car in her mind as large, hulking, a black sedan with its windows tinted, lurking in the formless dark. This car was just an old Ford the color of a stain.

Minnow drove by slowly, hunching low in her seat in case Jim was out in the yard or on the porch. Though the house showed signs of life—the front door was open and a sprinkler spat forlornly at the sun-seared grass—Jim was not visible. She drove to the end of the block and then swung back, slow, so slow, easing past his house once more. Still no sign of him. She idled the engine, daring to stop at the end of the driveway. She almost wanted him to see her. She waited for three minutes, then four. When the dashboard clock clicked over to five, she asked herself what she thought she was doing, and she drove home.

After that, Minnow returned to Jim's again and again, and she chose increasingly odd hours. She wasn't sleeping much anymore, which made it easier. She was losing track of time, losing track of when one was supposed to be sleeping or awake. Without the structure of her normal life, she looked at her phone and found it was eight P.M., three A.M., noon, and all those revelations were equally surprising and equally meaningless. One evening she made a thermos of coffee and a peanut butter sandwich and she drove over to Jim's house and sat outside it all night.

She felt good, tilting her seat back so that she could recline. She wondered why she had never done this before. It was calming. She was here, in her car, she knew where she was. Jim's house was there, across the street, she knew where Jim was. Everything fell into a navigable, understandable grid, defined by the relationship of those two points. When she tried to imagine Jim's face, she could summon only fragments: the throbbing forehead vein, a patch of red in his cheeks, a five o'clock shadow, the brim of a baseball cap, the cavern of his chanting mouth, the peanut-colored nubs of his back molars. Had she seen his molars, actually seen them, or was she imagining them? She turned the image from side to side but couldn't be sure.

When the sun came up, Minnow drove home slowly, her eyes burning and bleary. She parked in the lot behind her apartment, not bothering to put the car in a garage, stumbled inside, and slept for a blissful eight hours. She had not slept so well in weeks. She awoke into a hot midafternoon, early cicadas screaming in the trees. Sitting in front of the open windows, drinking coffee, she felt ecstatic.

When evening fell and the cicadas hushed, she found herself making another thermos of coffee, another peanut butter sandwich. It was not that she decided what to do, just that she did it. Her body had certainty and so she followed it—hands on the steering wheel, her sneakered toe on the gas. This time the lights were off in Jim's house and the driveway was empty, so she parked closer. Several hours into her vigil, a car eased around the corner into the cul-de-sac. Minnow slid all the way down in her seat as headlights spilled over her and Jim pulled in. He opened the driver's side door and music poured out into the night—a pop song that sweetened the air briefly before he turned it off. He stepped out of the car, swaying, and Minnow realized that he was drunk. He stood for a moment, his hands on the top of the Ford, and Minnow's heart beat quickly; had he seen her car, a lump of shadow in the many shadows cast by trees and shrub? But he was only searching his pockets for his keys. He found them, dropped them, fumbled on the driveway for them. Staggering upright, he slammed the door, loped toward the front steps, tripped briefly but regained his balance. She watched as he let himself inside.

Lights flickered on in the windows, tracking his journey from room to room. The hallway, then the living room, outlining the drapes in a rush of warmth. His shadow passed behind them; a long pause, and then lights flushed an upstairs room. A bedroom. It seemed he lived alone—or was his wife away? Was there anyone who would call to see if he got home safely?

The idea didn't occur to Minnow slowly. It came in a rush, as a vision: flames leaping up the curtains, consuming the stairs. Fire going everywhere that the lights were, the lights pointing the way for the fire to go. The house eaten from the inside, consumed in the way that Minnow was being consumed. The image was so clear that, in those seconds, it was as if it were happening. And then Minnow blinked, alarmed, and the night was dark and tranquil again.

*

She called her father in the morning. He had emailed her a set of news articles in the days after their fight: abortion activists who had been murdered in their homes; a clinic in the next state that had been bombed; a female doctor who had been stalked and shot. He had not included any messages with the articles, and the two of them had not otherwise spoken. Minnow understood that what he was saying was that he was afraid for her, but the emails fed a slow and steady anger inside her. She had considered replying to them, but every time she began, she found herself saying things that she knew she would regret. Ultimately she deleted each one and didn't write back.

Now, she dialed Christopher's number and waited, but he didn't pick up. Instead she got the old answering machine with her own child voice on it, recorded in middle school. *You've reached the Hunter residence, please leave us a message at the sound of the beep.* "It's Minnow," she said uncertainly, but then she didn't know what else to say and hung up. In the afternoon, she tried him again, and this time the phone rang and rang. He must have unplugged the answering machine, or else it was full.

When her cell rang a few minutes later, she leapt to it, but it was a school number, not her father. She let the call go to voicemail, and afterward she listened to Dean Kaye's voice with its diplomatic mixture of firmness and regret: "Miss Hunter, I appreciate what you must be going through right now. But the truth of the matter is that we will need your answer shortly. If you are making the decision not to leave of your own volition, the board will need to act on that. But I'd like you to have the opportunity to end this on your own terms."

She listened to the voicemail twice. The dean's voice was gentle. He spoke to her with sympathy. She hated him for that. She thought of Jim—how he offered her no sympathy, only hostility. It was comforting, the simple force of his hatred. After the second time, she deleted the voicemail and called her father again.

"Dad," she said to the ringing phone, "please." But Christopher didn't answer, and eventually she had to give up.

*

Two days before the fire, Jim spoke to Minnow for the first time.

He had shouted at her many times—or, more to the point, he had been in a crowd and had directed his shouting toward her—but they had never spoken. When she exited her apartment building and saw him leaning against the wall, her heart leapt into her throat. She expected that his goal was to frighten her with his presence alone, so when he spoke, it caught her off guard. His voice was a normal-sounding voice; a little nasal, even. Just a voice.

"Hi there," he said.

Minnow considered walking past. But the fact that she had been parked outside his house emboldened her; she knew something that he didn't. So she stopped.

"Hi," she said.

"I don't know if you know who I am—" he began.

"I know who you are."

He finished anyway: "I'm Katie's uncle."

"I know that," Minnow said. "I saw your piece in the newspaper." And then: "I've seen you around."

It was an outrageously casual way to describe how she had seen him, but Jim nodded. He adjusted his baseball cap; it was off-white, yellowish with sweat where it hugged his head. A logo Minnow didn't recognize was printed on the front. She could smell him and he smelled good: Old Spice mixing with a light aftershave.

"Well," Jim said. He seemed awkward. "I was hoping we could have a few words."

"Okay."

"You seem like a nice young lady. And I hear—I hear that you felt that you were helping my niece—that's what I've been hearing from a few folks."

"Yes," Minnow said, startled eagerness surging in her chest. Finally, they would have a chance to just speak to each other and he would understand. "Yes, that's right, and—"

"But I also hope *you've* been hearing," Jim kept going, "that around here, we don't consider that to be a good kinda help. Katie was raised to know better, and the fact that she did what she did . . . well, that's between her and God. But what *you* did, that's about community. That's about what you're bringing into a community and how your community is gonna feel about that. Do you follow me?"

Minnow swallowed, hope receding. "No," she said, although she had.

Jim frowned and rubbed a hand over his stubbled cheek. Minnow remembered how he had knelt in his driveway the night before, searching for his dropped keys. He had seemed vulnerable in that moment, exposed to her gaze. Now, however, he was solid as a tank.

"I guess what I'm saying," he said, "is that folks don't feel safe with you here. They don't feel safe having you teach their kids. I hope you can understand that, why that is. I think there's other places you might be a lot happier, and that's just—that's what I wanted to say to you. This place, we got different values."

"Mr. Curtis—" Minnow began, but he pushed through:

"It's time for you to move on," he said. "That's about as simple as I can make it, Minerva."

Something about hearing her full given name in his mouth sent a spike of cold down into her stomach. "Are you threatening me?"

Jim blinked at her. "I wouldn't call that a threat," he said mildly. "I'd call it an opinion."

The sun was hot on Minnow's bare forearms and the back of her neck. Sweat prickled under her arms. "Were you the one who smashed my windshield?" Minnow asked abruptly.

Something shifted under the surface of Jim's face and he sounded a little smug when he said, "I don't know anything about that."

"No," Minnow said. "I bet you don't."

"But if that kinda thing is going on here, maybe you'd agree, this isn't the place for you."

"Maybe," Minnow said, taking a step toward Jim. Caught off guard, he shifted from foot to foot. She took another step. He frowned and shifted. "Or maybe the problem isn't the place. Maybe the problem is a person."

"I told you," Jim began, but this time she cut through him:

"I'm sure you didn't have a thing to do with it. I'm sure you don't sit out in the parking lot from time to time, late at night, and smoke a cigarette, and watch me in my apartment. Just like I'm sure you didn't come home late last night, real drunk, lose your car keys in the driveway, turn on all the lights in your house."

"Now, wait just a minute," Jim said, but she didn't pause, and when she took another step, this time he backed away.

"I'm sure you're just a good guy, and you think all you have to do is show up and I'll get scared. I'm sure you think you can come and go whenever you want. And you probably think that that doesn't go two ways, Jim. You think when you go home at night, you're safe—because you're the one who decides when things are safe or unsafe. That's what you think. Isn't it?"

"Wait just a fucking minute," Jim said, his eyes narrow and color mounting high on his cheeks.

"A *minute*?" Minnow laughed out loud. "Jim, I'll wait all night. I'll wait all goddamn night. I'll wait in your driveway. I'll wait across your street. I will watch your house as you dream, I'll count the steps between your car and your front porch. I've got the patience of a saint. And now I'm going to work. Maybe I'll see you later. Maybe."

She turned sharply and walked down the path, gravel crunching under her sneakers. She waited for him to shout after her, but he was quiet. She didn't look over her shoulder, though she wished she could see what he was doing. It took her until the end of the path to realize that her hands were numb and tingling, shaking with adrenaline. She shoved them in her pockets. And she saw it again, the indelible image from the night before: a house alive with flame, and every bedroom burning.

*

She didn't go to Jim's house that night, though she did go out. It was habit by now: leaving her apartment as dusk fell, getting into her car, driving to where she could be nothing but a pair of eyes gazing in instead of the thing being gazed at.

She had never been to the dean's house, but she knew where it was.

He and his wife lived just off campus, in a small cul-de-sac close to the iron gate that signified the beginning of school property. Theirs was a large butter-colored house with a wraparound porch and white wooden columns. Wide windows faced out in all directions: onto the ivy-strung brick buildings, onto the small road that divided the cul-de-sac from campus, and on the north side of the house, into the woods.

The cul-de-sac itself was a loop of road studded with well-kept old houses, gardens richly decorated and already midbloom. There was more money here than in Jim's neighborhood, that was clear at a glance. As Minnow drove slowly with her window rolled down, she wondered for the first time what Jim would make of Dean Kaye. Had they met at any point? Had Jim showed up at his office, had he demanded that they speak? Somehow she doubted it. Jim would be intimidated and resentful in an office like that, she felt sure. She knew that Katie was the only one in the family who had gone to a school like Sewell. But the thought occurred to her that, were they to meet, Jim would home in immediately on what it had taken Minnow time to discover: Dean Kaye's slippery charm, his tendency to shape-shift depending on who he was speaking to and what they needed from him. Dean Kaye was not a man of convictions, Minnow thought, driving past his house. Jim at least knew what he believed, even if what he believed was that Minnow was a monster.

She reached the end of the cul-de-sac and circled back, driving more slowly this time to really take it in. Dean Kaye's driveway was lined with flowers on both sides. Who had time to plant them, she wondered. Did he have a landscaper or did the school do it for him? As the driveway neared the house, it widened to take in a carport right off the standalone garage. Lilac bushes flowered on each side of the porch; you would be able to smell their sweetness from the open windows of what looked like the living room or parlor. Minnow could make out the shape of bookcases through the windows. Though elegant, the house was not overly grand. It was a homey house, Minnow thought with bitterness, a house in which one might be happy.

She waited until she had exited the cul-de-sac and driven down the small road before she pulled over and parked. The grass grew higher here and the tree cover was unbroken; her car wouldn't be visible from any houses, although she knew it would look odd to a neighbor driving past. Well, that couldn't be helped. She sat, and the dusk thickened, and she sat. Time flickered and blinked.

When night had fallen, she left the car and walked. The road was dark, and almost immediately her foot hit a pothole and her ankle rolled. Minnow landed hard on one knee, pain radiating upward. Swearing under her breath, she fought her way to her feet and took a tentative step, then another. Pain lanced through her leg. She stood still, considering the version of this night in which she turned around, went home, iced her ankle. It was a good version. It was a version that belonged to a reasonable life in which she did reasonable things. It was a life she felt she could still glimpse from time to time, but it no longer felt like it was hers. She took a steadying breath and limped down the road toward Dean Kaye's house.

The lights radiated down the driveway and across the lawn. It was hard not to feel that they were, in some way, a gesture of welcome. She found herself ducking and weaving as she darted across the road, but the pain in her leg escalated until she realized she was whimpering, small hurt-animal noises, and she had to stop. In the end, she just lurched up the driveway as if she lived there, pausing in the shadow of the dark garage. Her shoulders were tight; she was waiting for someone to discover her; but the night was calm, the air heavy with the smell of flowers. Light spilled from the windows facing the lawn. No blinds, no drapes. The corner window was half-open.

What must it be like, Minnow wondered, to live a life wherein it never occurred to you that you might be under surveillance? Where you felt so secure that you wouldn't even pull the curtains? Well, she had had that, too, she thought. That had been part of her life on the other side.

Standing by the bushes beneath the parlor window, Minnow hesitated. She had not considered what to do here. During her stakeouts of Jim's house, she had never left the safety of her car. After a moment, she waded into the fragrant embrace of the lilacs and put her face against the unguarded glass. The scene inside was so calm, so lovely, that she found herself clutching the siding, her breath coming in heavy gulps as if she had been physically injured by it.

Dean Kaye was kneeling on the living room floor, wooden blocks scattered around him. A small child was balancing on one foot, a fat hand on the dean's shoulder as it surveyed the mess. A pink elastic secured a spout of wispy white-blond hair. In the background, the TV flickered—an animated child's show, Minnow realized, in which a blue fox was singing a song while he leapt about in what appeared to be the control room of a submersible. Dean Kaye lifted his head and Minnow ducked instinctively. But he wasn't looking at her, he was turning toward his wife, who entered the living room with a glass of wine in hand.

Minnow had seen the wife before at various formal events. She had always been pleasantly blank-faced, friendly but not conversational, making herself as absent as possible without ever being discourteous. Now Minnow took her in and found with a shock that she was beautiful, in an oversized knit sweater and L.L.Bean sweatpants, her thick brown hair pulled back into a loose bun. She looked like the model for an athleisure fashion line, someone who was at home in her body, her clothes, her life. Minnow felt a pulse of envy—of the wife for being effortless, and of Dean Kaye for having such a wife.

The wife dropped into a graceful crouch, pulling the toddler in for a kiss as it shrieked and wriggled, then releasing it again. "Have you seen my glasses?"

"Upstairs," Dean Kaye said, "bathroom counter."

"No, I brought them down." His wife vanished out of sight again.

Minnow watched Dean Kaye work at rearranging the blocks to recapture the attention of the child. It vanished out of sight of the window, but Minnow heard it screaming "Mama!" up the stairs.

Dean Kaye began to try and lure the child back, but—"I've got her," the wife called, her voice distant in the far reaches of the house. Alone, Dean Kaye turned off the animated television show, and flipped to CNN. He watched for a moment, then kept flipping. A movie in which a man in leather was riding a motorcycle very quickly past the Eiffel Tower, intercut with a series of scenes in which a speedboat was being driven recklessly down the Seine. Leaving the blocks scattered over the floor, Dean Kaye settled down on the couch, facing the television.

He was so untouched, she thought. He had thrown her to the wolves and then stepped back into the comfort of his home and forgotten about her and Katie both. Katie Curtis was something to be dealt with during work hours, but irrelevant to the pleasures of his daily life. It was not so with Jim. For all that Minnow disliked the man, he was as consumed by this business as she was.

Dean Kaye's wife was back in the doorway, glasses perched on her nose. They were stylish aviator frames, Minnow saw. "Will you heat up the leftovers?" she asked.

"Yeah, in a sec."

"I'll do bath time—maybe throw a salad together, the lettuce is going bad."

She turned toward the stairs without waiting for an answer. For long minutes after she had left, Minnow remained frozen in place. She imagined the wife submerging the toddler in a bathtub that would be large, white, maybe even claw-footed. Maybe the wife would sing to her or would tell her a story of some kind. She imagined Dean Kaye putting dinner together, the sweetness of this thing: cooking for those you loved, in a house you loved. Knowing you would all sit down together, and the outside world would recede even further.

Minnow turned away. She retraced her steps past the lilac bushes, back to the driveway. She wasn't even trying to remain unseen now, but still there was nobody to see her. She walked toward the stand-alone garage, curious, and when she pulled haphazardly at the side door, it opened in her hand. She stepped through, into a space that smelled hot and musty, and flicked on the flashlight of her phone. She played its beam over bags of sand, shelves of gardening implements, bottles of pesticides and cleaning fluid.

An Everlast punching bag hung from an overhead support, and Minnow considered it. She had never imagined that Dean Kaye would be a man with a punching bag hanging in his garage. Did he hit it? Did he hold his daughter up to it and let her pretend to hit it?

Was it a remnant of a different life for him, his bachelor life, that he hadn't been able to part with even after marriage? Each detail was a devastating reminder that he had a whole, fully furnished life into which to escape. Hers was falling apart like a sand mosaic in a high wind, and his was glorious, steady, each object telling a story of surplus and prosperity: the gardening shears, the work gloves, the orange-plastic-handled pliers, the red plastic jug of gasoline.

She blinked at it. She blinked at it. The image came, and she let it.

When she picked up the jug, it was heavier than she had imagined. The top was child-safety-proofed, tricky in her shaking fingers. She turned it, squeezed and turned, squeezed and pulled. It came open, and the smell hit her nostrils, bright and searing. She coughed, shook her head, coughed again. She lifted the jug in both arms, up to her chest, cradling it like a baby. And when she extended her arms, the jug in a dangerous parallel to the floor, the noxious liquid spilled out as if that was what it had always been made for. It flooded across the floor with a brutal simplicity, splashing walls and wooden rakes and leftover insulation, as if the answer to everything wrong in her life could be so easy, the most natural thing in the world: destruction.

1969

14

MARCH 5 WAS A WEDNESDAY. KEEN WENT TO LAB THE NIGHT before and cleaned up after his last experiment without starting the next one. He ran a wet paper towel over the top of his bench, arranged his things neatly. He felt calm and focused and even went to bed earlier than normal. But in the morning his stomach was acid and jittery; in the shower, his heart beat so quickly that he had to lean his forehead against the tile wall and breathe through the steam.

He knew the plan. They had gone over it and over it. It was a relief to surrender to a series of events that was already in motion. He ate breakfast mechanically, unhungry but following the directions that Olya had given all of them. He drank a second cup of coffee, then pulled on a warm jacket and left the apartment, locking the door after him. He walked from his apartment to campus, neither meandering nor hurrying, landing at Lowell Lecture Hall just before 9:45 A.M.

He filed up the steps and into the redbrick-and-limestone building with a group of other students. The printed fliers for Andrew Hungerford's lecture were taped to the exterior wood doors. He kept his face expressionless and his eyes down as he passed through the entryway, as if he were just another person who wanted to hear what Andrew Hungerford had to say about the American presence in Vietnam. As he entered the large lecture hall in the stream of students, he looked up and saw Daisy already partway up the aisle, settling into the third row. When he passed her, it took every effort to not make eye contact.

He settled into the nearly empty back row and took an aisle seat. Above him, the balcony was filling. Olya had forbid them from sitting there—it would take too long to get down to the floor, she said. As students filed into Keen's row, he shifted his long legs back and forth to make room. A few gave him dirty looks, perhaps wondering why he had taken the most inconvenient seat, but no one said anything. The lecture hall filled. He looked at the large clock on the wall over the podium. It was 9:53. His eyes dropped down and he saw Peter sitting in the front, legs stretched out, a paperback in hand. Just another student waiting for the lecture to begin. Keen started scanning the room with quick flicks of his eyes, trying to see who else he recognized without craning his neck or drawing attention to himself. Olya wouldn't come until later, he knew that, but even so he found his eyes lingering on any girl with brown hair.

At 9:58, Andrew Hungerford came in; or rather, two men came in, talking jovially, and one of them must have been Andrew Hungerford. Keen gazed from one to the other, shocked that he did not, after all this time, automatically know which was Andrew. The first was small and slight, dressed in drab khaki pants and a brown blazer. He might have been in his late forties or early fifties; his hair was thick and curly but sprinkled with salt-and-pepper, and he wore a pair of bold spectacles. The other was large and round—round shoulders, a round chin, a paunch protruding over his pants and visible beneath his navy blazer. Both men stood near the lectern and made conversation while students entered, the stream dying down to a trickle as the clock hit ten, and then 10:01 and then 10:02. Keen found that his breath was coming quickly, his chest tight, his hands balled into fists. He forced himself to relax, to spread his palms out on his knees, damp heat soaking into denim.

At 10:04, the rounder man gave the shorter one a clap on the shoulder and stepped to the podium. "Good morning, ladies and gentlemen," he said, in the cheerful voice of someone who is used to being listened to. "I am very pleased to see you here today, and a happy midweek to you all. It is my great pleasure to present to you a man whose scholarship is as extensive as his moral curiosity; who researches as deeply as he experiences, and whose breadth of work—"

And that was when the wooden side doors were thrown open. Even knowing that it was going to happen, Keen's heart bolted in his chest. Still smiling, a little quizzical, the professorial man turned, pausing minutely in the thread of his sentence, and Dwight Beachum's voice cut in, loud and authoritative.

"If you will excuse this intrusion, Professor Haggerty, Mr. Hungerford, and those who are gathered here today. My name is Dwight Beachum and I am here with the SDS, the Black Marxists, and countless like-minded individuals." Jack Gordon of the Black Marxists stood at Dwight's shoulder, with his arms folded. Behind him Keen made out Olya, Ethan, and so many others that they spilled into the hallway.

"Well, may I ask you to take a seat?" the round man, Professor Haggerty, began in a voice that was aggrieved but still in command.

Dwight Beachum cut him off again. "We will not be taking a seat, professor. We will not condone the murders that Mr. Hungerford condones, and we will not condone how he wishes to make excuses for the murderers. Quite simply, we are here to take over Lowell Hall."

Dwight turned to the audience of students, who were now leaning forward, rapt. Some were murmuring to each other in consternation, but most were focused on the front of the room, as if they had gone to see one movie and found a far more interesting one playing.

Dwight addressed the room. "You are free to go if you go now. You are also free to stay, but if you stay, do so knowingly. This is an action." He turned back to Professor Haggerty and to Andrew Hungerford, who both appeared to be stunned. "You may also go, Professor Haggerty—and, in fact, you must." With that, Jack Gordon and a stocky man—not a student, Keen thought—stepped to either side of Professor Haggerty. "You, Mr. Hungerford, will be obliged to stay here." And two more protestors stepped to either side of Andrew Hungerford, who turned his head from side to side, gazing at them in disbelief.

"What on earth are you doing?" he began, but his voice was lost. The motion of the two students on either side of him was Keen's cue, and with it, he and Daisy and Peter and a group of others rose to their feet as one. The students who were not plants swiveled their necks eagerly to stare at those standing, aware that the performance was taking on unforeseen dimensions. Keen knew that a handful of activists were already moving swiftly through the building, expelling faculty from other classrooms, securing room after room to make sure there would be no unwelcome surprises. He knew that they would chain the doors shut as soon as the exodus was complete.

Even as Professor Haggerty began sputtering, Keen and the others descended the aisles toward the front. Seeing a group of students moving toward him, Haggerty lapsed into quiet. Keen felt power rush through him, sudden and whole. He breathed easily and deeply, oxygen saturating the crevices of his lungs, the surface of every cell. His heart slowed. Now that he was in motion, he felt untouchable, and the sensation was akin to physical pleasure.

Andrew Hungerford said, "This is outrageous!" But objections meant nothing because the machine was moving. Professor Haggerty struggled a little for show but appeared relieved to be leaving. A few handfuls of students got up, collecting books and coats and scarves, and left hastily, throwing alarmed backward glances. Of those who stayed, some remained in their seats, eager to watch, while others descended from the balcony to mill about on the main floor. Keen wasn't sure who had been recruited ahead of time and who had simply decided that whatever was going to happen was far more interesting than what awaited them if they left.

He didn't have much time to contemplate, however, because Dwight turned to Keen and Ethan, as planned. "Comrades," he said, "will you please escort our guest to a safer location." Being addressed as *Comrade* made Keen want to burst out laughing, but Ethan's face didn't shift. He took Andrew Hungerford's arm forcefully, above the elbow, and propelled him into motion. Keen followed, unsure whether or not he needed to take Andrew Hungerford's other arm and finally choosing not to. Around them people fell away, clearing space for them to exit.

In the hallway, Keen was rewarded with a glimpse of Olya. She was passing, her face set, walking quickly toward the front doors. She didn't notice him, but it was enough just seeing her there. It filled him with certainty, and now he did take Andrew Hungerford's other arm, although he didn't need to. Hungerford was walking compliantly in the direction they were taking him. He was shorter than they were, and slighter; it would not have been hard to stop him if he had attempted to break and run.

Hungerford regained his voice when he saw where they meant to put him—a storage closet that had been emptied of its mop and bucket. "This is crazy," he said as Ethan opened the door and gestured him inside. He came to a stop, still not struggling but also not proceeding. "This is bizarre. I don't understand, who *are* you people? What do you want?"

They had debated about the storage closet around the table back at 5 Wellman. Peter had said to put him in a classroom—not one from which he could escape, but somewhere he might be comfortable for the next day or two. But Olya and Dwight and Jack Gordon had all chimed in here, firm in their disagreement. The man shouldn't be comfortable, they said. He didn't deserve it, primarily—"But most importantly," Olya had said, "we need him *un*comfortable. We need him to be in a frame of mind where—ten or fifteen hours in—he finds himself with a lot to say about how wrong he's been." And so: the storage closet: windowless, a bare lightbulb with a pull-chain, the floor scarred and pitted. Peter had wanted to leave him a chair, but: "No chair," Ethan had said grimly, and Olya had echoed this: "No chair."

"Get in," Ethan said now.

"But I don't understand." Andrew Hungerford swung toward Ethan, who grabbed his upper arm again and forced him forward.

"It's very simple," Ethan said. "This is where you go for now. So get in."

"I want to talk to someone," Hungerford protested. Keen had imagined this man as the apotheosis of all moral authority: a man the size of God who spoke with his father's voice. He had not been prepared for someone who was smaller than he was, whose voice was kind and a little quizzical. "I want to talk to your leader."

"We're all our own leaders," Ethan said—a line they had agreed on—and shoved Andrew Hungerford, swiftly and efficiently. Hungerford stumbled forward, catching himself, and Ethan closed the closet door neatly and locked it. Daisy had procured a ring of janitorial keys ahead of time, through unknown means. A moment of silence, and then Andrew Hungerford started pounding on the door with his fist and shouting.

Ethan turned to Keen, calm, the color high on his cheeks. Keen realized that he was riding his own tide of exhilaration.

"Good work," Ethan said. Keen flushed, first with pleasure and then irritation that Ethan should be the one to make him feel good. "I'm going back to help," Ethan added before Keen could speak. "You stay here and keep an eye on him."

"Wait," Keen said weakly. "I thought we were both supposed to stay with him."

"What's he gonna do, break the door down? Just stay here." And Ethan was off down the hallway, nearly running.

Left alone, Keen wasn't sure what to do with himself. He folded his arms, he put his hands in his pockets. He leaned against the wall, he stood upright and at attention. Inside the storage closet, Andrew Hungerford stopped banging, and Keen heard the slow murmur of his voice—was he cursing? Or praying? Keen put his ear near the door, but the sound had stopped. Then a dull thud and a sliding. Hungerford must be sitting down on the floor, his back against the wall. Keen felt the urge to sit as well—his knees were shaking, adrenaline coursing through him in waves—but he felt that it would be unprofessional. He would remain standing, ready for anything, authoritative and imposing. When Olya came to check on the containment of their target, she would be impressed.

Time passed. Keen stood, and leaned, and stood. Eventually he crouched, knowing the position was undignified but ready to spring to his feet at the sound of footsteps. He could hear commotion elsewhere—chanting, shouting, occasional crashes as if desks were being overturned or chairs knocked over. He wondered if the campus police had made it inside, and for a moment his heart flopped into his mouth, but then he comforted himself: the doors would be chained by now, there would be no way in.

Footsteps, close by, and Keen sprang to his feet. Peter rounded the corner, jaunty, and at the sight of him, Keen relaxed.

"How's it going out there?"

"Oh, there's faculty in front of the building," Peter said cheerfully. "They're pissed. Campus cops, too—and a bunch of students are trying to get in to join us. Dwight told them to rally outside in solidarity." He jerked his chin toward the supply closet. "How's it going in there?"

"Fine, I guess."

Peter smiled. "I had Haggerty," he said. "Two years ago, for Anthro. I've never met such a smug asshole. I wish we'd put him in the closet, too."

Hearing their voices, Andrew Hungerford began to bang on the door from the inside. "Help me!" he called, muffled but hopeful. "Help!"

Peter stepped to Keen and tapped on the door with one finger. The pounding died away immediately.

"Hello," Peter said.

"Hello," Hungerford called. "Can you hear me? I've been kidnapped."

"Yes," Peter said, winking at Keen. "By a very fearsome crew. I wouldn't draw attention to myself if I were you."

Silence, and then Hungerford flared into anger. "Who *are* you people! What do you want? You should be ashamed to interfere with free speech on a university campus—"

"Speech isn't free, Mr. Hungerford," Peter said to the door. "I'm sorry to have to tell you this, but that is one of the many great lies at the heart of this university, and also this nation. Speech costs, it costs a great deal—to those who speak it and to those who listen."

Hungerford was quiet, and Peter turned back to Keen. "So," he inquired, "how's your first day as a revolutionary?"

"Good," said Keen. "Where's Olya?"

"She's organizing food for tonight. Admin cut the phone lines in here—Jack and Dwight are talking to Dean Freeman from the windows."

"About what?"

"Freeman is saying they'll charge us with criminal trespassing if we stay." Peter laughed. "Dwight told him we charge them all with war crimes, so. Onward!" He turned to go.

"Wait," Keen said. "Where's Ethan? Is he coming back?"

Peter's tone didn't change but Keen thought there was pity in his face when he said, "Ethan's helping Olya with the food."

"Oh."

"He'll probably be back after that."

"Sure," Keen said, knowing they both knew this wasn't true.

After Peter left, Keen sat flat on the floor, his back to the wall, legs sprawled out. He tried not to think about anything. He listened for the vibrations of many bodies moving through the old building, many feet on many floors. He made himself empty.

"Hey. Is anyone there?" Hungerford's voice brought him back. "Hello?"

When Keen was quiet, Hungerford called louder: "Hello?"

"Shut up," Keen said, irritation rising.

"Who are you?" Hungerford demanded. It was not the first time he had asked the question, but now Keen heard the tonal switch from the broad *you* to a more specific, personal You.

"Christopher," Keen said. He never used his full first name, and so he was surprised to hear himself say it out loud. But it filled the air, it took a satisfying weight.

"Christopher," Andrew Hungerford said. "I'm Andrew."

"I know who you are."

"Do you? I don't understand why I'm the enemy." When Keen didn't reply, Hungerford sensed the misstep in his tactic and tried again: "What's going to happen to me?"

"Nothing," Keen said, "if you cooperate." They had discussed a series of uniform answers to the questions Andrew Hungerford might ask, and it pleased him that Hungerford had asked one of the ones they had discussed.

"What does that mean, 'cooperate'?" Hungerford demanded. "Nobody has asked me to do anything!"

"I'm asking you to shut up," Keen said roughly, and was surprised at himself. He was all the more surprised when Hungerford fell silent, obeying his command.

Time passed. The little hallway with its storage closet was far from the action—this had been part of the plan, of course, and it had seemed like a good idea, to have Andrew Hungerford safely tucked away. But now, exiled here, Keen felt increasingly jumpy and stymied. He wanted to be in the heart of the resistance, exchanging strategies, leaning out the windows beside Dwight Beachum and Jack Gordon, telling the deans they were war criminals. He wanted to be exchanging glances with Olya as Dwight delivered the overblown speech that he had anticipatorily drafted. Whatever was happening, Keen wanted to be with Olya, not here. He began to harbor against Andrew Hungerford a resentment that was similar to the loathing he had had for the man he had imagined in that dark December stretch.

"Christopher?" Hungerford's voice again, more tentative this time. "Christopher, are you there?"

"What is it," Keen gritted.

"I need your help."

"The answer is no."

"I need my inhaler."

"Your what?"

"My inhaler. I have asthma. I—I keep my inhaler in my pocket, it's usually in my pocket and I think it must've—when I was grabbed, it must've fallen out somewhere."

Keen had met a girl with asthma once. She had been a lab tech in undergrad, and she had had one of those devices, an inhaler. He had seen her use it before a particularly important exam. She had put it to her mouth like a kazoo, but then she had squirted and inhaled and held her breath. He had asked her about it, never having seen one before, and she had told him matter-of-factly that, as a child, she had had asthmatic episodes that landed her in the hospital. She had told him that her parents had been afraid that she would die.

"I don't know where your inhaler is," Keen said at last, uncertainly. "Are you sure it isn't in your pocket?"

"No," Andrew Hungerford said. "It's not."

Keen wondered if he was being tricked, but Hungerford's voice sounded thinner, a few notes higher, as if he were afraid.

"Well, I don't know where it is," Keen repeated.

"It must be in the lecture hall," Hungerford said. "When your friends grabbed me, it must've fallen loose. Will you—will you go check there for me?"

"No," Keen said automatically.

"What am I going to do, break out?" Hungerford rattled the unyielding doorknob to underscore his point. "I'm not going anywhere."

Keen was unsure. His orders had been clear, but then so had Ethan's, and Ethan had left thirty seconds after depositing Hungerford in the closet. Ethan was now drifting around the building with Olya, talking about *rations,* talking about the *revolution.* Were they kissing in a private corner, beneath the portrait of some famous alumnus? Were they making love in an abandoned conference room, Olya on a wide, polished conference table, her legs wrapped around Ethan's hips? Keen swallowed convulsively and dug his fingernails into his palm.

"Are you there?" Hungerford called, softly.

"I'm thinking," Keen said, resorting to honesty. They had not discussed this in their strategy meetings. He wondered if there was a way to summon Peter, or Olya herself, to ask what to do. But he would have to leave the closet to find either of them, so if he planned to step away from his guard post, he might as well go down to the large lecture hall and see if there was an inhaler lying abandoned on the floor.

"If I don't have it, I can't breathe," Hungerford said, muffled. Keen had to lean closer to the door to hear him. "I—I don't like small spaces, I—my chest gets tight in small spaces and . . . I'm going to need it, Christopher, very soon. I need it."

"Be quiet," Keen said, but fear had entered his own voice. "I'm trying to think."

If Andrew Hungerford needed the inhaler, he needed it. If Olya came by and Keen wasn't here, guarding—well, what did it matter? Hungerford wasn't a big man, the chances that he could break the door down in the five minutes Keen would be gone were slim to none. And if Olya demanded an explanation—well, Keen thought with satisfaction, he would give her one. It would start with Ethan's unplanned departure.

"All right," he said, getting to his feet.

"You're going to find it?" Hungerford's voice soared with hope.

"I'm gonna look," Keen said, "but I'm coming back in a few minutes. Okay? So no—no funny business, no yelling. I swear to God if you try to get out of here I'm going to throw your inhaler in the toilet and flush."

"I understand," Andrew Hungerford said. "Thank you. Thank you."

"Don't thank me," Keen said. "For God's sake, don't thank me." One more moment, glaring at the closet door, and then he couldn't help himself: "They're drafting me, you know."

"I'm sorry?"

"I got drafted. For your fucking war, your fucking morally imperative war. They're making me go."

Silence, and then Andrew Hungerford said: "I'm sorry."

This was not what Keen wanted to hear, although he didn't know that until Hungerford had said it. Keen might have said, beforehand, that he wanted an apology from Hungerford on behalf of the entire rotten system, on behalf of the entire rotten world, for every book he'd written and every lecture he'd given. Keen might have said that he wanted Hungerford to be forced to apologize for the whole lousy decade before they let him go. But now, hearing the sincerity in the other man's voice, Keen felt only shame and rage.

He could not reply, and so he swung away from the closet door and stalked down the hall in the direction from which they had come, hands shoved in his pockets, eyes trained on the ground in case he saw Andrew Hungerford's inhaler anywhere along the way.

2018

15

ON MONDAY MORNING, HOURS AFTER MINNOW RECEIVED NEWS
that the students were all on strike and so classes were suspended,
Charles showed up at her door with a bag of croissants. She stood in
the doorway gazing at him and he smiled back at her: "Am I
intruding?"

She had hoped he would come. That was the truth of it.

They stayed in bed for two days, leaving only to eat naked in the
kitchen or, briefly clothed, to drink Nespresso on the small balcony.
She watched Charles as he moved around her space, making himself
at home there. As he descended the ladder from the sleeping loft, her
eyes traced the long line of his spine, each vertebra notched like a
puzzle piece, the curve of his ass, the intimate splay of one bare foot
reaching down from the ladder to plant itself on cool kitchen tile. She
was learning the shapes and planes of his body, she was learning his
map of expressions and gestures and sounds, the way acute pleasure
made him shiver as if the temperature had plummeted. It was almost
painful, the intensity and speed at which she was learning these
things.

Before they had slept together, it had been a story she could tell,
laughingly, once she returned home: a beautiful young man—so
sophisticated, these Parisian youngsters!—who had had a crush on
her, and of course it was flattering, but . . . now it was a story that
could not be told, because it could not be laughed at. It would only

be a story that Minnow told to herself late at night, alone, to remind herself that it had happened.

"How serious, Minou." Charles was watching her from the couch. "Tu t'inquiètes?"

"No," Minnow said, drawing him back in: "Je m'inquiète pas, come here," and so he pressed her down on the couch and she rode his tongue with her eyes shut tight and a red swell against the backs of her eyelids, until they dozed again, the distant threads of sirens rising and falling in the background all through the long afternoon.

On the evening of the second day, Tuesday, they ran out of bread, wine, and sausage.

"We need to go out," Charles said, stricken.

Minnow laughed at his expression. "Do you even know where your underwear is?"

They were back in bed, and Charles propped himself on his elbow to glance around the room.

"It's been so long since I took it off."

"I'll go," Minnow said. "Wine and bread, I can remember that."

"No, no," Charles protested, "I'll come." And then his eye dipped in that saucy, delighted wink that was becoming familiar. "I'll go, how do you say, *commando*."

Out in the cold air, they walked through the streets arm in arm. Or rather, after a few steps, Charles took Minnow's arm in his. She stiffened briefly but didn't extricate it. It was unlikely that they would see any of the other teachers, she told herself. And besides, their faces were swathed in scarves and hats, amid all the other people bundled behind scarves and hats.

As if reading her thoughts, Charles joked: "Do you think people will look at us and think, Ah, the lovers, comme ils sont jolis?"

"No," Minnow said drily, "I think people will think, How sweet, that son and his aging mother."

Charles snorted. "You do not look old enough to be my mother."

"I could have had you very young."

Charles laughed out loud. "So, you are worried maybe they will look at us and think, She must have had him very young?"

Minnow started laughing as well, and then they were leaning against each other, shaking, and each time one would subside, the other would start again.

To her surprise, nobody seemed to notice them, though Minnow felt she must be incandescent with self-conscious lust. In the wine shop, Charles came up behind her and slid an arm around her waist, and Minnow nearly dropped the bottle she'd chosen. As they walked back to the apartment, she found herself pressing the side of her face into the side of his, glorying in his laughter. When they reached her apartment door she kissed him deeply and he pressed her back against it, his body tensile and strong underneath the bulky coat. They didn't end up cooking dinner that evening; they fell into bed, and hours later, they tore hunks off the loaf of bread and dipped them in olive oil, and that was dinner, and it was enough.

It exhilarated and alarmed her how quickly she adapted to his presence—not just his body in her bed, although the sweetness of that was piercing, but also how he folded into the other crevices of her life. Charles standing by the bookshelf as the morning sun streamed over him; Charles curled in her armchair reading; Charles standing in the small kitchen chopping shallots to fry or shaking vinaigrette in a jar; Charles stepping out of her shower with his dark hair wet, reaching for her even as she laughed and handed him a towel. Minnow had not known how lonely she was, until the hours were passing and Charles was everywhere, all the time.

*

It was midway through the first week of the strike that Minnow heard Luc's plan. It was framed less as a plan and more as an argument, and she did not at first understand what she was witnessing.

Charles had invited Minnow to his apartment in Saint-Germain, although he was bashful about it. He warned her ahead of time that it was not precisely his; it had belonged to his great-grandmother, and Charles and his brothers had each taken turns living in it as they attended school, Charles being the last of the three, and therefore the one who had remained. "None of us have dared touch it since my great-grandmother's time," Charles warned her. "We just live in her mausoleum, one by one. So you will find it very odd, and maybe distasteful."

"I want to see it," Minnow laughed, and Charles held up his hands in mock surrender.

"Luc is coming over tomorrow night—he has some business to discuss. Maybe you will come, too? He'd love to see you."

Minnow hesitated. Ever since the night of the protest in which she and Luc had gotten lost together, her feeling of unease about him had grown. She wasn't sure why; at the time, she had felt as if they were connecting. As if there was a shared understanding, even, in the way that he had talked to her about what Charles believed: as if she and he both knew better than that. It was only after the fact that his story had troubled her. When she imagined him standing outside his boss's door with a gun, she felt an instinctive recoil. But: "All right," she said, and was rewarded with Charles's smile, lighting up his face.

At first glance, Charles's building seemed ancient and grand, its façade ornate. When Charles buzzed her in, she took in the expansive marble floor of the lobby, the gold-framed mirror hanging on the wall by the elevators. But the elevator was out of order, and climbing the stairs, she caught the patina of grime on the walls and the damp musty scent of age.

Charles opened the door barefoot, his hair damp. He leaned in to kiss her, and she smelled his shampoo, underneath it the soap-and-cigarette scent of his skin. She kissed him back, already laughing at the hunger surging between them, and he broke the kiss with reluctance.

"Come in," he said. "Please."

The room was an odd shape, long and high ceilinged but oddly crooked, the old wooden floor rolling away at a slant toward the windows. Above them, high beams jutted out of ancient stonework. The walls were painted a fading green, silvery with age, and every surface that Minnow's eye touched was covered in small figurines. A wood stove burned in the corner. Beside it, in an armchair, Luc was sitting with a glass of wine, and as they entered, he looked up smiling. His eye was still bandaged, though the shadows softened the effect.

"Minou," he said, with what seemed like real pleasure. "Bien-venue."

She took in the ostrich feathers tucked behind a mirror and bent with dust, the green velvet of the low couch, the tall wide windows whose red velvet drapes were pulled back with gold ties like in a movie theatre. On a mantelpiece, what appeared to be the skull of a large carnivore. On the opposite walls, two lavish portraits that Minnow sensed were expensive, maybe even historic, renderings of Vernier ancestors. It was a carnival of oddities, assembled by a hand whose taste was as broad as it was distinctive.

Charles broke in, watching her gaze travel the room. "Don't be fooled by what you see. The roof sometimes leaks; the elevator is bro-ken, as I imagine you discovered; there is often no hot water." He waved a hand, mock-grandly. "The risks of a free ride. Can I get you a drink?"

"Thank you," Minnow said, and Charles's fingers touched the back of her wrist lightly, making the hair stand up, as he turned away to pour her a glass. She saw Luc watching her, a slight smile on his lips, and she flushed.

"Alors," Luc said. "Minou has come at the right time to weigh in."

"Weigh in on what?"

"On Luc's desire to write the next *Art of War*." Charles handed Minnow her wineglass.

Luc ignored him. "The answer to our problem," he addressed Minnow, "is a building."

Minnow opened her mouth to seek clarification on which prob-lem, but Luc kept going. "All battles are battles of symbols."

"Luc," Charles began, in a long-suffering voice, but Luc forged on:

"Symbolism is how you win or lose a war, because it is how you win or lose the minds of the people who are trying to decide if they are part of the war. All politics is theatre and so it follows: to win a victory, you need a *symbol* of victory. A thing people can point to when they say to each other, 'Well, you know, regarde.' Oui ou non?"

"Oui," Minnow said, interested. "Theoretically."

She was thrilled by the image that came to her, as if she were gaz-ing down from above: Minnow, sitting by the fire, with her lover and his friend, discussing the political landscape of riot-torn Paris. It was not an image she would ever have thought to situate herself in. The lancing exhilaration was akin to what she felt when Charles reached for her. The thought of Charles drew her eyes back to him. His face was unreadable; he was gazing down at the ground, listening, and she caught only the curve of his cheek, the fine shadows cast by his long eyelashes. She would have assumed that he was in agreement with Luc, but the tension between them suggested otherwise.

"Bon," Luc said with satisfaction. "Let us take it from theory to concrete example." He leaned forward, his one eye fixed on her, electric blue. "In every protest right now, the cops are always around the Arc de Triomphe. Have you noticed that? They let shop windows get smashed down the street—they don't give a fuck about public property, they just don't want images of the gilets jaunes taking a landmark."

"So you're saying the gilets jaunes *should* take the Arc?"

"Well," Luc smiled, pleased with himself. "We already did, once. It was a good trick."

Minnow had missed this, and she tilted her head, confused. "We . . . you did?"

"Acte 3," Charles said. His voice was rough. "December first."

"So . . . that was your symbol of victory, no?"

"Yes," Luc said, "but the point is escalation in the face of their escalation. The cops have doubled down—now they are huddled around the Arc like ants, so it can never be taken again. But imagine this: a building *near* the Arc, just near enough that all the cops are gathered but looking in the wrong spot. Imagine: right under their noses, in full view, we appear. A thing they never thought to guard. This says: We are unstoppable, we are powerful, we cannot be contained—"

"No," Charles said wearily. "I told you no, Luc."

"What?" Minnow looked from Luc to Charles.

"Charles's father has a building on the Avenue de Friedland," Luc told Minnow.

Charles stood abruptly. "Minnow," he said, "would you like a tour of the apartment?"

"The offices of his illustrious firm," Luc said sweetly, as if Charles hadn't objected. "Which are closed for the weekend. Though if someone were to use his keys and his codes for a larger purpose—"

"I told you," Charles said, his tone icy. "Where you bring in my family, it is too far."

"Your family," Luc said, half dismissing and half cajoling. "Your family will be fine. They have been fine for five hundred years. Listen to me, Charles, how can there be a too far when we have so far to go?"

Charles swung back to him. "We have different ideas about family. I respect yours, but you must respect mine." Minnow had never heard him sound so self-possessed, and Luc fell silent. Charles nodded to Minnow: "Well. The tour?"

Minnow followed Charles away from the warm circle of the fire. She had not realized how large the apartment was, how many rooms spilled into each other, some lamplit, others dark, the shapes of furniture hunched in shadow.

"It is a lot," Charles said apologetically, just ahead of Minnow. "Too much, even."

"Do you mean Luc?"

Charles sounded wry when he replied, "I meant the apartment." After a pause, he added: "But also Luc." He was turned away so she couldn't see his full expression, but his shoulder blades drew against each other.

"All right," Minnow said, defusing. "Tell me about your great-grandmother."

Charles's tone lightened. "She was rich. She was scandalous. She modeled for artists, in secret, when she was young. She was friends with all of them—Picasso, Modigliani—the women, too. Dora Maar! She loved to be looked at. I'm told they would all fall in love on a regular basis and it was very shocking."

Minnow smiled at the enjoyment in Charles's voice.

"Then, of course, her father disinherits her. But *then*—there comes the war. The first one, the second one. By the end of the second, her father is dead, her brothers are dead, there is nobody to remember that she had been disinherited. So in the end, she wins!"

"She sounds fantastic," Minnow said.

Charles's face lit up. "Would you like to see her?"

"What, are her bones in one of these bedrooms? Is she mummified inside a trunk?"

Charles laughed. "I feel certain she would have liked that," he said. "But no. Come." At the end of the hallway was a closed door. Charles pushed it open and stepped in, and Minnow followed. A mahogany four-poster bed sat against the wall; a lamp was on, perched atop a stack of books, and the lamplight flung strange shadows into the corners of the room. Minnow realized with a slight shock that this was Charles's bedroom. Somehow, impossibly, she had not imagined him in a bed outside of her own. As she turned, taking it in—the high ceiling, the piles of books and magazines—her gaze landed on what Charles had intended to show her: a giant painting of a naked young woman hanging on the wall opposite.

The woman looked, Minnow thought immediately, like trouble. She reclined on a divan, her limbs loose and supple, her chin tilted so that she was taking you in rather slyly from the side of her gaze. She was not smiling with her mouth, but the smile was in her eyes, and Minnow recognized Charles in her immediately—the shape of her face, yes, but also the warmth of expression, the way Charles looked right before he told a joke that was pointed at himself.

"She looks like you."

Charles laughed, but he was pleased. "You mean I look like her."

"The resemblance is striking. You've made your point: you come from a lineage of the scandalous and the disinherited." Minnow had meant it to be a joke, but Charles turned toward her, and she saw that he looked stricken.

"I didn't know that was my point, but now that you've said it, I think maybe it was." He smiled ruefully, hands jammed into his pockets. "I keep trying to impress you, but of course I keep failing."

"You aren't failing," Minnow said, startled, and then, catching herself: "What I mean is, you don't need to try and impress me."

Charles hesitated, and then, with the air of someone who was taking a plunge without knowing what was at the bottom: "Would you like to meet my family?"

"Meet them?"

"Yes," Charles said. "They have a party for the New Year—it's technically for my father's firm but it's become a whole thing. My parents' friends, our friends, friends of friends, people you've invited on a whim, people you've stopped liking but can't disinvite." He gave her his most charming smile. "A varied company, but mostly fun?"

Minnow hesitated, torn between flattery and anxiety. "But who will you say I am?"

"Minerva Hunter."

"But who will you say *we* are?"

"Nobody will care."

"*Au contraire,* is I think the phrase. If you walk in the door with a woman, your family will undoubtedly care." Minnow lifted an eyebrow at him. "A much older woman, too." Charles opened his mouth and Minnow pressed a palm against his lips: "I know, I know, Macron and Brigitte, but still."

Charles stuck out the tip of his tongue and ran it against her palm. When she pulled away, smiling, he said, "I will say that you are my good friend, how is that?"

"Don't emphasize the 'good.'"

"My good *friend*?"

"It's also suspect if you emphasize the 'friend.'"

Charles burst out laughing. "We met in the street," he said, "I invited you in, I don't yet know your name but I hope to fuck you in the coat closet before the night is out. How's that?"

"Possibly better," Minnow said. "Also, I'm not going."

"Nonsense," Charles said, "of course you are. Please come. Glamour, fur coats, expensive wine. Moi. On your arm, adoring."

Minnow pulled Charles close for a moment, her mouth on his mouth, sloppy and electric. Desire quickened between them. Without breaking the kiss, Charles slid a hand into the front of her jeans, the pads of his fingers brushing against her dampness. Her breath caught, and he slid his fingers beneath the thin fabric of her underwear as she gripped his arm.

"Say yes," he urged her, low and amused.

"Luc is outside," she whispered.

"I know."

"We have to go back out."

"I know." He began to move his fingers in small light circles, and she felt herself soaking them. He slid two fingers into her and she pulsed around them, gasping, as he began to move deliberately, in and out, his teeth against her jaw. Pleasure uncoiled at the base of her spine and spread outward like a ripple. She came in his hand, and as he stroked her through it, she surprised herself by coming again. For a moment she leaned against him, gasping, her knees weak. He slipped his hand back out, his eyes steady on hers, and licked his fingers.

"Now," he said, "we can go back out."

*

That night, in bed, Charles said, "You never talk about your father."

They had been reading side by side, wrapped in blankets beneath the saucy, dreamy gaze of his naked great-grandmother. The room was cold, and when the wind blew, it cut under the windows and sharpened the air. Flipping through a copy of *Le Monde* that she had found on the floor, Minnow felt exhilarated by this most normal of acts—casually domestic but with all the electricity of newness between them. Now, she realized that Charles had put down his book—Chekhov's stories, she saw, in French—and turned his face to her. He looked shy, almost vulnerable.

"What is there to say?" Minnow asked. "I've told you about him."

"That you're close," Charles said. "But—forgive me if this is—you don't seem to call him, or to speak. And I have wondered . . ." He let the sentence trail off. Minnow considered, and then nodded.

"My father hasn't spoken to me in months. So."

Charles's eyes were bright with curiosity. "Months?"

"Four. Give or take. I mean, a few emails, right before I came here." She had emailed Christopher her new address when she took the job and he had replied to wish her safe travels, as if she were going for a weekend. He had said nothing about what had transpired between them, or what had happened to make her leave. She knew that the things that wounded him most were the ones about which he spoke the least—her own mother was an example of this—and yet she was hurt and furious, and she hadn't replied. "I've thought about calling, but . . . well, he hasn't called me either."

"Why is that?"

Minnow sighed, directing her gaze up to the high ceiling, where off-white paint was peeling in strips.

"I took a student to get an abortion. At my previous job. That's why I was fired."

Charles stared at her, wide-eyed, and then sat up. "You are serious?"

"Yes."

"But this is enough to fire you?"

She hadn't expected that reaction. "I mean . . . in America, yes. Although—*fire*—it's complicated. Essentially, I was fired."

"And your father—he is religious?"

"No," Minnow said slowly. And then she laughed suddenly. "Well, maybe he is. Only his religion is privacy—not standing out, not doing anything to draw attention to yourself. You know, when I was a kid and someone would ask for his phone number or date of birth— like someone at a store or in a bank—he'd always go: Why do you need that? Like, every piece of information was so . . . carefully guarded. The idea that people would talk about him—that was his nightmare. And then people were . . . you know, saying my name on the radio."

Charles lifted an eyebrow. "It became so public?"

"It became," Minnow said tightly, "extremely public." She took a deep breath, trying to ease the pressure in her chest. "And of course he was scared for me. But then people started calling *his* house—to ask questions about me, or get a quote, or . . . I don't know, some of them were I guess just trying to fuck with him. *Your daughter's a whore,* that kind of thing. So then he felt . . . exposed, vulnerable. And he was . . ." Minnow took a shaky breath. "He was *so angry* at me. For bringing that to his door. Of course he was angry, he had every right—but I thought he would at least understand *why*—that at the very least, he'd agree that the girl needed help. When I realized I was wrong . . ."

An image leapt up in front of her eyes: Dean Kaye's garage, on fire.

How she had stood in the dark shadows of the trees and watched the blaze spill over everything, watched him and his wife pour out of the house, panicking, to stare at the garage, heard the long pull of the fire truck's wail as it raced toward them from the other side of town. How powerful she had felt, and at the same time, how bereft. How she had called her father later that night, and he had not picked up; by then, the answering machine was unplugged and he was not picking up any calls.

"Hey," Charles said gently, bringing her back to the present.

"I miss him," Minnow said. Her voice had become thin, and she fought to keep it steady. "I'm so mad at him."

Charles touched the side of her face, ran his thumb along her jaw. He studied her closely, as if he were seeing her for the first time, tender and a little awed. Then he leaned in and kissed her on the jaw, the cheek, on her nearest eyelid. Caught off guard, Minnow smiled. As Charles dropped his head onto her bare shoulder, his hair shaggy and soft, she asked the question that had remained at the back of her mind: "Does Luc really plan to take over your father's offices?"

Charles didn't lift his head, but his voice was ironic when he replied: "It is what he would *like*, but 'plan' requires my consent."

"What is it exactly he wants to do?"

"He wants to hang flags out the windows, banners with faces of the mutilés—you know: *You say that there are no injuries, look in our faces and tell us that again.* And of course if we take over a building—especially *that* building—the media will show up. They'll stand right outside and all of those pictures will be splashed across the daily news. And then Luc talks about running a kind of pirate radio from the offices: *Nous sommes ici, broadcasting from the Avenue de Friedland,* that sort of thing—a real fuck-you to the cops. And to Macron." Charles sighed. "And to my father."

"Right," Minnow said. "So . . . the answer was no."

Charles hesitated. And then, almost despite himself: "He's right that they won't show the real images, the news media—they won't show what really happens—just some anarchistes kicking over benches, maybe somebody flips a car and they show that, but the real damage?" Charles shook his head in disgust. "He's right that the world won't look unless you make them, and there aren't many ways to make them."

"Okay . . ."

"And he says nobody will get hurt. I mean, the building is empty on the weekends, there is nobody *to* get hurt. It could be more peaceful a protest than walking in the street."

Minnow lifted her hand and ran it through Charles's hair, once and then again, carding it with her fingers. "It sounds like you're thinking about it."

Charles turned his head so that her hand was on his face now; she could feel his eyelashes fluttering under her fingers. After a moment he said, "Our fathers . . . can we blame them for their lack of imagination?"

"I don't know," Minnow said gently. "Can't we?"

Charles shook his head. "I think it must be a slow poison to come up against the limitations of justice again and again. The more you see, the more poison accumulates. But what changes in the end is you, not the systems, not the structures. Just you. My father thinks he has figured out the game and won it, but that is his problem—that he has learned to look at it like a game, where some people win and most people lose."

Charles tilted his chin to look up at her. "They've been asleep for decades. They woke up in '68 and then they failed, so they went back to sleep, and they had us, and we were born asleep. And why should they wake us up? So that we can see how they failed? No—we have to wake up on our own, Minou. We have to wake up and wake each other up and stay awake. They can't help us because they don't know how." Charles smiled at her, and his voice was very soft when he said, "This is the great gift of our lives, that we could be here now, you and I. That we could be awake together. I feel pity for our fathers, that they cannot have this again."

*

By the second week of the strike, Minnow had never felt so far from her old world and so embedded in a new one. The Left Bank was often quiet, but on the Right Bank, fighting between police and protestors intensified. She and Charles spent their days together, either in his apartment or walking aimlessly through streets whose air seemed forever tinted with tear gas. Despite her exhilaration, Minnow was cautious, steering them away from one place to another when the energy churned into ugliness, and for the most part Charles let himself be led by her, especially if Luc was not there. She was unsettled by the intensity of Charles's admiration for Luc, the way he often spoke Luc's thoughts or observations as if they were his own. Only on the subject of his family did he seem able to disagree.

Luc was busier than he had been before, thrown into a fervor of activity that Minnow did not wholly understand. He seemed to be constantly relaying messages from one group of people to another. Sometimes he would call Charles late at night, his voice on the phone tinny and jubilant. When Minnow asked Charles what Luc had said, the answers were various and confusing. This group of activists had agreed to meet with that group, despite a grudge that had been nursed for years. Another group was planning an action of some kind outside the offices of the French national media company. Someone had begun another attempt at a written charter, to lay out in some form the demands of the people, but nobody who had read it seemed willing to agree that those were indeed the demands to lay out. During these explanations, Minnow thought of Luc's pleasure in explaining to her the value of chaos as a tool of resistance, and she wondered whether he was now questioning that methodology.

Some nights, they were alone together. Charles would read the newspapers, relaying to Minnow in detail what the government had done or said or promised and then walking through their statements with the accuracy and authority of a lawyer, poking holes, lifting contradictions up to the light. Other nights, Charles's apartment was full: Luc and Sophie and Julie and Flora and Rémy. One night Rémy was arrested and then released; he showed up late at their door, breathless with outrage and pride. He said he was coming straight from a holding cell, and a bruise had already begun mapping itself across his ribs where he had been struck with a baton. Minnow and Charles had been out in the street that day as well, and all three of them drank until dawn, wired with adrenaline.

From time to time, Luc would arrive with a band of friendly strangers whose names Minnow never managed to retain, and Charles would order takeout or run to the corner for a case of wine. They would all drink and watch the news, shout in French at the television and at each other, receive phone calls from other people who seemed to be shouting. The air hummed with expectation, though of what Minnow wasn't sure. Luc's guests always treated Minnow with deference—"As if I were your wife," she joked with Charles once, and to her surprise, he blushed. Though Luc was unfailingly courteous to Minnow, sometimes she caught him watching her and Charles with a keen blankness to his face. She couldn't tell what he was thinking, and when she met his gaze, he would smile and look away.

One evening toward the end of the week, Minnow found herself alone with him for the first time since they had gotten separated from the others at the protest. Charles and Rémy had gone around the corner to buy firewood for the old woodstove. Minnow had opened her mouth to volunteer that she and Charles would go, but Luc spoke first: "Minou and I will stay," he said with his catlike smile, and so the other two clattered out into the cold December air without her.

Alone with Luc, Minnow was unsure what to say. He leaned over, bottle in hand, and she held out her glass and watched him fill it. The wine was black ruby in the dim light.

"So," Luc said easily. "I hear you're meeting the Verniers."

Charles hadn't spoken to Minnow again about his family's party, but she knew it wasn't forgotten. He was waiting for a yes. Now, to Luc, she said, "Maybe. I don't know yet."

Luc smiled. "They're charming."

"Have you met them?"

"No. But I've read interviews—Charles's father is an eloquent man." Luc sipped his own wine, his eyes on Minnow. And then, without preamble: "Charles told me about what you did for that student. The abortion."

"Did he?"

Luc heard the tightness in her voice. "I hope it's all right that he told me."

Minnow sighed. "It's not a secret. My whole country knows."

"He respects you," Luc said. "And I see why."

Minnow studied Luc over the rim of her wineglass, trying to read his face. He had trained himself to a kind of blank stillness that was impossible for Charles, whose face was a faithful reflection of everything he felt.

"Charles misunderstands," Minnow said. "I found myself in a situation, I didn't go looking for it."

"I don't think that matters. We find ourselves constantly in situations we didn't look for—what matters is what we do there."

Minnow cocked her head. "I read you as someone who goes looking for things and then finds them."

"I make a practice of knowing what I want. But even so, the world can be . . . unpredictable." Luc smiled. "For example, one doesn't plan to get a flashball in the eye, but there it is."

Minnow studied Luc. "You're serious, aren't you?" she said. "About the Vernier building?"

Luc nodded.

"You think Charles will change his mind?"

"I think," Luc said carefully, "Charles has a tendency to say no before he says yes. It's understandable. So much of this is new to him. The way of thinking—the utility of sacrifice—these are not things boys like him are raised with. But he understands more than most what we're doing on the street. More than most, he wants change. A victory—a highly visible symbolic victory—is often the turning point inside a revolution."

Minnow considered blunting the edge of her question and chose not to. "Let's say he agrees. His father will never forgive him. His brothers, his mother—a wedge will be driven between him and his family. At his age, these things seem easily solved, but the reality is that they aren't. Aren't you sacrificing him to what he doesn't fully understand?"

Nothing changed in Luc's voice when he said, unhesitating: "Yes, no doubt."

"Yes?"

"None of us are so precious that, if we are useful, we shouldn't be used."

Minnow blinked at him, completely taken by surprise. "Do you really believe that?"

"Yes," Luc said.

Minnow turned this over in her mind. There was a simplicity and power to it that made something in her chest rise and turn, like an engine starting up.

"You should talk to him," Luc said. He had turned to look at the dying fire, and the injured side of his face was in shadow, the untouched side bright. His voice was light, nearly casual. "Your opinion matters to him."

Discomfort stirred in her. "You want me to tell Charles to help you occupy his father's offices?"

Luc's visible eye crinkled in a smile. "I want you to tell Charles what you think," he said. "What you really think. And let him consider that."

"What makes you so sure that I think this is a good idea? That I agree with you at all?"

Luc turned his face back to Minnow. She had bristled against the manipulation she felt was implicit in his words, but when he spoke, he was sincere, utterly without guile.

"I already know what happens if we do nothing and let things just carry on. I know what that looks like. I'm ready for whatever is next. I know you understand that. You burned a man's house down." He shrugged. "Maybe you agree with me and maybe you don't, that's for you to decide. But your instincts . . . Charles could learn something from those."

*

Six days before Christmas, Minnow came home and found her father standing on the sidewalk in front of the side door to her courtyard. He was tall, stooped a little, his face in profile as he gazed down the street in the direction of the Jardin des Plantes. He was wearing his old black peacoat, a coat he had owned for many years, with its ragged hems and torn blue lining. Shock reverberated through her.

"Dad," Minnow said, and he turned his head and took her in.

Christopher was not an expressive man, and although Minnow

had long ago learned to parse whole geographies of emotion from the slightest shifts of his face, this time she could not be sure what he was thinking or feeling.

"Min," he said. "It's good to see you."

"You're in Paris?"

Christopher's mouth moved in a wry smile that sent an ache of familiarity through her. "Merry Christmas," he said.

Minnow studied her father uncertainly. They always spent the holidays together: Thanksgiving, Christmas, New Year's. It had been an unspoken constant, no matter where she was or who she was dating—nothing that required discussion beyond which day Minnow was flying in. Seeing him here, on this Paris sidewalk, filled her with the sense of an alternate universe in which they had been talking this entire time. In which Minnow had invited him—"Christmas in Paris!" she might have said.

Reality flickered, and for a moment, Minnow imagined the normal version of this visit. Christopher, good-natured and interested in where she was living and what she was doing. Minnow, trying to impress him a little, showing him her favorite café, her favorite boulangerie, her favorite wine store. And maybe this was how it could be if she said nothing about what had happened in the intervening months. Christopher was not a man who felt the need to talk about difficult things. Both of them could take a synchronized step back into habit and routine: the food they liked, the jokes they shared, the music they listened to together.

At this thought, frustration flooded her—or was it despair? And then she heard Charles's voice in her head: *Our fathers . . . can we blame them for their lack of imagination? They can't help us because they don't know how.* The feeling drained out of Minnow with alarming suddenness, leaving behind exhaustion.

"Can I come in?" Christopher asked, and it was his uncertainty that undid her. Not trusting her voice, she nodded.

He closed the distance between them and held out his arms. They were not a physically demonstrative family, but she stepped into the embrace and Christopher held her tightly. Minnow took a deep breath and drew in the mingled smells of winter, the residual plastic of airplane air, and Christopher's own scent, something like wood and earth.

When he released her, he cleared his throat but said nothing. Minnow turned away to gather herself, stepping past him to punch her entry code into the keypad. The door unlocked itself. She pushed it open, took a deep breath, and gestured her father inside.

1969

16

KEEN WAS LYING PARTWAY UNDERNEATH A BANK OF SEATS, CHEEK pressed to the scuffed floor, when Ethan surprised him. Andrew Hungerford's inhaler must have gotten kicked, because it had come to rest wedged beneath the metal support of a row of seats—a tiny vital scrap of plastic. Keen scrabbled for it with his fingertips.

"What are you doing?"

Keen reared up, nearly hitting his head. "I—I dropped something," he said and then wondered why he'd lied.

Ethan leaned against the doorway, arms folded. He looked bigger and older—maybe it was the angle, how he was backlit against the hallway. Or maybe, Keen thought, the events of today had nourished him like a baby god, and now, in his pursuit of Olya, he would be unstoppable.

"Where's Hungerford?"

"Locked in his closet." Keen got to his feet. And then, tucking the inhaler into his pocket: "Where did *you* go?"

"I went to help."

"Okay, well, last I heard the plan, you were supposed to *help* by staying with me."

"Look, we don't need two men on a locked closet door," Ethan said, as if Keen was being petulant—and, in fact, a petulant note had entered his voice.

"Why don't you take closet duty," Keen said, "and *I'll* go help."

"I'm actually supposed to be with Dwight right now," Ethan said, neatly evading.

"Well, am I gonna trade closet duty with someone at *some* point?" Keen demanded, hearing and hating the whine just below the surface of his words.

"Do you feel like you *need* to trade it?" Ethan asked, and then Keen hated him more. "I'll have someone bring you food later," Ethan added, relenting, "and you can switch off then"—but Keen brushed past him and stalked down the hallway.

All the way back to the supply closet, Keen's fist clenched and unclenched in his pocket. He was squeezing the inhaler so hard that he made himself let go of it, in case it broke. Fucking Ethan, he thought. He had never had any intention of guarding Hungerford. Had he discussed this with Olya? Had she agreed? Had she said, "You're indispensable to me"? Had she said, "Look, why don't we leave Keen with the little author, and you come be by my side where you belong"? Had she said, "Just ditch Keen, make sure the closet gets locked and then ditch him"? Had she said, "I love you," Keen wondered miserably—had she said it to Ethan in exactly the same way she had said it to Keen? And then he reminded himself that she hadn't said it to him, not like that. She had asked: "Don't you love me?" But she had never said the phrase all together: *I love you, Keen*. Maybe she had said it to Ethan.

Keen reached the supply closet, shoulders tight, chest feeling as if someone had stepped on the middle of it. He tapped on the wood with a finger: "Hello?" His voice came out rough and gritty.

"Hello!" Andrew Hungerford's voice was a rush of relief. "Can you hear me? I'm Andrew Hungerford—"

"I know who the fuck you are." Keen worked to keep his anger shoved in his chest where it belonged. "I'm the one you sent to get your inhaler."

"Oh." And then: "Did you find it?"

"Yeah, I've got it."

"Thank you," Andrew Hungerford said, fervently. "Thank you."

Keen realized that he hadn't thought through the next part of this, the part where he opened the closet door. He glanced quickly down the hallway, but Ethan was long gone and the corridor was empty. They hadn't restrained Andrew Hungerford's hands, they hadn't tied him down; but then again, he was so small and his shoulders were so thin.

"Can I have it?" Andrew asked. It was the note of fear in his voice—as if Keen might have fetched his inhaler to tease him with it—that convinced Keen.

"Yeah," he said, "hang on."

He fumbled with the ring of keys jammed into the lock. It was stuck at first, hard to turn, and he almost laughed at the idea that now he wished to open the door, he might not be able to. "Hang on," he said again and gave the key a wrench, yanking at the doorknob at the same time. The door flew open, and Andrew Hungerford leapt straight at him.

Hungerford was a whirlwind of teeth and elbows and small hard fists, kicking legs, and at first, all Keen felt was pure surprise. One fist connected with Keen's sternum and he doubled over, wheezing, as Andrew Hungerford shoved past him. Keen grabbed his ankle and brought him down, hard, onto the floor. He hauled Hungerford back toward him, and the man lashed out, his leather-soled foot glancing off the side of Keen's head. Startled and angry, the pain cutting through his bewilderment, Keen slammed his fist into the nearest body part he could reach—a thigh—and Hungerford redoubled his efforts to escape, fingers scratching furiously, legs lashing. Keen managed to drag him back toward the open closet door, and as the other man's midsection came in reach, Keen slammed a punch into his stomach. Hungerford coughed and curled around himself, no longer scrabbling. As Keen bent to grab his shoulders and shove him the rest of the way inside, Hungerford darted his face upward and attached his teeth to Keen's cheek. It was such a shocking act, so vicious and delicate, that Keen was wholly unprepared. He howled and reeled backward, slick heat running down his cheek. Hungerford made a last-ditch attempt to stand at the same time that he tried to run. But his shaky legs gave way and, his center of gravity surging forward, he launched himself flat onto his face. Before he could get back up, Keen was on him, raining a storm of punches at whatever he could reach:

head, ribs, back. Some of them connected and Keen felt the impact
jar up his arms and into his shoulders. Once, he hit the floor by accident, and something popped in his fist. That was what stopped him,
or perhaps he would have stopped anyway, because Andrew Hungerford was not resisting him. He wasn't unconscious, but his arms were
over his head and he was waiting for Keen's fury to abate.

"Get up," Keen said, harshly. He hauled the older man to his feet
by the back of his blazer, and Andrew Hungerford rose willingly if
limply. His face was very pale and his nose was bleeding profusely.
His breathing came in short, constricted bursts. Keen dragged him
the few feet back down to the closet and shoved him inside, on guard
for more resistance, but Hungerford just slumped against the far wall.
He was holding his chest, his face tilted down. Keen slammed the
closet door and relocked it, and then slid to the ground himself, cata-
loging his injuries: the bite on his cheek, which was bleeding with
abundance; his right fist, which was swelling with alarming speed; the
bruises he could feel rising along his ribs and arms.

"Christopher."

"Shut up," Keen growled.

"Christopher." Hungerford's voice was tight. "I—do you have my
inhaler still?"

"You've gotta be kidding me."

"I need it."

"If you think I'm opening this again, you're crazy."

"I won't fight you anymore. But I need it."

Hungerford was trying to trick him, Keen knew. He could hear
that forced breathiness in his voice, a performative thickness. Any
moment now he'd start making fake choking sounds, anything to get
Keen to open the door so he could escape—and what if he actually
did this time? What if he got outside, got out to the campus police?
Keen would have to sit by the empty closet and explain to Olya—and
Ethan! Fucking Ethan!—exactly how it was that he had been tricked
into opening the door, not once but *twice,* and releasing their
prisoner.

"Christopher, can you hear me?"

"No."

"I . . . I really need it. I think . . ." Silence, then a wheezing. "Stress—arguments and stress—they can trigger—and the closet is moldy. I think there's mold in here, and that's also a trigger. Please—can you just . . ."

"*Arguments,*" Keen said bitterly. "Was what just happened an *argument*?"

"Please," Hungerford said. He was pitching his voice quieter, and Keen admired the theatrics of it. At the same time, he wanted to punch the man a few more times. Hungerford managed to inject a tight dry cough into the proceedings. "I'm begging you, please."

"I'm gonna leave now," Keen said. "I'll be back in a bit. So you can save your breath, I won't be here."

He started to make the sounds of leaving, stamping his boots, and then he thought, *Fuck this, what am I staying for?* He could at least clean up his face. He left his post and strode down the hallway, in search of the men's restroom. He braced himself to encounter others there but found it empty. He stood in front of the mirror and examined himself.

He looked tough, at least. The blood had congealed as it ran down the side of his cheek, painting a thick stripe along the side of his jaw. His lip was split, which he hadn't been aware of—one of Hungerford's wild kicks must have connected. He thought about washing the blood off and then changed his mind—what the hell, leave it as it was. "He tried to escape, and I stopped him." That was a good story. "He pretended he couldn't breathe so I opened the door, and then he attacked me, and I just put a stop to that real quick. Just real quick." Keen realized he was speaking out loud, delivering these lines to the mirror in a murmur. He glanced around, embarrassed, but the bathroom was still empty. Seeing himself looking so tough, an initiated revolutionary, Keen's anger dissipated. Hungerford was just doing his job, trying to get away—anyone would. And then Keen had done *his* job—admirably, swiftly—and stopped him.

Keen felt in his zippered side pocket and his fingers discovered the hard plastic of Hungerford's inhaler. Maybe if Ethan actually sent someone to take his place, the two of them could open the closet, subdue Hungerford, give him the inhaler, and seal him back up in case he did come to need it in the time he had left.

Exiting the bathroom, Keen heard a burst of laughter and four students walked past. All of them were wearing black armbands, and they were passing a joint back and forth. One of them saw Keen's face and his eyes widened. "Whoa," he said. "Whoa, man."

Keen gave him a sharp military nod and kept walking, pleasure suffusing him.

"What happened to you?" the student called after him, and Keen replied: "Combat, comrades. Combat." He made sure not to slow his purposeful stride until he had rounded the corner and then he walked more slowly, replaying the moment in which the other boys had been impressed by him.

The keys were sticking out of the closet door just as Keen had left them. He approached and waited for Hungerford to call out to him, but the man was quiet. Well, good. He must have finally figured out that the only people in this building were the ones who had taken it over. Keen sat against the wall, legs stretched out. Hungerford was still quiet. *He must not know I'm here,* Keen thought, and then, with disdain: *I notice there's no coughing now. He doesn't seem to be having any problems when he thinks I can't hear him.*

He lost track of time sitting against the wall. His mind wandered until he realized that he was light-headed with hunger. It was night, now, and he hadn't eaten since breakfast. When he realized that, it occurred to him that the hallway was deathly silent—Hungerford had made no sounds from the closet, not even the shift of shoulders against the wood paneling as he changed positions. Was he asleep?

Keen tapped on the closet door. "Hey," he said.

Hungerford was silent.

"It's Christopher. I'm back."

Keen pressed his ear to the door, trying to hear Hungerford's breathing.

"You still want your inhaler?"

It was the quality of the silence that made something drop in his stomach. A silence that had nothing human in it; a silence that was only absence. He fumbled with the keys, jerking the doorknob, adrenaline spiking through his chest and making his fingers tingle. The key stuck at first, as it had before, but he rattled and wrenched at it, and only seconds passed before the door came open in his hand.

It was dark inside the closet. The lightbulb must have burned out, or perhaps Hungerford had collided with it when he was thrown back in. Keen squinted, but it only took seconds for his eyes to adjust, and then he saw Hungerford, sitting against the juncture where wall met wall, just sitting, his legs straight out and his shoulders slumped and his head tilted down, and Keen knew at a glance—though he had never seen this before—that the man in front of him was dead.

2018

17

BEFORE CHARLES HAD OPENED HIS MOUTH, MINNOW KNEW HER father did not like him. Charles had worn a bulky leather jacket that made him look even younger than he was, and he walked into Minnow's apartment like he belonged there. She saw Christopher notice his ease and felt the unspoken judgment.

"Daddy, this is Charles. Charles, this is my father."

Charles held out his hand, and after a nearly imperceptible delay, Christopher took it.

"It is a pleasure to meet you," Charles said. Minnow could tell he was nervous. His voice was too chipper, too agreeable.

"Likewise," Christopher returned blankly.

His first two days in Paris, Minnow had debated whether or not to introduce her father to Charles, at the same time as she had debated whether or not to bring up the subject of Sewell School, of Katie, of the silence that had extended between them. Failing to come to a conclusion, Minnow had done nothing. She and Christopher spent both days together. He came over in the late morning, walking from his hotel, and they drank coffee in her apartment, staring out at the light drizzle. It had been raining for weeks now, and when the rain turned to a sharp mist, they crossed the street to walk through the Jardin des Plantes, their feet crunching on gravel. Both days, they came to a stop by the pen of damp and inconsolable wallabies and gazed in, and the wallabies gazed back at them, heavy-lidded and implacable.

On the second day the sun came out briefly, and they walked through the long aisles of winter trees where the lumières had been arranged: large installations of canvas, steel, and strings of lights. The lumières looked lumpy and charmless in the daytime, but Minnow knew that at night they would glow, magical creatures brought to life in the darkness. There was an orca you could walk through; just beyond it, a frog and a spider cavorted. The gate that led out onto the Quai Saint-Bernard was decorated with looming multicolored dinosaur heads, and both Minnow and Christopher paused, looking upward with delight. "We should come back after dark," Minnow suggested, and Christopher agreed, both of them enjoying the implication that there was more for them to share together.

On the third day, they went to the market on the Rue Mouffetard and Christopher held a series of bags as Minnow selected whitefish from the fishmonger, fennel and lemons from the vegetable stall, a fresh baguette from the boulangerie, a small wheel of Camembert and a hard wedge of Gruyère from the fromagerie. As they walked back to the apartment, Minnow came to a decision. "I was thinking I might invite a friend over for dinner tonight," she said, ignoring Christopher's unspoken dismay but feeling it all the same. Christopher didn't like strangers; Christopher didn't like guests. "I'd like you to meet him. He's been a big part of my life here."

Christopher had been silent, and then he'd said, diplomatically: "Whatever you'd like, of course," and Minnow understood that he was on good behavior, that he felt the need to make up to her, even if neither of them was bringing up what had occurred between them.

Now Minnow sensed that same resignation, as her father shook Charles's hand without enthusiasm. The desire to punish him drifted through her.

"Daddy," she said brightly, "why don't you and Charles get to know each other? I'll just throw the fish in the oven and be right back out." She turned on her heel and walked toward the kitchen, leaving her father and Charles together.

"Let me take your coat," Christopher said, a little haplessly, and then Minnow was alone in the kitchen. She realized her heart was racing. She felt bad for throwing Charles in at the deep end. She hadn't even kissed him when he'd arrived. She had planned to, something in her had wanted her father to see how casually and confidently she leaned over to kiss her young French lover. But then it had all been too much, too strange, and she had frozen.

Minnow was at the stove, sealing fish into foil packets of thinly sliced fennel and lemon, when a sound made her turn. Christopher stood in the kitchen doorway.

"Dad, what are you doing?"

"I thought I'd lend a hand," Christopher said. "Put a salad together."

"You should keep Charles company. He's in there all alone."

Christopher didn't respond to that, and when Minnow threw another glance over her shoulder, she saw he looked lost.

"How's the hotel?" Minnow asked, just to have something to say.

"Oh, it's fine. For what I paid, it's fine." He came closer, leaning against the fridge, watching her hands work. "I keep forgetting to bring them over, but I brought you a few things."

"Me? What did you bring *me*?"

"Warm clothes. You left some scarves and a really great jacket— a down jacket—at my house, and I thought . . . I didn't know what you had with you here."

"Dad." Minnow was laughing, despite herself. "You brought me the winter coat I wore in high school?"

"Is that when you wore it?"

"Yes! Senior year! That was twenty years ago!"

Christopher smiled with just the edges of his mouth and his eyes, so that to an outsider, he would not have appeared to be smiling. "That explains why it was in my house," he said.

"Oh, Daddy," Minnow said, realizing too late that the laughter stuck in her chest might be tears. She turned on the faucet to have something to do and rewashed the clean mugs stacked beside the sink.

When she was done washing them, the threat of tears had receded, and Christopher was standing at the kitchen window, looking out into the inner courtyard. The lights in the courtyard had motion sensors, and in the absence of human movement, the courtyard became an abyss of shadow.

"I came to Paris when I was your age," Christopher said. "Younger, actually."

"I remember."

"Did I tell you that story? About the three leather jackets?"

"You did."

"I thought I'd come back sooner or later, maybe live here." Christopher shook his head. "Some things, you get old and you realize you thought there would always be time, and then there isn't."

"Daddy you're not old," Minnow said automatically.

He snorted. "*You're* old," he said, "so I must be *really* old."

"Okay, very funny."

Charles leaned his head into the kitchen, looking confused, and gave Minnow a hopeful smile. "Ah, did you require sous-chefs? I am at your disposal."

Christopher looked away to the window again, and Minnow wanted to tell him to stop being childish.

"I'm almost done here," Minnow said lightly. "Charles, will you pour us some wine in the other room? And put on some music?"

"Madame," Charles said, with a light bow. He fetched the wineglasses from the cupboard over the sink, reaching up over Minnow to do so. For a moment she smelled the closeness of his skin, the fragrance of his sweat. He must have walked from Saint-Germain. She felt the dizzying impulse to lean into him, to put her mouth on the juncture of his neck and shoulder, and she restrained herself. As if he had felt the impulse, he gave her a wry smile over the tops of the wineglasses and whisked them out to the living room.

Left alone with her father again, Minnow studied him. And maybe it was because Christopher looked so lost, like a small boy in a strange place surrounded by the unknown, that something thawed in her. "I'm glad you're here," she said, and his face was transformed by relief as he lifted it toward her, as if he had been waiting this whole time for her to say so.

*

For the first half hour, Minnow thought the dinner might go well. The fish came out beautifully, juicy and citrusy, each piece cooked in its own little packet of acids and spices. Minnow had opened a bottle of white as a nod to the fish, and a bottle of red as a nod to her own preferences, and with the wine flowing, Charles was loose and expansive and Christopher was conversational.

They talked about films at first—it turned out both Charles and Christopher were fans of Werner Herzog, and they launched into a discussion of the ethics of *Grizzly Man,* and the fine line between documentation and exploitation. "But he was documenting *himself,*" Charles argued of the now-dead titular character, and Christopher returned: "If you exploit yourself first, does it make it impossible for you to be exploited by another?"

"But what is exploitation for one is not necessarily exploitation for another," Charles said. "Someone who sees self-exposure as self-expression, perhaps he cannot be exploited in this way."

Minnow had never watched the film in question, but she was relieved that Christopher was interested in the conversation and that Charles could hold his own. She kept seeing him through her father's eyes and noticing everything about him that made him look unbearably young. Christopher had not asked where they met; he had not asked Charles much of anything. He was behaving much the same as he had with Kenneth: cool, polite to a fault, courteous in a way that gave Charles no room to get to know him. It was as if Christopher had already surmised that, like all the others, Charles would not be permanent and therefore was determined to give him as little as possible before he went.

Minnow brought her attention back to the table just as her father said: "I believe that what a lot of people like to call *change* is just a continuation. So few people understand history that old things look gleefully new when sold in different packaging."

She glanced between him and Charles and realized that the two of them were serious, Charles most of all. The conversation had shifted into new territory, and she had an uneasy feeling she knew what it was.

"You mean history repeats," Charles said. "Yes? But I would say: history repeats less and less when you create governments that are capable of making new history."

"I would like to know what that *actually* means," Christopher said drily, and Minnow winced a little. She opened her mouth to try and lighten the air, but Charles rose to her father's challenge.

"A government, the way it works—these are just things that someone thought up, no? We imagine a thing and then we institute what we have imagined. And then we enforce what we have instituted, and it may feel as if it has been that way forever. But it hasn't! Someone, at some point, just made it up. When the imagination of a country is poor, everyone who comes next simply does what has come before, ignoring the ways in which it has not worked. This is the value of people who can come along and communicate to the whole country that there is a different way."

"And what is the way that the gilets jaunes are communicating?" Christopher asked. "To the outside eye, smashing up a lot of buildings doesn't seem like a particularly new message."

Charles sighed. "For me, what they are revealing is what our government is capable of doing to us in the name of crushing dissent. As a child, I was raised to think that I lived in the heart of civilization. But given what I have seen with my own eyes, now I must understand differently the people ruling me."

"All right," Christopher said slowly. "But state brutality isn't new. Is it? You're very young, so maybe that was a new thought for *you*, but—your father, for example, I will guess that he might remember very vividly the student protests of '68, here in your city."

Minnow could tell from Charles's expression that he didn't like being reminded of his age or his father, but he strove to keep his tone warm and open.

"That might be true," he said. "But before we can have what is new, we must get rid of what is old. And if the people understand that our leaders are not serving us, if we know enough to be dissatisfied, we can turn toward change."

"Well," Christopher said drily, "dissatisfaction and change are two different things. Dissatisfaction is the human condition. But *change*? Change is trying to roll a ball uphill."

"I don't think dissatisfaction is the human condition," Charles argued. "Maybe striving to transform, yes—but you can say there is a kind of satisfaction in that. Bringing into being the world we want to live in."

Christopher sighed. "Where is it?"

"I'm sorry?"

"The world you want to live in. Where is it? Is it here yet? If not, is it that you just need to try harder? You individually, *you*, Charles, you just need to try harder and then it'll show up? Is it not here yet because you're lazy?"

Charles opened his mouth but Christopher went on inexorably: "*Or* is it that your parents strove for that world—or maybe not *your* parents, I don't know your parents, but a lot of parents, and grandparents, and great-grandparents—and there were moments in which things were achieved, sure. Laws were passed, there were gains—don't get me wrong, some of them, in fact, were achieved by *our* generation and then undone by *yours*. But that's neither here nor there. Gains are not societal overhaul. And the problem, Charles, is that you aren't working with simple materials—a bad system that you need to make into a good one, a corrupt man that you need to replace with an honest one. You are working with humans, and the material itself is polluted."

"*Polluted?*" Charles laughed, but his laugh sounded strangled. "That is a very strong statement."

Christopher plunged through him, implacable. "We are greedy and full of ego, we are incapable of separating our politics from our self-interest, we think that whatever is good for us is what is good for society, we lie to everyone around us and especially to ourselves. And once you have begun lying to yourself you are entirely without value as a tool of transformation. If you can't even see your own motives clearly, you have no hope of seeing what you're trying to change." Christopher glanced from Charles to Minnow, as if by accident, but their eyes held, and then he turned back to Charles. "How do you build a house when all the building blocks are rotted through?"

"All right," Minnow said brusquely, "that's enough." To Charles: "Forgive my father, he's a pessimist."

But Charles seemed dazed. She could tell from the pinched look around his eyebrows that he had understood the depth of Christopher's contempt for him. Nonetheless, he leaned forward across his plate, almost pleading, and addressed Christopher: "But you can't believe this."

"Why not?"

"Because it is—because . . ." Charles seemed to run out of words. He shook his head. "Because then what is there?"

"What do you mean, 'what is there'?"

"You have to believe in the ability to improve your world; otherwise, why get up in the morning?"

"Because you have obligations," Christopher replied, and this time he sounded severe. "To your employer or employees, to your neighbors, to your family. Tangible obligations. To individual people, not to the world."

Minnow had not planned to participate in the conversation, but she heard her voice, caustic and brittle, as if it belonged to a stranger: "You didn't seem to think much of my obligation to Katie Curtis."

Christopher hesitated; she had caught him off guard. And then he met her eyes and said: "I thought you took an unnecessary risk, Minnow. One whose consequences you didn't understand."

Here we are, thought Minnow. She had wondered this entire time when Christopher was going to bring it up, and she felt a flash of elation that—in the end—she had done it herself.

"I didn't," Minnow said, "you're right, but what if I had? Would you have respected me then?" As Christopher opened his mouth she pushed further: "Was it my lack of *understanding* that you couldn't respect, or the fact I took a girl to get an abortion? Or that I didn't ask your permission, your opinion? Which was it, do you think, that you couldn't tolerate?"

"Minnow," Christopher said, seemingly at a loss.

"I'm sorry, are we not supposed to *talk* about this? Are we supposed to just pick up and carry on like it never happened?"

Charles got to his feet, a little unsteadily but understanding that the currents had shifted. "A lovely dinner," he said. "Thank you. I should . . ."

"You don't have to go," Minnow said, but she was glad that he was leaving.

"No, no." Charles gathered his coat and scarf even as he spoke. "You have so little time together. Mr. Hunter, c'était un plaisir."

"I'm sure," Christopher said drily. He rose to his feet but made no move to shake Charles's hand, and Charles, having shouldered rapidly into his coat and flung his scarf around his neck, made the decision not to try his luck.

"Bonne nuit." Charles leaned in to Minnow, and for a moment she was scared he would kiss her, but instead he kissed her cheek. He let himself out of the apartment and they heard his shoes clattering in the stairwell as he descended. Into the silence, Christopher asked: "How old is that boy?" And this, for Minnow, was the last straw.

"Forget Charles," she said, turning to face him. "*I* am thirty-eight years old, Dad. Whoever I would need to become for you to allow yourself to respect me on your own terms, that's never going to happen now. It's too late, do you understand me? So you have to make peace with who I *am*. You have to respect me for who I actually *am*. I don't know how to help you do that, but you have to learn how."

She didn't know what she had expected, but it was not the way her father looked at her then, with such deep sadness. "I love you," he said. It was not a thing they said to each other—she could count on one hand the number of times she had heard him say it. But even so, she replied:

"Love is easier than respect. And it means less."

"That isn't true," Christopher said. "Of course I respect you, Minnow—"

"But you don't! You think Charles is an idiot, I'm an idiot—anybody who wants to do anything other than just shut up and keep their head down is an idiot to you! When did you start confusing conviction for stupidity? And why did I listen to you for so long?" She had raised her voice, and she had the terrible feeling that if she stopped shouting, she would cry.

Christopher looked exhausted. "Minnow," he said gently. "It isn't that I think everyone is stupid and I'm the exception. It's that I have *been* stupid, remarkably stupid. And I have hoped . . . I hoped you wouldn't repeat my mistakes."

"But what does that mean?"

Christopher considered, and Minnow studied the side of his face, the hollows under his eyes. When she looked at him quickly, a glance from the side, he looked like a stranger, tired and old. At last, he said quietly, "You are so like your mother. Sometimes that scares me."

It was the last thing Minnow had expected him to say. "What exactly does *that* mean?"

Christopher's mouth moved in the ghost of a smile. "She was never careful—with herself or with me. Or with you. And so when you are not careful . . . the idea of losing you is not—it would not be possible for me to heal from that."

"Lose me? How would you lose me?" Minnow shook her head, trying to understand. "Did you really think somebody was going to come kill me?"

Christopher sighed. "There are so many ways to lose a person," he said. "Was I scared for you, physically? Of course I was. But also . . . we think we know ourselves, but we are infinitely malleable, we can be bent in any direction. Accidents, mistakes, they can change us forever. They can make us unrecognizable, even to ourselves. Do you know what I mean?"

Minnow shook her head. "You were worried I would *change*? Dad, of course I'm going to change, that's . . . that's what happens."

"I didn't want you to be shaped by what happened with Katie. That in particular." Christopher shook his head. "The . . . the guilt—"

"Guilt?" Minnow heard her voice lift and struggled to bring it back down.

"There's a way in which it corrodes you, guilt. Over time it eats away at you—it leaches the joy out of everything, you spend your whole life—"

"I don't feel guilty, I didn't do anything wrong."

Christopher was quiet and Minnow felt the abyss between them once again. And then he spoke, decisively. "When I was in my early twenties, the age of Charles, maybe, I was living in Cambridge—this part you know—for graduate school."

"Yes," Minnow said. "That's where you met Mom."

"That's right. And this was, let me see, '66 to '69, it would have been. Lots of protests, all the things your friend Charles is so excited to be inventing, here in 2018. I got caught up in all of that."

"*You* did?" Minnow ignored his dig at Charles. "I thought that was Mom, and you were, like, buried in your lab, this hermit who never had any fun."

Christopher smiled. "Yes," he said. "Well, I was. But then I met your mother and her friends, and we were all . . . For a time, we got involved."

"And because you couldn't save the world then, you decided it wasn't worth saving?"

"No," he said, coolly, "not exactly. We took over a building as part of a protest—and people got hurt."

Minnow leaned forward. "Wait, you never told me this. *You* took over a building?"

Christopher sighed. "And it was for nothing. Of course, it changed nothing, the war rolled on, it ended when it ended, and two decades later, we were in Iraq. Except for those of us who had been . . . damaged by it, and our lives stayed damaged. That's the other thing about people who talk like your friend Charles—they're so caught up in how good it feels to play revolution that they're completely unprepared when tragedy happens."

But Minnow didn't want to talk about Charles. "What happened?" she asked. "What do you mean, 'tragedy'?"

Christopher hesitated for so long that Minnow thought he wouldn't answer. At last: "Things got out of hand," he said. She could tell the admission was hard-won, but she had no idea what it meant. He took a breath, and she saw that he was searching for more words. At last he managed: "It affected me hugely. And your mother."

"But how?"

"We were not who we thought we were," Christopher said softly. "In the end, *I* was not. And what we believed in . . . it did not do for us what we had hoped."

Minnow studied her father, sensing the need to tread with care. As she racked her mind for ways in which to ask and re-ask the question until her father gave a more definitive answer, Christopher asked, delicately: "Have you heard from your mother?" Despite the softness of his voice, it was like a bomb detonating in the room.

"Have I *heard* from her?"

"She said she emailed you."

Minnow felt her jaw loosen in disbelief. "How . . . When did you speak to her?"

"She called—she was trying to reach you—this was a few months ago. She'd heard—on the news she'd heard about the situation at Sewell, and . . ." Christopher's voice trailed away. "She said she reached out to you," he said, defensively.

"I didn't—no, I didn't get it, I didn't hear from her." Minnow's mind was racing. "She must've emailed me at the Sewell account—it must have landed after they locked me out. You didn't say anything!"

"I didn't know if you'd spoken or if . . . I wasn't sure if I should . . ."

"You mean you weren't talking to me."

Christopher lifted his head, alarmed. "Minnow, I wasn't ever *not talking* to you."

"But you weren't," Minnow said. "We weren't, we were objectively not talking."

"I thought you wanted . . . space—I thought—I mean *you* weren't calling *me*—"

"Bullshit," Minnow said. "Don't you dare. You were ashamed of me. And you were angry at me. And you maybe didn't know what to say—or how to say it—but also, you felt those things. And you didn't know what to do, so you didn't do anything."

Christopher took a deep breath and studied his hands. After a moment, he lifted his gaze. "I guess that's true, too," he said.

In the silence, Minnow asked: "What was it like, talking to Mom again?"

Pained lines flickered across Christopher's forehead, but he was steady when he said, "It was nice to hear her voice."

"Nice?"

"And strange. Of course. I hadn't heard from her in . . . decades. I didn't know she still had our landline number."

Minnow had planned not to ask the question and so she was surprised to hear her voice soar an octave or two as she asked, "Was she worried about me?"

Christopher's tone was unbearably tender. "Yes, Min, she was worried."

"Where is she, anyway?"

"It sounds like she's living in Oregon." Christopher hesitated. Then, carefully: "I took her number. If you'd want to call . . ."

Minnow realized her palms were damp. She wiped them on her jeans. The food sat unattended on the table, half-eaten, Charles's wineglass not entirely empty. A deep weariness swamped her, and for a moment she entertained the fantasy of putting her head down on the table amid all the plates and going to sleep.

"You said once that she—you and she had an agreement. That if she had me, you would raise me, and she could leave."

"Did I say that?" Christopher cocked his head, startled. "I don't think I would have said it that way."

"I don't remember how you said it, but—that's what happened, right?"

Christopher sighed. "It was harder for her than that. After she had you, she was very—confused about what she wanted. She came and went and came and went. You wouldn't remember this, it was your first two years. But it was confusing for you, too, that sometimes she was there with us and sometimes she wasn't, and when she wasn't, we couldn't reach her. You—it upset you. Sometimes for months at a time—you'd be fine, but then she would appear or disappear and you wouldn't be fine anymore. And she loved you, Min, in her own way she absolutely loved you. So much so that when she realized she was hurting you, she just . . . she made the decision to remove herself from our lives. But I don't want you to think that the decision was easy for her."

"Why didn't she just—find a balance? Like, live down the street, take me once a month, that kind of thing? Or, like, do what she wanted but spend holidays with us? Why did it have to be all or nothing?"

Christopher sighed. "That was just Olya," he said. "She doesn't— *didn't*, at that time, anyway—understand the space between the extremes of things. She only understood the poles. The power, I guess, of pure commitment: you're all in or you're all out. And for me, who always lived in a gray middle space—you can understand, maybe, how infuriating and dazzling that was for me. Especially as a young person."

Minnow nodded.

"And maybe," Christopher suggested, his tone still gentle, "maybe at Sewell you were like her in that way. And it scared me."

Minnow realized with surprise that her face was wet. She wiped it with the back of her hand.

"I always thought I was like you," she said. "Until Katie. I thought you would've done what I did."

Christopher looked pained. "I understand how exhilarating it can be, to feel like you're . . . accomplishing something. I understand how everything in your life comes into such strong relief in those moments and you can think, you can almost think: *Ah, here it is. The point.* I've felt that before, too. It ends, though. That's the thing. It ends, and then . . . what are you left with?"

Sadness weighed in Minnow's chest, and she had to breathe around it before she could speak. She had wanted to ask her father to tell her more about what happened to him back then, in the building he and her mother had taken over, but now she realized she didn't want to know. What could he say that wouldn't break her heart? Whether it had been a small thing or a large one, he had given up—and so had her mother, in some way. If Christopher had given up on the world, Olya had given up on him. What good could it do Minnow now, to hear about surrender? When she looked around her, the whole world was a picture of the surrenders that had come before. They had nothing more to teach her, except for the value of the opposite.

"Maybe it doesn't have to end," she said to her father, hearing Charles in her own voice—and behind him, Luc. "Maybe it only ends if you give up too soon. Maybe if you go all the way and keep going, you actually start to get somewhere."

*

Three days before Christmas, the gilets jaunes staged acte 6, though Minnow gathered from the news that the number of participants had fallen across the country. Charles called her that morning, asking if she would join him, but she said no; she had agreed to spend the day with her father. Charles and Luc went instead, and Charles sent her a few pictures of the crowd—still thick enough, from what she could see, milling in their yellow vests, faces grim. There were more injuries than she had seen before. One of the photographs was from the protest at Versailles, although she wasn't sure if Charles had taken it or if it had been sent to him. She thought of Luc talking about the symbolism of warfare, and she watched the footage briefly on her computer until Christopher called from the hotel to say that he was on his way over.

Minnow and Christopher were good at being in each other's company, good at long and companionable silences. They went to the Pompidou to look at cubism, riding the long escalators up through their transparent tubes, staring down at the great square where pigeons scattered, men sold wares, students sprawled on the gum-flecked cement. Despite the protests, there were still tourists, and in those spaces a sense of normalcy reigned.

On Christmas morning, they walked all the way to the Eleventh and huddled at the café tables outside Chambelland as the rain tapered off, drinking hot coffee and sharing pastries. At dusk, they walked past the courtyard of the Louvre, with its Pyramid of glass and light. They strolled through a Christmas market and bought paper cups of mulled wine, but Christopher was nervous—a gunman had shot up a Christmas market in Strasbourg only weeks before. It felt to Minnow that between the protests and the shooting, the whole city was on edge, everyone glancing over their shoulders as they walked, and yet the trappings of Christmas offered a soothing illusion that there had been Christmases before and there would be again: gathered wreaths, string lights, lumières, and safety.

Charles called to wish her a merry Christmas, and hearing him on the other side of the phone filled Minnow with longing. It had been barely any time at all, and still she had missed him. He was at his parents' house, and she could hear voices in the background—muffled laughing, the clink of glasses. Somewhere, a dog barked. A picture coalesced before her eyes: Charles's father and mother, his two brothers, a roaring fire in the fireplace, a maid or two, a wolfhound. A nuclear family drenched in happiness and prosperity. She swallowed back what felt disconcertingly like envy and wished him a joyeux Noël.

"When can I see you again?" Charles asked.

"My father leaves the day after tomorrow," Minnow said.

"I promised my parents I'd help set up their party," Charles said delicately. "But after that . . ."

Minnow smiled. "If the offer is still standing . . . and if you're still in need of a date . . ."

She could hear Charles's smile in return. "As it happens, I am."

Minnow had not thought to get a tree, and so after dinner she and Christopher lit white taper candles that she found in her pantry. She had not thought about gifts either, and so she was surprised when Christopher took out a brown-paper-wrapped parcel.

"I only brought you one," he said with a rueful smile.

"I didn't get you anything," Minnow said, immediately apologetic.

"The past few days were my present," Christopher said. Then, amused: "I don't know if you remember this, but when you were very little, you used to help me wrap your own gifts."

"I did?"

"You really liked wrapping paper. And you didn't like it when I was in a room and you weren't allowed in. I would go into my bedroom to try and wrap your presents and you'd stand in the hallway and cry. So I started just letting you help wrap everything, and then I saw that you enjoyed that more than the actual things." Christopher laughed. "You liked unwrapping, too. You didn't care that you weren't surprised."

Minnow laughed with him. "I don't remember that!"

They were sitting in the living room; lit by the flicker of candles, her apartment felt like a tiny cocoon, placed somewhere outside the stream of time. Minnow held the present in her hand, shook it a little. "Can I open it now?"

"Merry Christmas."

Minnow eased the tape up off the paper with her thumbnail, lifting it open without tearing, and Christopher watched her, smiling.

"That's the way your mom used to open gifts."

They hadn't spoken of her mother since the night of the dinner, and Minnow felt anxiety pulse under her ribs. Christopher had given her the phone number, but she hadn't let herself think about whether she would choose to do anything with it. She folded back the broad edge of brown paper and looked down at the thin flat book, water-stained and dog-eared.

"What is this?"

Christopher turned his mug of tea in his hands, embarrassed. "It's silly, but—it was the first book your mother ever gave me. I've had it all these years and I thought maybe you should have it."

Minnow lifted the book and turned it in her hands. "Anna Akhmatova," she said. "I've never read her."

"'Why is this century worse than those others?'" Christopher quoted, and then smiled: "And she answers that question. Many times."

"Dad, I had no idea you liked poetry."

Christopher's smile lines deepened. "I don't. You know what else Anna Akhmatova said?"

"No," Minnow said, laughing, "tell me."

"'I was born in the right time in whole / Only this time is one that is blessed.'"

"She sounds much more optimistic in that one."

Christopher laughed. "It gets increasingly less optimistic from there. She was the poet of Stalinist Russia—maybe you already know this—but her work was banned. People would memorize her poems and then burn them, whisper them to each other, pass them along."

Minnow thumbed through the book. It was well-read, long loved. She tried to imagine her father reading it—in a dorm room late at night? In a shared apartment? In his lab?

"What's your favorite?"

Christopher smiled. "I'm ashamed to answer that question honestly."

"Oh, come on!"

"My favorite poem is your mother's favorite poem, which she identified for me when she gave me the book. And that is probably *why* it's my favorite poem, and not because I have any taste or discernment of my own. But to this day, it still is."

"Will you show me?"

Christopher reached over and took the book from Minnow. She watched the tenderness with which he turned the pages, as if the book were an old friend with whom he was visiting.

"This is the beginning." And he read out loud: "'Unmoved by the glamour of alien skies, / By asylum in faraway cities, I / Chose to remain with my people: where / Catastrophe led them, I was there.'"

Minnow felt unexpected tears prick her eyes. Christopher stopped reading, staring at the page as if he weren't seeing it. After a moment he said, without lifting his gaze, "You should call her, Min."

"Why?"

Christopher shook his head. "I have tried so hard not to tell you what to do when it comes to your mother—whether or not to pursue her, whether or not to consider her a part of your life. But even if she has failed you as a mother, she may still have something to give you. Maybe just because she is so different from me. And if so, you deserve that, too."

"I don't even know what I'd say," Minnow said. "I grew up without her. Whoever I am, that happened without her. What is there even to say?"

Christopher considered the question from all angles. She could tell that he was turning it over, examining it, turning it again. And in the end he lifted his hands a little, as if to say he didn't know. "You could start by telling her you're all right," he suggested. "And see where it goes from there."

1969

18

APRIL IN CAMBRIDGE WAS WET AND BRUTALLY COLD. IT DID NOT feel like anything could ever begin anew. Keen was constantly raw and chapped, his muscles clenched from walking hunched against the wind. The trials hadn't yet begun but they were all anyone talked about—the charges against Dwight and Ethan in particular. The implication that they had always been dissidents and anarchists but now were murderers, too.

Keen wasn't sure who had named them as leaders, or if the police had simply come to that conclusion because Ethan and Dwight were two of the activists who didn't run when the Boston police pulled rank on the campus police and broke their way into Lowell Lecture Hall at dawn. Perhaps because Ethan and Dwight had not run even when the police started beating students with truncheons, nor when they had thrown an English major out a window. Or perhaps Ethan and Dwight had been close to hand when the police had opened the closet door and found Andrew Hungerford's body, curled on itself. Or perhaps some terrified student, arrested and held overnight the way so many of the protestors were, had pointed the finger in the hopes of being released.

Keen had not been there by then. He had been gone for hours. He had fit his body through a ground-floor window; he had wriggled his way out and dropped like a stone to the hard ground underneath. He had walked away from the building with his shoulders tight and his jaw set, not looking back, fighting the impulse to run and therefore call attention to himself. No one had seen him go. No one knew that he had gone, not even Olya, who had been arrested in the initial wave before Hungerford's body was found. She had been one of many jammed into a Boston police cell, a somber, too-thin girl in a too-thin yellow coat. Nobody had looked at her and thought either *murderer* or *leader*. When the first swell of students was released into daylight, dazed and bruised, Olya had been among them. She would not be on trial when the trials convened. Either it ate at her or she was relieved; Keen did not know which, because he had not been to 5 Wellman since March.

Olya had called his apartment the morning after the occupation, the morning she was released from jail. She had been on a pay phone downtown; he could hear traffic close by. She had told him in an urgent rush that Ethan and Dwight were being held, but that she had just been released. She had told him not to tell anyone, not his lab-mates, not his roommate, who he had seen in the building or even that he'd been there at all. She had told him that the police had asked her strange questions, and that she had been given to believe that they were all being watched carefully. She had told him to stay away from 5 Wellman until things died down. She hadn't seemed surprised that Keen was home to pick up the phone, that he had somehow dodged arrest, and her lack of surprise made him feel like he'd failed her. She hadn't learned of Hungerford's death yet—he had realized that right away—and he had struggled with whether or not to tell her. In the end, the line had seemed too exposed and the moment wrong. He had said nothing, and she had hung up.

The night after the occupation, Andrew Hungerford was on the evening news. In the following days and weeks, he would be all over the newspapers. The most popular photograph of him was one in which he was young and very much alive, staring out at the world with calm confidence. Keen couldn't look him in his pixelated gray eyes. Keen couldn't hear his name. As pundits expounded on a world turned upside down by ruthless and drug-addled draft dodgers, Keen withdrew. He stopped sleeping again. Whenever he closed his eyes he saw Andrew Hungerford's face—not the face he had invented in his previous depression, but the actual man. Andrew's expression of alarm, of fear, of disbelief. The way his face looked when the muscles in it were slack, his neck tilting forward—the moment in which Keen knew what had happened but had not yet named it to himself. He stopped leaving his apartment. He lay in limbo, waiting. He knew that blame would fall like a whip wherever it could, and that, if he kept his mouth shut, there was a chance that it would miss him. Unless Ethan spoke.

That was the one constant at the back of his mind. Somewhere, at some point, Ethan would say: "We left a man to guard Hungerford." Ethan would say: "I don't know what happened, but you should ask that guy." Ethan would say: "Christopher Hunter"; and then they would all come looking for him, gathering on the sidewalk outside his apartment building, pounding on his door. Eventually, as he played this dark prediction out again and again, Keen began to long for it.

And yet more days passed. The world was on fire, the world was normal. The campus was quiet, wounded. People died by the thousands overseas and people went to work here. Nixon was president now, his voice was on the air talking about de-escalation, he repeated "Peace with honor" as if it were the title of a hit single. On local radio, anchors chewed and rechewed the bones of the Lowell Hall occupation, but then they moved on to other campus uprisings elsewhere. First gradually and then all at once, they stopped talking about Andrew Hungerford. Sometimes when Keen turned on the radio, his whole body contracted in a preemptive flinch, all he heard was Sly & the Family Stone's "Everyday People" or Creedence Clearwater Revival's "Proud Mary" or commercials for Pan Am and Raid and Kentucky Fried Chicken.

In bed, Keen stared at the ceiling and thought about March 5. Sometimes he thought about all the days leading to March 5. *I love you,* Olya had said, in a manner of speaking. If she had phrased it as the answer to his question, if she had not spoken the actual words themselves, what did it matter? When Keen replayed it in his head, he played it as *I love you,* putting the words in her voice, until he was so adept at this trick of concentration that he could put other words in her voice as well. *It's going to be all right,* this new Olya told him late at night in his silent bedroom. *Everything is going to be all right, Keen. You did what you had to do. You did exactly what I needed you to do. There are always casualties—Andrew Hungerford knew that; he said it himself, didn't he? There are always casualties in any battle of principles.* And when the sun came up, inevitably, again and again, when the sun came up and kept coming up like a stupid toy fueled by an endless battery, then Keen would blink his gritty, swollen eyes and wonder how much longer it could possibly take before he was arrested.

*

Keen stayed away from 5 Wellman for five weeks. During that time, he heard very little—almost nothing—about what was happening there. He told himself that it was safer not to know, but as time passed, he found a heavy panic had settled into his bones, one that he could not shake even when he was asleep. He startled awake at the smallest sounds; he could not concentrate to read; he could not concentrate on his experiments, and so he stopped doing them. In April there was another occupation on campus, and this helped turn the conversation away from Andrew Hungerford. It was shortly afterward that Keen went to 5 Wellman without calling ahead.

Peter was the one who let Keen in. He had been heating up rice and beans in the kitchen, and the smell of food made Keen's stomach rattle. Keen had been convinced that the whole world had changed, yet Peter looked exactly the same.

"Look who's here," Peter said, with seemingly sincere pleasure, and he hugged Keen. At his touch, something flooded Keen's chest and he held on to Peter with the grip of a drowning man. Peter must have felt his desperation, but he did not comment on it. All he said was: "Let's get you some food."

"Is Olya here?"

Peter released him from the hug, steering him toward the kitchen. "Yes," he said cautiously, "but she's upstairs right now."

"Upstairs?"

"She's packing."

"Packing?" Keen stared at Peter, bewildered. "Packing what?"

Peter hesitated, then said: "She's going to California. For a while."

"For how long? How long is a while?" The anguish in Keen's voice could not be masked. Peter shook his head. "I don't know," he said gently. "I think it's not a bad idea." And then: "Do you want me to call her down?"

"No," Keen said, "I'll go up." He was daring Peter to stop him. Was he hoping Peter would stop him? But Peter just stepped back, and Keen set off up the stairs, his heart racing in his chest.

He found Olya in her room on the third floor. She was kneeling on an overstuffed suitcase, bearing down with her full weight to close it, but at the sound of his footsteps, she lifted her head.

"Keen," she said. He couldn't tell if she was pleased.

"Why California?" he asked wildly. "What's in California?" Now that he was here, after so many days and nights of saying nothing to anyone, he couldn't stop the words from spilling out of him. He was transparent, he was a bowl of water, everything he felt flashed through him and was immediately legible.

"Who told you?" Olya asked, alarmed.

"Peter, just now, downstairs, Peter."

Olya's face cleared, and Keen realized that she looked terrible. She looked like he did—gaunt, pallid, as if she hadn't been sleeping or eating. He had always known her to be in motion, but now anxiety thrummed through her, her teeth worrying at her chapped lips, her head turning sharply when a dog barked on the street below. He had imagined Olya waiting out the storm in a state of calm, and he had been wrong.

Olya got off the suitcase and put her arms around him. He clutched her harder than he'd ever held on to anything, and even as she held him back, he felt her slipping through his fingers.

"Don't go," he said.

"I have to. It's bad here. It's gotten . . ." Olya hesitated. "Nobody's talked to you?"

"No. Do you mean cops? Who?"

"Anybody."

"I haven't talked to a goddamn human in a month," Keen said and started to laugh, and then realized he was crying. The more he tried to stop, the harder he wept. He felt Olya's embrace turn comforting, and he felt her exhaustion at having to comfort him. "I'm sorry," he said. "Fuck, I'm sorry."

"It's okay." Olya let him go and peered up into his face. "You heard about Ethan and Dwight?"

"No, I haven't heard anything."

Olya considered this and nodded slowly. "It's bad." She said again: "It's really bad."

"Are they charging them with . . ." Keen hesitated at the word *murder,* but Olya knew.

"Manslaughter," she said. "Nobody thinks it was murder—the guy had a condition—but I guess he got kinda banged up along the way, I don't know—and they're saying . . ." She hesitated and Keen guessed at the question before she asked it. "You didn't see anything?"

"See anything," Keen echoed. His stomach was lead. He had stopped crying, his entire body had gone numb.

"Yeah, like . . . was he coughing, or . . ." Olya shook her head. "I mean, before you left him, did he seem like anything was . . ."

"Left," Keen repeated.

"Yeah," Olya said impatiently. "You and Ethan dumped him in the closet and then Ethan came down to me and you went . . . wherever, and . . ." Her voice broke and she worked to repair it. "Ethan said that the guy seemed fine."

Tell her, Keen thought. *Tell her.* He felt almost elated: here was the opportunity, it had come to him at last. If he could say the words out loud, in the right order, then Andrew Hungerford's face would stop floating behind his eyes whenever he closed them. If he could say the words out loud, he would buy himself some peace. He knew this. He knew this to be true. All he had to do was tell her.

"That's right," he heard himself say. "He was fine when we left."

Olya nodded. "That's what I thought," she said. "They're fucking framing Ethan. Just because he had charges from before, they're making him the fall guy." She glared up at Keen. "I told him that if things went bad he had to be careful, he had to be especially careful. I told him not to stick around, you know? But he never *listened*, he wouldn't *listen*, he always thought he knew best."

Keen could hear the fault lines in her voice and for a moment he wondered if she would cry, if he would be allowed to hold her. But she swallowed, she shored herself back up.

"Some asshole said he saw Ethan being rough with Hungerford," she said. "Like, dragging him into the closet by his throat or something. That's bullshit, I mean that's bullshit. You were there when he put him in the closet, you didn't see that, did you?"

Some petty part of Keen wanted to object that he hadn't just *been* there, he and Ethan together had put Hungerford in the closet. He had played a role. But he understood that now was not the time for this—that there would never again be a time for this.

"No," he said. "I didn't see anything like that."

"I didn't think so," Olya said fiercely. "I didn't fucking think so."

"But why *California*?" Keen demanded, and it came out as a wail. He could only tolerate the conversation straying so far from this central wound. "What will you do in *California*?"

He thought Olya would have several answers ready, and that each one of them would be rock-solid and inarguable. But instead she was quiet. He had never seen her look so hollow—as if all the life had been poured out of her. "I don't know, Keen."

He thought he would say, "I could go with you." For a moment, he thought he actually *had* said it. What was it that closed his throat? The feeling was visceral, as if a hand had locked around his windpipe. He stared at Olya and he swallowed against the force of Andrew Hungerford's hand. *Tell her*, he thought. *Come clean and then you can go with her, then you can start over. Then there can be a place for you, somewhere in the world, to start over. Once you say out loud what you've done.*

Andrew Hungerford's hand tightened and tightened until Keen was coughing. He held his chest and coughed, and Olya watched him with wide vacant eyes, until finally she realized that it was still her turn to speak. And then she said, "Let's go downstairs. Peter's making some food, we both should eat."

"But will I see you again?" Keen asked.

Olya blinked at him as if he were speaking a language that she'd stopped knowing. "Of course," she said at long last. "I'm sure we will. Of course."

*

He did not know what day she left. He had asked her to tell him, that he might see her off, and she had flinched, as if even the idea were painful. Several days later, he returned to 5 Wellman, and she was gone. Only Daisy was at home, and Daisy was high. She was unsure at first whether or not Keen was real, and so he didn't trust her to accurately report when Olya had left, and what she had said upon leaving. "Did she leave an address?" he asked again and again. "Did she leave a phone number?" Daisy blinked at him, her eyes round and red, shaking her head slowly, in widening circles. "Oh no," she said at last, her voice coming from very far away. "I don't think she plans to be reached at all."

*

The letter from the draft board came in June. Keen felt nothing when he saw the envelope. He felt nothing when he opened it. Many, many months ago, he had imagined a letter arriving in response to his petition for deferment. He had imagined either devastation upon reading a refusal, or wild glee upon reading an acceptance. Now he felt completely disconnected from the letter, the hand that held it, the eyes that scanned it.

There had been an error, they wrote; his previous term of deferment, though on the record, had been accidentally overlooked. He did indeed have two years left to finish his education, after which he would be eligible once again. He put the letter down. He waited for a sensation to make its way into the front of his mind, but he felt nothing, vaguely bored. He had begun going to lab again, because it was better than staying home. He put the letter in the metal lab sink and lit it on fire, blowing it out before the smoke alarm went off. The lab was empty these days; he didn't know what had happened to anyone. If the undergraduate assistants ghosting through the hallways smelled paper burning, they said nothing.

That afternoon, he returned to 5 Wellman. He hadn't been there in weeks. This time the front door was locked. He rang the doorbell again and again, listening to the echo inside, but nobody came to the door. Eventually, he turned around and walked back to his car. He wondered if he felt desperate, but he couldn't locate any feeling at all in his body.

He was pulling the car door open when he realized that someone was calling his name: "Keen! Wait up, Keen."

He turned and saw Peter coming toward him along the narrow flagstone path. It was choked with weeds, as was the scrap of yard into which parties had once spilled.

"Sorry," Peter said as he got closer. "Reporters have been coming around, we just don't answer anymore. But I looked out in case Jonno forgot his key again and I saw you."

"Reporters?"

Peter gave him an odd look. "Yeah," he said. "You didn't hear?"

Keen shook his head. "Hear what?"

Peter's face shifted, and Keen saw that he had decided not to tell Keen whatever it was he hadn't heard. Instead, he said: "I have something for you—I was waiting for you to come back."

"For me?"

Peter held out a book. "Olya left it behind," he said. "I thought maybe you'd want to have it."

Keen blinked at Peter. It took a moment to realize that Peter was holding the Akhmatova book from which Olya had once read to him. After a moment, Keen took it. It was so light in his hand, barely there, the pages rumpled and stained. He remembered Olya reading aloud, the way her eyes had glittered in the near-dark. A bookmark was shoved carelessly in place, and when he opened to the page, his eyes fell on the first few lines: "Unmoved by the glamour of alien skies, / By asylum in faraway cities, I / Chose to remain with my people . . ."

Olya had not chosen to remain. Had she left the book because she no longer wanted it, or because she hoped it would find its way to him? Was he an idiot, always trying to read more into her most meaningless of gestures, destined to never be satisfied by the answers?

His throat tightened, an unbearable ache, and he closed the book hastily. "Thanks," he muttered.

Peter's voice was gentle when he said, "You look really bad."

"Do I?" Keen hadn't looked himself in the face in months. It had become unthinking habit never to look in a mirror, never to chase his own reflection.

"Yeah." Peter hesitated and then he asked, "Wanna take a jaunt?"

Keen imagined himself going back to lab. The emptiness of it, the silence. Whatever was going on in the university, it had trickled all the way down to the Mallinckrodt basement. Cavener didn't even come anymore. He imagined going home, and his whole body rejected the idea. Sheila had moved out, and though Keen felt relief at her absence, the apartment had become a tomb.

"Sure," he said.

"Let me drive?"

"Sure."

He slid into the passenger seat, and Peter crossed around to the driver's side. Keen didn't ask where they were going, because it didn't matter to him. When the engine started, he closed his eyes, and faster than he would have thought possible, rocked by the motion of the car, he fell asleep.

*

When Keen opened his eyes again, the car had come to a stop. They were parked at the end of a long spit of land that jutted straight out into the ocean. Tough spindly trees grew in close clumps on sandy, unforgiving soil.

Keen dug his fists into his eyes. "Hi," he said.

"Good afternoon," Peter said from the seat next to him. He opened the car door and the wind blew in, sharp and briny. Peter unfolded himself, stretching, and began to walk into the thin line of wind-warped trees. There were no houses here, no other cars. Keen followed. They broke through the trees, arriving on a crescent shaving of rocky beach. Beyond it, the sea unspooled into the gray haze of the sky.

Peter toed off his socks and shoes, leaving them where they fell, and walked barefoot into the damp pebbly sand. After a moment, Keen followed in this as well. The cold on his bare skin was a shock that jolted upward through his spine. It was pure feeling, like someone hitting an on/off switch between his body and his mind. *Oh,* he thought, shocked. *You're still here.* Without looking to see if Keen would follow, Peter walked down to the tide line and came to a stop. Keen joined him and they stood shoulder to shoulder, watching the waves reach for them and then slip past them.

"What is this place?" Keen asked at last.

"I come here sometimes."

"How'd you find it?"

"Someone showed me." Peter smiled. "Lost him, but I kept the spot."

"I'm sorry."

Peter hitched one shoulder in a shrug. "It's okay. The spot suited me better than the relationship, it turned out."

"Was that recently?"

"Oh, no. God, no. Years ago. When I first moved here." Peter pulled his jacket tighter against the wind. "He was married, and I knew it was a bad idea from the start, but I was crazy about him. I mean, I thought I might actually lose my mind. And when we broke up . . . I remember I just felt like *How is it possible that everybody else is okay?*" Peter laughed. "I remember walking around Cambridge and just . . . looking *so* closely at everybody I passed, because I thought, *They can't possibly be fine. I'm in so much pain it can't just . . . not matter.* Right? Except of course everybody *was* fine—or they were in their own private pain, which was completely unrelated to mine. It's strange, how our own feelings are so large that, for us, they blot out the sun. But meanwhile, everybody else is getting a tan."

Seagulls arced overhead in widening loops, their plaintive voices carrying down in shards of sound. Keen shook the hair out of his eyes. His voice sounded gravelly with disuse to his own ears. "Why did you break up?"

"Well. There was the whole wife thing."

"Did she know . . . ?"

"I think, in the interests of preserving the parts of our lives that we

like, most of us work very hard not to know the things we know."
Peter turned then, his eyes warm on Keen's face. "But then . . . at a
certain point, it all leaks through. Doesn't it? And it just knocks us
out."

Keen hadn't realized that he was biting his inner lip until the taste
of copper warmed his mouth. He heard himself speaking, unsteady
but unable to stop. "When we first met, Olya said that I was thinking
in a vacuum—that everything I care about, scientific knowledge,
there's a human application that corrupts it. And I thought, *What a
sad and limited way to see the world.* But now I think she's right. I
think I'm . . . corrupt in a way that I never . . . And given that, it's
hard for me to . . . I don't know. Get up in the morning. And she's
gone and I just. I don't know, I don't know what to do, just that I
should've done everything differently." Keen cut himself off, shaking
his head. "I know how this sounds."

"How does it sound?"

"Like so much whining. Ethan is on fucking trial, and I didn't
even get sent to war after all, not this year—and I'm . . . what? *Sad?*"
Keen sliced the word with his teeth. "Fuck me, I'm sad."

"Hey." Peter put a hand on Keen's arm, briefly. "Things got fucked
up. We all get to be sad."

Keen wondered if Peter knew what he'd done. For a moment, the
impulse he had had with Olya was alive once more: *Tell him, tell him.*
But what would the words be? How would he build the sentences to
say the thing that he had practiced never saying?

"You seem okay though," Keen said, instead. "Actually, you always
seem okay."

"Do I?" Peter laughed. "Maybe so. I didn't used to be."

"How?" Keen asked, and realized he was asking from the heart,
nearly pleading. He wanted to clarify the question—*How do I do it?*
maybe, or *How is it possible?* But Peter seemed to understand
anyway.

"She didn't leave *you*," he said. "She just left. She just—hit her
limits, and she had to go." Keen opened his mouth but Peter kept
speaking, his voice soft.

"People give you what they can," he said, "within their limits. This is what I've learned. It's the same with a country, with the world. Beauty, within limits. If you learn to value the least of what is possible, you'll never go hungry. You'll always have a reason to get up in the morning."

*

That night, alone in the lab, Olya's book tucked inside his jacket, Keen thought carefully about what Peter had said. He turned it over and over in his mind, considering the idea as a map, tracing a path along which you might walk for the rest of your life—a straight and steady road that did not take you off the edge of a cliff. It seemed at odds with the ideas that had formed a map for Olya and Ethan and the others: that the world could not be borne as it was, that it must be reshaped, no matter the cost. But perhaps it wasn't a contradiction so much as an addendum, Keen thought. The world must be remade, but if it could not be, perhaps you could derive a measure of happiness from the crumbs. Or perhaps: the world must be remade, but the remaking takes time—generations, even—and so this is how you manage your lifetime without surrendering to despair.

When he thought about it this way, it seemed to Keen that he could see a bigger picture emerging, but every time he began to look closer, it drifted away. He was more exhausted than he had ever been, but afraid to go home and watch the darkness shift into gray light across the ceiling of his bedroom. He put his head down on the top of his lab bench and sat that way for a time, the wood making grooves in his forehead. He fell asleep and woke up, disoriented and still bathed in the subterranean glow of fluorescent lighting. He thought he had only been asleep for a short time, but when he went upstairs to go home, he found that it was already dawn.

Walking home across the sleeping campus, his body ached, but his mind was, for the first time in a long time, unalterably clear. *The least of what is possible,* he thought to himself. One after another, images came to mind and were replaced by other images: Olya laughing across the table at 5 Wellman; Olya rolling her eyes at Dwight Beachum; Olya running toward him across the parking lot on the day of the Dow recruiter. Olya staring at him with her fierce, despairing gaze as she asked: "You were there when they put him in the closet, you didn't see anything, did you?" One after the other after the other, and then they were gone, and Keen was alone in the gathering dawn. *The least of what is possible,* he told himself, and this time, he pointed it toward his future like a promise.

2018

19

THE OFFICES OF MICHEL VERNIER WERE IN A BEAUTIFUL OLD building tucked off the Avenue de Friedland. As Minnow's cab navigated the traffic circle around the Arc de Triomphe, she leaned her forehead against the cold glass and gazed up through a haze of lights. Traffic was heavy, and from a standstill, she watched groupings of tourists who had clearly hoped to outstrategize other tourists—and possibly also the protests—by coming to the Arc in the evening. The air was calm, although only days earlier this exact scrap of earth had been the site of bloody skirmishes: the police in their body armor, the gilets jaunes dashing forward and falling back. Minnow had watched the footage later, and Charles and Luc had been right—the camera's focus was on the Arc, rising coolly above it all, this time uncaptured. Minnow saw no footage of the less iconic streets where cars and barricades had burned.

The cab pulled loose from the roundabout and slid to a stop alongside the Vernier compound. Large indigo double doors marked the entranceway, a gold plaque shining dully on the right-hand door. A high iron fence encircled a lush garden. As the cab pulled away, Minnow hesitated, unsure how to proceed. She was saved by an arriving couple, who buzzed, announced themselves, and then held the heavy blue door open for her to follow. The man was wearing a well-tailored suit and the woman wore an expensive green silk dress. Minnow felt painfully underdressed in her own black jeans, the nicest of her sweaters, her gray peacoat. She had washed and brushed her hair, she had even applied makeup—something she rarely did—but somehow she had not stopped to ask if the best of the clothes she had would be good enough.

Cheeks burning, Minnow followed the couple into a large court-yard. The air was cleaner and denser here. The smell of wet leaves, the sound of water rushing. They crossed the cobblestones to a building directly across from the entryway, and the man pressed the second buzzer. When the door buzzed open, he nodded to the woman to precede him, then took Minnow in and gallantly nodded to her to precede him as well. She did, to be polite, falling back as soon as she had entered and pretending to fumble for something inside her pock-etbook so that she could trail behind them.

She heard the sounds of the party before they emerged at the top of the stairs, into the open stretch of wide, high-ceilinged rooms. People milled and swam before her eyes in a sea of suits, vividly col-ored dresses, the flash of red lipstick, the shine of earrings. Glasses of wine and champagne lifting and touching, a great glass chandelier spilling fragments of light across the walls. She could always walk out now and tell Charles she hadn't been able to get here. The traffic, maybe, or she had gotten lost, or—

"Puis-je prendre votre manteau?"

Minnow turned to see a pretty girl with matte red lipstick and a black turtleneck. "Oh," Minnow said uncertainly, reluctant to hand her coat over and expose the insufficiencies of her sweater.

"Minnow!" Charles slipped out of the press of bodies. It took her a moment to recognize him in a dark blazer and well-fitting black pants that she had never seen before. His hair was combed so that it didn't fall into his eyes. He looked poised, wealthy, and again she felt a gnawing unease in the pit of her stomach that she had not under-stood correctly how to pass in this world.

"You actually came." Charles sounded surprised, as if he had read her mind.

"It might not have been for the best," Minnow said. "I think I'm underdressed."

"But that's ridiculous, you look perfect."

Because the girl was still patiently standing there, waiting for directions, Minnow gave in and handed over her coat. Charles pressed a glass of wine into her hand in return.

"Here." He leaned in and kissed her briefly and she smelled the familiar scent of his skin, and the less-familiar musk of a cologne she didn't know. "Taste this obscenely expensive wine, and then have a few more glasses, and then eventually we will be home in bed." He leaned in again and said low, his lips brushing her ear: "Yours or mine."

As she moved slowly through the press of bodies with Charles at her side, Minnow's anxiety began to ease. Bowing his head to murmur into her ear, Charles described the couples he walked her past: "That's Guillaume Leclerc, he's one of the partners in my father's firm; that's his wife, Jeanne, she's a former dancer and an alcoholic; that's Sophie Jusseau, she's a famous theatre actress; her husband is—oh, over there, that's him, he runs a fancy restaurant in le Marais; that's Yannick, my older brother; that's his girlfriend Marie, she's much cooler than he is, but unfortunately she is also a lawyer; oh, right there, do you see the man with the jowls? (That is the word, yes, *jowl*?) He is also a close friend of notre ami Emmanuel Macron, speed dial in the mobile, don't ask me what he does, but he has money."

"And who's that?"

Charles lifted his head to study the target before he lowered it again: "He is a judge, and that man beside him is his boyfriend, but they both have wives, and the wives . . . oh, the wives are over there, at the bar, they may also be girlfriends at this point, the arrangement has lasted so long."

"You're joking," Minnow said, laughing into her drink, and Charles's smile lived in his eyes, though his mouth stayed serious as he said: "Am I?"

Charles had just obtained each of them a new glass from a circulating tray when he glanced over Minnow's shoulder and his face shifted. "Ah," he said, almost to himself, and then to Minnow: "Don't panic, but my father is coming to say hello."

"Did you just say 'Don't panic'?" Minnow demanded, even as

Charles was saying, with a level of formality that Minnow had not heard from him before: "Papa, puis-je te présenter à mon amie, Minerva?"

Michel Vernier was a tall and imposing man, dressed simply but elegantly in a tuxedo jacket and slacks. Minnow could see his son in his face—the clear-cut cheekbones and the jaw—but his eyes were his own: pure and polished gray, eyes that showed very little and missed even less. He held out his hand and Minnow took it. His grip was firm and warm.

"Minerva, welcome," he said, as if it were natural that he should address her in English. Minnow wondered what Charles had said about her ahead of time. "I am so pleased that you could join us tonight."

"Monsieur Vernier," Minnow said. "Thank you for having me."

"How are you enjoying your sojourn in Paris?"

Minnow thought briefly of racing through the dark streets hand in hand with Charles, the police line closing behind them, and she said, "Very much, thank you. It is a beautiful city."

"I've spent some time in Washington," Vernier said, "and New York. I don't believe I've had the pleasure to visit much else of America."

"You missed very little," Minnow said.

Charles's father smiled politely. They made small talk, Charles resolutely at her side. Minnow knew that the words they were speaking were not what was actually happening. Vernier's courtesy was a smokescreen behind which a series of swift calculations were occurring, though she could not read what they were. Minnow kept her face arranged to a similar blank pleasantness, but she felt her chest tightening.

"Charles, chéri, je te cherchais!"

The voice made them turn, and Minnow knew right away that she was looking at Charles's mother. She was the one from whom Charles had gotten his large dark eyes, and they shone out at Minnow. Her mouth was thin, her face rounder than her son's, and there was an air of grandeur that didn't eclipse her warmth. She peered at Minnow with a gaze that made Minnow certain she had been watching from across the room, although all she said as Charles hurried to make the introduction was: "Bienvenue, a friend of Charles is a friend of ours." Her English was lightly accented but nearly perfect.

"Thank you so much for having me," Minnow repeated, and shook her hand as well. Her grip was lighter than her husband's, but she held Minnow's hand for a beat before she released it. She had given her name as Suzanne, but Minnow was uncertain whether or not to use it.

"It's our pleasure, of course. You are from the United States, yes?"

"I am."

"I lived in California," Suzanne said. "When I was much younger—I studied for a time at Berkeley. Do you know it?"

"Yes," Minnow said, "of course."

"I loved it. It is very different from the rest of America, I think, it is very . . ." Suzanne made a gesture and settled on the approving adjective: "European."

"Maman," Charles said, a gentle warning against a well-worn topic.

"What? I am not allowed to talk about Berkeley?"

"You are of course allowed to talk about whatever you like," Charles murmured into his drink.

"Charles thinks it's embarrassing when I talk about America," Suzanne said to Minnow, but the teasing was for her son. "Or art, or literature, or wine."

Charles smiled at his mother over his glass. "You're always permitted to talk about wine," he said. "As it's a subject on which we agree."

Watching Charles and his parents, Minnow had a new vision of him: a precocious boy staying up late in the midst of adult conversations, more at ease with his parents' friends than with children his own age. She had not expected his comfort here, although of course she should have. This was his world, after all. But what surprised her was that this was a world in which he seemed not just placed but rooted.

As Charles's mother talked about an exhibit of American artists that she had curated, back when she still ran a gallery, Minnow shot a glance at Charles. He stood with his shoulder grazing hers, sipping from his glass while his eyes traveled over the room. A new thought struck her: in a circle like this, there would be only so many things you could do to shock your parents in a way that was both irreproachable and stylish. Drugs would be tacky, refusing to attend college would be banal and probably boring. But a girlfriend who was American, incorrectly classed, and much too old—that would be a coup, because what could your parents do but greet her and make small talk with her, what could everybody in the room do but dart glances at your parents as they were forced to extend their hospitality in the wrong direction?

Minnow felt her palms get cold. Was that what this was to him? But—no, she told herself swiftly, that could not be *all* this was. Some of it, maybe. Maybe even unbeknownst to him, some of it. But certainly not all. Charles skimmed the back of her hand with one finger, still gazing in the opposite direction, their hands hidden from his parents.

"You've come at a very tumultuous time," Suzanne was saying. Minnow noticed that Vernier had taken a back seat to his wife, although he was following the conversation, his eyes moving between his wife's face and Minnow's.

"Have I?"

"Yes! You can't have missed it, all of the . . ." Suzanne made a gesture toward the outside.

"Oh," Minnow said. "That. No, I—I haven't missed it."

" 'That,' " Suzanne echoed, and laughed. "I love how blasé Americans can be. But then your country also has a long history—when I was in Berkeley, too, so many riots!"

Minnow couldn't help her gaze sliding sideways to Charles, who was primed to say the word *protests* automatically whenever he heard the word *riots,* but to her surprise, Charles was quiet, his eyes cast downward at the carpet.

"Yes, well," Minnow said uneasily. "I suppose change comes at a cost everywhere."

She thought she had kept her voice entirely neutral, but Vernier's keen eyes landed on her. His voice was jocular when he said, "Yes, of course, there are people who want change of some kind, but I find that gets lost when the majority starts burning and looting. It is an unfortunate thing, because then everybody stops listening."

Again Minnow waited for Charles to speak up as he had done with her own father, but he sipped his wine, his eyes skating across the room. Someone nodded at him and he nodded back.

"I'm no expert," Minnow said, keeping her tone as easy as Vernier's, "but my impression is that in the absence of noise, things often get buried. It's very easy to sweep *silent* people under the rug."

Tension radiated off Charles's body beside her, but still he said nothing.

"That is a gracious euphemism for what is happening," Vernier said. " 'Noise.' But tell me, this is also the problem in America, no? There are those who want concrete actions, but then the mob weighs in, and . . ." He made an elegant gesture: *And so it goes.* "Discourse happens between two or five or ten people. The idea of democracy was never to listen to the mob—it was that a small group of people might engage in discourse on behalf of everybody else."

"Men," Minnow said, without meaning to.

"I'm sorry?"

"A small group of men. No?" She searched Vernier's mild gaze for contempt but couldn't be sure whether or not she found it.

"It doesn't have to be," he replied.

"But that *is* what it looks like, generally? And when all the decisions are made by a small group of men—perhaps they're men of privilege, whose understanding or experience doesn't account for the realities of everyone else—the decisions they're making don't really solve everyone's problems. Do they?"

Once again Minnow glanced at Charles. He didn't meet her eyes. She felt the shock of betrayal.

"I don't think *anyone* can solve *everyone's* problems," Vernier said tolerantly. "Do you?"

Minnow felt her heart speeding up in her chest. She could not call his tone condescending, exactly, and yet he was not speaking to her as if she were his equal. She felt as if she were back at Sewell, standing before Dean Kaye, summoned to account for herself.

"I think that people who understand and share the problems of the majority are more likely to understand what the solutions look like," Minnow said. She heard an unsteadiness in her voice and hated it. Vernier was not a man who would respect unsteadiness. And suddenly she wondered why she was always in a position where she was working to earn the respect of men who never once thought to earn hers. The flare of anger turned her toward Charles: "Charles," she said pointedly, "what do you think?"

His eyes jolted up to meet hers, and she saw he was alarmed. Vernier's eyebrows twitched upward, but his face was impassive as he turned to his son, courteously. "Charles?"

Charles was silent. He looked anguished. After a moment, he mumbled something.

"What did you say?" Vernier inquired.

"It's complicated," Charles repeated, his voice so low it barely lifted above the din of the room.

Minnow stared at Charles, aghast. She found that she couldn't recognize this boy who stared at the carpet, at his wineglass, at strangers bobbing and nodding across the room, anywhere but at his father. She had understood that there was tension between Charles and his father, of course, but she had assumed the tension came from Charles's conviction and his ability to articulate it, not his timid, dissociated silence. Minnow caught a flicker of discomfort on Suzanne's face.

"Darling," Suzanne murmured. "We should . . ."

Vernier ignored his wife and son, speaking to Minnow. He knew he had won, and he managed to sound both triumphant and sympathetic. "In the last two years, I have seen things in your country that genuinely defy belief. Truly, I think all of Europe has been shocked by the behavior of your leader, as I know many Americans are. But even in the case of America I would say, the imperfect practice of democracy is not an excuse to abolish it entirely." Vernier smiled at her. His teeth were very even. "I'm sure you would agree."

"My love." Suzanne took her husband's arm, even as she lifted her hand in a wave to a group of women across the room, who waved back gaily. "I told Martine we'd be right over."

"It was a pleasure to meet you," Vernier said gallantly to Minnow. "I hope you enjoy yourself this evening."

Before Minnow could respond, Suzanne steered her husband firmly into the crowd. In the silence, Charles took a deep breath. Minnow became aware that she did not want to hear him speak now that his father was gone. She felt something in her throat that tasted like disgust. Even as Charles opened his mouth, she cut him off: "Where's the ladies' room?"

Charles nodded toward the stairs. "The alcove," he said, and might have said more, but Minnow was already slipping through the throng. The wood-framed alcove that Charles had indicated contained a small door with a stained-glass window; just beyond it, a set of broad marble steps led down and up, to offices on other floors.

Minnow let herself into what turned out to be a single cubicle with both toilet and sink, locking the door behind her. Alone, she exhaled slowly, then leaned in to examine her face in the mirror. She looked tired. Lines carved at the corners of her eyes; below her eyes, the skin bagged, thin and purplish. She did not apply makeup often and therefore she did not do it well. What had Charles's father thought, looking at her face? He must have thought she was tacky on so many levels—for the fatigue and aging she hadn't effortlessly concealed, for her American voice with its flat nasal vowels, for her bad sweater and her legible indignation. Was that why Charles had been rendered speechless? Had he been ashamed of Minnow? Had he felt himself unable to defend his opinions when standing beside her?

She had been looking forward to seeing Charles ever since her father had left the day before. She had wanted to tell him about her time with Christopher, what he had revealed to her, even about having been given her mother's phone number. She had imagined Charles as an antidote to her father's exhausted pessimism. Now disappointment weighed heavily on her.

Enough of this, Minnow told herself. This is stupid. She would find him and tell him that she was going home. He could stay here and play the part of the good son, but she had no such obligations. She didn't want to see him like this. It made him small.

Minnow flung open the bathroom door and nearly walked into Charles, who was waiting for her just outside.

"Fuck this," Charles said. "Let's go."

Caught off guard, Minnow blinked at him. "You want to go?"

Charles ran a hand over his face. He still couldn't quite meet her gaze, but a muscle jumped in the side of his cheek. "I think it's best."

"Okay," Minnow said. "Then let's go."

*

Out in the street, Charles lit a cigarette and offered her one as well. She shook her head and he stuffed the packet back into his coat pocket. The night had become cold, and Minnow wished she had dressed more warmly. She should have known that she did not have what it took to be stylish, and then at least she could have been warm.

They walked for several blocks without speaking, and then Charles said, into the tense quiet, "I'm sorry."

Minnow considered pretending that she didn't know what he meant. In the end, she said nothing.

Charles glanced at her. "I say I won't let him get to me, but . . . Every time, it takes him nothing."

"Did he get to you?"

"Yes, and he knew it." Charles shook his head. "He wears you down—there's no arguing, there's no—he always has an answer."

"But you weren't arguing." Minnow tried to keep the accusation out of her voice and didn't succeed. "You didn't say anything."

Charles flinched. "What was there to say?" he muttered sullenly.

"You didn't seem to have any trouble finding something to say to *my* father," Minnow said, and then regretted it. She took a breath. "I'm sorry."

"No," Charles said miserably, "you're right." They walked together for half a block, the sound of their shoes loud on the pavement. Then: "This is the thing about my father. He never misses a moment of your failing—his eyes have been trained for weakness, and he sees it every-where. And when you are the child of such a man, no matter what is said or not said, this becomes the biggest thing between you: how he sees your weakness and how you see him see it. And over the years . . . the way to win is not to fight. Show him nothing, not even an opin-ion. But seeing you stand up to him . . . The way you spoke to him . . ." Charles turned to Minnow then, meeting her gaze steadily. "You had no weakness."

Tenderness engulfed Minnow. She slid her arm through Charles's and shook him gently. "He's just your father," she said. "I know what it feels like—how hard it is to look him in the face and say, 'You're wrong.' But you have to. There's a whole chapter of your life that lies on the other side of standing up to him—it can't begin until you do."

"Is this your new chapter?" Charles asked, gesturing a wide arc to the streets around them. He was joking, but Minnow answered him seriously.

"Yeah," she said. "I think it is."

Charles pulled her closer to him. "I'm glad to be in it," he said. His voice was rough, though he was staring straight ahead. And she thought that was the end of the conversation, so she was surprised when, several blocks later, Charles said into the hush: "I'm going to do it."

"Do what?" she asked, and he replied:

"Give Luc the offices."

2019

20

THE MORNING AFTER SETTING THE FIRE, MINNOW HAD FELT FULLY, astonishingly alive.

Within days, she would doubt herself. Within a week, she would feel ashamed, she would ask how she had been capable of such a thing. Three months down the road, her plane touching down in Paris, she would summon the memory of Dean Kaye's garage and feel as if she had been suspended in a state of madness. But that morning, with the smell of smoke still in her hair, Minnow had woken and the world had looked different to her. It was as if a film had been peeled away, and she could see with an incandescent clarity.

She was ravenous that morning. She made herself a full breakfast, although normally all she had was a cup of coffee. She scrambled eggs, she buttered toast, she had no bacon but she sliced apples and oranges and put them in a bowl. She ate standing at the kitchen counter, too hungry to carry the food across the kitchen to the breakfast nook. After she had finished, she washed the dishes, showered, put on her nicest jeans and her teaching blazer, and went to Sewell School to resign.

Dean Kaye's secretary looked nonplussed when Minnow walked in. Minnow had never spoken with her beyond a sentence or two. Now she looked at the other woman and felt pity for her, that her whole life revolved around serving a man who was not in control of his own destiny.

"I'm sorry," the secretary said. "You don't have an appointment with Dean Kaye, do you?"

"He's been trying to get ahold of me," Minnow said.

"I just—I'm sorry, he's just not in today is the thing. There was an unplanned—he had sort of a family—emergency."

"An emergency," Minnow repeated. Her heart sped up in her chest, but her voice was smooth, completely normal. "Oh no. I hope everything's all right?"

The secretary lowered her voice, although they were the only two people present. "His house burned down," she said. "Last night."

"His *house*?" Minnow shook her head. "That's terrible. His whole *house*?"

The secretary frowned. "I'm not sure," she said, backtracking, "but there was a fire. It started in the garage, I think? Dean Kaye called this morning and said he wouldn't be in."

"That's terrible," Minnow said again. Her voice oozed sympathy. Her veins coursed with adrenaline.

The secretary frowned a little. "Maybe I can take a message?"

Minnow wondered if her tone had sounded slightly wrong in some way. More gleeful than sympathetic. Guilty, even? But she didn't feel guilty. She felt the desire to lean across the desk between them and say: *I did it. It was me. See how I can leave my fingerprints on this place, see how I won't lie low and be hunted.*

Minnow reined these instincts in and cleared her throat. "Well," she said, "I was coming to tender my resignation."

The secretary took a second look at her, and Minnow saw, to her own surprise, that the woman was recognizing her for the first time. She had thought of herself as marked, instantly familiar to anyone who saw her face. But in truth she must have looked like just another teacher, relatively indistinguishable from all the other white women with mousy brown hair and unremarkable blazers.

"Oh," the secretary said, flustered. "Oh, of course, I didn't . . . Miss Hunter, is that right?"

"That's right," Minnow said. She heard her own voice, and it sounded cheerful.

The secretary seemed even more flustered by this. "Ah," she said. "Yes. Well. I'll let Dean Kaye know that you stopped by."

"Thank you," Minnow said. She turned to go. Then she turned back: "Do they have any idea how it happened?"

"I'm sorry?"

"The fire—was it electrical, or . . . ?"

"I don't know," the secretary said. "He didn't say anything about that, he just said—you know, that he won't be in today."

"Well, I hope everything turns out all right," Minnow said generously and walked out without looking back.

For the rest of that long, sunlit day, Minnow took herself through the town as if she had never seen it before. She parked on the main street and walked past the small galleries and shops, the little cafés, the mom-and-pop restaurants. She walked all the way to the far end of the stretch, where it got less cute and towny: the Walmart, the coin laundry. When people looked at her, she stared straight back at them—not defiant or braced against their contempt, but utterly curious. She absorbed their details: the fine lines around their mouths and in their foreheads, how their faces shifted as they glared back or glanced away. She had thought of all of them as a faceless, malevolent force, a great wave of hatred rising up to crash down over her life. That afternoon, she saw them as a scattering of droplets, each droplet unique and fragile, capable of being destroyed by her.

Why did nobody tell me this before? she wondered, walking back to her car in the long late shadows of the afternoon. *My whole life, everybody just told me to watch out—for bad men, trouble, danger. Why did nobody tell me I could be dangerous, too?*

*

The night before the Vernier occupation, four days into the new year, Minnow called her mother. She did not know she would do it; she was not certain until Charles had fallen asleep, and even then she held out the possibility that she wouldn't. Curled in bed under the portrait of Charles's great-grandmother, listening to the soft even cadence of his breathing, Minnow gently extricated her shoulder from beneath him. He stirred but didn't awaken. She searched for her clothes, found neither her underwear nor her shirt, pulled on her jeans and sweater. Making her way into the hall, she shut the bedroom door behind her.

The living room was dark except for the orange glow from the woodstove's bed of embers. Minnow sat cross-legged on the floor, warm boards creaking as she settled. She asked herself if she was really going to do this. When there was no answer, she fumbled with her phone, hands shaking as she searched for the number that Christopher had given her. She hadn't even put it in her contacts list—she had not been ready for that—and now she went through her Notes app, scrolling until she found it. No name attached, just the number itself. She did the math in her head quickly: it was just after midnight here, which would make it late afternoon in Oregon. She dialed, and as the phone rang, she considered hanging up. Christopher had said the number was a landline, so Olya might not even know that her daughter had tried to call. Minnow could just disconnect and it would be as if she had never—

"Hello?"

The voice of a woman, a little breathless, as if she had rushed for the phone.

"Olya?"

"Oh, just a sec." The woman must have covered the receiver with her hand, because her voice was muffled as she called: "Olya! Phone for you, sweetie!"

Minnow realized, with a dropping sensation in her guts, that she had assumed she would recognize her mother's voice. But she hadn't heard it since she was a baby—how could she possibly know what Olya would sound like? She had only ever imagined Olya alone—isolated, regretting her decision to leave them. It hadn't occurred to her that Olya would live in a place where someone else might pick up the phone when it rang, where someone might call her sweetie.

"Hello?"

When she had imagined making the call, Minnow had not walked herself through this next part. She had not planned what to say, because it had been important to her to believe that she would not actually call until she did. So it should not have felt like such a failure of composure when the word tumbled out of her mouth: "Mom?"

There was a winded silence, and then: "Minerva?"

"Minnow."

"Minnow. Hello." Olya's voice was careful, as if she were afraid she would scare Minnow off the line.

"Is now an okay time?"

"Yes, of course. Yes. Just—give me half a second." The sound of her mother moving across a room, an ocean away. Then Olya's voice, close and clear again: "The phone is in my study, so . . . I was just shutting the door."

Her study. Minnow tried to see it: bookshelves? A desk? A rag rug? Would it be cozy, this study, or would it be coolly minimal? What did she use it for? What did Olya do with her days?

"Are you still there?" Olya asked.

"Yeah, yes."

"Did your dad give you this number?"

"Yeah."

"I'm glad." Olya was quiet, then: "He said you're in Paris now? Is that right?"

"You've been talking?"

Olya cleared her throat, as if the question embarrassed her. "He called me to let me know he'd seen you and that you were okay. I hope that was all right."

Minnow wasn't sure, so she said nothing.

"Are you still there?"

"Yes," Minnow said again. "I'm still here."

"I wrote to you." Uncertainty was in her mother's voice now. "Keen said you never got it?"

"I think I'd already been fired from Sewell by the time you emailed me there."

"I'm sorry that happened," Olya said. "I heard—I was following the news, and when I realized— It was a crazy thing, the way that was handled. By the town and the school and . . . A lot of media outlets, they made me furious, trying to 'both sides' the thing, and it was like—there are no 'both sides,' either you believe that a woman— fuck that, a *human*—gets to control their body or you don't."

To her everlasting surprise, Minnow's eyes filled with tears. This she had not anticipated, but hearing the fierce sincerity with which Olya defended her filled a void she had not known was present. "I know," she said, trying to keep her voice steady. "I know."

"You know the part that makes me scream?" Olya sounded more comfortable now, as if this were territory she understood. "When it comes to *men,* everybody in the country agrees that they've gotta be in charge of their bodies. You know? If you're killed in a car crash or whatever, your organs aren't up for grabs. You have to expressly be an organ donor. Even though you can't even use it anymore, it's understood that your decision about your body matters. But that argument goes right out the window when it comes to women and sex."

"I never thought about that," Minnow said. "The organ donor thing."

"I didn't either," Olya admitted. "Some young person posted it on social media, one of those platforms—I'm not really on any of them, but Linda told me about it. She's got all that stuff, Facebook and whatever."

"Linda?"

Olya hesitated. "I don't know if your dad mentioned . . ."

"He didn't mention anything."

"Oh . . . Linda is my . . . my companion."

In the silence, Minnow thought about all the things *companion* could mean and made the choice not to ask. There were limits to what she wanted to know about her mother, and limits to what she wanted to say. At least this time.

"Are you still—"

"Yeah, I'm right here."

"I'm sorry, I guess I'm . . ." Olya exhaled hard into the phone, a sort of laugh. "Nervous. I'm really nervous. I didn't know if I'd ever hear from you."

"No, that's my line," Minnow said. She was too disconcerted to be angry, but she heard her own voice and it sounded icy. "*I* didn't know if I'd ever hear from *you.*"

"Okay," Olya said quietly. "That's fair." The air stretched thin between them, and then Olya sighed. "You know, I've asked myself over the years what I would say to you when you came calling and you had questions or . . . you were angry or . . . What would I say about myself that could possibly . . . But I never found anything good to say, so I just swore I'd be honest. Whatever you want to ask me, Minerva—Minnow—I'll tell you. Honestly."

Inside the small glass-windowed door of the woodstove, embers shifted. Flames licked upward briefly without conviction, fire moving in the coals like it was twitching in its sleep. Minnow had had questions her whole life. Christopher had not been a place to put them and so she had stored them away, one by one, inside her chest. Now she could summon nothing. Her mind was an utter blank.

At the thought of her father, she asked: "Did Dad tell you that he and I weren't talking?"

"No," Olya said. "He didn't say that."

"Before he came to Paris, I mean. We hadn't been talking."

"No, he didn't say anything like that."

"What *did* he say?"

"He said . . . Well, he told me a little bit about you. He said you'd grown up to be . . . just a really good kid. I'm sorry, a good *person*. And I asked him how you'd been doing, of course, with all that horrible Sewell stuff . . . and he said you were really strong."

"Is *that* what he said?" Minnow laughed, then realized her voice had lifted, and she dropped it again, hoping not to wake Charles.

"You sound surprised." When Minnow was quiet, Olya tried again. "You helped that girl when other people wouldn't have. I think that's strong."

"I don't think I helped Katie." Minnow hadn't intended to say this, but it spilled out. "I know I'm not supposed to say this, but I don't think I did her any favors. Her family pulled her out of school, they're horrified at her, she feels—felt, maybe feels?—that she's going to hell . . . I mean, how exactly did I help?"

"She doesn't have a child that she doesn't want and can't take care of," Olya said staunchly. "That's how you helped."

"I guess you'd know about that," Minnow said, without intending to. In the slapped silence that followed, she was as shocked as Olya. "I'm sorry," she said at the same time as Olya said, "It's all right. It's fine."

"No, it's . . . juvenile," Minnow said. "I didn't call you to be an angry teen. I'm sorry."

"Why *did* you call me? I'm—delighted that you did, please don't misunderstand the question, but . . ."

Minnow thought of Charles, asleep beneath his great-grandmother's portrait. She thought about the offices into which, tomorrow, they would pour. For a moment, she hesitated. Where to start? She could ask Olya why she had left them, but Minnow already knew the answer would be an entire lifetime of complication, a lifetime of choices that couldn't be summed up in an explanation that would satisfy her. She could ask if Olya still loved her father, but to hear her mother say yes would be just as painful as hearing her say no. If she asked questions like that, she would get answers she couldn't use.

"When you and Dad were . . . back when you were in school, Dad said . . ." Minnow hesitated. "You were protesting, I guess, but he said that nothing *changed*. That was how he put it. That you did all these things but nothing *changed*. And that there just—I think he stopped seeing a point to . . . any of it. I guess what I'm asking—is that how it seems to you as well?"

"No," Olya said without hesitating. "That's not how it seems to me."

"No?"

"Your father was always—" Olya caught herself, and Minnow heard the moment in which she chose a kinder tack. "Sensitive," she said. "Which I—I think that can be a real gift. But I guess I'm just not that sensitive. I think things take time, and you do them again and again and again, and eventually the small victories start to build up. And you have to *count* the small victories, you can't just look around and say, Oh god, everything is terrible, nothing will change. If you don't pay attention to the details, how can you see the whole picture?"

"Like what?" Minnow asked. She realized that she had a hand on her chest, her fingers spread as if she were trying to cup her heart in her own palm. "Like for example what?"

"Well," Olya said thoughtfully, "I live in Oregon, as I guess you know, and we had some developers come into town last year. There's a sort of walking trail that everybody likes to use—to walk their dogs, look at birds, that sort of thing. These developers were going to turn it into a series of condos. And we just—Linda and I weren't having that. What a fucking waste, what an outrage! We fought them for a whole year, we got a bunch of neighbors involved—I mean, we were picketing town hall! We were picketing their offices! We were writing petitions! We made a real stink. And last month, the town bought the land that the trail is on and kept it zoned as parkland. And every time I go for a walk, which is just about every morning, I look around and I think: *I did that.* In part, I did that. And that's the whole picture, too," Olya said. "Or it contributes to the whole picture. Do you know what I mean?"

Minnow heard the pride in Olya's voice and something in her reached toward it, like a tendril toward light. Though the question might have been rhetorical, Minnow answered it anyway, with her whole heart: "Yes," she said. "I know what you mean."

*

Minnow had imagined their occupation of the building as an adrenaline-fueled high-wire act, but instead, once it began, nothing happened for many hours.

Holding hands and shivering in the predawn cold, Minnow and Charles entered the Vernier compound by a side gate to which Charles had the keys. The side yard was empty, but when they circled around to the front they found Luc sitting on the steps of the Vernier building, having a cigarette. "Bonjour," he said, as casually as if it were any morning. Charles glanced around and Luc assured him: "Nobody's here but us. We already did a sweep." And then, standing, as if he were the owner and they were hoping for a tour: "I'll take you up."

The stretch of offices had been transformed since Minnow was last there. Stripped of party regalia, the rooms were austere and elegant. The occupiers had turned the wide reception area into base of operations: a ceramic coffee table was strewn with paper bags of pastries and empty coffee pods from a Nespresso machine; boxes had been dragged in and dumped here and there; microphones and ring lights were heaped in a corner. Among them sat expensive objets d'art—tall, fragile ceramic vases and an array of small, dense marble sculptures that Minnow had no doubt Vernier would not have liked them touching. She wondered what he would think of the crumbs, the stains, the banal populism of the coffee pods.

As Luc led them in, they passed Flora and Julie setting up the microphones in a little windowless office filled with file cabinets.

"The broadcast studio," Luc said with a smile. "Very high tech." Rémy and two other men staggered up the stairs and into the reception area, grunting under the weight of sandbags. "For the doors." Luc nodded toward the high windows of the reception area, then to the offices over his shoulder where windows faced out onto the courtyard. "We've got plywood and heavy curtains for these, which will help with tear gas."

"You think we're going to be under attack?" Minnow's pulse quickened.

"I think they will try a variety of tactics," Charles said. Luc had been able to suppress whatever excitement he was feeling, but Charles's nerves were in his voice. "My father will not want this to be the main news story. So at first he will want to talk with us—scolding, bargaining. But then they will have to get firmer."

"And . . . that's a good thing?"

Luc smiled. "It is a riveting thing," he said. "It is a thing the whole country will look at. And while we have their attention, we will make use of it."

Charles was on his knees by the file cabinets. Minnow realized that he had been picking the lock, because now he slid the drawer open, a bent paper clip held in his mouth. He leafed through the file cabinet with curiosity. Surprised, Minnow found herself imagining him as a teenager. Had he picked his father's locks before, and felt a small satisfaction by doing it? Or was this a trick he had learned more recently—from Luc, perhaps?

"Try your father's study," Luc suggested. "None of the good stuff will be out here."

Charles smiled. "My father would never take notes on the good stuff," he corrected Luc. He toed the file cabinet shut with his sneaker. "Let's go get the banners."

The two men vanished down the hallway and Minnow stood at the window, looking down. The sun had risen all the way, and the courtyard was filled with dusty light. Rémy crossed below from the side gate, his body sending shadows swinging wildly over the cobblestones. He was dragging a heavy roll of what Minnow realized were stage curtains, dense and fireproof. Luc and Charles met him cheerfully, and Charles hoisted the other end of the roll up onto his shoulder. He and Rémy wrestled it through the front door, disappearing from view, while Luc slipped back out the side gate. Sophie came in with bags of snacks and water—she had driven to a nearby Franprix that was not yet boarded up—and everyone seemed as excited about the snacks as if a siege had already begun.

The banners were hung from the windows facing onto the courtyard, in easy view of the front gate, which would be unlocked when the time was right. Visitors would find themselves immediately confronted by the long swoop of silk-screened cloth decorated by bloody faces, missing limbs—square after square of suffering. Minnow leaned out one of the windows, scrabbling for purchase as she looped her end of the banner through a metal fastening, and as the fabric caught a breeze and billowed, she found herself face to face with a grainy version of Luc as he must have been in the days straight out of the hospital: his face disfigured and swollen.

Julie turned on a small television mounted in the wall of a corner office, and as soon as the TV was on, people gathered around, watching the protests starting up again all across the city: acte 8, the eighth consecutive weekend in the streets. The room vibrated with electricity, but when the same familiar images chased themselves across the screen—men and women in yellow vests, burning barricades, a camera spiraling above the Arc de Triomphe—the watchers lost interest and returned to their tasks. Minnow perched in the deep windowsill and leaned her head back against the pane. She hadn't imagined that she would accompany Charles to an occupation and feel sleepy, of all things, but in the limbo of waiting, she found her eyelids slipping lower and lower.

Later, Minnow would come to know how busy the city had been across that long morning and into the early afternoon. She would come to know that a flaming restaurant boat bobbed in place along the Seine like an apocalyptic omen; that only blocks away from the offices, protestors fought hand to hand with police beneath the bursts of flashballs; that police dodged rocks and broken chunks of paving and responded with curtains of tear gas. Over on Rue de Grenelle, protestors smashed down the door of a Ministry with a forklift while the government spokesman fled through the garden. The crowds and the police were diminished, their numbers worn down by previous weeks of combat and by the winter chill, and yet the fighting was no less vicious. Later, Minnow would wonder if, together, these distinct fights formed an interconnected neural network; if each small violence communicated itself to the next one so that the city responded like an animal, flinching and tossing.

One moment, the offices were suspended in limbo; the next, Luc had received a call and put it on speakerphone, and everyone gathered around to listen. The man on the other end of the phone spoke a gravelly, fast-paced French that went by too quickly for Minnow to grasp, and when he was done, he hung up without waiting for Luc to respond. Charles said, "Alors, on y va," and he and Luc went into the recording studio and closed the door. Almost immediately, Minnow heard Luc's voice, a smooth announcer's rhythm:

"Bonjour à toutes et à tous, nous émettons depuis les bureaux de Michel Vernier, tout près des Champs-Élysées . . ." His voice rolled out, powerful and in control.

"J'ai le grand plaisir d'être ici en compagnie de Charles Vernier, le fils de Monsieur Vernier," Luc said, and Minnow heard Charles's voice chime in, lighter, clearer.

"Bonjour," Charles said. "Je suis Charles Vernier, et nous sommes à deux pas de l'Arc de Triomphe où la police et les gilets jaunes s'affrontent depuis de nombreuses semaines. Nous sommes ici pour vous apporter la vérité dont nous avons été témoins, des choses que le gouvernement, la police et les médias—et mon propre père—ne veulent pas que nous vous parlions."

Listening, Minnow caught the reference to Charles's father—*what even my father doesn't want you to know*—and she understood fully what Charles had already grasped and come to terms with: Charles and his father were the story; how could they not be? And a story only ever belongs to those who tell it.

Charles's voice rose and fell, intimate and mesmerizing. Unlike Luc, he didn't have an actor's smoothness or projection. Instead, he sounded sincere and young, a little nervous but confident in his righteousness. A voice you would listen to if it gave you directions.

"Ça va?" Flora was leaning in the doorway to the small office. Her eyes darted to the images flickering across the TV screen.

"Good," Minnow said. "You?"

Flora smiled, wide and exhilarated. "We are getting—what do you say? Views. Many views."

"What's the next step?"

"It could go one of two ways," Flora said, "and then we will know they heard us. The first is that we start to see our own videos there"— she jerked her chin to the television. "You can check through the channels if you want, run through them and let us know."

Given a task, Minnow slid off the windowsill and searched for the remote. She found it underneath a half-eaten Danish, wiped the stickiness on her jeans, and aimed it at the television.

"What's the other way?" she asked.

"The cops arrive," Flora said cheerfully and vanished back into the hall.

*

One moment the courtyard below them was empty, and then it was not. The cobblestones rang with the shiny black boots of riot police. They came pouring in the front gate as Luc and Charles had intended; it was the only gate they had left unlocked and unbarred.

Charles and Luc stood by the open window of the foyer, gazing down. Though the sound of boots in the courtyard had drawn her, Minnow's gaze lingered on the two of them for a long moment. Luc looked relaxed and ready, his hands in his pockets. Charles looked blank and uneasy. Minnow wondered if he was wishing he hadn't agreed to this. Luc nudged him with a shoulder and said something low and Charles turned to smile back at him, swift and radiant. Whatever Luc had said, it was exactly what Charles had needed to hear. And again Minnow felt that old discomfort, that Luc could read him so simply and move him at will. Charles turned back toward the window and his expression shifted, the smile dropping out entirely. Minnow knew instantly who she would see below. And, looking down, there he was: Michel Vernier.

He stood in front of the line of police, gazing up at the windows. He was wearing a dark coat, and the drizzling mist made him gleam as if he'd been polished. His head was tilted upward, his eyes squinting, and though Minnow felt as if he were looking straight at her, she knew that he had eyes only for his son. The look on his face was untranslatable.

"Charles," she said.

He didn't look at her. A muscle ticked in the side of his jaw.

At his shoulder, Luc smiled. "Now we're getting somewhere."

Luc gestured and Rémy stepped past Minnow, phone in hand, filming down into the courtyard. Minnow wondered, briefly and guiltily, if she had shown up on le livestream. It hadn't occurred to her before, but for the first time she imagined Janet or any of their other colleagues watching the news, seeing footage taken from the Vernier office occupation, reacting as Minnow flashed across the screen.

"M'sieur Vernier," Luc called down. "Bienvenue. Nous aimerions aborder avec vous le sujet de vos relations avec notre président, Emmanuel Macron. Pourriez-vous répondre à quelques questions?"

Vernier ignored Luc completely. He spoke to his son as if the two of them were alone together. He didn't lift his voice, but it carried clearly. Minnow made out a few words here and there—he was asking Charles to come down, to discuss this. Something about the police—he didn't want Charles to find himself in trouble that was beyond his ability to comprehend. If he came down now, this could all end quietly. This was the translation that Minnow put to the words she salvaged, and watching Charles's jaw tighten and nostrils flare, she knew she had been correct about at least some of it.

Charles replied coolly, but there was a flaw just under the surface of his voice. Minnow knew, with a flash of clarity, that he was furious but unsure of himself. No matter how often he and Luc had gone over their plan, there had been no way to rehearse for the reality of his father's disappointment. Minnow wondered if Charles had lived his whole life trying to avoid this exact moment.

Minnow leaned over to Flora. "What are they saying?" she whispered, but Flora just shook her head, her eyes darting between Rémy with the camera, Charles in the open window, and Luc at his shoulder.

Luc broke in, speaking in his smooth orator's voice. His words were directed at Vernier, but Minnow knew that this was for Charles's benefit. Luc was showing him what it looked like, the character he had come there to play. Charles swallowed convulsively—once, twice—the lines of his throat leaping. His hand, hidden by the windowsill, twitched and clenched.

Vernier responded, but once again it was not to Luc. "Charles," he began, "assez avec ces jeux. Je comprends ce que tu veux faire, mais ce n'est pas la façon d'y parvenir." Minnow worked backward to thread the words together. He was saying that he knew what Charles wanted, but this wasn't the way to accomplish it. And before that: *Enough of these games.* What must Charles feel, hearing his political convictions framed as a game?

Luc responded before Charles could—his tone was mocking, and Minnow knew that he was throwing Vernier's words back in his face. Vernier did address him then, directly but coldly.

"Je parle à mon fils," he said, and Minnow understood that sentence clearly: *I'm talking to my son.*

"Et bien," Luc said carelessly. "Parlez. Mais nous sommes ici pour la même raison." He gestured to Charles with his chin, including him in the declaration: *Go ahead and talk, but we are here for the same reason.*

"Non," Vernier corrected him. "Non, vous avez des raisons très différentes. Je me suis renseigné sur vous, Luc. J'aime savoir qui mon fils fréquente." And then, calling up to Charles: "Est-ce que tu connais bien l'homme à côté de toi? Demande à Luc si . . ."

Vernier kept speaking, but more slowly now—he was making a point that he felt had power, like a man laying down a winning hand of cards—and Minnow received each word with a thrill of individual understanding. *How well do you know the man standing beside you?* He had asked. And then: *I've looked into you. I like to know my son's friends. Ask Luc if* . . . but the last words were unfamiliar. She looked to Luc and Charles and saw that all of the blood had gone out of Luc's face.

"Demande à Luc ce qu'il a fait à son patron," Vernier called, "et dis-moi que c'est l'homme que tu veux comme ami."

Minnow put the words one after the other, carefully, her mind leaping ahead even as the meanings fell into place around the blanks. She remembered the story Luc had told her, of standing outside his boss's home holding a gun. But he had done nothing, he had said. He had realized that there was nothing he could do that would change the shape of events, and so he had done nothing. *Ask Luc what he did to his boss, and tell me if this is the man you want as a friend.* Charles and Luc stared at each other, wide-eyed. Charles's face had become a mask of doubt.

Luc saw this and began speaking rapidly, his tone a mixture of dismissal and pleading, but Charles caught his arm.

"What does he mean by that?" Charles demanded. Minnow knew he had switched to English so that she could comprehend fully, and it touched her, even then, that he would feel that he needed her in this moment. That her understanding would mean something to him.

"You know the story," Luc said, brusquely, including Minnow in his gaze. "I already told you the story." He switched back to French. But Charles cut him off.

"Yes, but how does my *father* know it?" Charles demanded. "If there was nothing that happened there, then how does *he* know?"

"Tu penses bien que j'ai fait mes recherches sur l'homme qui a tant influencé mon fils." Vernier from below, his voice cool and imminently reasonable. He was saying again that he had looked into Luc, Minnow gathered, but what did that mean? Luc's expression was unreadable, his eyes narrowed.

Behind Vernier the line of riot police stirred, frustrated by the exchange, unsure what was happening. One of the men—a captain, perhaps—approached Vernier and spoke to him quietly. Vernier shook him off. The man spoke again, insistent. Minnow wondered if he was demanding permission to extract them from the building.

Vernier shook his head again, his voice too low to be heard. Whatever he said, he said it with authority, because the police captain stepped back.

"You think your father has some kind of special truth for you?" Luc began mockingly. He included Minnow once again, as if asking her for help to get Charles back on track. "You know he will lie to get whatever he wants. *You* have said this about him to me."

Charles swung toward Minnow, and she saw his confusion—he wasn't sure what to do. His father had shaken him badly. Luc glanced at Minnow, then back to Charles, and the open doubt on Charles's face made him switch to a softer tone, more intimate.

"This isn't about me," Luc said. "You are thinking for yourself, on your own, and that terrifies him. Don't let your father distract you right now. What we have come here to do is larger than either of us. If you want to throw it all away, you tell me that. Look me in the eyes and tell me that whatever you think of me is more important than history, and I will go downstairs and open the door myself."

In the hush, Minnow heard the tick of the wall clock. Sounds filtered in from the one open window—not from the courtyard, which was ominously still, but from the streets beyond. Faraway chanting and shouting, a whistle blowing, sirens. Charles's eyes skidded toward Minnow. He looked torn, panicked. She couldn't help remembering how he had looked the night of the Vernier party, confronted by his father. How small he had seemed, how confused and defeated. Something must have shown on her face—could it have been a shadow of disdain?—because Charles looked stung. Before Minnow could speak, he turned back to Luc and nodded.

And with that, Luc leapt into action. He called over his shoulder in French and Sophie and Flora appeared, reaching for the final panel of plywood that had been leaning against the wall by the secretary's desk. Minnow realized that Luc had switched plans—it was too dangerous for Charles to speak to his father, regardless of how useful the footage might have been. Vernier had a hold on his son, and he would use it to his advantage if given the chance. The window had to be sealed off, the offices turned into a siege-worthy keep from which Luc could regain control of the narrative, broadcast that carefully crafted version to the hundreds of thousands of eyes that had turned toward them. Rémy and Flora dragged the plywood sheet across the floor toward them. Minnow's eyes followed the groove the panel left in the smooth floorboards, a scrape that would last after this day. Her attention was wrested back when Luc said her name. He was nodding toward a small piece of sculpture that rested on a low table parked between the windows.

"Move that," he said.

Minnow lifted the sculpture in her hands and found it surprisingly heavy. It was made of white marble and looked like a large ammonite. She wondered if Vernier was the one who chose the art for his office, or if it had been someone else who had seen and liked this thing. She cradled it against her chest like a dense animal, using her hips to shove the display table away from the path of the plywood.

Beside her, Charles turned back toward the window, to his father. "J'suis désolé, Papa," he said. He might have added more to his apology, or perhaps that was all he planned to say. Minnow would never know. She would remember, later, that he didn't even finish the last word, *Papa.* The world split its seams before the syllables left his lips.

If Minnow were to try and arrange the events in chronological order, perhaps it would have looked something like this: As Charles spoke, Luc reached for the window. His eyes were bright and he was almost smiling, as if he could feel the day steadying beneath him, returning to the path he had planned for it. The CRS officer directly behind Vernier must have understood that the time for talking had ended and that the office was sealing itself off. The man lifted his arm, and in one swift gentle motion, he threw a tear gas grenade in a high arc, up and over their heads and through the open window. It hit the wood flooring behind them, a hard metal *thunk,* and it rolled. As this happened, without hesitation, without even a moment's thought, as if the motion upward had triggered a motion downward, Minnow threw the sculpture out the window. And it seemed that when Vernier fell to the cobblestones, he fell at exactly the same moment as Minnow released what she held, although of course this was not possible; of course it could only have been subsequent to the throwing, because it was not that he fell but rather that she struck him down.

21

KEEN HAD NOT BEEN RAISED ON FAIRY TALES, IN LARGE PART because Roger Hunter, as a man of God, believed that they were slightly too adjacent to the devil. But Keen was aware of their rhythms: after ten years, the sleeping princess awakens. After a hundred years, the family curse ends. When, in the spring of 1979, he opened his door and found Olya on the doorstep, the moment itself did not feel to him like a fairy tale. Rather, it felt as if the past ten years had been a fairy tale and his real life had suddenly resumed.

He was living in Connecticut by then. He was an assistant professor of chemistry at Wesleyan. He lived all alone in an old Victorian house that was not unlike 5 Wellman, and he had chosen it for that reason. His landlady, an aging Polish woman, lived on the first floor. She approved of him because he had neither friends nor girlfriends; he did not play music; he did not turn on the television, because he did not want to know the news. He maintained a steady, cool equanimity that was fueled by his talent for compartmentalization; he parceled his attention out among his students, his classroom, his lab, and the papers he was writing. That and nothing else.

When the doorbell rang that May, he traveled down the three flights of stairs to answer it, assuming it was a delivery. He opened the door to Olya—thinner, gaunter, her hair longer, wrapped in a patched red coat—and it was only then that his steady numbness was punctured like a soap bubble and everything flooded in: louder, brighter, more overpowering than he could bear.

*

The gas from the grenade was unbearable. That was the only clear thought in Minnow's mind as the world splintered into chaos. All of Minnow's senses were wiped clean by a heavy, unoxygenated fog, a searing thickness that made it impossible to see or breathe or think. They were staggering, they were choking, Charles was crying out for his father. Someone had shut the window, but then someone swung it wide again to try and get clean air into the room. Someone nearby was retching and weeping, but Minnow had no way of knowing who or where.

She staggered, with one hand holding her T-shirt up over her nose and mouth and the other flailing—colliding with the walls, with other bodies, trying to make sense of the room. Her outstretched hand found the cool length of a wall and she followed it, blinded by chemical tears. The wall opened into a small room—a bathroom. She shoved the door shut and battered herself around the space like a moth until her hands lit on what could only be a sink. She turned the knobs, frantically, and shoved her head under the rush of cold water that ensued.

Under the water she could hear nothing, but the burning began to ease, and with the easing, the ability to think returned to her. This had all gone wrong, impossibly wrong. She saw again the fragment of image: the grenade swinging up and Vernier falling down. Was it possible still that it could not be her fault? Could there be any other explanation?

The door to the bathroom burst open, and Minnow swung around, water arcing wildly outward from her face and hair, splashing on the tiles. Through her bleary red eyes she made out a tall, wiry form, shoving the door shut behind him. Relief swamped her.

"Charles, here." She guided him toward the sink, helped place his face under the water. He gagged and spat, turning from side to side to flush out his eyes. When he emerged, she had found a fistful of paper towels under the sink, and they patted their faces dry. Minnow's whole head felt swollen, her eyes ached as if they had been rolled in sand and shoved back into her sockets. In those first seconds of silence, Minnow had no idea what to say to Charles, how to begin, but then he said, "My father was hit," and she knew he had no idea that it was her fault.

She opened her mouth and only a question came out: "He was hit?"

"I need to get outside," he said.

"Did you see what hit him?"

"It all happened so fast but I saw him fall."

This is the time, Minnow thought. This is the time to say out loud what you did, what happened. There will not be a time after this one in which you can be anything other than a liar. So say it now. But Charles kept on, even as Minnow drew in a sharp breath to speak.

"I have to get down there. Luc has the doors barricaded. If we go down the stairs they'll arrest us before I even get to my father. We have to go out the other way."

"What other way?"

Charles was rifling in the wooden cabinets behind them, and he turned around with two hand towels—thick expensive ones that would not look used no matter how often you washed them. Even now, Minnow could be impressed by wealth. He wet them under the faucet and then handed one to Minnow, tying the other over his nose and mouth.

As he moved toward the bathroom door, Minnow stepped in front of it. "Wait—"

Charles's eyes were inflamed and teary but his face was stony. He took her shoulders gently. "Are you ready?"

"How are we going to—?"

"Follow me."

He flung the bathroom door wide and the thick, acrid gas drifted toward them in a haze. Somewhere beyond that haze, beyond these walls, down the stairs that Minnow couldn't even see—somewhere out there was Vernier. In a flash, Minnow saw again the crack of red that spilled from his forehead, how unexpectedly it had appeared. Had the moment passed? Could she grab Charles's sleeve, even here, in this poisonous mist, and whisper the truth into his ear?

Charles charged forward, turning away from the chaos, down a hallway toward the back.

It was a relief, in the end, just to follow.

*

Keen asked himself sometimes if it had been a mistake: that first evening in which he let Olya into his new house, let them back into each other's lives. Or was the chief mistake falling in love with her again? But how could he have done anything else? He had never fallen out of love with her, so it was not a return to a thing so much as a continuation of what was.

Olya had changed, it was true. She was harder to read. She had always lived on the surface of her skin, all nerve and reaction, and now she was somewhere much farther away. She would not tell Keen what exactly she had been doing over the past ten years, although she gave him bits and pieces. She had been with a Berkeley chapter of the SDS; she had been with a San Francisco chapter of a guerilla group that was comprised solely of women; she had been living on a farm, somewhere out past the Marin headlands. When she talked about the farm, her face softened; it had not been a place of conflict but of respite. She had gone there after giving up on the world: "I decided to tend to my own small corner of it," she said, and so a friend had given her an address and she had gone out there and stayed and stayed. In the end, though, she had returned to the world: "If we stay in our small corners," she told Keen, "the center falls through." He wasn't sure whether she was sharing with him what she had come to realize, or admonishing him for the smallest corner of all: the one into which he had retreated.

Keen asked her, that first night, why she had come back. He meant *to him,* but he phrased it as if he were asking about the East Coast in general.

She considered the question for a time without answering. He had seated her at the rickety card table he used as a dinner table, fenced in by mismatched thrift shop chairs. He had wanted to summon the devil-may-care flavor of 5 Wellman but had succeeded only in creating a space that seemed shabby and cheap. He hadn't realized this until now, watching Olya sipping coffee from a chipped John Deere mug. But she herself didn't seem to have any judgment of his surroundings. Instead, she was turning over the question he had asked, and at last she said: "They released Ethan. Early."

A spark of terror passed through him. Keen had not heard this name in years, not since the trials had concluded and Ethan and Dwight and a handful of others had been sentenced. "Did you see him?"

"Yeah—Peter called me to let me know Ethan was getting out. The two of us went to pick him up."

"Peter called you?" It hadn't occurred to Keen that Olya would be callable. After she had left, Keen had not had a number for her—nobody had seemed to—and though Olya had sent the occasional postcard to Keen's apartment, there was never contact information on the back. He had put off moving for an extra year because he had not wanted to lose the chance that a postcard might show up, but when he was given the Wesleyan job, he couldn't turn it down on the basis of a reason so slim, so shameful.

Olya was nodding now—yes, she said, Peter had let her know that Ethan was being released early, so she had come back. Peter was still living in Boston, which Keen had also not known. They had fallen out of touch soon after Olya had left—it had been too painful for Keen to maintain the friendship. Olya and Peter had helped Ethan adjust to his first week back in the world. Eventually Ethan planned to fly to Indiana, to see his family. Olya related these facts simply, without emotion.

"How was he?" Keen asked. He knew the question was stupid, but he couldn't ask what he really wanted to know. *What did he tell you about me? Is he okay? If he isn't, is it my fault?*

But Olya was shaking her head. "It's a brutal system," she said. "It's not made to heal, it's made to punish. So he was punished."

"Did he seem . . . like himself?"

"No," Olya said after a long pause. "But then neither do you."

In the silence between them, Keen felt a great tenderness well up in him at the thought that she had remembered his details carefully enough to know that he had changed. The tenderness warred with fear, and he was prepared for almost anything she might say, but not for what she did say:

"Can I stay with you tonight?"

Keen stared at her. Then: "Here?" Then: "Yes, of course, yes."

He did not ask if she would stay longer than the night, or why she wanted to, and possibly because he did not ask, she stayed with him for almost two years.

*

It was easier than Minnow had thought, the path of escape. Charles led the way with the instinct of a born fugitive. It took him a moment to crank open the skylight in the second bathroom, down a hallway that Minnow had never traversed. Minnow had assumed Charles would clamber up through it, but he jerked his head for her to go first. She approached, gingerly, her eyes still streaming, her throat swollen beneath the protective shield of wet towel. He knelt, gesturing for her to step on his shoulder. When she did, he stood, steadying her legs with his arms so that she could climb up through the skylight and onto the sloping mansard roof.

In the sunlight, the cleanness of the air was overwhelming. She tore the towel off her face and took in gasping lungfuls while Charles pulled himself up behind her. She could have lain down on the slanting tiles, but Charles was already calling softly—"This way, stay down!" She followed him, hunched over, the two of them navigating the length of the roof. Below them, the edges of the courtyard spun into view and out again. She could hear the commotion drifting upward, but she couldn't see what was happening. She wondered if others had escaped, or were being arrested, or were fighting.

Charles took them across the raised center of the roof, a flat straight catwalk, from which the roof slanted downward. If Minnow didn't look to either side, it was as simple as walking a narrow sidewalk. They navigated a cluster of chimneys, climbing around them, and when they reached the opposite edge, Charles gestured to a skylight partway down the incline: "In there." When Minnow hesitated, he encouraged her: "I've done this before, it's a short drop."

"*When* have you done this?" she demanded. Despite the seriousness of the moment, she felt incredulous laughter rising.

"In high school," Charles admitted. "A few times. Come on!"

He went first, prying the skylight up, swinging his legs over the edge, supporting his weight on his arms briefly, and then dropping through. Minnow peered over the edge and Charles was beneath her, staring up. His whole face looked raw, his eyes bloodshot. She saw his lip was bloody, as if he'd bitten through it without noticing.

"Vas-y, Minou, I'll catch you."

She swung her legs over the lip and lowered herself. He caught her around the waist, and for a moment they looked at each other, and she wondered wildly if this would ever be possible again. Then he set her down and turned away. They were in an office space not unlike Vernier's offices. A heavy oak desk, a black desk chair behind it and two brown leather chairs facing it, the floor covered with a burgundy carpet instead of the clean wood flooring. The carpet muffled their steps as Charles opened the door and they crept out into the hallway and through a warren of uninhabited offices. Sound traveled to them through the walls and windows, coming from the courtyard and the streets, but Minnow found it hard to hear over the roaring of her heartbeat in her ears. In the stairwell, they descended rapidly, taking the stairs two at a time.

"Doesn't this take us to the courtyard?" she demanded, breathless at Charles's shoulder.

"There's a service exit through the basement."

Charles didn't turn around, and Minnow had only the back of his neck, the plane of his shoulders, to try and read. As they descended stair after stair, Minnow held against herself briefly the Charles that she had known—his sweetness, his compliance, his eagerness to believe the best was possible. She did not want to imagine who he might be after this, and who she might be to him. They worked their way deeper into the earth, and she felt the world recede.

*

Keen knew that they were playing house. He knew that they were pretending, if only because—after that first evening—they never talked about either the past or the future, and it requires a great and unnatural application of will for any human to remain solely in the present. But it didn't matter. He had never in his life been so happy.

It wasn't that he would get home to find the house warm and smelling of cooking, as had happened so often at 5 Wellman. Sometimes he would get home from teaching and find Olya sitting in the cramped living room where he had left her that morning, staring out the window. Other times, he would find her in bed, and he wouldn't know whether she had returned there in midafternoon or whether she hadn't yet gotten up.

They slept together but they didn't have sex. They didn't touch. That first night, Keen had gallantly made up the couch for himself and Olya had stopped him. "Please don't," she'd said, and he had understood, from those two words, not that she wanted him but that she didn't want to be alone. Olya had nightmares, which she did not explain. Again and again he woke up to her thrashing in the sheets. Sometimes she cried out. Keen would bring her water and she would drink it, and then they would go back to sleep. He understood that to ask her questions would be to lose her, and so nothing that she did or said occasioned inquiry from him. And this was the right choice, because as the weeks passed, he would get home and find her reading or hanging her laundry to dry or, increasingly and to his great relief, playing records from his collection.

Three weeks after her arrival, he came home and found his apartment empty. He panicked. He searched for a note but found nothing. He was sitting, trying to calm his racing heart, when the front door opened and Olya let herself in. He saw at a glance that she was carrying two brown paper bags of groceries, that she had simply gone out to get them food. She looked at him, sitting collapsed in a chair with his face ashen, and each of them understood in that moment what had happened. It would have been too dangerous to say out loud: how easily she had become the core of his whole world, and how unclear it was what she planned to do with that.

That night in bed, for the first time, Olya reached for Keen. Later, when he was torturing himself, he would wonder whether she'd felt like she owed him something—whether this was the way she had

chosen to alleviate her own guilt for not being able to give him what
he was so willing to give her, which was: everything, everything. But
in the moment, it hadn't felt like pity or obligation. It had felt like
something in her was waking up, coming back to life. Like the life in
her was reaching out to him, with curiosity, with determination. The
image that had come to his mind that night was of a swimmer in the
middle of a dark sea coming across an unexpected raft. Would you
not cling to it? And then he banished all that was not her body and
his, and he didn't remember until much later that he had had this
thought at all.

*

Following Charles down into the basement was like stepping below
the city into a different century. The damp air smelled heavy and
secret. Charles turned on the flashlight of his iPhone and Minnow
fumbled for hers, only to realize that she didn't have it. She had lost it
somewhere—back in Vernier's offices? On the roof? Somewhere else?

"Charles," she whispered, the air swallowing her voice. "I don't
have my phone."

If Charles heard her, he didn't reply. He swept his light from side
to side and Minnow followed it with her eyes: ancient stone, block set
against block, long coppery pipes running across the ceiling. Something darted in the shadows and Minnow pressed a hand to her
mouth so that she wouldn't scream. Charles kept moving, and with
him went his light, so she followed closely. A vibration rumbled under
her feet. Was it a boiler, a train, or the revolution outside?

Charles got turned around in the cavernous depths and Minnow
trailed him as he wheeled from side to side muttering to himself, his
flashlight illuminating damp stone after stone. At last he found what
he was looking for: an old metal door, set deeply into the wall. He
unlocked it, his hands coming away rusty, and pulled it open. Just
inside, a flight of narrow stone steps rose at a steep angle. Both of them
stared upward, listening. Men's voices above them, shouting—running
footsteps, close, then passing, then gone. A car alarm. Minnow hesitated, turning back to Charles. The chilly quiet of the basement
seemed like sanctuary, though seconds ago it had been frightening.

Charles looked uncertain as well. He had pulled the towel off his face, and he sniffed at the air. "There'll be more tear gas up there," he said. "Still have yours?"

Minnow nodded, her fingers shaking. "What happens when we get up there?"

"You run," Charles said.

"And you?"

Charles gave her something that was almost a smile. "I need to find my father," he said, as if in apology. He might have said more but a deafening rumble from above stopped them both in their tracks. The walls shook, dust and fine silt rained down on them. Then silence. Had something exploded? Had the Arc itself toppled over? They stared at each other, wide-eyed. Then Charles stepped past Minnow and began climbing the stairs, trudging toward the light. Minnow bit back the questions that were rising up, laced with panic, and followed close behind as the sounds of conflict grew louder.

*

It was in the second month of Olya's stay that Keen learned two things. The first was that there were police in San Francisco looking for her, and the second was that Olya was pregnant. Olya was not interested in explaining the circumstances of the former. Keen understood that she would not have told him this much if she had not felt that it was necessary. She said that she had lived under a different name in California and so they were looking for her by that name, but that it was important that Keen not talk to anyone about her, and that he should let her know immediately if anyone—no matter how innocuously—began asking about her. Keen knew that something must have changed for her to feel the need to share this with him now, but he didn't ask what she had heard or what she had done. For a moment, for the first time in many years, Andrew Hungerford's face swam before his eyes. He had no right to ask anyone what they had done. He said only, "I understand."

Looking at him, her face softened into an unbearable tenderness. They were sitting in the cramped kitchen; Olya had made carrot and ginger soup; she reached across the card table and took both his hands in hers. That was when she told him the second thing. She blurted it out as if she hadn't intended to say it.

"Oh," Keen said, before his mind could catch up with his mouth. "Oh wow. Oh my god. How?"

"Well," Olya said, "When a man and a woman . . ."

"No, I just meant . . . I just mean . . . Are you sure?"

"I'm late. About three weeks late, and I'm never late."

Keen realized that she was talking about her period and felt himself flush to the roots of his hair. Olya laughed out loud. "You asked!"

"I did, I do, I want to know," Keen said with painful sincerity. "Is it . . . am I . . . ?"

Olya stared at him for a moment and then nodded. "Yeah, Keen. It's you."

Keen found that his thoughts were racing so hard he couldn't keep up with them. As they flashed past like small meteors, he found that the only thing that felt clear was the elation mounting in him. A baby. *His* baby. Their baby. A child was glue, a child was a promise. Olya would never leave him now. And together, they could . . . Together . . .

"Are you all right?" Olya leaned across the table, studying his face. "Are you going to faint?"

"No," Keen said. "No, I'm . . . oh my god." He surged to his feet, pulled her up with him. He stepped awkwardly around the side of the card table and enveloped her in his arms. She laughed at first, surprised and charmed, but then as he hugged her, the laughter drained out of her. After a moment, she hugged him back. She lowered her face to the side of his neck, breathed him in, and then put her head on his shoulder. He had never embraced her like this. In the exhilaration of it, he felt like a different person. He felt his whole life start over.

"Marry me," he said on impulse, and it was only when he felt Olya stiffen in his arms that he realized that—after all the space he had given her and the questions he had not asked—he had managed a dangerous misstep after all.

*

In the thickness of tear gas, day became night. Bodies streamed past and vanished. Minnow and Charles had come up into the streets beyond the courtyard, but despite having surfaced, Minnow had no sense of where they were. She caught fragmented glimpses: a riot cop with his visor down and his black baton raised as a man in a yellow vest charged him; a girl staggering and weeping, her hands over her eyes; two policemen restraining a man, tearing his respirator mask off his face while he coughed and gagged.

"Down," Charles shouted, just as Minnow heard the champagne-cork sound of an incoming flashball. She dropped into the smog, and they heard the hard *thunk* of metal hitting asphalt, although it was impossible to know whether it was near or far.

"Charles," Minnow said, but her voice was lost in the explosion. Eyes closed, she waited for pain and did not feel it. The flashball must have been farther from them than it sounded. As she straightened, a man came racing out of the haze and barreled into her, knocking her down. Struggling to her feet, her hands encountered the tacky slick of blood on her face.

"Minnow, are you okay?" Charles knelt, helping her back up.

"I'm bleeding."

"That's his blood," Charles said. He felt her cheek and forehead with his fingers. "I saw him, he's the one bleeding. You're all right. Come on."

A Star Wars–helmeted riot cop charged past them through the mist, baton raised, swerving toward the clatter of metal on asphalt. Another ran toward her—or perhaps toward the barricade at her back, which was now on fire. Anger rose up in her at the men with their shiny black helmets and segmented body armor, ants pouring out of every crack in the sidewalk. She bent down, picked up a chunk of paving stone, and hurled it at the CRS running toward her. It glanced off the curving metal flap at his shoulder and he staggered a little, startled, then enraged.

"Quick, quick!" Charles was yanking her arm. "Behind the barricade!"

The heat of the fire singed her lungs through the damp towel as they threw themselves behind a stack of burning Christmas trees and rubbish bins. The smoke was thick here and they crouched, jackets over their heads. Footsteps behind them, in front of them, the sounds of men shouting, women's voices lifted high and wild.

"He's gone," Charles said on her left, a blurred shape. "You're crazy." But there was a note of admiration in his voice.

"Fuck them," Minnow said, and suddenly she was talking about all of them—the CRS with their tear gas and flashballs; the Sewell men who had slowed down beside her in their pickup trucks as she walked to the grocery store and shouted, "Hey, it's Professor Baby-killer!"; her beloved father, who had changed nothing about the way the world worked and who had not taught her to believe that it could be changed. She wanted to throw stones and bottles and hand grenades, she wanted to tear down everything around her. A rage rose in her like she was nothing more than the thin skin containing it, and she shook with it.

"Okay," Charles said, his voice close to her ear. "We're going to crawl around the side and then you can run down the alley there—do you see?"

Minnow squinted through the tears and smoke and made out the wavering mouth of a narrow street diagonally across from the burning barricade. "Yes." Then: "What do you mean *me*?"

"The offices are the other way," Charles said, and the apologetic note was back in his voice, hoarse as it was from coughing.

"You can't seriously be going back there. You'll never get in! Your father isn't still there anyway. If he—if he was hurt, they'll have taken him in an ambulance."

Charles hesitated. Under the grime, he looked childlike, uncertain. "I don't know," he said.

"Listen to me: if you go back there, you're just going to get hurt or arrested. We need to get out of here and then . . ." Minnow heard the lie in her voice, the implication that everything would be all right once they were no longer here. She forged on anyway: "You can call your mother."

She watched Charles's mind work—one thought chasing another—and finally, after what might have been seconds but felt like hours, he nodded. He lifted himself to peer over the top of the barricade once again, and then came back down. "There are five cops, they are putting men into a van—when their backs are turned, we go. One . . . two . . . three . . . We go!"

Charles seized Minnow's hand in his and, bodies bent, they ran.

*

After a few days had passed, Olya came to a decision. And when she had arrived at it, she presented it to Keen firmly. She was going back to California, she said. She knew a doctor who could relieve her of this problem. After she had had it taken care of, she would go stay in Marin for a time, on the farm. She couldn't expect Keen to disrupt his whole life. They were not their parents, they didn't have to get married just because they'd had sex.

"But I *want* to," Keen said, wide-eyed, uncomprehending. "I want to be with you."

Olya's face was sorrowful. "Keen," she said. "Look at us. That's not who we are."

"But why not?" Keen demanded wildly. "Why *not* who we are?"

"Keen . . ."

"No, what? Explain to me why! I love you. I *love* you! And you— maybe you don't feel the exact same way about me, but it's okay, maybe you don't have to. You trust me, and that counts for something. You and I—"

Olya cut him off. "You left Andrew Hungerford dead in a closet," she said gently. "And I shot a man—though, last I heard, I don't think he died. But that isn't the point. We weren't made to be parents, you and I. We have to *change* the world, not just live in it."

At another moment, this revelation would have captured Keen's attention fully. He had spent months wondering what had sent Olya fleeing back East. But hearing Andrew Hungerford's name unlocked something overpowering and unstoppable in him, and so instead, he heard himself asking: "You knew? You knew this whole time?"

He realized he was crying, and then without warning he was crying so hard that he couldn't stand. He sank to his knees on the floor, and after a moment, she knelt by him. She didn't touch him, but he

felt her tenderness. He had to repeat his question before she understood it. Then she shook her head.

"Not the whole time, no. It came together for me, eventually."

"Did Ethan tell you?"

"No."

"Did you tell him? When you saw him—when you and Peter went
to get him—"

"We didn't talk about you." Olya put a light hand on the back of
his neck. "We didn't talk about that day at all." She stroked the short
hairs of his nape, soothing him.

"I never meant it to happen," Keen said. He lifted his face to her,
raw and wincing. "You have to believe me that I never meant—he
attacked me, I let him out and he attacked me, so then when he
started saying he couldn't breathe, I thought—"

Olya ghosted her fingertips over his mouth, silencing Keen. "I
don't care about him," she said. Her voice was calm, the gentleness
still in it. "I don't give a fuck about that man. He deserved to die."

"He . . ." Keen blinked at her. He felt as if the ground had shifted
violently underfoot. "Nobody deserves that, Olya—"

"He was ready to send any number of boys off to die, he based his
career on that." Olya shrugged. "He's no great loss, I don't care about
that. That's not what I was trying to say."

"But *I* care," Keen said, anguished. The tears had dried up now,
but he was leaning his head into Olya's hand like a cat. "I couldn't
stop thinking about him for years. I still—I thought you *left* because
of that."

"I left because it was a fucking disaster," Olya said. "The whole
thing, all of it. And I wanted to go somewhere where I could actually
do some good. And I did—I *have*. Raising a kid doesn't do anyone
any good."

Keen lifted his head to look her in the eyes. "I don't think that's
true."

Olya frowned, confused. "You want a child?"

"I want to raise a child with you."

Olya was quiet after that. She retrieved her hands from Keen's hair and they sat on the bedroom floor, a floorboard's width of space between them. Finally she asked, "How can you be so sure?"

Keen reached across the space between them, slipping his fingers into hers. Her hand was cold. "I've always been sure of you," he said.

"You shouldn't be." She wasn't looking at him, but her voice sounded wry and wistful, more like the Olya of old. "*I'm* not sure of me, so you *definitely* shouldn't be."

"I think we could be happy," Keen said. "And I think that right now, in this country, being happy is a fucking revolution. We can change the world by living in it, Olya."

And with that, he made the decision not to ask her—never to ask her—about the man she had shot. Everything that happened in the past had to stay behind them; if they could achieve that, they had a chance.

He thought she would dismiss him right away. She had already decided, after all. But instead he felt her hand tighten around his, and all of his heart was in his throat when she asked, "Do you really think we would be happy?"

*

The line of police appeared out of nowhere, out of the haze, a chain of human bodies blocking the path to freedom. "La nasse," Charles bit out. "Opposite side, go." But Minnow couldn't see three feet ahead of her; wherever the opposite side was, it was unreachably far.

One of the policemen was shouting at them to stop. Minnow's lungs burned despite the damp towel, and she let go of Charles's arm to adjust it. Even as she let go, he was plucked backward from her; she turned, horrified, and saw him hit the pavement hard, with two CRS on top of him. One was holding him down, the other fastening his wrists behind his back with zip ties, his arms bent at a painful angle.

"His head!" Minnow heard herself shout. "What are you doing? Be careful of his head!" Charles lifted his face from the stones. Blood was already streaming into his eyes. "Run!" he shouted at her. He said something else, but it was lost as the CRS officer behind him slammed his face back down onto the asphalt.

Two of them were coming at Minnow, and she made a split-second decision—she wheeled away from Charles and ran. The street came up to meet her feet, the air burned her eyes and lungs. She had lost the towel and now she was half-blind and reeling. She collided with something hard and screamed, thinking it was one of the officers who had come after her, but as it bounced away from her and overturned with a clang, she realized it was a rubbish bin.

She lost her balance and fell, then lay for a moment, her cheek against the sidewalk. Someone raced past her and stepped on her back, but before she could shout, whoever it was had passed. Minnow pulled herself to her knees, realizing the danger of staying still, realizing also the danger of moving. Where was Charles? What was happening to him? She couldn't think about that now. Or Vernier lying in the courtyard, blood spilling from his head, too. No, she couldn't think about that either. Run and then we'll figure it out. But all the *we* was gone, Minnow thought with a panic that clutched her chest. There was no more *we,* there was only Minnow, alone once again.

On her feet, she tried to move toward wherever the opposite side would be. As she pushed forward, the smoke thinned, and the sounds of combat seemed to be receding. Hope began to rise in her. She imagined the mouth of a new street opening up in front of her like salvation, and she would take it, and the air would be clean, and she could breathe, she would be able to call someone to help.

This thought brought her up short. Who was there to call? And if she did, what would she say? She heard her father's voice in her head, dry and laconic—What was it he had asked her and Charles that night? She had recoiled from the question, but now it came back— *How do you build a house when all the building blocks are rotted through?*

But, Minnow thought, is a rotten house not better than none at all? Is a large rotten house, one that can shelter many more bodies, not better than a small rotten house built for only a few?

She was weeping, stumbling on bits of trash and debris, but out of the smog now. She drew lungfuls of air, greedily sucking down more. She wiped the back of her hand over her eyes and nose, and when her vision cleared, she saw an empty passageway had opened up in front of her: a narrow vein of sidewalk between two close buildings. Relief lifted her like wings. She took a step forward and then another, and when her arms were seized from behind, her first scattered thought was that it was her father after all, that Christopher had returned to find her.

Instead, Minnow was jerked in a half circle, coming face-to-face with two gendarmes—not the CRS but two young men in uniforms who looked as grimy and nervous as she was. They shouted at her in French, and Minnow tried to hold her hands up in surrender, then remembered she was being restrained. When she coughed from the center of her chest, the force of it doubled her over so that the two gendarmes ended up supporting her weight.

The first was speaking to her in rapid, commanding French, telling her to do something. It was too loud all around them. On her other side, his partner kept hold of her arm, as if otherwise she would bolt. The first one lifted his voice again, frustrated and angry, and before she could think, she heard herself saying, "I don't understand you, I'm sorry. Je ne comprends pas."

He paused then, and a look of confusion came over his face. "Touriste?" he asked, and then asked it again, enunciating loudly: "You are touriste?"

Later she would wish that she had paused longer than she did before she replied, nearly weeping in shame and relief: "Yes, yes, je suis touriste."

*

As the two gendarmes walked Minnow down the alley to the far edge of a wide and unfamiliar avenue, they spoke to her in stern but more solicitous French, occasionally finding English where they could. They had, by now, seen the tearstains and blood on her face, where her jacket was ripped, the muddy footprint on her back in a man's size twelve boot. They told her that this was a riot, that it was not safe for people like her, that it was quieter on the Left Bank and she should go there, but mostly that she should stay at her hotel today, Saturdays were not good days, Saturdays were dangerous.

Minnow let them guide her and lecture her. She barely heard them. She was struck dumb by the vastness of her own treachery.

"Est-ce que vous avez mal?" One of the gendarmes was leaning in to look at her now, and she realized they had reached the edge of the avenue beyond the net of police. They had walked her free and clear. Though she could hear the popping of flashballs drifting through the air, it could have been happening in another world.

"Madame, are you all right?"

"Yes," Minnow said. "Thank you, yes. I'm sorry, thank you."

"Go home now, yes?" And they left her, turning reluctantly back toward the chaos.

Minnow was crying again without knowing it. She mopped at her face with the backs of her sleeves and felt her skin burn; the tear gas had formed a chemical coating on her clothing. Even so, she found herself peering after the gendarmes, hesitating. Charles would be long gone now. She knew no one else here. What was she waiting for? What *was* it that wouldn't let her go?

The crowd surged abruptly, breaking through the net of riot police. They were running in her direction, their voices lifting on the wind. And for a moment, Minnow saw herself from a bird's-eye view: ragged and rotten and mesmerized by the multitude stampeding toward her. And then she launched herself toward them, running to meet them, and though she could not have said what she was running toward, she felt it all around her, beating the air with its great wings: the future, flickering and wild, waiting to be seized.

*

Minnow was born on a gray Wednesday morning, just before noon.

Keen had come to accept a variety of things by then. He had come to accept Olya's growing dissatisfaction, the restlessness that had pursued her across the forty-one weeks of her pregnancy. He told himself a story wherein Minnow's arrival would make everything all right, but he had come to accept that he did not know if he believed that story. None of it mattered. When the nurse came to fetch him, he was pacing the scuffed linoleum floors of the hospital waiting room, drinking paper cup after paper cup of bad burnt coffee. She led him into the room, with its strange cacophony of smells both medicinal and primal, and his eyes went straight to the alien creature, gray and pink, swathed in blankets and lying on Olya's chest. It looked like an emissary from another world.

"Can I . . . ?" But Keen was already reaching for it, even before his eyes found Olya's—she was exhausted but beaming.

"Go ahead," Olya said.

Keen lifted the creature in his arms. It weighed nothing. He thought it would be dense as a bowling ball, but it felt like a scrap in his hands. He looked at its face, and though it did not look entirely human to him, he felt all the love in his body surge to meet it. Every cell inside him was sending a nuclear-powered blast of love in its direction. As if it felt that blast, it opened its giant eyes and looked at him. She looked at him. Her gaze was dark and calm. She had come on a long, strange journey to get here and, having arrived, she was determined to be upset by nothing.

"Minerva," Keen whispered, trying out the name that Olya had liked. It had felt overly grand to Keen, a name too heavy for a baby to shoulder. But now, staring into her depthless gaze, he felt the name slide into place. "Minerva, hello."

Many days would unfold after this first meeting. Many nights, too, although eventually, those nights would become ones that did not include Olya. In the nights that followed Olya's departure a year later, Keen would find himself alone once again with his pain and regret, with Andrew Hungerford's face, which would sometimes recede and sometimes return and never seemed to go away entirely. On those nights, Keen would go to his daughter's crib, even if she hadn't been crying, even if she was deeply asleep, and he would lift her in his arms and walk back and forth across the floor the way that he was doing now, here, in this hospital room. And on those nights he would sink deeply into the tethering reality of Minnow's body against his chest, her need of him, her trust in him that existed independent of knowledge. He would believe again what he had said to Olya, that living in the world fully could be what remade it.

The new world was not who he might become as a father; the new world was Minnow herself. It was already too late for Keen, he thought. It had been too late for him even before he closed the door on Andrew Hungerford. He was not capable of dreaming up a brave new world, because nothing in him was brave or new. But Minnow was both. Minnow had nothing timeworn and failing inside her, Minnow was all time, all potential. All he had to do was keep her safe. All he had to do was give her everything he had, and keep her safe, and keep her safe, until she could become the inviolate future.

Historical Note

In the spring of 1969, Harvard students occupied University Hall and were violently evicted by state police. The occupation of Lowell Lecture Hall is made up, as are its reasons and circumstances, but the tenor is influenced by the real event. Likewise, the multiple actes of the gilets jaunes are real, as are the weapons used by the police and the injuries suffered by civilian protestors, but the Vernier building takeover is a fiction.

Acknowledgments

My love and thanks to:

My agent, Allison Hunter, who fiercely championed this book long before it was written, when it was still an idea I was describing over lunch.

My editor, Caitlin McKenna, whose instincts and epiphanies are my guiding principles. You make me a better writer and thinker.

The whole Random House team, especially Andy Ward, Rachel Rokicki, Erica Gonzalez, Cara DuBois, Katie Zilberman, Windy Dorresteyn, Madison Dettlinger, Maria Braeckel, Erin Richards, Fritz Metsch, Rachel Kuech, and Noa Shapiro.

Kimberly Burns, for whose wisdom and wit I am ongoingly grateful.

Alex Grace Paul, researcher extraordinaire, whose historical research provided detail and texture to draw on. Viktor Cohen, for his careful read and nuanced notes on the French side of things.

Edward Bonver, for granting permission to include the translations of three Anna Akhmatova poems. All three poems were translated to English by Yevgeny Bonver and can be found on poetryloverspage.com. They are: "I Was Born in the Right Time" (written in 1913, translated in 2000, edited by Dmitry Karshtedt); "Why Is This Century Worse . . ." (written in 1919, translated in 2000, edited by Dmitry Karshtedt); and "Requiem" (written over three decades, between 1935 and 1961, and translated in 2005).

MacDowell, the National Endowment for the Arts, the Guggenheim Foundation, and the kind people who work for these vital organizations. Thank you for meaningful support at a crucial time.

The friends & artists who kept me company—across dinners, walks, phone calls, and collaborations—while I wrote this book. Among them: Michael Arden, Kevin Artigue, Robert Atterbury, Rachel Bonds, Billy Carter, Jessica Chase, Erin Chen, Michael Yates Crowley, Dana Delany,

Mike Donahue, Augustus Donahue, Renata Friedman, Swan Huntley, Matt Kelly, Daniel Kluger, Basil Kreimendahl, Ely Kreimendahl, Ted Malawer, Andy Mientus, Roberta Maia Pereira, Max Posner, Matthew "Maude" Rauch, Tyne Rafaeli, J. T. Rogers, Samantha Sherman, Phil Wei, and Nick Westrate.

My parents, Mark and Sue, who gave me a childhood in many places, among them Paris.

My brother Chris, who was and is my best friend in every place.

The Brachwitz, Silverman, Laffrey, and West families.

Dane Laffrey, ç'est toujours toi.

ABOUT THE AUTHOR

JEN SILVERMAN is the author of the novel *We Play Ourselves,* a Lambda Literary Award finalist; the story collection *The Island Dwellers,* longlisted for a PEN/Robert W. Bingham Prize for debut fiction; and the poetry chapbook *Bath,* selected by Traci Brimhall for Driftwood Press. Silverman's plays have been produced across the United States and internationally. Their honors include fellowships from the National Endowment for the Arts and the Guggenheim Foundation. Silverman also writes for TV and film.

jensilverman.com
Instagram: @this_panda_is_sad